THE BROCKHURST FILE

A MAT LADIES NOVEL

Lynne Adair Kramer

Jane Dillof Mincer

Wellsmith

ISBN: 0990764508
ISBN 13: 9780990764502
Library of Congress Control Number: 2014915140
Wellsmith, Northport, New York

CHAPTER ONE

Lucy Bennett glared down at the little red light on her phone. Someone had picked up line two. Her desk finally clear, the last of the day's flurry of faxes and phone calls at an end, she was about to escape the office ahead of the worsening storm. Only one person in the building was clueless enough to pick up an outside line once the phones were switched to service.

The head of Bennett and Birnbaum buzzed the new intern.

"Tell me you didn't pick up line two."

"Yes, there's a Skippy Brockhurst for you and she sounds very upset. She says it's an emergency." Melissa was thrilled to be pitching in, just as her first week at the law office came to a close.

"We're in the business of emergencies. Everyone thinks their call is an emergency. That's why we have to put the phones on service. After hours, we only pick up the private line."

"Oh, whoops."

"I assume you said I was still in the office."

"Yes," came the feeble answer.

"You know what this means, don't you? Now, I have to take the call. And I could be stuck here all night."

No response.

"Did you hear me? I could be stuck here all night! In a goddamned blizzard!"

Knowing she was going to hate herself, Lucy picked up the phone.

Her associate, Claire, popped her head around the edge of Lucy's office doorway. A weekend's worth of homework trailed behind her in a rolling briefcase. She was hoping to review a few documents with the boss, but could see it was futile.

"Hey, Skippy. My God, it's been so long. How the hell are you?" Lucy managed to sound enthusiastic.

Claire shot her employer a sympathetic smile as she took a seat across from her. There was only one Skippy Brockhurst. It was never an easy call.

"What was that, Skippy? You must be in a bad zone."

Andi Birnbaum appeared at the doorway, files tucked under her arm. Lucy signaled to her partner to pull up a chair.

"Skippy, I can't hear you very well. I'm going to put the phone on speaker. I have some of the attorneys in my office with me, is that okay?"

"Fine, fine," Skippy said, her voice coming through the static. "Look, my son is in serious danger."

Melissa, who had crept over to the boss's office, caught the client's words. She stood in her tracks just outside of Lucy's doorway, afraid to step into the lion's den. Unless she was wrong, everyone was still at the office and in that room on account of her. She peered in. The boss did not look in the mood to send any thanks her way.

Skippy's voice, with its overtones of clubby lockjaw, was painfully familiar to the roomful of attorneys. Each had worked on her hotly contested divorce case. The villain on the other side of the divorce and custody battle was Everett, the heir to the Brockhurst fortune.

The man had made an impression on every attorney at the firm. On first glimpse, Claire described him as a fellow of "the proper pedigree," but later referred to him simply as "the wastrel." Another associate, Meg, had taken an instant loathing to him despite his good looks and the charming grin: "He's one of those skinny WASP men who's 'light in the loafers' — and I don't mean gay. His type never wears socks, even in the dead of winter." Andi called him an "old school guy with some old money," to which Lucy added, "Big money, probably offshore." After a few more conferences, Andi became familiar enough with Everett to consider him a clever guy who might have been more than a little rich, if he hadn't chosen drugs and alcohol above everything else.

Skippy Brockhurst was undeniably the better parent, but her disdainful attitude and obnoxious behavior made it almost impossible to represent her. Lucy had toughed it out, but after she got Skippy one helluva deal, all her client did was complain about her bill. Lucy restrained herself from pointing out that Skippy's own need to discuss and fight over every detail had made the charges so high.

When the case was over, the entire office had rejoiced to see the client move on. Skippy seemed satisfied to have secured her standard of living, and almost gleeful to have evicted Everett from the mansion.

Now the Brockhurst file, sealed up for more than three years in the dusty archives of Bennett and Birnbaum, threatened to make a reappearance.

Meg, who had hoped to stop by the boss's office for just a moment, saw she was going nowhere. She pulled off her hat, unzipped her coat and plopped down on the couch. Andi sensed a lengthy discussion ahead. She brushed past Melissa, still frozen in Lucy's doorway, and ran off to fill her large wine glass with water. The piece of crystal stemware, a client's gift, was never far from her reach; it was a reminder to stay hydrated. It improved the attorney's mood to pretend she was enjoying some Cabernet on the job, and the staff was used to seeing her waft down the office hallway, water-filled glass in hand. She never explained it to the puzzled clients who sometimes caught her mid-sip.

Melissa saw Andi return to Lucy's office with a full wine glass and cringed. Had her own actions set off a drinking binge? Ms. Bennett said they might be here all night — and it was her fault. She waited outside the door and held her breath.

"I'll explain it once more, since you obviously didn't get it the first time. I said there's reason to believe Beau is in danger. Look, Lucy, I need to talk to you — in person and right away. I can get to you in half an hour or so."

"Skippy, how is your son in danger? I need specifics."

"He's home with the nanny. But someone is trying to get to him."

"Who? And why?"

"That's what I need to talk to you about."

"Is he in immediate danger?" Lucy asked. "I mean, would this person be lurking outside your house, somewhere? Should we call the police?"

"No, not the police! I won't have the police!" Skippy shouted, her voice shrill.

"Should I set up surveillance? I could do that. Or a bodyguard?"

"No! I need to speak to you in person."

Meg made an abrupt gesture to signify that she was blowing out her brains with a very short pistol.

"No emergency!" Andi muttered a little too loudly.

"What did you say?" Skippy asked. "Was that Andi?"

"Hi, Skippy," the lawyer said. "Yes, it was me. I said snow emergency. You must know how bad the roads are."

Meg covered her mouth to suppress her laughter. She let out an inadvertent and most unladylike snort that, fortunately, did not transmit clearly over the speakerphone.

Lucy smiled. This particular client had cried wolf so many times before. If it was a real emergency, why had Skippy turned down her suggestions for taking immediate measures? Whatever the problem was, it could wait.

"Skippy, I'd be willing to stick around for you, but it's really getting awful out there. From what you're telling me, nothing will happen while Beau's on your watch. Is this your weekend with them?"

"It's always my weekend with them," Skippy said.

"Well then, how about I see you first thing Monday morning, before I have to be in court?"

Skippy hated early morning appointments — something about her circadian rhythms — but the offer to meet at the crack of dawn was calculated to make the client feel that she was a priority. Besides, how much sleep did the woman need? The lawyers of Bennett & Birnbaum ran contests to see which one of them could get actual REM sleep, two weeknights running. Skippy could try functioning on a few less hours of sleep, if only for one day.

"I can be there at eight o'clock on Monday morning," Skippy said.

"Perfect," Lucy confirmed. "And of course you know I pick up messages over the weekend. One thing, though. What about school on Monday? Will Beau be safe?"

"I'll have Bridgette drive the children over to school, and she'll walk them in."

Lucy instructed Skippy to get hold of Beau's passport and to safeguard it. "Call me if anything urgent happens," she said. "And Skippy, you do know what I mean by urgent, right?"

The attorneys began to disperse, Melissa in the lead.

Desperate to get home, Lucy worked along with her office manager to clear the files from her credenza, letting Ruby vent about the day's vicissitudes and the nightmare of trying to fit all of the clients into the schedule for Monday afternoon.

Ruby had been the first to set off warning flares when they took Skippy on as a client. Right from the start, Skippy treated Ruby like a go-fer, with a barrage of requests for iced water, coffee, more ice, aspirin, tea, all within the allotted hour.

Ruby had also noted that immediately after the initial consultation, Mrs. Brockhurst had gone back to the waiting room and spent an inordinate amount of time scribbling down notes. Ruby assumed she was making a record of her meeting with Lucy. On that basis alone, the office manager predicted they were in for it, having observed a common modus operandi among certain other clients over the years. The ones who studied their own cases from the beginning thought they were smarter than, and could outsmart, their own lawyer.

But, as her boss always reminded her, it wasn't Ruby who paid the bills. Turning away a high-maintenance client along with a mighty retainer was simply bad business.

Ruby was like family. She had been around a long time and knew more about the law than did many seasoned lawyers. Her street smarts and no-nonsense approach to the world matched well with Lucy's own direct and practical manner. Over the years, the two women formed their own mutual admiration society. Lucy recognized how far Ruby could have gone if she'd been fortunate enough to get the education she deserved, and Ruby was perpetually impressed with how much her boss could accomplish in a single day.

They were a study in contrasts: Ruby, statuesque with her thick auburn hair fastened up and out of the way, and Lucy, with her wiry, athletic build and a head of curly hair that seemed to have a will of its own. Lucy favored tailored suits, her shirt tucked in neatly, a belt always at her waist. For the most part, she displayed her style through well-chosen jewelry and scarves, with certain clients insisting on finding out the source of each intriguing item. Ruby dressed plainly, intent on downplaying her curvy figure by covering up in loose-fitting clothes.

The assistant and her boss agreed most particularly on one thing: they couldn't abide a phony. To Ruby, Skippy Brockhurst was just that, a poser with no right to be a snob, a girl who clawed her way up from some mid-western town and managed to snag a society guy with a fortune. From her viewpoint, Skippy didn't deserve any of it, especially the coup of getting to live in the Brockhurst mansion. Worse, the client had never expressed appreciation for the work Ms. Bennett had done for her in negotiating the settlement.

Lucy, however, saw Mrs. Brockhurst in a more favorable light. She was a good-paying client, and the source of several excellent referrals. And Lucy didn't see her as a phony. To her, the client was exactly as she appeared: a woman who went out and got what she wanted, and who was not going to let her background impede her in any way. Skippy was a self-made woman.

The two ladies were finally on their way out of the building, negotiating the slippery stairs when Ruby just had to say it.

"How much you wanna bet she calls the office over the weekend?"

"Why would you even need to ask? The only question is how many times."

As she turned her car out onto the highway, Lucy wondered how Skippy Brockhurst could have climbed out of the woodwork and back into her life on one of the shortest days and longest nights of the year.

CHAPTER TWO

It was late when Lucy arrived at home, her truck tires gliding silently across the fresh blanket of snow covering her driveway.

"Jake! Adam!"

No one responded. They were still where they were supposed to be, she realized: at the Greenes' house, most likely enjoying hot chocolate after an afternoon playing in the snow. Her children knew how to turn early dismissal from the Jay Fletcher Middle School to their best advantage.

As she finished lugging the first of her briefcases up the back stairs, she heard the boys' voices coming from the garage.

"Will one of you guys bring up my other bag?"

Lucy could not hear the words, but they were clearly arguing over whose turn it was to help her. She'd be happy to see either of the boys come up the stairs with her second briefcase. Instead, it was Dan's face that greeted her.

"Don't look so shocked," Dan Hammond said, kissing his wife. "For once, I took your advice and came home before they closed the roads." He held up her other briefcase. "And I settled the boys' dispute."

"Looks like they settled it. In their favor."

"Guess they learned something from their mother."

"Did you get anything at all in return?"

"I'm working on it."

Their most enthusiastic greeting of the day came as they tried to get from the mudroom to the kitchen. The door was open only a crack when Torts used his forceful snout to wedge it open the rest of the way. He pounced on his masters with a great, leaping, barking, wiggling welcome that nearly bowled them over, but lasted only until the appearance of the boys. The dog's happiness gave way to hysteria as he bounded around Adam and Jake in mad circles, distributing the snow from their coats and boots throughout the tight space of the mudroom.

With a wet and woolly start, the weekend at the Bennett-Hammonds was on. There was no room in it for Skippy Brockhurst.

CHAPTER THREE

At precisely 7:35 Monday morning, Lucy pulled into her office parking lot. The morning's mixture of drifting snow and black ice made the trip to work extremely challenging. Schools, businesses as well as the courts were closed, in view of the second storm that had struck overnight. Andi was stuck in Vermont, where the storm had continued straight through the weekend. Ruby was trying to dig out from the blizzard's second round. Lucy anticipated that she'd be on her own for at least part of the day, so there she was, prepared to handle the elements in her snow boots and behemoth coat, viewing the icy lot with a singular thought: lawsuit waiting to happen.

As she began to haul her roller-case behind her, she looked up at the handsome brick building, noticing the heavy icicles that had already formed along its front gutters. In the past, her ownership of the property had been a source of pride, since it reflected her business success. Lately, she thought more about the burdens of ownership than its blessings. The immediate burden in front of her was making sure the property was safe enough for her staff and clients. Although the plowers had come the night before, blowing snow covered up the sand they'd spread and left the pavement full of icy patches. Lucy was determined to get across the parking lot and up the steps without breaking a major bone. The micro-spikes would have come in handy, but her son, Jake, had already absconded with them. She made it up to the building and to her relief, found an unopened bag of ice melt wedged behind the abandoned umbrellas in the back of the coat closet.

It was only to be expected that Skippy Brockhurst would arrive just in time to witness her lawyer casting ice melt along the front stoop and stairs, huddled in an unfashionably bright red coat, her homemade scarf flying in the brisk wind, and clumping along in what seemed to be oversized hiking boots.

In one glance, Skippy assessed the scene simply as Fashion Don'ts. She found it impossibly irritating to have to return here. It was worse than going to the dentist; it was a nightmare come back to haunt her. This time, under Lucy's acute inspection, she was likely to wither. Gathering her courage around her like a warm bodyguard, she stepped out into the biting wind to meet her fate yet again.

"I'm sorry it's freezing in here," Lucy called from the kitchenette. "I can't remember if you take caffeinated or decaf."

"Caffeinated at this hour, and half and half with one Splenda," returned Skippy, who had settled into the well-appointed office, placing her giant Prada bag in the next chair. She removed her Burberry scarf, revealing a thick head of hair pulled back tightly into a youthful ponytail. As had been promised, her colorist had achieved the goal of matching her hair color to that of the first wisps of blonde hair sprouted by the fairest Scandinavian babies. Skippy had been a brunette when she had last met with Lucy.

"My God, should I call you Marilyn?" Lucy asked, as she handed her old client the custom-made cup of coffee. "I'd have doughnuts and bagels, but Ruby's having a difficult time digging out." Lucy wondered how they'd managed to lighten Skippy's skin and eliminate her freckles, and whether her client was anorexic.

"I can't eat that stuff anymore," Skippy sighed. "High cholesterol."

"Well, are you okay? Something up with your health?

"What, you don't think I look healthy?"

"You're about half the size I seem to remember — and that wasn't all that long ago."

"It's the stress."

"Don't tell me it's stress. You went out and did this to yourself," Lucy scolded. "You must be a size 0!"

"In petites," Skippy confessed.

In some bizarre region of her brain, Lucy pondered what it would be like to be that skinny. Would a mini-bagel show up in profile? A grape? She tested the heating register with her hand, and noticed that the air was still cool.

"Have you seen yourself in the mirror?" Lucy went on. "Are you deliberately trying to get rid of your body?" The attorney had found that many of her female clients suffered from an eating disorder; they were either stress eaters, or they could barely eat at all. Extremes just seemed to be part of the divorce terrain. Sometimes, the extremes turned deadly.

"I had a full check-up and other than the cholesterol, I'm healthy," Skippy said.

"Yeah, your hair looks really healthy, but — how much weight did you lose?" Lucy asked. She moved from window to window, raising the blinds to let in the brightening sun.

"Well, I did have these removed," Skippy looked down at her chest. "Look, I had them since I was twenty-two and they were always way too big for my frame. Honestly, they never brought me any luck — just the opposite."

Lucy couldn't be bamboozled. She smacked the thermostat to wake it up and asked as casually as she could muster, "Are you still seeing your shrink?"

"Now and then."

Lucy looked squarely at her former client. "I think it's vital — no, essential — that you make an appointment with your therapist, which you are going to do as soon as we're done here." Lucy's welcome back had concluded. "Now, what's going on?" she asked, as she sat down, took a big sip of coffee and then swiveled around to the credenza behind her to grab a large bag of candy.

Skippy needed her help desperately, but despised being in this room, its all too familiar décor pushing its way in between her thoughts. She saw the framed photos of Lucy's smiling family, her trophies, diplomas and letters of accolade. She remembered that same still life painting and how she had focused on the knife sitting pleasantly by the apple when she first sat in this seat, hoping for an easy way out.

Lucy emptied the bag of candies into the crystal bowl so familiar to Skippy, who could remember little hands reaching in. Damn, she was starting to tear up. This wasn't happening. Through the whole ordeal of the interminable divorce, she had remained strong, collected and unbroken. Lucy with that damned chocolate was just killing her. One tear stung as it escaped, then another.

"I'm just a mess right now."

Lucy's habitual gesture was so smooth, the tissue seemed to appear from nowhere.

"I loved only twice in my life," Skippy uttered with a drama that took even her by surprise, and added in a strained falsetto, "Emma and Beau."

The names of her children were barely audible to Lucy, who thought that she might have underestimated Skippy. Another voice told her that this was not possible.

"And now...I just don't know how to deal with this."

"Where are they?"

"At home, with Bridgette. My sister was supposed to get here to help me out, but her flight was delayed. I would have brought the kids with me, but the roads...."

"Of course," Lucy said, commiserating.

"Gary Vaughn." Somehow, Skippy spit it out. "I had an affair with him. He might be Beau's father." The words hung in the air between them.

"Hello, hello!" sang a voice from the waiting room. "Hello, Lucy, I know you're here 'cause I saw your car!"

Lucy's heart sank. It was Consuela Birnbaum. She and Max were supposed to be in at 10:00 a.m., not nearly this early.

"I'm with a client," Lucy called across the first floor of the building.

"Darling, it's an emergency! We have to leave for the airport, PRONTO!" Consuela answered in her lilting voice. For reasons unknown, Consuela proceeded to tap the front bell. The fax machine came to life at the same moment, along with the phone, which rang as if to complete the three-part harmony.

"Oh, God, I'm sorry," stammered Lucy, who let the phone go to service, but was astonished to see Consuela heading into her office.

"How did you...?"

Then Lucy saw her. Eager Melissa, the new bane of her existence, had made the supreme effort to get to the office early, in her trusty Subaru. And she had been given her own shiny new key to let herself in.

"She went right past me —" Melissa started, but Lucy was in no mood to listen. The intern remained out in the hallway, thinking about fleeing the scene. She hadn't realized that another client was already in her boss's office, and although she couldn't see her face, imagined that the woman must have been pretty annoyed by the interruption. Another mistake, she thought, and it wasn't even nine o'clock.

"Well hello, Consuela," Lucy said as she greeted her partner's mother, who walked right up to her desk to exchange a big hug and a kiss. Consuela showed no concern that another client was sitting in the room.

"Great to see you, but I'm afraid your appointment was for 10:00."

"I know, I know, but we have to make the flight and we need more time with the roads such a mess." Consuela was gaily arrayed in a flamboyant white and navy blue sailor suit that further announced its nautical theme through the brightly-stitched anchors and patterns of little dancing whales. Her white snow boots took nothing away from the effect. She was determined to make it to the airport and then to Florida and the cruise Max had been planning with her for over a year. She was not going to miss the flight, nor the cruise, nor the big send-off in Miami with relatives to show up from as far off as Atlanta.

Melissa had remained in the hallway trying to keep her distance, but Lucy called after her to get Ruby on the line, "NOW!"

Lucy took a long look at Mrs. Max Birnbaum and prayed that she would not see a matching sailor hat perched on that huge head of teased hair. Consuela and Skippy politely ignored one another, and Lucy took control of the standoff by gently guiding her partner's mother to the conference room.

Max was already seated comfortably at the conference table, having managed to work his way out of the waiting room and into the office by subterfuge, convincing Melissa he needed to use "the facilities." From there, he helped himself to some coffee and a seat, and prepared for the signing of the two wills. Melissa had helped him off with his coat, beneath which he wore a dapper navy blue suit, with a crisp white handkerchief, embroidered delicately with his initials.

To some, Mr. Birnbaum was a dead ringer for George Burns, "only older" as Max loved to add. His actual age was a secret he closely guarded. Despite his advancing years, he still held onto his irrepressible spunk, retained all of his faculties other than his hearing, and kept nearly every tooth. His brilliant business acumen came through to his patient listeners by way of parable and anecdote. To those who showed an interest, he generously expounded on his philosophy of life, leading some to swear he was a guru or saint. The few who on account of his long-windedness thought him a bit senile made a grave mistake, especially those who first met him at the blackjack table. Max loved to gamble and was still a stud at his favorite game. He was eager to get back on the dance floor with Consuela, whose one-eighth Cuban blood accounted for their title as best mambo dancers at any affair. They were going to strut their stuff on this cruise, and he'd had a new tuxedo custom-made for the occasion.

The tiny blonde with the naturally tiny nose and oversized handbag, sitting in Lucy's office, was not going to stand in Consuela's way. She and Max were determined to update their wills before they stepped foot on a plane or hazarded a journey at sea. With their son's marriage looking shaky, the couple decided to tweak their respective wills to safeguard their grandchildren's inheritance. Max came up with some clever ideas, refined by Lucy, and all was in order. They were ready to sign their new wills and they wanted to do it right away. All Lucy had to do was conjure up the necessary witnesses, along with her trusty assistant to serve as notary.

The phone rang again. Lucy prayed that the ever-helpful Melissa would not answer it. If they started taking calls before the staff arrived, they couldn't take care of the Birnbaums or Skippy. With that thought in mind, Lucy excused herself from the Birnbaums to slip back into her office and see how her client was doing.

Skippy seemed frozen in her seat, whether from the continued chilliness of the office or from the fact that her great revelation had been upstaged by all of the commotion.

Having no answer as to Ruby's whereabouts, Lucy devised a way to handle the competing clients.

"Skippy, I'm really sorry about the interruption," she said. "You certainly don't have to do what I'm going to ask, but this really is an emergency for the Birnbaums. They need you as one of the witnesses for their wills, or they're going to miss their cruise."

"I thought I recognized her. Isn't that lady Andi's mother?"

"Actually, yes," Lucy said.

"I seem to remember bumping into her once in Andi's office." She sighed, still clearly agitated. "Well, Andi was the only one here who ever really cared."

It was like a slap in the face to Lucy, who had devoted so much time to Skippy's divorce, time that might have been spent with her own family and with clients who were in far more serious financial or emotional straits. As was so often the case with her practice, Lucy's soulful, patient partner received whatever shred of gratefulness the client could give. Funny that it was Lucy and not Andi who had been called upon to meet with the client before hours on this icy morning. If her former client's help wasn't vital at this particular moment, Lucy might have given way to at least a minor rant, but she restrained herself and led Skippy into the conference room, where formal introductions were made.

Debonair as always, Max kissed the back of Skippy's hand and offered to help both the blonde and her immense handbag to their respective seats.

Meanwhile, Lucy flew up the stairs to the second floor to find her intern, who wasn't answering the intercom. They nearly bumped into one another as Melissa threw open her office door, cell phone held high in front of her like a prize fish. "Here she is!" she shouted in her boss's face. Lucy winced, grabbed the phone and greeted Ruby with a pissy, "Where the hell are you?"

"I'm around the corner, with provisions by the way and I had to dig myself out for the second time this weekend. And thanks for asking how I managed to get out at all this morning!"

"You're a goddess," Lucy returned, remembering full well who actually ran the office. "The Birnbaums showed up early. I'll tell you the whole story later. But we do need you here ASAP!" The boss returned the phone to Melissa and gave her a quick run-down on how to witness the wills. "Don't make any comments, please, since it's already a delicate situation with our client, Mrs. Brockhurst, serving as the other witness," warned Lucy.

Things in the conference room had heated up considerably. Consuela had taken the opportunity to give the once over to the woman sitting beside her. Observing Skippy's reddened eyes and the tissue still clutched in her hand, she leaned over. In words that must have come to her from some bygone movie, she whispered. "Whoever he is, honey, he really done you wrong. You just have to go back out there and find one like Max, who really knows how to treat a lady."

Having heard none of this, Max smiled and nodded as though in agreement, while adjusting his hearing aid.

"You need to eat something, sweetie. Doesn't she need to eat something, Max? You look like Catherine Daley on 'Young Hearts,' you know? Very pretty, but she had that awful thing, what was it…that disease where she couldn't eat. I hope you don't have that, it's horrible."

"Anorexia nervosa," Max said, properly tuned in, enunciating each syllable. He could see for himself what Skippy failed to observe in the mirror: she was painfully thin. Lucy's client viewed the Birnbaums' concern as criticism and was silently reconsidering her offer to help out when Consuela went on.

"You know that enormous handbag could be part of the problem. My chiropractor told me that I had to 'lose the purse or get a hearse.' Lugging that leather sack around all the time nearly destroyed my whole shoulder, and then I used my other shoulder and almost fell down the steps at the post office. And will you look at that?" She indicated the view through the picture window, where Ruby was crossing the frozen tundra, hauling her own oversized bag over her shoulder, files squeezed up under her arm and shopping bags clutched in each glove. "She's gonna fall flat on her face if she doesn't watch it."

Lucy headed for the conference room, Melissa tagging along behind her. As she followed Lucy into the room, she realized that despite the change in hair color and the obvious weight loss, she recognized Mrs. Brockhurst.

A sudden snapshot of "the fiasco" flashed across Melissa's mind as she recalled the party at Cedar Beach Club, where she used to work as a lifeguard. A children's swim party was in full blast when Mrs. Brockhurst made her grand entrance as a guest for the day, along with her own children and their nanny. While the other mothers were arrayed in their conservative one-piece bathing suits or tankinis, they cooed over Mrs. Brockhurst's slender yet curvy figure when she revealed her spectacular leopard string bikini. She headed straight for the mother's Sangria table, where she settled down to pose and drink. At some point later in the day, Mrs. Brockhurst got up from the table, and started to slowly make her way through the line of kids at the diving board. In retrospect, some suggested she'd been more than a little tipsy when she lost her balance by the edge of the pool. Her backwards spill into the water narrowly missed the tail end of a child's cannonball dive.

Melissa came to the rescue, jumping in to help Mrs. Brockhurst get to the side of the pool. In her effort to help her, Melissa inadvertently pushed aside a portion of the lady's bikini bra, revealing to the poolside crowd a goodly portion of oversized breast. While Mrs. Brockhurst was coughing up water and catching her breath, Melissa tried to subtly reposition the bra, but Skippy recoiled and then realized the problem.

"I'll handle this!" she hissed. Mrs. Brockhurst mustered enough composure to climb out of the pool and into the huddle of helpful mothers gathered at the top of the pool ladder. But, as Melissa could see, some were enjoying the show at the woman's expense. Skippy and the family left soon thereafter. That was the last Melissa had seen of her.

Praying desperately that she wouldn't be recognized as the lifeguard who blew it, she found herself involuntarily staring at Skippy's chest, much to her own discomfort and to the exasperation of Lucy, who tried to snap her out of it.

"Melissa, this is Mrs. Brockhurst, who will be the other witness to the wills."

Oh my God, the lady had lost her chest. It was concave, gone. Melissa panicked. She struggled to get back to the business at hand, but her mind shrieked that Mrs. Brockhurst had lost her breasts to some terrible disease. She just couldn't help herself as she stumbled along, and in reaching over to greet her, said ever so sweetly, "It's a pleasure to see you, again, Mrs. Buh, Mrs. Buh...Brockhurst."

Skippy stared blankly at her and said, "I'm afraid I don't recall, but it's nice to meet you."

Lucy glared at Melissa, placed the documents on the table and said, "Okay, we're all here. Now all we need is Ruby. RUBY!"

"Stop shouting, I've got the food!" answered Lucy's assistant, entering the room with a plateful of bagels and cream cheese and a pitcher of water. She took one look at Skippy and said, "Whoa...look at you!"

Perhaps it was more than Skippy's condition; in fact, it might have been the strong scent of the bagels along with the terror-stricken look on Ruby's face that pushed her over the edge, but Skippy started to "green up." She leaned slowly to one side and fainted into the next chair. Luckily, her immense handbag caught the brunt of her slumping torso, sparing her any serious injury. So much for Consuela's warning about her bulky purse.

Instantly, the room was aflutter, but quickest to the rescue was Melissa, who went into lifeguard mode, methodically pushing Lucy and Ruby back as she took charge. She gently pulled Skippy back into a sitting position, supporting her head and back with her strong arms, then reached into the pitcher and splashed a bit of water on Skippy's face. She came to almost immediately, but dizzily gazed around the room, finally coming to focus on Melissa's face. She had a sudden feeling of déjà vu, but wrote it off to the circumstances.

"Feeling any better?" Melissa offered, hoping that the look in Skippy's eyes signified consciousness only, and not sudden recognition.

"See if you can drink some," Lucy suggested as she watched Melissa offer a sip of water to her client. "We're going to get you some help." The attorney was caught off-guard by her intern's take-charge behavior and was impressed, much to her own surprise.

"No," muttered Skippy. "Please don't call anyone. This happens..."

"This happens?" Lucy and Ruby asked in unison.

"Once in a while," Skippy continued. "I'm always okay. I'll be fine. Just give me a minute."

Melissa released her slowly and then helped her take another sip of the water. Max and Consuela, who were standing at the table, turned their eyes from Skippy to one another, wanting to help, but feeling helpless.

"Let's get on with it," Skippy said weakly. "These people are going on a cruise."

Everyone in the room froze. Could she serve as a witness? Was she back to the land of the living? Was this kosher?

"Let me do this one thing." Skippy insisted.

It was incredible to all in the room that this client wanted to see it through, though just having emerged from a state of collapse.

"If I'm not okay in fifteen minutes, you can call for help. But if I am okay, I'm your witness."

"Fine, but I have one caveat, too," countered Lucy.

Mrs. Skippy Brockhurst came back to herself within the allotted fifteen minutes, and became heroine for the day as the wills were read, signed and notarized. Their affairs in order at last, the Birnbaums set off for the trip they'd almost missed. Just after they left, and to the chagrin of Ruby who saw this as a terrible precedent, her boss revealed that Skippy promised to let Lucy drive her directly to the office of Dr. Howie Gassner for possible confirmation of the diagnosis made by wise Max Birnbaum.

It was unusual for Lucy Bennett to get so involved in the life of a client that she would send her directly to a doctor. But early in her practice, Lucy resolved that she would serve as an attorney only for those clients clearly interested in helping themselves. That was, of course, unless cash flow at the office turned decidedly slow.

Following Lucy's instructions, Skippy sent word to her sister to take the airport limousine to Dr. Gassner's office. Luckily, the sister caught the text message in time, and was able to respond that they'd meet up at the doctor's. From there, the Brockhurst sisters were to use Skippy's car to get home, and Lucy would take the limousine back to her office.

The roads were still poor, but Lucy found that her client's car handled well, as she followed a snowplow down the turnpike. Skippy used the visor's mirror as she carefully reapplied her make-up and tidied her hair. She checked her cell phone for messages, texted several memos to her office and muttered to herself about the cancellations in her schedule.

After driving along in silence for some time, Lucy finally asked, "Okay, so how did you meet Gary Vaughn?"

"How could I miss him? He was working with all the developers and so was I. Somewhere along the line I found out you handled his divorce, too. You're one of the only things he and I really had in common. Until now."

"When did you start seeing him?" Lucy inquired. Getting further details from her client was going to be tricky. Typically defensive, Skippy disliked opening up about herself. Consuela had barged in just as the client was about to make her confession. Now it would be like peeling an onion to get the rest out of her.

Her instinct was correct. Skippy felt trapped in the car, and was unsure if she could reveal more without losing control again. There was a long pause before she gave an answer: "I never started seeing him. It was a one-time thing."

"One time? You had sex one time with the guy and you got pregnant?"

"Well, it wasn't one time. I was at a real estate convention in Vegas. Look, Lucy, I have to call Bridgette and see what's going on at home."

Lucy reminded her as gently as she could that Skippy had called home just before they got in the car. "I really can't help you unless you tell me what's going on. Isn't that why you came in to see me today? The urgent matter?"

Skippy took a big breath and tried to sum up the facts as succinctly as she could.

"Well, what else can I tell you? We kept bumping into each other in real estate, since he was an architect with his own construction company, competing with all the big guys. He would help develop the property, and if it worked out, I'd get the listing. And there he was at this convention. It was a really weak moment for me."

Weak? thought Lucy, barely suppressing a smile. She was well aware that Skippy Brockhurst usually managed to control her every move, as well as everyone else's. By her brief calculations, she figured Beau to be about seven or eight years old, so this affair must have occurred after Gary's divorce, and long before Skippy's. As Lucy faintly recalled, Skippy once mentioned a problem with fertility that she and Everett had early in their marriage. She gave it as an illustration of Everett's generally uncooperative attitude throughout the relationship. He put the blame on Skippy for their failure to conceive, and then when the doctor told them that Everett might be the problem, she had to beg her husband to even call the doctor.

"I ended up spending a day or two with Gary," Skippy said, cramming the whole episode into one sentence. More silence ensued. Skippy pulled the visor down again to re-examine her make-up. She looked into her own eyes and saw those little flecks that Gary had pointed out. Red and gold. Little flecks she had never noticed until he had found them.

She had escaped the last portion of the day's third seminar and gone back to her hotel, settling in at the same blackjack table where she'd won a few dollars the night before. Perhaps, she thought, it was her lucky table. She sat there in her royal blue Tahari suit, proudly bearing the grey and green Barstow-Taft real estate tag with her title as the firm's top producer. A familiar voice broke through her concentration, just as she was doubling on a pair of fours.

"I thought you said you hate to gamble, Mrs. Brockhurst," Gary Vaughn murmured over her shoulder.

"Well, if it isn't Mr. Vaughn," she laughed, looking up at the man. She thought he looked pretty good in his polo shirt, trim, tan, wholesome, his light hair receding back just enough to mature his boyish features. She could sense his ease, a confidence that was magnetic. It must prove very effective in business, she thought.

"I never said I hate to gamble. I said I hate to lose."

"Well, shove over and I'll show you how it's done," Gary boasted, nudging her aside as though they were an old, intimate couple. The afternoon went on as Skippy watched how easily a bundle could be made and lost, the drinks flowing and the pair's small talk turning from friendly to flirtatious.

After he had bottomed out, Gary whispered in her ear, "Don't look so sad. It's only money. Wanna see what I get for supporting the house?" Champagne glasses in hand, she and Gary went through the busy lobby, past a guard station and to a secluded bank of gilded elevators. From there they rode up to his lavish suite with its towering vista over The Strip. Gary smiled broadly as they stepped out onto the flower-bedecked limestone terrace just as sunset began to settle onto the elegant cocktail table, already set for two.

"What if it hadn't been me you found downstairs?" she asked coyly.

"Well then, I guess I would have been spending a long night all alone," he answered, folding her into his arms.

As the car swerved onto the Expressway, Skippy's reverie broke. She dreaded the possibility that Lucy had read any of her thoughts. The whole episode in Las Vegas was so out of character for her, so melodramatic, like one of those romance novels she couldn't help picking up at the airport. She looked at her attorney, who had stopped asking questions.

Actually, Lucy was waiting. The silence might pressure her client into revealing the whole story.

Skippy took the bait. "Before we left Vegas, we agreed to drop it. You know, like the saying goes. And then when we got back, Gary handled his real estate deals exclusively through me, and I gave him my referrals. My work really took off. I have to say, I owe him a lot for that."

"Did Everett ever have a clue?"

"No. He never knew anything about it, only that Gary was a great help with my career. While I was pregnant, things were better at home. Everett was more attentive. After years of giving us grief, his folks finally seemed to come around. And when Beau was born, they told us they were expanding their apartment in the city and giving us Laurel Hall. It was something we never expected. It was the best time in our marriage, so I had no reason to look back. I never considered that Gary could be Beau's father."

Lucy was more than a little skeptical about this.

"Or maybe I just shut it out," her client said.

"Did Gary ever mention it to you?"

"What, the possibility that Beau was his? Of course not, he was in the middle of a mess at home — you know, his own custody thing. The last thing he needed was to learn he might be some other child's father. Maybe he thought about it, but he never said anything to me. Until recently," she added, as they pulled into the parking garage of the medical building. The car came to a stop.

"He wants to take Beau for a DNA test," Skippy said. "I've told him no, that it wasn't going to happen. I told him over and over, and when I finally refused to answer his calls, he accosted me outside of work. It was on Friday, just before I called you. He told me that I'd better cooperate or he'd take matters into his own hands." Again, her voice began to quiver, and she looked away. "Sometimes, I can't believe my life."

"You and everybody else."

The two made their way through the doors of the medical office. It wasn't long before Howie came out to give Lucy his usual big bear hug and to shrug off her profuse thanks for accommodating the "emergency" patient on such short notice. After the two kidded one another about being the only shmucks to show up early to work on a snow day, Howie ushered Mrs. Brockhurst in for a brief examination.

Luckily, Lucy had warned him ahead of time that Skippy was a skillful negotiator and would be resistant to any ultimatums he might lay down. Indeed, he found that she initially denied the problem altogether. While taking her vitals, however, he learned enough through casual questioning to diagnose not only anorexia, but possibly bulimia. Howie told her that she could avoid immediate hospitalization only by promising to return later in the week for a full evaluation.

After walking the patient out to the waiting room, he turned to the two women and said as he frowned at them both, over his bifocals, "Mrs. Brockhurst, you are not going to wait for your doctor to get back from Aspen. And since you don't seem to like his partner, I would advise that you get back in here within two days. My secretary will work you into the schedule. Are we all on the same page?"

It was rare for Lucy to see this side of Howie, since her visits had always had an informal cast. She was glad he spoke aloud to them both. By doing so, he was able to keep his friend in on the plan. Skippy made an appointment, just after which her sister stepped into the waiting room. She struck Lucy as a down-to-earth version of her client, attractive but in a more natural way. Georgina's long, dark hair was streaked with grey, her face unadorned by make-up. Extending her hand out to her sister's attorney, she gave her a welcoming smile and personally thanked Ms. Bennett for having gone the extra mile.

The gesture surprised Lucy; this was something Skippy would never have done. On parting, Skippy confirmed she'd meet Lucy later in the week to determine how to handle Gary's threat. For now, the instruction was for the sisters to keep close guard of Beau, and to call the office if anything seemed unusual.

CHAPTER FOUR

O n her way back to the office in the airport limo, Lucy got hold of Howie and thanked him again for seeing her client. Their respective professions often came down to the same thing: handling people in crisis. Controlling what happened after they left their offices was a different issue. No matter how sound the advice given, their clients were going to do exactly as they pleased.

She tried to get through to Ruby, but her assistant was still finishing up on the phone, calling clients whose court dates were canceled due to the weather. Ruby reassured them that the firm was working on rescheduling their matters and that she would urge the court to take the emergency cases on the next available date. She had completed her last call when Lucy arrived, asking her to get the rest of the firm on a conference call to coordinate the next day's schedule. While Lucy would normally have taken advantage of the rare day without appointments to remain at the office and catch up on work, Ruby wouldn't leave unless she did.

"Buzz Melissa and tell her we're closing shop early."

"Did I hear you right?" Ruby asked.

"Yeah, and let's do it before something else comes up."

The doors of Bennett and Birnbaum officially closed at two-thirty that day, an unusual occurrence.

Even though she left the office early, Lucy still had her afternoon and evening's work cut out for her, needing to prepare for the next day's full morning in court. However, as she pulled up to her house, she took the time to notice, if not admire, the mighty, six-foot snow and ice superhero gracing her front yard, sparkling in the bright sunshine for all to see. The boys had placed a Bud Light can on the giant snowman's raised stump of an arm.

Yet for all the boys' diligent work outside, the driveway and walk remained unplowed and un-shoveled. They could build a monument, Lucy mused, but shovel a path or clean the driveway? Obviously, the thought hadn't crossed their minds. The only path to the house was the choppy clearing cut by the boys' snow boots as they had trekked in and out of the house with their buddies. She figured the boys were off with their friends, sledding on their boogie boards over at the elementary school. They hadn't yet outgrown that sort of fun.

Her driveway still snow-covered, Lucy wondered why the plow guys hadn't come by. She had yet to pick up her phone message saying their truck was stuck on the turnpike. Dan was still at work and had told her he couldn't get home early. She refused to let the snowy muck turn into ice overnight. So, for the second time that day, Lucy scrounged around for a package of ice melt and cast it along the front steps. She spent a good half hour shoveling the front path and chopping at the areas that were already icing over.

"I'll blame you all if I pull out my back!" she shouted aloud to the wind. Kristen would have had something decent cooking, the house clean and cozy. But her au pair was back in Idaho, having been called home on the death of her grandfather. Lucy stepped inside her home to face the mess left behind by her unchaperoned boys and their buddies. In the hallway and along the banister, there were piles of rejected coats, hats and gloves, on the kitchen floor, puddles of melted snow, in the sink a dozen dirty mugs, on the table, empty packages of hot chocolate-mix and on the counters, a field of crumbs from pizza bagels. When, exactly, had she stopped praying for snow days and started to dread them? Hadn't she promised herself that she would never grow up, never grow old, always love the snow?

As she placed the clothing back into the closet, she came across a pair of fuzzy green mittens. She recognized them from years ago, gloves for a child's small hands. She would have thrown them out on the spot, but, as with so many other things from the past, it was hard to let go. Perhaps that accounted for all the recent arguing with the boys. She, who had protected and guided them all their lives, was not about to abandon her maternal role anytime soon, no

matter how much they resented her hovering. She was their advo-
cate, their champion. It was the same for many of her friends and
certain clients, who focused on their children's welfare above all
else.

She saw it in Skippy Brockhurst, who beneath her arrogance and
condescension, seemed determined to do her very best for her children. And yet, that once invincible woman appeared vulnerable and
unsure, frightened. Perhaps it was partially due to Skippy's weakened
condition, thought Lucy, as she considered what sort of strength her
client would need to get through her current dilemma.

***

The client was asking herself the same question. The agency's "top
producer" hadn't been to her office in days. Instead, she was stretched
out on her favorite couch, watching her sister start to unload the boxes
of Christmas decorations. The children were busy with their aunt,
who chatted on about the excitement ahead of them: Beau's birthday,
Christmas, and a trip to Disney. The cozy domestic scene and the scent
of holiday cookies baking in the kitchen all but dispelled Skippy's anxi-
ety. The light-hearted chatter went on around her, and as she closed
her eyes, she saw the immense stretch of leaf-covered lawn before her.
It was only a few months ago...

September, and the intoxicating smell of the bonfire of leaves burning
at "Oleander," the Downing property. No one would think of lighting
even a small fire without the Town's permission but on the vast old
estate, things continued as they had years ago. The smoke lost itself
within the acres of forest and what little drifted off beyond the land's
perimeters seemed to bother no one. She and Gary were walking what
she called the "North 40," surveys in hand, the sun warming them on
the cool, autumn day. She had brought him another rare opportunity,
a job as the architect to design the restoration of the Downing mansion. In addition, he would be designing an elegant conservatory to be
built beside the old greenhouses.

They approached the bonfire and waved to the estate's caretaker. The old man, in his tweed cap and worn suede coat, barely seemed to respond. He was intent on supervising his small crew of men as they carefully added barrels of leaves to the bonfire. As Skippy had explained to Gary, there was a covenant that ran with the sale of the property, allowing the caretaker to continue maintaining the greenhouses as long as he was able, and to live in the cottage until his demise. The property seemed to enchant Gary, who commented favorably as to the old mansion, the gardens, the site for the conservatory and most of all, the sweeping meadows.

Skippy thought at the time that Gary looked unusually pleased, so different from his demeanor at the Aston Fall Homecoming Concert, when he'd seemed distracted rather than his usual friendly self. He attended the concert at the headmaster's invitation to celebrate the kick-off event for the school's new performing arts center. Skippy had lobbied long and hard for the arts center's renovation to go to the Vaughn Design Group, and when coming over to exchange mutual congratulations with Gary, she proudly pointed out Beau. Her son, with his violin, was climbing on stage with his classmates as they prepared to perform.

Gary nodded as he spotted Beau, but made no comment. He didn't smile back at Skippy as she might have expected. Later, rather than give her a cordial goodbye, he left without a word. Bad business, she had thought, to give her the cold shoulder rather than thanks for all she had done on his behalf.

The day they met at the Downing estate, he seemed to be right back to his old self. He mentioned, as they stood watching bonfire, that the smell of the burning leaves always brought back old memories. He turned to her with what she assumed would be some reference to the one old memory he loved to bring up, despite their mutual promise to leave it alone. Perhaps he imagined that mention of their Las Vegas interlude would give him a little leverage in whatever deal they were handling. Or maybe he just liked to rattle her. She could tell he found the whole thing amusing. It always ended with her telling him to "cut the shit" and get back to business.

As they walked slowly away from the bonfire and back toward the mansion, she was prepared for him to start up once again with his foolish innuendos.

"You know," he started, "I used to have a nickname...when I was a kid."

"Oh, yeah?" Skippy responded, in her best smart-ass tone.

"Yep. It was 'Flame.'"

"Oh," Skippy laughed. Would he never stop trying? "Isn't that the name of some horse I once rode?"

"You should talk. I definitely rode a horse named Skippy."

"Oh, here we go again," she muttered.

"Yep, they called me Flame. I was quite a redhead," he said. "Wouldn't believe that, seeing me now, huh?" he chuckled lightly, roughing up his light brown hair.

Every bone in her body froze. It was not funny, not in the least. She didn't even need to look at him; she knew what he was driving at. The nausea had started then and never stopped.

"See, Mom, I made a happy face," Emma giggled. She placed a fresh-baked cookie into her mother's hand.

"Oh thanks, Emma," Skippy said, rousing slowly. She did her best to take a nibble, then looked up at her sister, who was carrying a plateful more.

"It's you, me and the cookies," Georgina said sternly, placing the goodies on the tea table. "So, sister, let's get to work."

***

Lucy was just about finished with her cleanup, when she heard the shouts of her kids and their friends out front and snow balls pelting against the kitchen window as the snowball fight picked up in earnest. As she started to prepare dinner, she found a moment to peek outside to catch the boys' ridiculous antics.

"Uncle! Uncle!" Rahme was screaming, caught between what could have been two of the school's best wrestlers had they actually liked school sports. The Morrell brothers preferred horsing around and stuffing snow down their victim's coats. Her boys pulled the "wrestlers" off and started in on them using their best short-range pitches. Rahme, with a devilish shriek, knocked off the heavy stump of the snowman's arm and charged ahead with it into the melee.

"Oh, man, you wrecked Super Frosty! Man down, man down!" Adam shrieked as the snowman stood dismembered, the beer can disappearing into the snow.

"It's WAR!" The battle switched into full gear, whoops and shouts bursting from the warriors, snowballs flying in every direction as the first major snowball fight of the season turned deadly; in the cross fire, Super Frosty was utterly destroyed.

Lucy cranked open the window just a crack. "Hey guys, someone's gonna get hurt!" She didn't need speed dial for the office number of her boys' pediatric orthopedist; she had it memorized. Her boys seemed to take delight in calling her from the site of their latest injury to let her know what bone had been newly broken and in what position it had ended up. Each had their own personal list of fractures, with total visits to their orthopedist now topping twenty. Today's possible contusions wouldn't qualify, nor snow "raspberries," and definitely not frostbite.

She shouted again, but it was of no use. The rampage eventually ended out of the teenagers' sheer exhaustion. Rahme and the Morrell boys straggled home, while her own boys trudged in completely covered with snow, still trash-talking one another.

"Hey!" Lucy called from the kitchen. "I just finished cleaning up your mess, so listen up! Boots off, coats and stuff in the dryer." They went on harassing one another as though they hadn't heard her, but managed to follow her orders.

By the time Dan got home, the scene was quiet, the house was cleaned up, dinner was ready and the boys were hanging out in their rooms, as if it had been an orderly and peaceful afternoon. Lucy was sitting at the table, reviewing a separation agreement.

Dan wondered aloud about the great lump of snow that had formed in the middle of their front lawn.

"Apparently, you missed all the fun," Lucy said.

"Hey, why don't we sit down to a nice dinner, just you and me?" Dan proposed, knowing that this would never happen.

"What, and miss the day's entertainment?" Lucy chuckled. The entire idea of dinner was based on the fact that the boys would provide a measure of comic relief for the day's usual horrors. Lucy looked up at Dan as he leaned over for a kiss, and as always, thanked her lucky stars that this was her man.

CHAPTER FIVE

S he tapped on the courtroom door just as Pete, one of her favorite court officers, was unlocking it. "How are we today, gorgeous? What do you have on with us?"

"I think it's the Lucy Bennett part this morning," she laughed.
"Can you mark me here on Kornblum, Nixon and Hecht? Look, I'll
be right back, I swear, but if one of my adversaries arrives, please tell
them not to move."

Lucy started down the hall toward the bathroom when out of the
corner of her eye she spied one of her favorite adversaries. "Glen!" she
called. "Do me a favor, big guy, and check in with Judge Thorpe's part,
first. I'll get you right in and out if you just wait there one second. I
think we'll be the only case ready for conference."

"No problem," Glen replied. "I'll be talking to Mr. Kornblum and
by the time you're back, I'll be ready."

"You're on."

The Kornblum conference would prove to be Lucy's easiest of
the day. The judge insisted on keeping close control of his cases and
wanted to make sure everything was moving along as it should. He
also insisted on the clients appearing each day that the case was on in
court, rather than just meeting with the attorneys.

Of course, when there was nothing to be accomplished other than
to check on the status of the case, this made no sense. But no one
wanted to take the chance of annoying Judge Thorpe. After all, with
five judges in the matrimonial part, he was likely to have one-fifth of
the cases of any divorce lawyer in Abbott County. He was picky. He was
a stickler. Whatever he wanted, Judge Thorpe got.

It was easy to spot her client. The pasty-faced, pudgy lady with jet-black hair sat cross-legged, her deep red lipstick outlining thin, pursed lips. "Good morning, Felicia," Lucy said to Mrs. Kornblum. "We just have to tell the judge that I'll be deposing your husband this afternoon. Once we do that, you can take a break and then meet me at my office at one-thirty. The deposition should start around two, but in case there's anything you'd like to make sure I delve into, why don't we spend a little time together just beforehand."

"Do you think that's going to give us enough time?"

"Felicia, have I met with you every time you've asked for an appointment on this case? And do I sound like I know your case pretty well? And you must know by now that I don't particularly like your husband, right? Trust me, I spent at least five hours reviewing his records over the weekend. Nothing will give me more pleasure than getting him. You probably won't even need a half hour." Mrs. Kornblum did not look convinced.

"You ready, Glen?" Lucy called to her adversary from across the back row of the courtroom. "Pete said the judge is ready for us."

"Yeah, let's do it."

"Pete, can you do me a favor and if any of the other guys show up on my files, just bring them in after Glen."

"If they're here, no problem," answered Pete, ushering her into the judge's chambers.

"Good morning, Your Honor," Lucy said as she took a chair at the conference table. Glen took a seat across from her. The judge joined the lawyers, taking a seat at the head of the table. As opposed to many of the other judges who personalized their chambers, this room was unusually spartan. His "dress," as he called it, hung on the metal coat rack beside the door. On his desk were a few family photos in simple frames, and along one wall a plain cabinet with the requisite law books that he used on a daily basis. A large calendar dominated the room. Had she been in Judge Oser's chambers, Lucy would have already been offered some coffee and fresh bagels, and would have been admiring the lovely artwork that made her room so much more welcoming. Instead, the attorney's stomach was growling.

"How'd you make out with all the snow?" Lucy asked the judge.

"My wife took the SUV, but surprisingly my little Honda did the trick. How'd you do?"

"I have to admit I keep a big truck just for this sort of weather, so I actually got to the office yesterday. Sometimes, I'm sorry to be so mobile."

"Okay," the judge started, "Where are you folks on the Kornblum case?"

Glen jumped in. "The bloodsucker over there is deposing Mr. Kornblum this afternoon."

Lucy's nostrils flared. She wanted to say something about fightin' words, but she and Glen were notorious throughout the courthouse for taking potshots at one another, just for the fun of it. She let him go on. With a wink at his opponent, Glen said, "We'll have a better idea of whether this thing can settle after we see what Lucy gets out of him."

"How about you two come back after the holiday, in about three weeks and let me know where we're heading. What's good for you?"

Lucy whipped out her iPhone. Seeing that she'd be back in the judge's part during the week he mentioned, she coordinated a date with Glen. "Get that coffee ready for this afternoon, my friend," he warned as he stood up to leave. "It's going to be a long haul."

"Extra sugar, just for you," promised Lucy.

"Judge, do you mind if I stay here with you?" Lucy asked as Glen left the room. "I've got the Hecht and Nixon cases to conference with you, and Pete said he'd be on the lookout for Bill Davies or Nick DeBello."

Just then, Pete entered the conference room with Mr. DeBello, himself. "Good morning everyone!" The burly lawyer's deep, raspy voice filled the room. There was nothing quiet about Nick.

"Hey buddy, nice to see ya'," Lucy responded, matching his big hello, but ready to plunge right in. "Tell me, Nick, does Mr. Nixon have any cash on him today to pay the back child support?"

As he took a seat across from Lucy, Nick sighed. "Listen, this guy wouldn't tell me if he had ten bucks or a million bucks. He tells me that business has been slow. And who am I to know what's going on in his diner?"

"Well, you see, Nick, that's the thing. I actually do know what's going on there. I sent my PI over to see how busy the diner was for two days last week, and two days the week before. She's prepared to tell the court that business is booming."

"I think she's got you this time, Nick," Judge Thorpe cautioned. "What do you say we go on the record after Lucy finishes her next conference with me? Don't leave for another courtroom, Mr. DeBello. I do not want to have to hunt you down. I will take the bench in about ten minutes. Have your client ready."

"Okay, Judge," Nick offered in a tone more subdued than usual. "We'll be waiting."

As Nick started out of the room, the court officer walked past Lucy with a knowing glance. He was partial to lawyers from his county, and Nick wasn't one of them. Pete enjoyed seeing Lucy get the best of him.

"Judge, I have Bill Davies on Lucy's last case. Can I bring him in, now?"

"Sure, Pete, that'll be fine."

While the judge couldn't show even a hint of partiality, Lucy knew that he, just like Pete, liked to see the lawyers from his own county do a number on the out-of-towners. Lucy was glad she'd had the foresight to have Maria DioGuardi keep an eye on the diner for a few days before court. This way she'd get enough information to give the judge a basis for taking the action her client needed. She was tired of the guys in their cash businesses claiming instant poverty, thinking no one would ever discover the truth. The local divorce bar had created a name for the people in these types of businesses. They called it SAIDS, Sudden Acquired Income Deficiency Syndrome.

Pete strolled into the judge's chambers with Bill Davies. The tall, athletic-looking attorney carried a small file, and was impeccably dressed in a dark suit. "Good morning, your Honor, and to you as well, Lucy."

Lucy liked Bill. He was a stand-up guy: smart, realistic and honest. She couldn't recall having a case with him that didn't eventually settle. They each knew their stuff, advocated strongly, but in the end tried to come up with something that would be effective for both parties. Each needed to win on a point or two, but working that way was far better than gambling on what might happen at trial.

"Judge, Lucy and I need a little time on this one. Mrs. Hecht was admittedly taken by surprise by my client's announcement that he didn't want to be married to her anymore." Lucy was grateful that Bill was taking the heat on this one by providing the court with an explanation as to why her client hadn't made progress with the financial statement. In the initial stage of all matrimonial actions, the court required each party to prepare their affidavit of net worth, disclosing their income, expenses, assets and debts. But getting a client like Mrs. Hecht to sit down and address her financial situation at the start of the case, her most vulnerable moment, was no easy task.

"Bill is correct, your Honor," Lucy added. "My client is just starting to realize that her husband is not coming back. Judge, I have to say Mrs. Hecht really didn't see this coming. After thirty years of what she considered a happy marriage, his announcement hit her like a ton of bricks. I've gotten her into therapy and she's just starting to lose the deer in the headlights look. Now that her therapist has her under a little more control, I think I can start working with her on some numbers. It's amazing what the right doses of Xanax and Lexapro can do for a person."

Lucy looked to see if she was making any headway with the judge. He remained poker-faced. "Anyway," she went on, "Mr. Hecht handled most of the finances, so I'm going to need at least another six weeks to work on getting some realistic numbers from her. She has no idea as to what she's spending now or what she'll need to live on. Remember, she's fifty-five and hasn't worked for a living in over thirty years." Already setting up her case, Lucy paused to add emphasis to her last point. "I've spoken with Bill, and he's indicated that he'll have his client try to provide some of the numbers for her."

"He's not a bad guy," Bill explained to the judge. "He wants to do the right thing, financially. He just can't live with her anymore."

The judge regarded the two attorneys before him, and thought of his own wife. Carol would be a basket case if he showed up one day and said not to take it personally, but he just couldn't live with her anymore. "All right," he said, "This case is pretty new, so I can give you people some time. Pick a date in the next two months that works for you and your clients, and we'll see you then."

Lucy was relieved for Mrs. Hecht. The judge could just as easily have set a tighter deadline that would have caused her lady immeasurable stress. She explained to her adversary that the judge was about to come out on the bench on her other case, and that there was bound to be fireworks. They'd have to coordinate their schedules quickly, before the "show" started. As much as Bill enjoyed watching one of the judge's spirited displays, he had cases on elsewhere in the courthouse, so hurriedly worked with Lucy to confirm a mutually convenient date.

Lucy came out of chambers at last, prepared to juggle her clients. She signaled to Mrs. Kornblum that she'd be with her in a minute, then turned to Mrs. Hecht and asked her to wait for a few more minutes until after Judge Thorpe had handled the Nixon matter. It never hurt to have her clients watch as the Judge reamed out the other side on one of her matters. Of course, this could create false expectations for the observer, but on balance, Lucy thought it made her clients feel better when they saw her winning.

Pete asked for counsel and their clients to take their places at the counsel table so that he could bring the judge out. The courtroom was pretty well packed, since it was still early in the day. Lucy sensed that the judge liked to take the bench under those circumstances, showman that he was. He seemed to relish making an example of someone in front of the whole room so that all would be advised not to fool with him.

"All rise," Pete called out as he banged on the door and Judge Thorpe entered the court. "This is the matter of Nixon versus Nixon, your Honor." The court reporter was already tapping away. "Counsel, your appearances for the record."

"Lucy Bennett of Bennett and Birnbaum, 1500 West Olive Street, Newtown, New York, for the Plaintiff."

"E. Nicholas DeBello of Chatman, DeBello and Hanniff, 500 County Road, Rye, New York for the Defendant," Nick boomed in one breath.

"Mr. Nixon, I've been told that you are not paying your wife the support that I ordered you to pay. Is that true?"

"Well, your Honor," Mr. Nixon stammered. "I've had a hard time keeping up. Business at the diner has its ups and downs."

Lucy could scarcely believe it. Hadn't DeBello warned this guy about her PI's information?

"Sir, are you telling me that you are not current with my order?"

"Yes, your Honor, but it's not that I'm not trying."

"Mr. Nixon, do me a favor and empty your pockets, would you?"

Mr. Nixon looked at Nick with horror in his eyes. Was this something they could refuse to do? Nick was absolutely still, signifying he could do nothing to intervene. Mr. Nixon fumbled in his back pockets and jacket pockets for a minute or two, and a murmur arose in the courtroom as it became clear that Judge Thorpe was losing his patience. Finally, the noise level rose too high and the judge banged the gavel and asked for silence.

Once the room quieted down, the judge spoke again. "Mr. Nixon, let's go with the right pants pocket, shall we?"

And then it happened. There wasn't a thing Nick DeBello could do as his client pulled out a roll of cash from his pocket. These guys just can't help themselves, Lucy thought. Didn't they know better than to have wads of cash in their pockets while claiming poverty? She had seen the judge do this before, and each time there seemed to be a pocketful at the critical moment.

"Now, hand that over to your wife," the judge instructed. Mrs. Nixon wasn't sure whether to laugh or cry as she started counting out the fifty and hundred dollar bills that were handed to her. And then she heard Judge Thorpe say, "Mr. Nixon, let's try the other pocket, shall we?" Another roll came out, as the gallery in the courtroom started to titter. This pocket contained the fives and tens that Nixon kept in a roll for change on smaller purchases.

"Mr. DeBello, instruct your client that he has exactly one week to get current with my order or he can come back here with his toothbrush, ready to be taken to the county jail."

Lucy and Nick both knew that Mr. Nixon was entitled to a hearing before being carted off to the slammer, but neither was going to mention it, and certainly not when Judge Thorpe was on the bench. Nick debated whether or not it was worth his while to make a record on the hearing issue so that he could go to a higher court if he needed to appeal. Truthfully, though, he was no fan of Nixon's; he'd been a royal pain in the ass and after this demonstration, he was sure to be able to find the money. The judge had made his point to the audience and to the Nixons. As he left the bench, Judge Thorpe was fully aware of the buzz he'd created.

Lucy's moment of satisfaction was brief. She had to attend to her clients, explain to each of them the results of the appearances, and reconfirm their court schedules. She took Mrs. Hecht aside for a few minutes, and firmly advised her that when they received Mr. Hecht's financial information, she would have to finalize her net worth statement.

Seeing her client's paralysis, Lucy gently touched her on the arm and said, "I know this isn't going to be easy for you. But the only way I can get you what you're entitled to is for you to tell me what you'll need to live on."

CHAPTER SIX

Lucy considered the upcoming afternoon of depositions with mixed emotions as she headed to her car. She enjoyed these examinations before trial, especially in a case like Kornblum, but the hours needed to interview witnesses could have been devoted to meeting potential new clients, a more profitable use of her time. Nonetheless, if she was going to keep getting the big cases, she had to keep handling her fair share of the depositions. Otherwise she'd risk having an important client complain they'd hired Lucy Bennett but weren't getting her services.

That was one of the interesting challenges of running her sort of firm. Lucy had a thriving practice that had grown to be one of the top divorce firms in the county. As in other busy law firms, the more successful they became, the more staff they needed, the more cases they needed to take to support the staff and so on, thereby creating a vicious cycle of never-ending work for Lucy and the troops. And as was true with all of the most successful divorce firms, the client hired the firm, not only one individual. The retainer agreements made that very clear.

Nonetheless, Lucy was constantly in demand, since she was the most experienced attorney at the firm, but primarily because of her reputation as "the barracuda." She tried to vary the hourly rates between herself and her associates, so that the clients would be tempted to save money and work with someone else. Certainly, she wasn't needed for the day-to-day problems and frankly, the other lawyers were often more patient than was she.

She told prospective clients that she would handle the settlement conferences and critical parts of the cases if they wanted her, but that her staff was there to cover the routine issues that arose. While depositions could be handled by either her or an associate, certain cases such as Kornblum required Lucy's expertise in analyzing financial and business records.

Lucy looked forward to the day's deposition, despite her client's difficult attitude. The proceedings could actually prove enjoyable, at least in the sense of a sporting event. She understood clients like Felicia, who had been spoiled during the marriage. The woman appeared in Lucy's rear-view mirror, driving en route from the court to the attorney's office, her mouth working endlessly as she chatted away on speakerphone. The client spent her marriage living in a palatial home, in an affluent area, with four children, and a cleaning lady who came in twice a week. Felicia hadn't worked outside the home for over a dozen years, and was a member of The Hunt Club, where she was satisfied to play on a USTA 3.0 team. She sandwiched her games between her shopping and salon appointments.

As Lucy well knew, nothing about this sort of lifestyle was considered at all extravagant or luxurious to her client. In fact, in comparison to many of her friends who frequented the country's finest spas, traveled overseas several times a year and stepped out in only designer clothes, Felicia considered herself a simple housewife, with a simple formula for living: Mr. Kornblum made the money and she got to spend it. That was the deal, and the thought of it ending terrified her.

As Lucy approached her office, she felt a certain annoyance in having to knock herself out for a person who took it all for granted. At times Lucy envied Felicia's life of leisure, but only briefly, because she'd never be faced with her client's terror; Lucy was capable of financial independence, something she was trying to make sure was being taught to all of her clients' children. No one should find themselves in Felicia's shoes. Despite her client's whining, which clearly came from her current state of desperation, Lucy resolved to do her damnedest to make sure the lady and her children remained quite comfortable. The attorney loved to win, and her competitive attitude kept the clients rolling in. She might have lost a bit of empathy along the way, but one thing was sure: if anyone was going to get her clients their money and lifestyle, it was Lucy Bennett.

***

Ruby greeted her boss with a long list of problems.

"Whatever it is, it'll have to wait," Lucy said as she flew by her assistant. "She's already here." The attorney had seen Felicia's car enter the parking lot behind her. Time would fly if she didn't get started with the client right away. She instructed Ruby to bring in Mrs. Kornblum as soon as she came through the door.

Naturally, Felicia chose to sit on the handsome, hand-carved chair, an antique. Lucy let her vent about her situation, and then went about making sure that the client told her everything she knew about her husband's business. Lucy had learned as much as she could from the poorly-kept records and the rest was going to come from Mort explaining how they could live as they did, if he was as piss poor as he claimed to be.

Glen and his client already assembled in the conference room, Lucy walked in followed by her client. She gave a warm greeting to the regular court reporter, Peggy, who was there to take down the day's testimony. Lucy liked to use Peggy's services because she was accurate and prompt in getting the transcripts completed. Likewise, the reporter enjoyed working for Bennett and Birnbaum, since the firm paid on time and since Lucy always made the depositions more entertaining than did most of the other divorce lawyers.

In accordance with Lucy's usual instructions, snacks and water were set out on the table, and coffee had been served all around. Seating was not random at these "examinations before trial." There was a certain protocol, and Lucy saw that because her experienced adversary knew the deal, there was no need to play musical chairs. The rule of thumb was for the person doing the questioning and the person doing the answering to sit closest to the reporter, who could then clearly hear their words and accurately memorialize them. Accordingly, Lucy sat down next to Peggy and directly across from Mort.

Ms. Bennett began with the customary courtesy explanation to Mort that she would be asking some questions, and that if he didn't understand one or couldn't answer it, he should let her know and she would rephrase it. She relaxed back into the comfortable leather chair, took a large sip of coffee, and smiled into Mort's eyes, as though she was truly eager just to get to know him.

Lucy started slowly, asking Mort about his work history, then building up to how he had gotten into the hotel trade. Based on her experience with deposing business owners, she was not surprised that Mort loved to talk about himself and his vast success. He was proud to say how he started with nothing when he was first married, and ended up with the lavish house, cars, boat and a thriving business. The fact that these assets were acquired during marriage made them marital property, to be shared with his wife. He spoke of all the hours he'd had to put in on the job, while Felicia was home.

The more he talked about the amount of time he spent away from home and what Felicia did to run the household, raise the children and entertain their friends and his business associates, the more he made Lucy's case for her. She was grateful that, long ago, New York wisely changed its divorce laws to provide for what was termed "equitable distribution" of marital property. While there was no presumption of a fifty-fifty split, the longer people were married, the more likely it was that this would be the result. More importantly, New York recognized the value of a wife's taking responsibility not only for the children and personal aspects of her husband's life, but also considered the value of entertaining the spouse's clients and business prospects. By doing so, she freed her husband to work, gave him social contacts with prospective customers and facilitated his success. This made her his "partner," deserving to share in his prosperity. The rules were the same regardless of gender and so, Lucy had many a male client share in his wife's successful business or practice.

By the time they were an hour or so into the proceeding, it was as though Lucy and Mort had become old friends. Peggy revealed no trace of what she was thinking, but she knew Mr. Kornblum was doomed. This was what the reporter liked so much about Lucy's depositions. There was no drama, no attack from Lucy's front. Rather than a battle, the examination took on the appearance of an informal conversation. As in this case, Lucy's witness typically fell under the spell of her seemingly casual approach. She disarmed her hapless victim into giving away more information than he or she realized. She often started in areas that didn't seem central to the job at hand, but which gave her the ammunition she needed to benefit her client down the road.

"So, Mort," Lucy began after taking another sip of coffee, as though the two of them were chatting over lunch at the local diner. "How often does a place like Hillside Suites have its bedspreads cleaned?"

Mr. Kornblum answered, "Oh, gee, the valet service only does them about once a month. I know he thinks I'm a chazar — you know, cheapskate — but I think the valet is a goniff, who's always trying to talk me into more cleaning. How does he expect me to make a profit if I'm always paying him to clean things?"

"Mort," Lucy interrupted, "can you tell the reporter what goniff means so that we have a clear record?"

"You know, a thief. I figured you knew what I was talking about, smart Jewish lawyer like you."

"Mort, is it the same with even your most expensive hotel, what is it again —?" Lucy rifled through her pile of documents, as though she hadn't memorized the name of every one of his accounts. "Oh yeah," she added as though just recollecting, "The Mayfield?"

"Yup," Mort answered. "Same as everyone else."

Lucy did some rough calculations in her head and concluded that she would never, ever again sit, other than completely clothed, on a hotel bedspread. If the Mayfield could handle its linens this way, God only knew what really went on in the lesser establishments.

"So Mort, I assume you have no choice with the sheets? You have to pay the valet to change those every day, and sometimes even more, right?" Lucy asked.

"Well, the better hotels like the Excelsior and the Grand wrap sheets around the blankets and then change the sheets and pillows every day, even for the same guests. That way the guests know their sheets are clean, and can comfortably pull the blankets over them. And I can charge those guests at that level of hotel for making things clean and tidy for them. That's what they expect from a five-star hotel. Makes everyone happy."

Lucy could only think that her opponent had drifted off, perhaps dreaming of a nice stay at the Excelsior, when Mort continued, unchecked.

"Now, a motel like Baybridge, those guests don't give a shit. Oh, excuse me," Mort apologized to the court reporter, who didn't flinch. He continued, blithely. "The people going there don't worry about wrapping up blankets. My valet service just changes the sheets as many times a day as the room requires. When the mood in the city is depressed, the execs and CEOs and brokers are in there all day fucking their brains out. When their business is in the crapper, they mess up plenty of sheets. And I make lots of money renting the same room out to more than one lovely couple a day. So, I do plenty well even if I have to pay the valet service for people, you know — coming and going all day long." Mort was the only one to laugh at his raunchy joke.

Glen shot a look at Mort. Before the deposition, he had carefully instructed his client to provide only the briefest answers and nothing more. But his client disregarded his advice, eager to speak in front of his captive audience. Lucy had often found herself in her adversary's shoes, but used other techniques to alert the client. In this case, she would have called for a brief pause in the proceedings, giving her a moment to rein in her client.

Perhaps, she thought, Glen realized it was futile. After all, there was Mort, grabbing another slice of bagel and looking around the room as though wondering why the conversation had stopped, oblivious to the fact that he'd just blabbed away any chance of getting out of this cheaply.

This deposition was turning into a field day for Lucy. She let Mr. Kornblum swallow his mouthful.

"Mort, other than the linens and bedspreads, is there anything else you have regularly cleaned in your hotels?"

"Well, let's see. The drapes are supposed to be done every three months, except Mayfield does it every two and Hillside every four. Then there's the carpeting, which is on about the same schedule."

Lucy silently vowed never to go near a hotel room's drapes other than to pull the cord very carefully, nor ever to walk barefoot across a hotel room. Lucy took Mort through a variety of other areas involved in the hotel industry from the maid service, to major repairs and general staff expenses. Then they covered the bedbug epidemic, a new and very expensive problem that had already started to take a bite out of Mort's profits. As it turned out, Mort had already managed to turn the problem into a goldmine by advertising that his was the first hotel chain to offer a safe, natural preventative that beat the varmints before they could get in.

When Lucy got to the hot sheet trade, things got a bit more dicey. There were none of the written contracts like with the big boys, and none of the monthly checks. Payments could be made at any time, and were rarely reflected in the checks listed in Mort's ledgers. While he rambled on about the crazy goings-on in the motels, Lucy was busy calculating the unreported income that Felicia should share. Mort liked his life, and as much as he'd grown tired of his wife, Lucy figured that he'd prefer to pay his soon-to-be-ex some extra money rather than have to pay massive taxes, interest and penalties that could easily be arranged by a simple phone call to the IRS.

Eventually, as the sunlight started to fade through the conference room window, Lucy's questions drew to a conclusion. After the long day, she had been able to get Mort to disclose what he figured his profit should be on each type of room in each level of hotel and motel. She reserved the right to inquire further after Mort produced some additional records. Glen would be willing to talk settlement after the plethora of unwitting admissions made by his client. Lucy asked him to stay for a minute while she placed Felicia in her office and Mort in the waiting room.

Facing Glen in the conference room, Lucy looked at her old friend with the slightest hint of the devil in her eyes. "Has your guy said enough yet, or do you wanna do this again?"

"I'll talk to him tomorrow. I guarantee you he still doesn't realize what he gave you today. How about I call you late on Monday?"

"Terrific," Lucy said. "I'll tell Felicia you'll be getting back to me by then, and Glen? Hopefully with some kind of reasonable offer."

They each left the room to speak with their respective clients, as Peggy packed up for the day. Lucy advised her that the manuscript was not a rush job, that a few weeks would be fine. Lucy made a point of making realistic requests as to when she'd need the transcripts. That way, when it was vital to get something done quickly, she was bound to get it. Lucy treated the other people in her "support team" the same way, and in turn, the process servers, investigators and expert witnesses, as well as the other court reporters gave Lucy their best service along with the courtesy her behavior engendered.

Lucy returned to her office to do a post-mortem with Felicia. For a change, her client was smiling. She couldn't quite get the words out to say "thank you" or to tell Lucy she had done a good job, but Felicia's good mood came close enough.

CHAPTER SEVEN

Meg returned to the office from her morning conference in Family Court to find Skippy Brockhurst in the waiting room, busily scribbling notes in her journal. Playing with a magnetic puzzle at the children's table were the two children and their nanny. There was no avoiding Skippy on her way through the room, and though Meg tried to look nonchalant, it was hard to cover up her feelings.

Rather than speak directly to Skippy, she concentrated on the kids. "You've gotten so big since I saw you last!" she said.

The receptionist, Dina, who had been happily observing the well-behaved children, added, "And so good! Like little angels!"

A brief, perfunctory smile crossed Skippy's lips, as she dismissed the various compliments by attending to her cell phone. No one had to tell her that her children were good. She knew it all too well, and dwelling on it would only add to her sense of doom, as their little world was threatened yet again.

Her words of praise eliciting no comment from the client, the receptionist made a mental note that Mrs. Brockhurst seemed very uppity, someone who probably pawned the children off on their nanny just like she was doing right then and there. Dina had seen enough in her many moons to feel sure that this was exactly how children could end up sweet despite their sourpuss mothers: the kind nannies did all the raising.

Meg was relieved that she'd have nothing to do with solving Skippy's current problems. The two women just weren't a good mix. Lucy had already told her that because of Skippy's precarious state, she and Andi would be best suited to handle the situation.

Meg stared straight ahead as Dina buzzed her through the waiting room doors and into the main office. She plopped down her briefcase in the hallway, grabbed her stack of phone slips from her message clip and as she passed Ruby's desk, whispered, "Watch out…it's the devil lady out there."

"Will you please stop it!" Ruby laughed. Lowering her voice, she added, "So she doesn't like you, get over it. Who the hell likes you, anyway?"

"Oh, fuck you, Miss Ruby," Meg retorted.

"Ruby!" Lucy called out from her office. "Would you bring her in?"

A moment later, her assistant ushered in the whole Brockhurst entourage, including the nanny. As Beau and Emma entered her office, Lucy smiled, trying to cover her concern. She could not possibly converse with Skippy in front of the children or Bridgette. It astounded her that so many of her clients chose to have their children by their sides while discussing the most intimate details of their marriage. Worse, they had no compunction about name calling or making disparaging remarks about the children's other parent. Lucy was disappointed to think that Skippy might be among those engaging in this sort of behavior. She was relieved to hear her client's explanation.

"I wanted you to see the kids before we had our talk."

Lucy went straight up to Beau to give him a high-five, and then tousled a hand through Emma's curly hair. "Wow, did you guys get big or what?" Lucy remarked. "What the heck are they feeding you?"

Beau, lately suffering under the weight of too much female adulation, didn't mind Lucy's brand of it and returned her smile. The attorney was too clever to mention his dazzling red hair; she knew from her own boys which territory to avoid.

"You guys into sports these days?" Lucy asked.

"He likes baseball."

"Sorry, Mom, I wasn't talking to you." Lucy said. "Beau, whaddya think of this?" She reached behind her desk and tossed him a baseball signed by Jorge Posada.

Beau caught the ball, to his own relief, and checked it out. "Cool," the boy answered. He had never been to a Yankee game, but knew all about the famous catcher.

"And this," Lucy added, handing him a picture of her boys just behind the dugout, almost within reach of Derek Jeter.

"I like baseball, too," Emma chirped.

"Oh, ya do?" Lucy asked. "Well, I'll keep you both in mind next season. Sometimes I can get a few extra seats at Yankee Stadium." Beau's wide eyes reflected some degree of skepticism, which Lucy alone could discern. She thought she knew why. All the broken promises, another casualty of divorce. "Now, let's see, I am putting this in my schedule." Lucy held up her iPhone and turned it around so that the children could watch as she typed in the words. "Call Mrs. Brockhurst as soon as I get the Yankee calendar, and figure out when Beau and Emma can make a game. Done!" Beau looked up at his mother as though for permission and she smiled back at him. "Oh, and who wants candy?" Lucy pointed out her infamous crystal bowl, toppling with goodies, wondering if the children remembered briefly stopping into this same room, just a few years earlier. They each politely took a piece.

"Okay, now, I've gotta chat with your Mom for a while," Lucy said. "Ruby, let's set the kids up in the conference room."

Ruby guided Bridgette and the kids out of the office, leaving the two women to face the serious issue before them.

"I've gotta hand it to you. You done good," Lucy said. It was true. Skippy had raised those children pretty much on her own, shielding them as much as she could from their parents' difficulties.

"Thanks."

"Their school break started already?" Lucy asked, recalling that the private schools usually scheduled slightly longer vacations.

"Today, at noon. They'll be going to Disney next week, so I won't be as worried. Everett and his parents will be with them."

"Your sister still at your house?"

"No, she just left to go back to her own kids. And her husband's been sick with the flu, so she's got her hands full. I flew her in to talk all of this over with her, but once she was here, I don't know, I just couldn't tell her. She knows I'm under the weather, but seems to think I'm in pretty good hands."

"And how are you feeling?"

"I'll be back at Dr. Gassner's tomorrow. Georgina tried to fatten me up with cookies and her homemade lasagna, but I just don't have an appetite."

"Well, we'll see what Howie can do. I agree with your sister. You're in good hands with him."

Lucy let out a sigh and set her legal pad out before her to signal they were about to get started. "Okay, so let's see where we are. Have you heard from Gary?"

"No, and I don't expect to. I was so angry the last time he called that I don't think he's going to keep trying. I think he'll do something, instead."

"Like?"

"Like take Beau to get tested, or…take him away somewhere. And I can't live this way, thinking it could happen at any time. Isn't there something we can do, like get an order of protection?"

"Look, there are ways of protecting Beau, but if you go that route he's going to have to know," Lucy said.

"I'm not going to allow that," Skippy protested. "How can you expect Beau to deal with something like that?"

"I don't expect him to deal with it. But let's go over our alternatives. You can get the police involved, given the threatening phone calls, and if so, Beau will know about it. But at least he'll be protected. Or, you can take a completely different course and confront Gary to see what he actually has in mind."

"Call him?"

"Yes. At least you'd have an idea what he's up to."

Skippy smacked her hand on the desk. "I should call Gary Vaughn and negotiate? Over my son?"

"You know that's not what I mean. We have to find out what Gary is willing to do. Perhaps we can get the answer in a very simple way. We could have the test done ourselves and see if he really is Beau's father. If the test shows he's not, we can send Gary the results and it's over."

"And what if the test shows he is the father?" Skippy returned, stridently.

"Well, if we could get a sample of Gary's DNA, then perhaps we could do the test surreptitiously and tell him only if it's negative. If it's positive, then we'd have to talk about it and decide what's best for the children."

Skippy glowered at her attorney. "And how would we do a test like that?"

"Well, we've got a private lab that we work with. They handle testing for drugs, DNA and all those things. Remember when we tested Everett for drugs? And no one would need to know about the results unless we want them to. Our only problem will be getting to Gary, to get a sample."

"And how would we get a sample of DNA?" Skippy clipped her words.

"I take it you don't watch TV much," Lucy chuckled. So many of her clients considered themselves to be experts in the law due to their obsession with legal TV dramas; the attorney often had to remind them that it was only fiction. They shouldn't be getting their legal education that way, she instructed. However, in this case, the prior evening's episode of 'Law and Order: Special Victims Unit' had done a pretty decent job of explaining the collection and use of DNA evidence.

"Well," Lucy told her client, "if you'd caught last night's show, you would have learned how easy it is nowadays to gather a sample of someone's DNA. It doesn't take much. I could try to meet with Gary. Maybe even here," she suggested. "All he has to do is take a cup of coffee to his lips and we've got his DNA."

"Why would I want to help Gary prove he's Beau's father? Wouldn't he end up with some sort of right to see him?"

"Well, we don't know if we'd be helping Gary or not. Remember, the person we're trying to help here is Beau." Lucy sat back and let her words sink in. Then she continued.

"You wanna know what the law says? It says a child born during a marriage is presumed to be the legitimate child of that marriage. That's one of the strongest presumptions in the entire body of law. It was designed to protect children, so that their parentage wouldn't be questioned and so that no child would have to suffer the label of being illegitimate. In addition, the law favors stability in a child's life. Everett is the only father Beau has ever known. Therefore, a court might say it would be too disruptive and certainly not in the child's best interest to allow another man to step in as his long lost dad at this late date. An attorney taking that position might employ a legal concept known as 'equitable estoppel,' where someone is 'estopped' or stopped from proceeding on their claim because it's simply not equitable, fair, or the right thing to do. In this case, Gary might be estopped from asserting that he's the biological father on the basis that it wouldn't be right for Beau. So, from this perspective I could certainly use that argument to try and keep Gary away from Beau, if that's what you want."

Lucy waited for Skippy's reaction, but the woman didn't move a muscle.

"On the other hand, it could be argued that Everett has been such a neglectful and indifferent and irresponsible parent that it would be in Beau's best interest to have a chance to have a real father, and therefore Gary shouldn't be stopped from coming forward to make his claim. So the question comes down to this: would a court allow Gary to proceed with his request for DNA testing of Beau? And you know me, Skippy, I could make a good argument either way. Although, frankly, the odds favor your ex-husband."

Skippy faced Lucy. Her attorney was telling her to decide what was better for Beau. She was asking her to decide which argument should be made to the court. Skippy hadn't considered that her own position in the matter might make a difference. Instead, she hoped that the law would be certain and that her attorney could assure her that Gary had no chance in hell, that a strongly worded letter from Bennett and Birnbaum would put an end to the whole matter.

"I just don't know," the client pondered aloud. "Gary's been saying over and over that if Beau is his, he'll be the father Beau deserves. You know about his daughters… they're pretty much grown up by now, and of course you know he has no son. I wish I hadn't told him anything about Everett."

"The two of you talked about him?"

"Oh, Lucy, you know, we worked together and just like anyone else when they're mad at their ex, I vented." She paused, while her attorney looked as if she wasn't buying the explanation. "Okay, so maybe we had more of a relationship than even I realized. But I guess I let him know over the years what kind of father Everett's been and he's sure reminding me of that, now."

"Yeah, and there's another thing to think about. Your daughter."

"Yes, what about Emma?" Skippy lifted her head, turning the question back at her attorney.

"Well, I've given that some thought. There's a bunch of issues we're going to have to talk about. For example, if it turns out that Gary is Beau's father and ends up with regular visits with his son, it could be tough on Emma if she's not invited to go along with them. And in that case, it gets really confusing in terms of visiting with Everett. I recognize he hasn't been reliable, but we'd still have to figure out what happens when he's actually visiting with Emma. Would he still get to see them both? Would he want to see Gary's son? We can't force him to see Beau. So, it's conceivable that each child could go with a different father on the same weekend."

"Well, then the law is all fucked up, because that would destroy our family."

Lucy turned to her credenza, opened the lower drawer and pulled out a new plastic tub of Trader Joe's chocolate chip cookies. While Skippy might not eat a crumb, Lucy hoped that the distraction might diffuse her client's panic. The lawyer worked the top of the tub, but the plastic was caught. She kept fiddling with it and getting nowhere, when her client finally reached across the desk and grabbed it from her. She ran her long, perfectly groomed index fingernail across the crease of the lid and had the tub open in an instant. She pushed the tub back across the desk at Lucy, scowling at her.

"I know how much you've suffered with this, Skippy. Obviously. But I need you to calm down and give me some honest answers." Her client looked away. "You know, Skippy, after all this time, I know what you're up to. You can't tell me that on some level you're not fighting to protect your perfect world..."

"Perfect?!" Skippy interrupted.

"Come on, you're at the top of your game at work, back in with your buddies, running the board at school. You could have a lot to lose if the situation comes out — and Everett's financial responsibility to Beau could come to an end."

"This has nothing to do with money," Skippy huffed, "if that's what you're insinuating."

"Okay, so if it's not about money, you and I both know it's really about who's going to make a big difference in how Beau is raised. He's only eight, with all those tricky years ahead of him. What we really should be thinking of is the importance of a father's influence on Beau, not to mention a good father."

Lucy took a few cookies from the tub, and offered some to Skippy. Her client raised a hand in refusal. The intercom buzzed in the office, and Lucy picked up only to say "Not now!" to her assistant. No matter what the emergency might be, Lucy was about to start her most important questioning of the day.

"When's the last time the kids saw Everett?"

"He was supposed to see them last weekend, but then that thing came up in Houston and he had to be there through Monday."

"I asked when he last saw the kids."

"Okay, before that, well, let me check my cell phone, it was... November 12th at the latest. He saw them on November 12th."

"For how long? For the day, the night, an hour?"

"For the day. He took them to his office and then dinner."

"Sounds nice. When was the last time they stayed overnight with their dad?"

"Oh, we dropped that some time ago, Lucy. It wasn't working out, so he agreed that the day visits were a better idea."

"So you dropped the night visits, and it sounds like he hasn't been sticking with the day visits either. When's the last time he actually stuck to his visitation schedule for a whole month?"

"A whole month? Oh, God, who knows. A month? Frankly, I can't remember him ever following the schedule for a whole month."

"Since you got divorced?"

"Yes, I guess so. I never really thought about it."

"Did he go to Beau's Little League games?"

"I think he made at least one this year. Uh, one for sure."

"And how long is the season?"

"Well, I suppose they have at least a dozen games or so."

"Does he go to his concerts? Parent-teacher meetings?"

Skippy shook her head, and shifted her gaze away from Lucy.

"So really what you're telling me, Skippy, is that since the divorce you've essentially been a single parent." Her client was better off recognizing this particular fact. "What you really have to go home and think about is this: if it turns out that Gary actually is Beau's father, is your son better off having an active father in his life?"

Skippy was silent. She had covered for Everett throughout their marriage and could feel the old habit return as her mind grappled in vain to excuse his behavior.

Lucy leaned forward and added, "So why don't we just keep this between us, and you think it over. Let me know if you want me to make arrangements to find out if Gary is Beau's father. All you have to do is call me and tell me that's what you've decided."

Skippy glanced at her watch and sighed, exhausted. "God, I've gotta get out of here."

As she walked out of the office, Lucy called after her, "You'll let me know if you want me to do it, right?"

Skippy continued down the hallway and out the door.

CHAPTER EIGHT

Had Gary known that Skippy was back in Lucy Bennett's office, he could have told both women that they were wasting their time. They would have been better off just giving him a call. He already knew the answer to their basic question. After considering all of his options, Gary had figured out the best method of getting what he needed from Beau. He managed to return to Aston's performing arts center on the pretext of having to "tweak" a few engineering problems at the auditorium. No one at the school had questioned his need to do so, and Gary's insistence on reviewing the acoustic adjustments himself was taken as a sign that he was a perfectionist, and perhaps even a bit of a diva.

Gary put the on-site opportunities to good use. He easily struck up a friendship with the band director, Dave Ames, who held band practice several times a week after school in the room across from the auditorium. Dave learned that Gary played blues guitar, and had once considered teaching music. As Gary explained, it was like old times listening in on band practice, if only for a few minutes now and then. Within days, Gary was able to schmooze Dave into lending him his sacred Les Paul McCarty to check out some resonance issues in the auditorium. Gary played a few numbers by Clapton, well aware that Dave and his students were apt to wander in once he started wailing away. Indeed, an audience soon crept into the back rows of the theatre and offered hearty applause at the conclusion of Gary's performance.

On Gary's last afternoon of testing, he brought in his sound design expert and they discussed their final review of the acoustics. Band practice was in full session, the children plodding through their drills several times over when Gary knew he'd found the perfect moment.

He knocked on the band room door, and Dave greeted him. Gary was right to imagine the students were ready for a break. They seemed relieved by the interruption.

"I'll be heading out, and wanted to say good luck to all you guys. A lot of talent in this room!" There were groans and laughter. "Hey, I've got an idea. My truck's filled with Gatorade the crew never got to this week. It'll be my parting gift, okay?" Gary and his associate brought in the cartons, offering a small bottle for each child. Of course, Dave suggested the kids would like a parting song as well. Gary, grabbing the Les Paul once again, wowed the class with an amazing and animated rendition of Stevie Ray Vaughn's "Scuttle Buttin'." Gary was kind enough to gather all the bottles after the show was over, and carried them off with his assistant. It was as easy as pie. And as it turned out, well worth the effort.

CHAPTER NINE

Claire moved into Lucy's office from her position in what the lawyers called "the interrupt spot." Lucy was accustomed to being interrupted whenever she didn't have a client sitting in front of her. Whether she was working with Ruby, on the phone or trying to read something, if a client wasn't actually sitting there, the lawyers considered it open house to speak with the boss. To Lucy's amusement, not only did the lawyers think nothing of interrupting her, but if several of them arrived at her office at the same time, they thought nothing of interrupting one another. The lawyers always seemed to be standing in the same place, just beyond the entrance to her office and slightly into the room where they could not be ignored for long. Lucy had named the location, so there would be no question as to why any of the lawyers was standing there. Now and then the thought crossed her mind that it might be easier to just have everyone take a number.

Claire began to speak with Lucy, ignoring the crowd that was gathering in the interrupt spot behind her. Before long, the others straggled into the cozy corner office, to take part in what had long been the routine at Bennett and Birnbaum: as the workday ended, the group met to share in the events of the day and to brainstorm about the matters ahead. Other than the lawyers and the current intern, Ruby was the one additional member of the staff who usually participated.

Lucy looked around the room at her colleagues. They were a team, a rather close-knit one, and didn't mind sitting cheek-to-cheek along the couch. Ruby monopolized the first few moments of the meeting, running down the list of the most pressing emergencies that had arisen during the day.

Andi was comfortably seated in one of the side chairs, an ornate heirloom with its own special charms, named on the day of the infamous "incident." On that day, Lucy had been meeting for several minutes with Ms. Rhoda Bower on a consultation, when the woman sprang from her chair, announcing that she had to use the restroom. While waiting for the client to return, Lucy buzzed her partner's office to give her a heads up about the potential new client. All she could say was, "So far, kinda jumpy."

Rhoda returned, finished up the consultation, but never mentioned anything about her little emergency. In fact, the lady had no intention of retaining the firm. She had made the appointment for the sole purpose of preventing her husband from hiring Lucy's well-known firm; once she divulged certain confidential information about herself, she knew it would be a conflict of interest for Lucy to represent her husband. In this manner, Rhoda methodically eliminated the best attorneys all around town, all the while planning to hire a relative.

It wasn't until just after Ms. Bower left that Lucy noticed the large dark red stain on her chair. She screamed out for Andi and Ruby, who commiserated, recalling how they'd eased Lucy's fears about allowing the lovely antique into the office. It was so delicate, so precious. They all stood dismally regarding the violated chair.

"Well, you said it was a period piece," Andi said.

The horror of the joke set the two partners laughing and crying in equal measure, as they worked alongside Ruby to try and clean up the telltale stain. Ruby wasn't laughing or crying, just bitching. After that day, Andi felt especially attached to the poor, forlorn chair, and made a special effort to show it her respect by sitting in it whenever possible.

Andi was now curled up in the infamous chair, draped in a voluminous hand-knit shawl as she threaded through her phone messages. Ruby finished up with her to-do list and turned the meeting over to the boss. Andi and Claire, who'd been working on the Kornblum file were waiting to hear what had happened at the deposition. Lucy was eager to relive her success. She regaled the room with tales of the hotel business, doing a decent rendition of Mort's performance. By the time

Lucy finished with the details about the cleanliness and lack thereof of the New York City hotels, there wasn't a woman in the room who didn't feel somehow besmirched.

"I've never in my life used a hotel pillow," Claire said. "You might as well rest your head on the back of the seat in the movies, or on an airplane. But bedspreads and curtains — that's something I never thought much about"

"Only one solution," said Andi. "Never travel. You got that Melissa?"

The group was unanimous in agreeing to avoid hotels altogether whenever possible, and when not possible, to bring along plenty of Purell, keep their clothes on for as much of the time as possible and to never touch a bedspread or curtain unless wearing protective gloves, preferably two layers.

"Thanks, Lucy, for sharing," Ruby said. "I'm sure each of us is going to be looking forward to our next romantic stay at a hotel."

A light flashed on the private line designated for use by the staffs' families.

Lucy picked up, and a puzzled expression appeared on her face. "Yes, I'll accept the charges." Her expression turned from concern to an irrepressible grin as she pressed on the speakerphone.

"Hey, Toots!" Max's voice came through the room as clear as a bell.

"Honey, are you wearing the shawl?" rang Consuela's question.

In unison, the whole room shouted, "Yes, she is!"

"We're here on St. Thomas for the day!" Max shouted.

"And buying up all sorts of tchotchkes," Consuela said. "You girls are gonna love 'em!"

Lucy and her partner exchanged knowing looks.

"Thanks, Ma, they can't wait," Andi called. "You should see their faces." The crowd was rolling. No one could resist the Birnbaums. "Ma, Dad, we're in a meeting, so I have to go, but I love you and have fun! Call me later in the week, okay?"

"We love you, we love you!" the couple sang together as the phone call ended.

"Oh, God," Andi sighed, with an apology for the interruption. "Welcome to my life," she laughed as she looked at Melissa, who was beginning to get the picture. Their daughter was a big-shot lawyer, but still every bit the Birnbaums' little girl, whether she liked it or not.

Lucy took a look at her watch. If she didn't leave within ten minutes, she wouldn't have time to get home, change her clothes, and go with Jake to his basketball game that night.

"My God, I've gotta get out of here. Let's deal with the rest of this tomorrow after court, okay?"

The group moved into action, each person grabbing her briefcase and several files, throwing on their coats and charging out the door together into a very cold December evening.

CHAPTER TEN

Howie regarded the lady before him. She seemed to listen intently to his instructions, nodding as he spoke, and placed in her handbag his batch of prescriptions for further tests and various nutritional supplements. Still, she seemed to look right through him as he talked about the advisability of her seeing a therapist. He gave her permission to travel, under the circumstances that she'd explained. Apparently, her husband was unable to take the children to Florida, so she would be taking them instead. For a woman on her way to Disney, she looked singularly weary. Of course, her illness was the obvious culprit. With the nanny along for help, and her in-laws accommodating the family, Howie felt his patient could manage it, as long as she limited the time at the Park each day.

Not that he was rushing Skippy out, but as soon as she left, Howie grabbed the phone to call his accountant concerning a few year-end matters. After all, he was running a business. Their chat was brief, leaving just enough time before lunch for a call to Lucy to let her know her client had actually come in for her appointment. As he waited for Ruby to get Lucy on the line, he was half aware of the sound of a siren approaching the building. What caught his attention was the sudden screech of brakes as the siren came to silence.

Howie swung his chair toward the window, and stood up as he held the phone. An ambulance had stopped directly beneath his office window, and the EMS crew crouched over something in front of the vehicle. Within seconds, a group started to gather. Lucy's voice came through the phone.

"So, Doc, what's the good word?"

"Lucy, it went fine but I can't talk now. Call you back." He rushed off the phone and joined the others at the scene.

"Perfect!" Lucy shouted. "You interrupt my conversation for Howie, and now he's too busy to talk! Can you get Mrs. Caufield back on the line?"

"You know, other people have things to do, too." Ruby called back from her desk. "They can't wait all day to talk to you. Especially doctors."

"Well, just get Mrs. Caufield and I'll try to make nice to her about the interruption. If Howie calls back, take a message."

Ruby didn't know where to start with the mountain of work piling up on her desk. Her job required that she deal with people every minute of the day, constantly draining her of the time she needed to handle the endless stream of routine work. She fantasized about having a day when she could make it to the bottom of the pile. In her many years with Lucy, this dream had yet to be realized.

When she finally got through the layers of assistants at Braintree Designs and was connected to its President, Julie Caufield, she was almost sorry.

"I only have a minute," barked Julie Caufield over her speakerphone. She had hung up on the attorney, unwilling to wait while Lucy put her on hold to take another call. She wasn't the owner and CEO of Braintree because she liked to wait on her lawyer — or anyone else, for that matter.

"Can you hold a minute for Ms. Bennett?" Ruby replied, in her most abrasive tone. She was hoping to save her daily ration of tact for a more considerate client.

"Just get her," demanded Julie.

Lucy apologized to her client, and listened to her collection of recent complaints, including the fact that her soon-to-be-ex had now decided to play hardball. He wanted to renegotiate the informal deal struck at the recent conference.

"Now he wants a part of the business," Julie said, "as though he ever bothered to walk in here and give me an ounce of help or one word of encouragement. I built this place with my own bare hands!"

Lucy popped jelly beans, once again having missed any chance of getting a real lunch.

"So, what are my chances of him starting with a whole, fucking evaluation, and all that shit? What I really don't need is a bunch of auditors and accountants going through my books and making my CPA come up with mounds and mounds of my records."

The attorney was about to respond when she noticed Ruby standing at the door.

"It's Howie!" Ruby said in a loud whisper. "He says it's really urgent!"

Lucy waved her away, intent on answering her client's question. She had barely gotten through one sentence when Ruby approached her desk.

"He says you have to take this call." Her assistant looked flushed and angry. It was only mid-day. Already, the fuses were blowing.

"Look, Julie, I need a good amount of time to explain this in depth, and I'll have to get back to you." Lucy said. "Let me call you a little later. I have a bit of an emergency."

"Lovely!" Julie snarled, and hit the speaker button.

"Howie, what's the big emergency?" Lucy was now popping peanuts, to add another food group to her lunch.

"It's Skippy." Howie's voice was very low and barely audible. "I'm sorry, Lucy…she's uh…had an accident. I don't know how to tell you this."

"Howie, will you speak up? I can't understand you," Lucy said.

His voice louder, there was no mistaking the doctor's words. "She's gone, Lucy. Skippy's gone."

The attorney was speechless.

"Are you there?"

It took a moment for Lucy to compose herself, as she tried to comprehend what she'd heard. "I don't understand. What are you telling me? She was just in your office, right? She went to see you. I don't understand."

"We were all out there, trying to help. She must have been crossing the road just as the ambulance came around the corner."

"An AMBULANCE?" Lucy shrieked, losing all trace of her usual cool.

For a doctor, Howie was having a hard time breaking the news to his old friend. "I know, I know, it's unbelievable. And obviously, they were right there on the scene to try and save her, but I guess the impact was just too severe and she…didn't make it."

"So you're telling me she's dead? She's dead?" Lucy yelled into the phone.

Within seconds, Ruby was back in her doorway. Facing Lucy, she mouthed, "Who's dead?"

"I'm sorry," Howie said.

Lucy sat in shock, her thoughts racing as she tried to comprehend what she'd heard. Beau and Emma flashed through her mind. At that, she started to tear up. She grabbed for the tissue box usually reserved for weeping clients, as Ruby stood by motionless.

"Skippy," Lucy finally said. "Dead."

Andi burst into the room with her usual smile and the promised Starbucks caramel lattes, but the look on Lucy's face told her that something was terribly wrong. Ruby gave no explanation, unable to speak.

Lucy stared at her partner, on automatic pilot as she repeated over and over into the phone, "I see, I see, I see," but she couldn't see at all. It was a nightmare. The woman who relied on her usual self-control wept silently as she sank back into her chair.

Across from her, Ruby and Andi spoke in low voices, Lucy oblivious to them. She dropped her head into her hands. The children's small faces appeared before her, wearing the same sweet expressions she'd seen just days before. As demanding as Skippy had been at times, Lucy genuinely admired the fine job she'd done with Beau and Emma. She'd raised them carefully with tremendous attention, and it showed. Now, the children's lives were turned upside-down and in a far worse manner than during the divorce.

Lucy tried to suppress the dreadful thought that she herself might have caused this tragedy. If she hadn't sent Skippy to Howie, if she hadn't been so insistent, so controlling, would her client still be alive?

That strange old feeling of mortality crept in, the one that nipped at Lucy's heels whenever someone close to her own age died. It was unthinkable that a hard-working, active, young mother could disappear from life without any warning, leaving little children behind. Lucy envisioned her boys without her and shook her head, as if to erase the image.

As she looked up, she saw Ruby and her partner. They'd asked her a question.

"Want me to call everyone in?" Ruby repeated.

"Yes, of course. Just give me a minute." She stood up. "You know, if I hadn't pushed her to go see Howie..."

Ruby interrupted her boss. "As much as you think you can control the world, you didn't make this happen." The assistant was tempted to joke about the number of times she had ineffectively wished some client dead, but kept that to herself. She looked at Lucy who, for an instant, seemed fragile. The boss walked past the women, heading for the bathroom.

Andi had yet to take off her coat. She remained in her partner's office, the cardboard box of coffees on Lucy's desk. Distributing lattes at a time like this seemed absurd. She met Ruby's eyes. "Want me to call them?"

"Nope, I got it."

Andi gave her a pat on the back and dropped her coat over the back of the chair. She watched as Ruby got on Lucy's phone and buzzed the other staff members, telling them each in a flat, perfunctory tone that they were to meet immediately in Lucy's office. She gave no further information.

***

Lucy stood at the bathroom sink, her mind a jumble. The only thing that seemed definite was her pivotal place in the inevitable shit storm that was about to hit. It was sure to become all-consuming. Someone other than Skippy was now going to raise Emma and Beau, and there was no certainty whatsoever that it was going to be Everett Brockhurst.

In fact, the last words she'd ever heard from Skippy opened the door to an entirely different option. After her last meeting with the client, the woman had left a phone message that puzzled Ruby but which was clear to Lucy. "Just do it," Skippy had said, signifying that she wanted to go forward with the DNA test. Those few words meant that she wanted her lawyer to find out if Gary Vaughn was, indeed, Beau's biological father.

The next step for the attorney and her client would have been to figure out what role, if any, the man would play in the boy's life. They'd never gotten that far.

It dawned on Lucy that as soon as Gary heard the news about Skippy's death, he was likely to make his move.

The attorney washed her face with cold water, hoping to regain her composure. It was one thing to let everyone know how hard she was taking this, but under no circumstances did she want to appear out of control in front of her staff. She pushed her hair back, as though it would make a difference. Staring at her blotchy face, she thought that if she ever used make-up, now would have been a very good time to apply some. As it was, she had no cover-up.

Her office was silent as Lucy returned. Neither Andi nor Ruby had said a word to the others, who were trying to figure out what was up. Full staff meetings in the middle of the day were rare, since the staff had recently expanded to fifteen. While the entire staff met together monthly, unscheduled meetings only occurred in the face of a disaster or crisis. The group of secretaries pulled in their own chairs, filling the room to capacity. The attorneys were gathered in the room, some in chairs, some clustered together on the couch.

Lucy peered over her half glasses and ended the suspense. "We lost Skippy Brockhurst today."

The staff could tell from her eyes and the tone of her voice that she was not speaking of a client defection, but rather something more serious.

"She was hit by an ambulance as she left Howie Gassner's office," Lucy said. "She died instantly."

A shock wave reverberated through the room.

"Even with all of those EMTs and doctors right there, there wasn't a damn thing anyone could do for her."

The room was silent for what seemed to be minutes. In contrast to their tough, high-powered image, the group of women sat together quietly, like a stricken family. They all waited to see if Lucy had more to say.

When Meg could no longer endure the silence, she blurted out what most of the staff was thinking. "Is that piece of shit going to raise those two beautiful kids?"

The room filled with buzzing about what an asshole the children had for a father. Each member of Bennett and Birnbaum took a personal stroll down memory lane, recalling what had gone on during the Brockhurst custody battle. Claire suggested that while the kids might be in Everett's custody, she was sure that the nanny would be the one taking care of them.

Lucy listened to the chatter in her office as each woman opined as to what was to be, their voices blending together and then fading from her. Her eye was caught by the prism that had formed on the back wall of the office, as it refracted through the glass case of the Posada baseball. Tracing the light up along the wall, her eyes and mind seemed to sharpen into focus. She could imagine her client's voice resonating in the room, the determined voice of a mother fighting to make things right for her kids. Staring up at the colorful light as it played on the ceiling, Lucy silently vowed that Skippy's children were going to be all right. She would make sure of it. She wasn't being noble and she wasn't on a mission, but she'd have to do what she always did. She would pull herself together and rise to the occasion.

CHAPTER ELEVEN

Over the phone from Florida, just before Vivian boarded the plane for New York, she and Bridgette agreed that it was a must. Unlike her earlier calls, in which Vivian expressed her grief over Skippy's death as well as her grave concerns about her grandchildren, this call was limited to practical matters. Vivian pointed out that despite Bridgette's remarkable efforts, she was still only one person, whose duties had always been strictly to serve as the children's nanny.

Under Vivian's shrewd cross-examination, the reticent Scottish woman conceded that parts of the vast home had been overlooked for quite some time, although she had to add in defense that the housekeeping staff had been reduced to but one employee, Teresa, after Everett's departure.

In Vivian's estimation, it wouldn't do, not for this occasion. Aside from the family who would be staying at the home for the next few days, hordes of people would be coming through to express their sympathies, not to mention the press nosing its way in. After giving Bridgette the financial nod, she instructed her to gather a staff together. They would need household help comparable to what they'd had for the family's former grand events.

It had been years since Vivian took a close look at the old estate, but she still knew every inch of it, inside and out. The house would have to stand up to it all: the countless eyes upon it, the whispering, eating, fussing, chattering, gossiping, splattering, and inevitably, the breaking of some piece of fine china or crystal, perhaps this time an heirloom vase. Some would come by as genuine friends, but most would show up simply to ogle. It had always been so at this grand home, and despite the often unwelcome notoriety, she missed it. No one was better equipped to brush the cobwebs off of Laurel Hall and put it back on its feet again than its former mistress, Vivian Masters Brockhurst.

***

Barely off the phone with Vivian and trying to imagine where, at this late hour, she could possibly find the army of workers required, Bridgette continued her desperate attempts to distract the children. After persuading them to come down to the kitchen, she tried to harness their help in unwrapping some of the enormous food packages that had arrived. Emma was making some effort, while Beau was sitting silently at the table, immobile.

"Be a love and find me those sharp scissors, would you?" Bridgette asked Beau, as she and Emma tugged at the tight ribbon on the largest package. Beau looked up at her, but didn't respond.

There was a soft tap at the kitchen entrance, and a welcome face appeared through the door pane. It was Georgina, at last. Bridgette dropped what she was doing and ushered her in, but before either could even utter a word, Emma sprang into the arms of her aunt. Georgina folded her in a tight embrace, weeping with her little niece for what seemed an eternity. Beau slowly rose from the table. Finding him through her tears, Aunt Gina pulled him into their tiny huddle. As distraught as he was, Beau couldn't cry. The end of his lips fell so low, they might have slipped off of his face, but not a tear came. He was numb. "It's gonna be okay, it'll be okay," Georgina repeated over and over, lying to them as she knew she must.

The tragic scene playing out before her started Bridgette on yet another crying jag. Blowing her nose with a few loud honks, she barely heard the phone ring. Please let it not be Vivian calling back, she prayed, since at this moment the last thing that seemed of any importance was a further discussion about "keeping up appearances" at the house. Her voice failed, and all she could do was listen to the unfamiliar voice on the other end of the wire.

"Hello? It's Consuela. Consuela Birnbaum, a dear friend of Mrs. Brockhurst's. I just wanted to know if you got the food. I'm hoping it came in time for your dinner. It's from the gourmet deli, some packages from Abe's Kosher. I can't seem to get through to them after hours to see if the delivery went through. Are you there? Hello?"

The woman's chatter seemed to restore Bridgette's composure. She honked into her tissue once more and began to regain her voice.

"Yes, this is Bridgette," she started, "the children's nanny…and yes, we did receive your packages. They arrived just a bit ago, and, well… we thank you so much. So good of you."

"Oh, what a relief. I'm hoping they included the chocolate-chip cookies for the children. Oh, it's so terribly sad, those poor little kids. Let me know if there's anything I can do to help. Anything at all."

"Well, actually —" Bridgette said quietly as she took the phone into the back hallway, "You wouldn't happen to know the name of a good employment agency?"

"You can't be serious!" said Consuela. "You're the nanny! The children need you now more than ever!"

"No, no, I'm staying, of course," Bridgette whispered, "it's just that we need some help to get the house prepared for all the people."

"Oh, thank God. You really gave me a start! Sure, I see. You need help there. Yes, yes, I know a great company. Miracle, they could do it. Miracle Employment, over in Craig County. Let me make the call."

"No, that's okay. I'll find them in the phone book. Thanks ever so much."

"My pleasure, under the circumstances." Consuela hung up the phone and sighed, trying to think of whatever else she could possibly do to help. At least the children had a loving nanny, she considered. And Bridgette's voice seemed to confirm it. Consuela couldn't help but try a bit of the lilting accent herself. "Thanks evah so much. Evah so much." It made no difference that Bridgette was Scottish. Consuela imagined her as the very British Mary Poppins, and felt positive that the children were in just the right hands. She headed back to her bedroom to unpack from the spectacular cruise.

CHAPTER TWELVE

The morning alarm went off at six, as it always did in the Bennett-Hammond house. Lucy needed a good two hours to do all that she had to before leaving for work each day. She rested her head on Dan's shoulder in their oversized bed, as she did every morning, and listened to the radio with the morning weather and headlines. It was going to be another miserable winter day. No precipitation, but wind gusts of thirty-six miles per hour, enough to make it feel at least ten degrees worse than the twenty-three degrees registering on the thermometer. She bitched out loud to Dan for a few minutes and then slowly made her way out of bed. She tried to avoid looking in the bathroom mirror, since there was absolutely nothing to be gained and much to be lost by seeing her wintry pallor and matted hair. A clear view of either would be enough to send her back to bed.

First things first, though, meant that Lucy and Dan had to get their workouts over with. Although it made their bedroom look more like a gym than a resting place, Lucy was glad to have her treadmill and exercise bike right there beside her, knowing that either instrument of torture was sure to help her burn off the necessary calories within a half hour. Dan got his exercise outdoors, jogging with the dog each morning, while Lucy enjoyed the relative warmth of her bedroom gym, watching "Today in New York."

This was a treadmill morning for Lucy. As she moved along, her sons both made brief appearances. She inspected them to see that they were properly dressed and not wearing shorts in the dead of winter, and took a moment to consider them with pride.

They were nice-looking boys, just at the start of their pre-teen years. Jake, her eldest, held out a permission slip and a pen, fully expecting his mom to sign the paper with one hand while going through her paces. Meanwhile, Adam recited the poem he'd memorized for the day's quiz. She wasn't done with the boys until they confirmed that their homework was finished and packed away along with their books and sports uniforms. With a kiss and a wave, she sent them off to meet the bus.

At Lucy's fifteen-minute mark, her next audience appeared. Kristen, her *au pair*, was having a hard time settling in again after her time away. Her to-do list was longer than usual and she didn't seem too pleased about it. Lucy tried to make it a little easier by asking her to throw together some pasta for the kids' dinner and telling her that she and Dan would fend for themselves.

At the end of her half hour of misery, Dan came in with the daily paper. Lucy rarely had time anymore to read the news before work, but Dan made a point of telling her anything of moment in the local section so that she could be on top of things when she got to court or the office. From the way he handed her the paper that morning, as though he was delivering a summons, she could tell that there was something in the morning paper that she needed to see.

She opened to the third page where she saw two photos: one of the accident scene with an ambulance stopped in front of Howie Gassner's medical office, and another labeled "the Brockhursts in happier times." The family was posed along the seashore, Skippy holding the baby, and Beau waving a stick at the camera. Everett was wearing the frozen smile that Lucy had detested when she first met him.

"Ambulance Mows Down Brockhurst Beauty," screamed the headline. An inset led with the title, "Poor Little Rich Kids" and included mention of the fact that the parents had gone through a bitter divorce.

"I guess I shouldn't be surprised it made its way into the paper. But really, how tasteless can you get?" Dan grabbed the paper away from her, seeing it wasn't helping with their start to the day.

"Run over by an ambulance? Right in front of a medical center? Could you believe it?" Lucy muttered. It made no more sense to her now than it had the day before. Yet, it happened. The reality of her client's death was there in black and white, for everyone to see. She prayed that "everyone" did not include Emma and Beau Brockhurst.

Dan and Lucy showered, dressed and packed their respective files up for work, gave each other a comforting goodbye hug and promised to be home no later than half past six, so that they could make it to the basketball game on time.

***

When Lucy got to the office, the parking lot was still empty. Even though she was the boss, she was often the first one there in the morning and last to leave at night. Now and then, Ruby took the opportunity to point out that this was not normal behavior.

"Normal bosses take their time getting to the office, eat an actual lunch, take out a guest from time to time, and get home at a reasonable hour," she liked to claim.

The attorney found her assistant's lectures amusing, since it was she who scheduled Lucy's calendar, arranging appointments from the crack of dawn through the early evening. And if a particularly promising or needy potential client called, Ruby would find a way to squeeze them in as well. But, they were partners in crime, each one wanting the same thing: to bring in the most business and to win as many cases as they could.

Lucy had just powered on her computer to open the calendar and retrieve the day's schedule when the first call came in. It wasn't yet nine, and the day had begun. She liked to screen the calls by waiting until she could hear the caller start to leave his or her message on the answering machine. This morning was no different, and after the fourth ring she heard Gary Vaughn's voice as he started to leave a message saying he had an important matter to discuss with her. She picked up the phone.

"Gary, is that you?" Lucy asked. "What's this 'rather important matter' you need to talk to me about?"

"Glad you're there, Lucy. I don't know if you heard the news this morning, but a friend of mine – I think you handled her divorce — well, she died yesterday in a horrible accident. Her name is Skippy Brockhurst."

"You bet I heard. I'm still trying to process the whole thing."

"Well, I don't have the time to process much, Lucy. I've got something that has to be handled immediately."

"And that is?"

"Are we speaking confidentially?"

"Of course."

"It's not something I brag about. In fact, no one else knows about this."

"Come on, Gary, out with it."

"Well, here it is: about eight or nine years ago, I had an affair with Skippy." He waited, assuming that Lucy would practically fall off of her chair. When he heard nothing on the other end of the phone, he continued. "We were at a convention in Vegas. Somehow, we ended up on our own and you know how charming I can be…."

"I wouldn't know," Lucy quipped.

Gary gave a short laugh. "Well I can be irresistible, so, you really can't blame her. We had a fling, and left it at that. But, in those few days together, she let me in on what her life was really like. Most of us knew about Everett, but she told me it was even worse. The family made her feel like an intruder. In fact, she seemed to be a pretty lonely person. After the trip, we made a few jokes about Vegas now and then, but nothing more happened between us. I think she knew I would have liked to see her, but I kept my promise. We just went back to doing our deals, helping each other out in business. After all, there was no reason to spoil a good thing by talking about what happened."

"So why exactly are you telling me all this, Gary?"

"Because, Lucy. I'm Beau's real father. He's my son."

Although she knew more about all of this than Gary could imagine, Lucy continued to play dumb.

"Do you know this Gary, or are you just guessing?"

"Have you seen Skippy's son Beau?"

"In fact I have, quite recently," Lucy said.

"Well, that's me about forty years ago."

"And I looked like Miley Cyrus forty years ago, but that doesn't make me her mother," Lucy said.

"Yeah, but DNA doesn't lie, Lucy. I am Beau's father and I'll be damned if that dirtbag is going to raise my son."

"Okay, Gary. Back up a second. What did you mean when you said 'DNA doesn't lie'?"

"I've done my homework, Lucy."

"Meaning exactly what?"

"You want the entire story?"

"Yes, if I'm going to be of any help to you," Lucy said.

"I was hired to design the new auditorium at Aston Academy, you know, where the Brockhurst kids go to school. I saw the boy at the opening concert. You could have knocked me over. It was like looking at my old grade school pictures. Once I saw him, I couldn't put it out of my mind; I had to find out the truth. So I called Skippy and told her that we needed to get together right away about some potential new business. And I told her what I suspected, right there in the middle of a fancy dinner.

"That put a pretty quick end to the meal, as you can imagine. Skippy went ballistic on me, though I know it would have been much worse if we weren't out in public. She ordered me to stop in my tracks, saying that she and the kids were finally on an even keel after the divorce, and that the last thing she needed was for me to rock the boat. She stormed out and I think she was hoping I'd drop the whole thing."

Just then, Dina came by the entrance to Lucy's office and gave a loud, cheerful hello, not realizing that her boss was on the phone. Lucy violently motioned to Dina to shut the door. Her receptionist obliged, silently marveling at how rude some people could be first thing in the morning.

"She was dead wrong," Gary continued. "I wasn't about to let this go. I tried to arrange another meeting, but she made it clear she didn't want to speak to me about the matter. 'Why shouldn't I be a part of my son's life?' I asked her. We'd both made the same mistake and yet she got to see Beau and be with him every day, and I was supposed to have nothing to do with him. That just didn't make sense to me. Of course, she was also concerned about this whole thing getting out and hurting her family and even her business. From what I knew, she could never really count on getting child support from her ex, so she needed every cent she made. And then she went on and on about what would happen if those snooty mothers at Aston got wind of the story. They'd talk about her behind her back, she'd be disgraced, and with all the gossip, her kids would end up hating her. I think she really blew the whole thing up in her mind."

"I don't think she was blowing it up at all," Lucy said. "This could really have had a big impact on both her kids and her business."

"Well, in any event, I told her I would think it over and then do what I thought was best for Beau. And believe me, I tortured myself over this thing. Maybe it would have been different if Everett was a good guy. Maybe I would have backed off. But over the years, Skippy told me more than once how he neglected those kids. He didn't seem to give a crap about them. And as far as what I ever saw of him, he was just an asshole. I went to a few of those fundraisers for that charity run by the Brockhursts, and I don't think he ever made it past the cocktail hour able to stand up straight. No one disagreed when Skippy decided to dump the guy.

"Anyway, all I've been doing is wracking my brain about this day and night. I even went to see a therapist about fifteen miles from here. I spent weeks going over the situation with him."

Despite all that Gary had told her, Lucy still needed to hear more about one thing in particular.

"Gary, I hate to interrupt and I do appreciate you telling me all of this, but you still haven't explained about DNA not lying."

"I was just getting there," he said. "I begged Skippy to get Beau's DNA tested. If it turned out I wasn't his father, then she had nothing to worry about. If I was, then we had to deal with it. She knew the way I took care of my daughters, how I gave them my heart and soul. But even so, Skippy always went back to what she called the 'complexities of the situation.' She kept putting me off and avoiding my phone calls, so I finally took matters into my own hands."

Lucy prayed he hadn't done something stupid like corner Beau, stalk him, or God forbid, try to steal him away. Without realizing it, she was already preparing to defend his actions. But, when Gary explained how he'd obtained a sample of the boy's DNA, she felt reassured. Gary had taken the course of action she herself might have suggested.

"About a week after I gave the material to the lab, along with my own samples, I got the results. The report said there's a ninety-nine percent chance I'm Beau's biological father."

"Did you ever get to tell Skippy?" Lucy inquired.

"No, but I was just about to. And then, well you know. It was too late."

A moment went by. It was still hard for either of them to believe that Skippy Brockhurst was gone.

"Lucy, you know me. I only want what's best for my son. Some people might think I'm a little rough around the edges, but no one could say I'm not good with children. I mean, how many teams did I sponsor in town for other people's kids? And you, of all people know how good I've been to my own girls — and what I gave them in the divorce settlement. In fact, as I recall, you told me I was being too generous. And even so, I never missed a payment. You didn't see anyone hauling me into court for being some kind of deadbeat. I did what I promised in that agreement and more. You have to admit, my kids turned out pretty good, didn't they?"

His attorney listened closely, but gave no response.

"Lucy, I need you to make sure I'm part of Beau's life. It's that simple."

"It's not that simple. This boy is eight years old and he doesn't even know you. There's a lot to talk about, and I'd prefer to give you legal advice in person. I'm sure you remember, I don't like to do this stuff over the phone. Can you get in here to meet with me?"

"How soon can that be?"

"If five o'clock tonight works for you, I could squeeze you in. We'd have only a limited amount of time, like maybe, an hour. I have lots of time tomorrow if you can wait 'til then."

"No. I'd rather see you tonight, if that's okay with you. I need the best shark lawyer out there on my team, the sooner the better."

"Gary, you know I am going to need some serious money in order to represent you on this one."

"What does serious mean?"

"Can you get twenty thousand for tonight?"

There was a short pause, during which Lucy doodled a tiny dollar sign on her yellow legal pad.

"Yeah, I can do it. I'll see you later, then, with the money in hand."

Lucy put the phone down and started to contemplate what would be her first move after being retained. She got back on the phone to tell her partner.

CHAPTER THIRTEEN

By early morning a long caravan of cars had formed along the winding drive up to Laurel Hall, carrying almost a dozen housekeepers. As they assembled in the massive kitchen, the women's chatter soon filled the room. They stood in wonder around the immense marble-topped chopping table, gazing at the age-old cabinetry that rose high to the lofty ceiling, the exquisite Wedgewood place settings on display behind the mullioned glass doors and the assortment of copper pots hanging over the stoves from the wrought iron rails.

As the women awaited instructions, word spread among them of the terrible end that had come to the owner, a beautiful woman who'd left behind two young children and this amazing mansion. Teresa's small voice attempted to rise above the din, but was easily swallowed up. She was hoping Bridgette was finished with yet another phone call, but there was no sign of her. Overwhelmed by the amount of fellow housekeepers barging in on her private domain, and knowing that the house was looking run down, Teresa was horrified to bear the crowd's inspection.

"Wanna get their attention?" one of the housekeepers offered as she picked up on Teresa's dilemma. Before there was time for any response, Amanda Gray, plucked out of the employment agency on her day off at "The Excelsior," let out her best two-handed shrieking whistle. The room came to an instant standstill.

"Works like a charm every time," Amanda said.

Wondering when if ever she'd regain the hearing in her left ear, Teresa thanked her and then turned to address the room full of women. "Uh, hello," she said, "I'd like to show you through the house, now." Teresa tried her best to direct the group, guiding them through the kitchen and off to the rear hall with its small cluster of pantries, work rooms and offices. Rather than give any clear instructions, she apologized in every breath for the areas that had been neglected, trying to explain that the house was just too big for her to handle all on her own.

Bridgette, after taking yet another phone call, finally joined the group and worked her way up to the front of the line, suggesting to Teresa that they get right down to the supply rooms on the lower level. The women followed Bridgette and Teresa along a narrow corridor and then down the staircase into the dark expanse of the basement.

Bridgette, who was up at dawn to get as much in order as she could, had helped the children to get out with their aunt. She knew what had to be done in terms of Vivian's decree, but felt woefully inadequate to organize an entire staff on the spot. Although she wished Georgina could be there to assist her, she was glad for the children's sake that their aunt had taken them out to breakfast. Within hours, the house would be once again filled with guests. There would be meals to be made and requests to be met.

Yet Bridgette was resolved that despite all the fuss that was to come, she would protect what little was left of the children's world. Believing she could get away with it by making some sort of excuse, she locked the mahogany double doors to the ballroom.

"Off limits," she told herself as she hid the key. She placed it on the delicate presentation table just outside of the ballroom, behind the silk flower arrangement and beneath the faded guest registry book. It was her one bold statement in the face of the ordeal. She was filled with doubt about shutting off the room, but far more concerned about the real, larger issues facing the children. As to those, she had no say and would have to let others make the right decisions. It occurred to her that the person who would have been best at getting them through the painful and perplexing days ahead, was no longer with them.

At the bottom of the basement steps, the women stood waiting. Bridgette drew in her breath, ready to launch into a recitation of the long list of tasks she'd hastily compiled, when the front bell with its lingering melody sounded from the floor above.

"Please see who it is," Bridgette asked Teresa. The housekeeper bounded up the stairs, relieved to be off the spot, while the nanny continued with her speech. "I want to thank you all for being here on such short notice. I'm sure by now, you may know that the owner, Mrs. Brockhurst, died and therefore this is a difficult time for the family." The lights flickered and the room went black. When the lights came back on, Bridgette could see that several women had gone pale. One jumped forward with a little start, brushing a cobweb from her hair.

"Just the wind, ladies," continued Bridgette. "So, as I was saying, we truly need your help today to ..."

"It's Mrs. Brockhurst!" Teresa shouted down from the top of the stairs. "She's at the door." The terror in her voice came through loud and clear. The women gasped almost as one.

"Well let her in, for God's sake!" Bridgette called.

"I did." Teresa crept down the top few steps, and stared down into Bridgette's eyes with a look that begged not to face Mrs. Brockhurst on her own.

Bridgette excused herself. As she hurried up the steps, the gaggle of women burst into a frenzy of questions. Wasn't Mrs. Brockhurst dead? How had she come back? Didn't the cellar look pretty creepy? What were they doing stuck down here in a God-forsaken dungeon?

The lights flickered once again, and then the basement returned to total darkness. "The next thing you know, they'll lock the door on us!" chuckled Amanda. "We'll be lucky to get out of here alive," she added with a private grin.

The lights came on again, but it was too late. Without further ado, the women started to clamber past the cackling Ms. Gray and up the stairs, moving as fast as they could along the passageway and back into the sunshine and safety of the kitchen. All but Amanda, who fearlessly strolled on through the expanse of the basement rooms, getting the lay of the land.

"Not bad compared to the 'Celsior," she mused. "Not bad at all."

The majestic front door still stood ajar to the icy air and gusts of wind, while Vivian stood before it in the vast foyer, wrapped formidably in her old stone marten. At the portico, a stretch limousine idled while its driver strode through the doorway to deposit several suitcases at Mrs. Brockhurst's side. Vivian waved him off, reminding him to stop first at the church, then the funeral parlor.

"Bridgette," she demanded, "Kindly find us someone to bring up the luggage."

Teresa came forward, out of shadows, only too glad to oblige but with no idea as to where the luggage should go. The Master bedroom? But with all of the mistress's belongings still there? She stood in confusion, then grabbed a suitcase in each hand and took off down the hallway, opting to figure it out when she got upstairs.

Bridgette instinctively reached forward to embrace Mrs. Brockhurst, but the woman shrunk back from her.

"Don't start," Vivian warned. "The children don't need to see me like that. Hugh feels the same way. He's had quite a difficult journey." It was a moment before she was able to collect herself. "Well, where are they? Where are Beau and Emma?"

"I'm afraid Georgina has taken them out for a bit... to breakfast," Bridgette explained, helping Vivian out of her coat.

"I see. Well, I've sent Mr. Brockhurst to meet with Reverend Davis, then on to the funeral home. I'll need the name of the florist we talked about, and the caterer, Wilhelm, or Williams."

It did not occur to any of the Brockhursts that someone else might have preferred to handle the funeral arrangements, or that Skippy herself might have had any particular wishes in this regard. Divorce or no divorce, the Brockhurst family formed ranks where the public was concerned. Whether anyone liked it or not, this funeral was going to bear all the hallmarks of a Brockhurst event, with the Reverend T. Lloyd Davis officiating.

"I did as you asked, and the women arrived a few minutes ago," Bridgette offered. "I was just giving them some direction."

The raucous voices of the staff filtered out from the kitchen, where Amanda had rejoined the crowd and was mercilessly teasing those she'd managed to frighten when they were downstairs. Spirited name-calling and high-pitched laughter followed each of her jibes.

Without another word, Vivian stormed off toward the source of the commotion, Bridgette at her heels. She passed through the familiar rooms leading to the kitchen, and then, with just the right amount of force, swung open the heavy kitchen door. Vivian assessed the situation: chaos reigned. The few who had not witnessed her entrance continued to babble on.

Above their voices, Vivian announced, "I am Mrs. Brockhurst, and this is not a party!"

Stone silence.

Amanda had done some assessing of her own: *Bitch.*

Still, she liked her style.

"Please be so kind as to follow me!" Leading the obedient pack back down to the dungeon, Vivian pointed out each and every portion of the working rooms, the lower kitchen, cleaning supplies room, linen supply room, washing room, drying rooms, lower pantry, lower larder, mechanical supply rooms, and on and on until she was done with the entire level.

Vivian always took pride in the fact that the basement was designed in the mode of a battleship's belly, functional and spotless. Unlike most of her set, Vivian was hands-on and had always taken an interest in attending to every detail of the home's operation. She noticed at once that the grey floors and white walls were terribly dingy.

Vivian turned about to the women after she'd finished the basement tour. "Have you all got that?" she asked. The women nodded obediently. That is, all but Amanda, who was humming to herself. No one had yet realized she was happily plugged into her MP3 player.

"On to the main level," Vivian continued. She guided them in the same fashion through several rooms of the main floor and eventually approached the double doors to the ballroom, where she stopped.

"There are some rare and irreplaceable pieces in this room, so I ask that you be very careful as we walk through, and of course, when dusting."

Bridgette had dreaded this moment, and was regretting her decision to have blocked it off. She thought Mrs. Brockhurst might be busy with other concerns under the circumstances, but in her presence, she realized that this woman would never overlook any aspect of her former home.

"I'm afraid the room is…under renovation," Bridgette blurted out.

Vivian looked at her. "Renovation? The ballroom? Has something happened to the ballroom?" A flush came over her face.

Vivian had made it clear, especially during her son's divorce, that the mansion would be preserved as part of the Brockhurst heritage, with its ownership to travel down the lines of succession as in the royal lineages. No major changes were to occur without her explicit authorization. There was to be no replacement of the marble, tile or cabinetry, no alterations of any kind unless needed for repairs, or in an emergency. The restrictions were stated clearly in her son's divorce decree, and Vivian had been sure to get her own copy from Everett. Unauthorized renovations were forbidden. Period.

"There's been a bit of a change — so, it's not really…"

"Get this door open," Vivian said, as she pulled on the two large door handles to no avail.

"I, uh —"

"Bridgette! I'm telling you to get this door open!"

Amanda was enjoying the tug of war between the two women.

"I'm afraid I've misplaced the key," Bridgette tried, in a feeble attempt to delay the inevitable.

Teresa, who'd lagged behind, was finally feeling brave enough to catch up to the front of the group. "Oh, I found it this morning when I was dusting!" she chirped brightly. "Right here on the table." She held up the Holy Grail for all to see.

Vivian grabbed the key from her, and had the heavy doors open wide in a flash.

The sight before her took her breath away. Gone were the fine furnishings, the Scalamandre drapes, and what had become of the mantelpiece? The marble floor was covered by a huge patchwork of area rugs across which were a mini-trampoline, mini-golf course, treadmill, and God knew what other types of sports equipment, and even a bowling contraption that ran the length of the room. One corner housed easels and art supplies, another had a drum set surrounded by guitars and what appeared to be some sort of recording equipment. Overstuffed sofas sat happily facing one another in front of the mantelpiece, over which Great Grandfather Brandon's portrait used to preside. A tremendous TV screen now sat in his stead on the wall.

"She's let them run rampant!" Vivian said, in her horror forgetting that Skippy was gone.

It was at that precise moment that Georgina and the children stepped into the room.

"Hello, Grand," Emma said softly as she and Beau approached their grandmother. "Don't you like our room?"

Vivian was caught off-guard, something she detested. But one look at those small, sad faces melted away her anger almost in an instant. They had a sacred place in her heart, maybe now more than ever. She just couldn't hurt her grandchildren on account of their mother's foolishness. "Oh, my poor little dears, of course I do, I love your room," Vivian murmured as she held them in her arms, "My poor, poor little dears."

CHAPTER FOURTEEN

Despite the fact that Lucy's client was already waiting to start her appointment, Ruby chose to put the call through to her boss. She knew from the name of the caller that Lucy would want to speak with her.

"Hello, Mrs. Bennett, it's Georgina Fiske. Thank you for taking my call."

"Georgina, I'm so sorry about your sister. She really was a very special person. I can't imagine what you must be going through — and the children…"

"I'm doing whatever I can do for them." There was a break in her voice, and after a pause, she continued. "They seemed to be doing a little bit better out at breakfast. At least they had some quiet time away from the house."

Lucy had spoken with Georgina once or twice during Skippy's divorce, and again recently at the doctor's office. In their short encounters Lucy had found her to be level-headed and, true to Skippy's description, "an artist without artistic temperament." Her face reflected a calm resolve, a quiet determination that Lucy could now hear in the cadence and tone of her voice.

She would have been impressed to see Georgina's steadiness in action, in her level handling of Mrs. Brockhurst only minutes earlier when the two women had wrestled over the children's afternoon plans.

"You must have a lot on your hands," the attorney said.

"I do. But that's partly why I called. It's so hard to handle practical things at a time like this, but I don't know any other lawyer up here. So, I was hoping you might be able to help me with some of these difficult matters. Do you happen to know who drew her will?"

Lucy could overhear a loud commotion on the other end of the line.

"Ms. Bennett, I'm sorry, I'll have to take this in another room." Georgina slipped into the small alcove off the back of the kitchen. She continued in a low voice, "Everett's mother seems to be taking over the house. And now there's some problem among the housekeepers she hired. I'm staying out of it as much as possible, so I can focus on what's important."

"Georgina, I was the one who drafted her will and in fact, she named you her executrix. Do you have a copy of the will?"

"No, but that's just one of my questions. I guess I'm wondering if you might know of any instructions Skippy might have left or about documents as to a burial plot. I've been in touch with the funeral parlor, but there seems to be some question even about that. Apparently, the Brockhursts have already been making their own arrangements."

"We don't usually put burial instructions in a will," explained Lucy, "since the burial often takes place before anyone's even had a chance to look at the document. So, we tell our clients to make sure someone knows about their wishes or that they leave instructions along with their important papers. I take it Skippy never talked with you about what was to happen if she died."

"When my sister was going through her divorce, we talked about a lot of important things, but never about burial instructions. Mostly, we talked about the kids. We agreed that if anything happened to one of us, the other would help take care of the children. We both agreed that we didn't want to stay alive if we were brain-dead. That was about it; we didn't talk details. Not about burial wishes. Not about finances or money…other than Everett's nonsense with child support." Georgina moved further along the narrow alcove as a deliveryman tried to get past her with a huge package of food. Amanda followed him carrying yet another package, loudly barking out directions as the fellow made his way down into the basement.

"I can get you a copy of the will," Lucy said, "but the Surrogate's Court is going to want the original document for filing. Is it possible for you to take a prowl around the house or ask Bridgette if she knows where your sister kept her important papers? If you and Bridgette can't find anything dealing with burial instructions, then you and your folks will have to duke it out with the Brockhursts. If so, remember, you are Skippy's living relatives, not her former in-laws."

Ruby stood at the door, gesturing toward the waiting room. Lucy lifted her hand. The attorney wanted to add an important suggestion while she still had Skippy's sister on the line. "Georgina, you've said how much it bothers you to talk about practical things at a time like this. Well, it bothers me, too. But, since you called about legal issues, there is one other one thing I want to mention. Has anyone discussed the idea of pursuing a wrongful death action, so the kids could get something out of this disaster? I think it's something that should be considered."

"A wrongful death action?"

"In a situation like your sister's accident, where someone dies as a result of someone else's negligence, you can bring a lawsuit to recover money for what's called wrongful death. Seems to me, someone or more than one person is going to bear some responsibility for your sister's death. For instance, could be that the driver of the ambulance was going too fast, and if he was, he or his boss or maybe both could be held responsible for Skippy's death. Or maybe there was something wrong with the ambulance's brakes or maybe a flaw in the roadway. Whatever the cause, there's probably going to be some liability, with the children getting money from one source or another. I just want someone to make sure they get it. I think we owe that to Skippy."

Lucy realized that Everett and his entourage of advisors were probably already exploring the options. Most likely, he'd been informed that under New York law, the surviving parent automatically becomes the children's custodial parent, with standing to bring an action on their behalf. How irritating, thought the attorney, to know she couldn't participate in the case. Skippy was young and a decent earner, so the matter was bound to be worth some serious money. As Everett's former adversary and now Gary's lawyer, Lucy was shut out of what could be a substantial fee.

Georgina was hoping for answers, but now felt besieged by even larger issues than the ones she'd imagined. "I'm sure you're right, but I guess it's all just too much for me to think about, right now. I'll give you a call to let you know whether or not I find the will. Thanks for everything, Mrs. Bennett."

***

After she signed up her new client, the day seemed to get away from Lucy. She had one meeting after another, the staff unable to break through to her with their own headaches. Normally, the attorneys would have ended up in the boss's office at around five o'clock, but Gary Vaughn's name waited on the calendar. She was just about to call Dan when Ruby announced her former client's arrival.

"Give me a minute to hit the bathroom, and then show Gary in, will you?"

Her assistant was muttering about something or other as Lucy passed her on the way to the bathroom. By the time the attorney walked back, she could overhear the other Ruby charming Gary, despite his agitation. Ruby was the real deal. She had a tremendous amount of common sense and a feel for saying the right thing to a client. She could usually smell a bad guy, and though it was a little presumptuous, Ruby weeded out those types before Lucy ever got to meet them. Before setting any appointments with her boss, she cross-examined people who called for a consult. If they couldn't give a straight answer to her initial questions or they objected to paying the consultation fee, she wasn't about to waste the firm's time.

As Ruby brought Gary back to Lucy's office, the attorney stuck out her hand to give her usual firm handshake. That handshake was a gift from her father that had always served her well. There was nothing wimpy about it. It instilled confidence.

"Come on in, Gary. It's been a while since you were in one of my chairs. Have a seat," she said, pointing to the "period piece," "and then we'll figure this thing out.

"Thanks, Lucy. Here's your money: fifteen thousand in check and five in cash, okay?"

Ruby was right behind him, as forewarned. She took the money and placed all of it into the firm's safe, to be deposited the following day.

"Can you believe this whole thing?" Gary began. "I mean, as rotten as she was to me about Beau, well, that was one fine lady."

"True," Lucy agreed. "It's a shame."

They sat in silence, each with their own thoughts. Lucy leaned back in her chair. Gary seemed haggard compared to the last time she'd seen him. The situation with Beau might have been more difficult for him than she'd imagined.

"Well, Gary, when we spoke earlier today, you said you were Beau's father. Did you bring the lab report with you?"

"Of course," the man said, pulling the report out of his portfolio.

"How about I take a look while you read and sign the necessary paperwork?"

"Fine, just give me the stuff to sign," Gary answered, impatient to move on with the matter.

"Listen, I'm going to walk out of this room and give you enough time to read through all of it. What you do with the time is your business, but you know I can't sit here and watch you sign something you haven't read."

"I read it before, last time. But, fine, I'll do it again."

Lucy left the room with the lab report in hand. She walked over to Ruby's desk. "Take a look at this and tell me what you see."

Her assistant scanned the sheet. "Okay, it's a lab report saying that there is a ninety-nine percent chance that some kid belongs to Gary Vaughn. So who's the lucky winner?"

"Keep sitting. The kid we're talking about is Beau Brockhurst."

"Are you fucking kidding me?" Ruby's voice was just a little too loud.

"Nope, that's why I took a big retainer. You can just imagine what this is going to be like. He wants Beau. No one knows about this, and now this whole miserable situation is about to become a three-ring circus."

"Jesus, what are you going to do?"

"I'm certainly going to wait until after the funeral, but I've got to get things moving right after that. Georgina and Everett have to know before they think everything's settled with the kids."

Ruby closed her eyes and rubbed her temples. It was the beginning of yet another horrible chapter in the Brockhurst saga, and the firm was going to be at the center of it.

"I have to tell you, Ruby, I really feel bad about Georgina. I think she's a good person, who's been thrown into a hornet's nest and she's trying to do her best in a rotten situation. I'm pretty sure she was expecting me to handle all of the legal work for her while she was up here, but obviously, now I can't."

"Well, if she means just the estate stuff, you really don't have a conflict, do you?"

"Yeah, I do. She told me in our phone call this morning that she once promised Skippy she'd take the kids if anything ever happened to her. You can bet the loyal sister will try to honor her wishes and get the kids."

Ruby frowned. "You know, I understand that we're a business and everything, but are you doing the right thing, representing Gary? Shouldn't you be representing Georgina?"

"Actually Rube, I am doing the right thing. Remember when I was representing Skippy in her divorce and she left town to visit her sister? She was going off to get her head together for a few days."

"Not really."

"Well, it didn't help her head at all. When she came back she told me it was just as bad in its own way at Georgina's house as it was at hers, but without the money. Apparently, her husband ran the house like it was under martial law. Skippy told me the guy was all over them with suspicion and questions just because the sisters wanted a little time on their own. He even interrogated Skippy about taking his kids out to a different mall than the one they usually go to — and he banned the videos she brought the kids as a gift, saying they were too 'mature.' For God's sakes, we're talking stuff like *Harry Potter*, and the kids were practically in middle school. Skippy seemed really concerned about her sister. She told me she never realized how bizarre her brother-in-law's behavior was until she stayed at their house. One long weekend with 'that Nazi,' as she put it, was more than she could tolerate."

Ruby shook her head.

"Well, you can see that I can't let those kids end up living with the great dictator. So yes, I think I really am doing the right thing. And the good news is that Gary Vaughn can afford to pay me to do it." Lucy returned to her office, leaving Ruby to her own thoughts.

She collected Gary's paperwork and took her seat across from him. He seemed to be searching her face for answers.

"I looked over the lab report and it does say exactly what you said it would. But be prepared to hear that it's unreliable."

"What does that mean?"

"It means you may have to re-do the test at a lab suggested by the court; that is, if you get that far."

"What the hell is that supposed to mean?"

"It means this isn't such a black and white situation as you might think. These kids have to be a mess, as it is, and you can bet someone is going to argue that dropping this additional bombshell is not good for them."

"But Lucy, come on, it's right there in the report. I'm Beau's father! Doesn't that make me entitled to be in his life? And let me ask you something, if I'm his father, why shouldn't I have custody instead of Everett?"

"Just a second, Gary. On the phone, you said you wanted to be a part of the boy's life. That's tough enough. But custody brings up a ton of other issues. Like, what about Emma? No one's going to want to split up those kids, and with their mother dead, it's even more unthinkable. And frankly, under the law, your chances of getting custody of her are practically nonexistent. Even if you wanted to take her, I don't think the court has the authority to give you custody of Emma. You're a total stranger to her. At least with Beau, you have a biological connection."

Gary got up and grabbed the back of his chair. For just an instant, Lucy wondered if he was going to throw it at her. What had she promised him? Nothing at all, and now he appeared to be incensed to hear that custody was going to be a big problem. In fact, she had to complete the picture for him.

"And then, let's face it. Beau is eight years old already. The only father he knows is Everett. You could be a day late and a dollar short."

"Bullshit," Gary exploded. "Do you want this case or don't you?"

"Of course I want the case," Lucy said. "I wouldn't be seeing you tonight if I didn't. But if you remember, I always tell you the truth. That means the good and the bad. That's all I am doing, Gary. And so far, we've only talked about Everett. If you thought from the little you knew about him that he was such a lousy father, you can only imagine what Skippy must have told her own family. I would bet that her sister, Georgina, is going to try and get those kids away from Everett. After all, she doesn't even know anything about you or where you fit into this picture."

As Gary tried to digest this unwelcome information, Lucy was already beginning to expound on the law.

"Speaking of where you fit in, you need to know that the New York courts have the power to stop you from even making your claim. In cases where a father shows up five or ten years down the road claiming that he's a parent, a court might say that the kids are doing fine with the dad they know, and that it wouldn't be good for the children for the court to upset the apple cart."

"Even if the guy's the real dad?"

"Yes, even then. But that certainly isn't always the case. I would argue that you had no reason to know you could have made a claim earlier, and that once you did know, you took immediate action. Even more important, I'd argue that Beau is not doing fine with the dad he knows. The dad he knows is a loser who couldn't give a rat's ass about his son."

"And how do we know if the court is going to stop me from bringing my claim?"

"We don't know. But we can make it harder for them to go in that direction. The more bad stuff we can show them about Everett, the more willing they'd be to explore other possibilities."

"So, what do we have to do?"

"I'd advise you to hire a detective right away to start working on getting the dirt on Everett. Do you know someone? If not, I like the detective we've been working with for years."

"If you've been working with him and you like what he's done, let's go with that. Do you have a name and number for him?"

"Sure, but it's not a 'him.' Is that a problem for you?"

"Come on, Lucy. I'm in your office, aren't I? What do you think?"

"Sorry, good point." Lucy called for her assistant. "Can you get Gary the number for Maria DioGuardi?" Lucy scribbled it down on a scrap of paper and handed it to Gary. "Just give her a call and set up an appointment to get her on board. When you meet with Maria, make sure to tell her you're my client and be ready to give her the basics of the case. Tell her you need all the dirt she can get on Everett, and ask her to call me."

"Fine, but what's this you were saying about the sister? Didn't you just say she might get involved in all this?"

"The way I see it, chances are good that she's going to try to get custody of the children away from Everett. If that happens, my goal would be to get you joined in that same custody lawsuit. But in order to make you a part of that case, we first have to show the court that letting you bring your claim would not be bad for Beau. That in fact, staying with Everett might pose the biggest risk. That's exactly why I'm sending you to Maria, so she can get the dirt on Everett. As for Georgina, who could be the better parent, that's something we might have to deal with down the road. That is, if we get you into the case."

"Why don't I just start my own lawsuit?"

"Because, my instincts tell me that Georgina isn't going to wait long to take action and that it wouldn't be such a bad thing for both of us to be throwing stones at Everett. If the two of you both come up with negative things about him, you have a stronger chance for the court to consider you as a possible alternative."

While finishing up with her explanation, Lucy had started to put on her winter boots. "Now I really have to throw you out. I've got to be at my son's basketball game in a little while, and you know how that is. Just call me after you talk to Maria."

Some lawyers might not have told their client about the game, but would have come up with an excuse for some business meeting or other event. That was not Lucy's style. She'd been around long enough to let people know that she, too, was human. She had the same problems as they did with juggling their schedules. They could take her or not, for who she was. That would be their choice or their loss, as Lucy's mother would say. She said goodbye to her client, packed her things up and headed out to her car to make the game on time, as promised.

CHAPTER FIFTEEN

Beau didn't want to see any of his friends except for Chris O'Neill. *His best friend is a lifesaver*, thought Georgina, as she greeted the boy and his mother at the door. Mrs. O'Neill handed her a basketful of handwritten cards from Beau's classmates and told her that the whole Aston community was there for them. All she had to do was say the word.

"Chris is the best help Beau could have right now," Georgina responded.

The two watched as Beau came down the hallway to meet his friend. Bridgette, holding the playroom door open for the boys, exchanged hopeful glances with the women. It was a first step.

✳✳✳

Amanda continued to stir up her usual brand of trouble, just as she'd been doing ever since she set foot in Laurel Hall. She managed to be the one Vivian asked to assist at the mansion through the evening.

"You call these clean?" the housekeeper scoffed.

Teresa glared back at her. She knew this was being done for the benefit of Mrs. Brockhurst, who'd just entered the dining room. Vivian took the bait, and came in for a closer view of the Baccarat. That afternoon, the hundred or so glasses stored in the basement were carefully carried up to the pantry, hand-washed and hand-dried by Teresa and the other housekeepers. The glasses were set out in precise order upon the two huge breakfronts in the dining room. Teresa needed a well-deserved break after working out the dinner arrangements for the Brockhursts and Fiskes.

"Of course," added Amanda, "If you're not fussy, I suppose they'll do."

Vivian could see nothing wrong, even up close. But this did nothing to stop her from expressing her disapproval. "Well, there's no time to wash all these again, so just attend to the worst ones and move on." Vivian stepped past Teresa and out of the room, leaving an icy silence in her wake.

"Thanks," Teresa muttered in Amanda's direction.

"Just doing my job. Thought I'd save you the embarrassment."

"I appreciate it."

Amanda recognized that her gig at Laurel Hall gave her a once in a lifetime opportunity. She could run circles around Teresa, tie her in knots and even get her fired if she so pleased. She led off her campaign by spreading word that Teresa was to blame for the general neglect of the house, then moved on to more specific complaints about the disorganization of the kitchen and laundry, and finally called into question Teresa's ability to handle just about any task. She sprinkled little comments that displayed the same disdain for Bridgette's abilities, as well as for those of the temporary housekeepers she deemed inferior. While the housekeepers were busy obediently following Mrs. Brockhurst's orders, Amanda was busy sabotaging their efforts in the hope she'd be singled out as the only one on the ball. After years of hard sweat and toil at the Excelsior, Amanda had finally come upon the person she wanted to work for, and she was resolved to make it happen. Mrs. Vivian Brockhurst was her ticket to a better life.

There was one little point that was lost on Amanda, however. No one played Vivian Brockhurst; the lady played you.

CHAPTER SIXTEEN

The telephone was ringing as Lucy unlocked the door to her office. She often wondered what it was about people that made them call after hours or before 8:30 in the morning. She figured out that it was the "Tag, you're it" syndrome. Certain people really didn't call to speak to anyone and in fact would rather not speak to anyone, but wanted to leave a message to say they called. Later, they could say they'd tried to reach the firm, knowing this would put the onus on the attorneys to try and reach them. It was annoying. It forced Lucy to start each day a few steps behind the eight ball with about a dozen messages to handle. The tactic bordered on unethical when the caller was some sleazy adversary, who was supposed to give her notice of something happening and made the call so late that there was absolutely nothing Lucy could do about it.

Then there were the lawyers who after dropping a bomb, proceeded to turn off their fax machines and place their phones on service, to avoid being contacted. Lucy was in the middle of a case with just that sort of snake. Heidi Herzog's routine was to send out a nightly fax canceling the next day's visitation for Lucy's client. Heidi would then turn off her firm's fax and put on the answering machine to keep Lucy from getting in touch to protest. She wanted to throttle the woman. At the expedited conference, she planned to tell the judge about Ms. Herzog's behavior. By now, all the judges were aware of Heidi's modus operandi, and Lucy hoped they'd finally consider imposing sanctions.

Alone in the office, Lucy passed the receptionist's desk and caught the tail end of a client's message. Here it was, 8:22 in the morning and the client was calling to complain that her husband had ordered her to "go and perform a physically impossible task" and asking Lucy exactly what she planned to do about it. As the attorney went to grab some coffee, she could hear another phone message come through. This time, it was the voice of Georgina Fiske.

Diving for the phone, the attorney practically shouted, "Georgina! It's Lucy Bennett here. How'd you make out with your search for the will and instructions?"

"I was hoping I could reach you. Lucy, I found the will, I found her financial papers, but no burial instructions. Mrs. Brockhurst thought Skippy should be buried at Saint Agnes' cemetery, but I put my foot down on that one. And my folks backed off about burying her at their church back in Oklahoma, after hearing my objections. She wasn't very religious, but I did know that she talked several times with the pastor at the Unitarian Fellowship. I guess something must have stuck with her, because she told me that Pastor Bill helped her clarify a lot of things when she was going through tough times. She mentioned that he not only understood her need to get away from Everett, but made her think God would understand it too. I tracked him down and he suggested that maybe my sister would have preferred to be buried in his church's small, local cemetery. I went to check it out yesterday afternoon and it seemed like a beautiful, serene setting. Anyway, we all agreed, even the Brockhursts, that the Fellowship cemetery would be suitable. Thank goodness, we got that settled."

"Glad to hear it."

"Also, I wanted to let you know that we're holding a memorial get-together at the house tomorrow evening, to celebrate Skippy's life. I thought since you've been such a big part of her life these last few years, you and Andi might like to be there. We'll be expecting people after seven in the evening."

"Thanks for letting me know. We'd be honored to be there."

"Ms. Bennett," Georgina continued, adopting a more formal tone, "To tell you the truth, I didn't call only to talk about the arrangements. I need to speak to you about the children's future. Do you have another minute?"

Lucy had a full list of items to get through before the day officially began, but she assured Georgina she had the time.

"Well, I've been thinking about it, and in my mind, there's no question: Skippy would never have wanted Everett to raise the children. In fact, she hated that he had anything to do at all with raising them. That was one of the main reasons she divorced him. I was wondering if I could come in to see you about trying to get custody of Beau and Emma."

At these words, Lucy could no longer speak with her. As soon as Georgina verbalized her desire for custody, the attorney had a definite conflict of interest, having already been retained by Gary Vaughn. She could not turn back, so came out with it.

"I'm sorry, Georgina. I can't help you with that."

"Excuse me?" Georgina asked, wondering if she'd misunderstood the attorney's words.

"I said that I won't be able to help you with that."

"Why not? Is it because of your relationship with Skippy? 'Cause if it's that, I don't see any problem: I'm only doing what Skippy would have wanted."

That wasn't the reason, but confidentiality kept her from getting into the details. "I can't really explain it all to you, Georgina, but I know things that make it impossible for me to represent you. I'm really sorry."

"Well, you're the only lawyer I know up here and Skippy thought you were great…well, maybe a little bitchy and hard at times, but she thought you did a very good job for her. Are you sure you can't help me?" Lucy could hear the rising tension in Georgina's voice.

"I wish I could."

"Well then, could you recommend someone else to me?"

"I honestly can't do that, but you can certainly call the Bar Association for a referral. Or you can take a look online for some options, if you prefer that."

Georgina was flabbergasted at this turn of events. "I can't believe I have to deal with this now, on top of everything else." She hung up the phone without saying goodbye.

CHAPTER SEVENTEEN

"**R**on, keep it down!"

"What, you really think they can hear me clear across the house? And what if they can? I'm not taking any more of their shit!"

"Please," Georgina said, "You'll wake the kids!"

"It's you who should be pissed off. And the way they insulted your folks, and Vivian pretending to be so devastated while she hustles us and your parents off to our little wing here in the back."

"I chose to be in the children's wing. And this is where we should be, right next to the kids. They need us here beside them, and Skippy would..."

"Enough about what Skippy would do. I'm sick of it already. Your sister's gone, and now it's up to us to make the decisions. Oh, and by the way, if she was here, she'd be telling Vivian where to shove it!"

Georgina felt herself crumple. She could handle almost anyone else, including the likes of Vivian, but Ron knew how to sting her every time. She turned her head away and continued unpacking his things, knowing his tirade would continue until he was just too tired to go on.

"Oh, and here's a cute one for you. Did you know she's planning a Christmas party? To try and cheer them up."

"Yes, I heard."

"I'm telling you, Gina, it's bad enough being shoved around and railroaded into the kind of funeral they wanted, but you better get ready to kiss your niece and nephew goodbye, because they're going straight downhill with Everett and his fucking..."

"Stop it!" Georgina exploded.

Ron stared at her. Over the past days, his obedient wife had been showing new colors and there wasn't one that he liked. He opened his mouth to answer her in kind, but she turned on him again.

"Just stop it," she repeated. She looked down at the bed, wondering how in the midst of her sadness it could feel so good to finally give it back to Ron. But she couldn't go any further. She couldn't dare provoke him again. Not here.

"Okay, Georgina, fine. But they're running this show, and you refuse to see it. You better wake up or I'm telling you, in a few years those kids won't even know who we are."

He left the room, slamming the door behind him. He passed one of the housekeepers along the upstairs hallway, nearly knocking her over, and headed downstairs to the library in search of Everett. Perhaps, thought Ron, the two of them could arrange one of their lively face-offs, just for old times' sake. He was certainly in the mood.

CHAPTER EIGHTEEN

Bridgette sat in her room, a picture of Skippy and the children in her hands. They'd be leaving for the service within minutes, but she needed to collect her thoughts. There she was, sitting in her old black suit that had been stuffed into the back of the closet. After getting the children's clothes ready that morning, the nanny found a moment to try and steam out the worst creases from her outfit, and locate a decent pair of boots that might not look too bad. Her own needs and worries were lying somewhere under the surface; her sole concern was for the children, especially for Beau. He hadn't cried since his mother died, or at least, she hadn't seen the tears. Last night, she'd joined him in the ballroom, where he and his father were sitting together on one of the couches, quietly talking. It almost looked to her as though things might be falling into some semblance of order.

And then Vivian and Hugh walked in, and the whole atmosphere changed. There were some terse words between Everett and his folks, and soon after, Beau said he felt tired. Bridgette escorted him up to his room.

It wasn't long afterwards that she heard the shouting. She prayed that the children were fast asleep, including the Fiske boys, who'd gone to bed earlier. But she knew in her heart that Beau had heard the fighting.

Bridgette set her mind to figuring out how she would help that child get through this particularly difficult day. She walked down the hall to the children's rooms. Meeting Georgina along the way, she grasped her hand.

"The limousine is here," she said as softly as possible.

"I know," said Georgina.

"I'll be right there beside you," promised Bridgette.

***

Although there seemed to be standing room only, Lucy found a seat at the end of the aisle. The funeral service at Grace Episcopal Church fit with what she imagined to be the Brockhurst tradition: reporters waiting outside along with a line of limousines, throngs of people, lavish flowers overflowing the altar and pipe-organ music and choir voices resonating throughout the towering old church. The tone of the service was reminiscent of a state funeral. The soft-spoken, silver haired pastor with his porcelain skin looked and sounded like something straight out of central casting. The whole scene seemed almost too perfect.

She spotted Georgina, the children and their nanny in the front row. Next to them, the two boys who she imagined were Georgina's, were poking one another at the slightest provocation, unaware that their antics might be noticed. The man sitting next to them didn't seem to care.

A touching speech written by Georgina and her parents was read aloud by Leeann Parker, Skippy's former sorority sister and close friend. The head of the Graham-Darcy Real Estate agency and several co-workers shared a few thoughts about their colleague's dedication and hard work, but Lucy wondered about the sincerity of their words. Skippy used to describe them as high-powered, but also high-handed and full of ego, and unlike the friendly, supportive agents from the smaller company where she'd started, more interested in competing with one another than working as a team. As star of the national firm's Dover Plains branch, Skippy stayed above the fray. Lucy wondered if some of those same teary-eyed co-workers were silently praying to get a good slice of all the deals now left up in the air on account of Skippy's death.

At the end of the service, Georgina wrapped her arms around Beau and Emma and gently led them down the aisle. It was as though the children's aunt had stepped into the shoes of their mother. Lucy assumed that the man following Georgina was her husband. If Skippy's description of Ron Fiske was at all accurate, he would be of no help to his wife. This was one woman Lucy would have wanted to assist. At least, she would have liked to give her a decent explanation as to what was preventing her from doing so, thought Lucy, her eyes falling upon a man at the back of the church: Gary Vaughn.

***

The mansion was as ready as possible under the circumstances. The myriad of houseguests straggled down the stairs into the large front parlor, each person trying their best to be civil, their brief conversations starting and stopping. Meanwhile, Amanda positioned herself in the upstairs hallway, prepared to pounce as Vivian emerged from the master bedroom. At last, the woman entered the hallway.

"I thought I should mention something to you, Mrs. Brockhurst. I really couldn't talk in front of anyone else."

"This is really most inappropriate, Ms. Gray, and certainly not the time for us to talk."

"It's just that I need to tell you something important," Amanda said. "I overheard some arguing last night just before I left and I thought you should know about it sooner than later."

Vivian said nothing and let her continue.

"Well, you know I stayed very late last night to be as helpful as I could. I was placing the extra towels in the linen closet and I heard some shouting. Mr. Fiske and his wife were having an argument and they were really going at it. He was so loud, I couldn't help overhearing him. But then I thought, if I could overhear him, so could the children, with their rooms so close by. His language and all the yelling, well…your grandchildren really shouldn't have to hear that sort of thing, especially right now."

"Your point, Amanda?"

"Well, it's not hard to see that you and Mrs. Fiske don't see eye to eye. So I just thought that you might want to know, with Mrs. Fiske being so close to your grandchildren and all."

Vivian didn't move a muscle other than her mouth, which opened just enough for one small word to slip out. "Dismissed." Then she moved abruptly past the housekeeper and strode on down the hallway. But Amanda was satisfied that their little bond had formed as neatly as she'd hoped.

***

Doris and Charlie were red-eyed and numb. They had met with as many people as they could, accepted the condolences of people they knew, those they had never known or hoped to know and held off their grief for as long as they could for the sake of their grandchildren. By the time Lucy squeezed through the crowds in the entrance hallway and found the couple in the front parlor, they were aching to collapse in their room upstairs. At first, they didn't seem to recognize her.

"I'm Lucy Bennett, Skippy's attorney." She extended her hand to each of them in turn.

"Oh, of course," Doris said.

Then there was silence. Had Georgina told them about it? That Skippy's attorney had deserted their one living daughter? "I'm so sorry about Skippy. I really liked her."

"Thank you." Doris managed. "It's been hard." She didn't mention that she and Charlie never cottoned to their daughter's nickname; she would always be their Suzanne, now and forever.

"I can't even imagine…" Lucy started, then saw the broken look on Charlie's face. She murmured, "If there's anything I can do…" The funeral rhetoric escaped her lips before she could stop it and her attempt to gracefully retreat was ruined as she stepped backwards directly onto Vivian Brockhurst's right toe. "Oh, I'm so sorry!" Lucy uttered.

"Aren't you the lawyer?" Vivian blurted out as she shifted her weight onto the other snakeskin pump.

"I'm a lawyer, yes. I was Skippy's lawyer, in her divorce. I hope I didn't hurt your foot." At this point, Lucy wondered what she could possibly have been thinking when she accepted Georgina's invitation. Was she looking for punishment? After all, she was the one who sent

Skippy off to the scene of her own death. Now, she'd put herself in the position of having to face the whole family.

"I'm fine." Vivian responded, bluntly, bending down to rub her foot. Lucy knew she had literally stepped in it, but did not expect to hear the next words.

"What the hell are you doing here?" It was Everett, drink in hand and actually thinking he'd made a joke. "My favorite lawyer!" he added.

"Hey, Everett. You hangin' in there?" Lucy's easygoing demeanor worked especially well when she was faced with a client's ex-spouse. She was actually relieved to see the old son of a bitch. She noted, also with relief, that Vivian had disappeared into the crowd. For a moment she could understand all of Everett's nonsense, knowing Vivian had been in charge of his life for so many years. Perhaps he was an example of normal wear and tear in a Brockhurst. But it didn't excuse his treatment of Skippy and the children. Everett had been given too many chances to make an effort, and threw away each and every one.

"I guess so, my dear," said Everett, with his usual charm. The perfect, model smile must have been the thing that cinched the deal, thought Lucy. The glare of those extraordinarily white teeth must have blinded Skippy and frozen her brain. That and the fortune. It seemed to Lucy that his good looks hadn't entirely vanished, despite the years of abuse he'd put his body through. "I'm managing," he said, knitting his eyebrows in an attempt to look more somber. Instead, he looked downright silly.

"Sorry about the kids. It's just awful." Lucy chose a glass of club soda from a waitress offering drinks, but Everett took the opportunity to take a glass of Scotch before tossing back the remains of the tumbler already in his hand. "Well, at least they've got family," he said.

"Yes, they do indeed," Lucy responded, thinking this a rather strange way to put it. She realized they were probably having their last civil conversation. Once he learned about Gary, she wouldn't simply be Skippy's former attorney, she would be the mortal enemy of the Family Brockhurst.

"They'll be in good hands." He leaned in toward her ear, as though they were in confidence. "I believe there's a pretty good wrongful death case."

Lucy cocked her head slightly to the side, as though daring him to continue.

"Not to mention the life insurance," he went on.

The fact that Lucy was glaring at him didn't seem to register as Everett continued on his predictable tack.

"And the house..."

Lucy felt the first pang of what she thought might be a migraine.

"And they've got me!" he announced before taking another hefty gulp.

"Everett, I need to ask you something important." Lucy said.

"Anything, sugar."

"Where's the nearest bathroom?"

Everett smiled. Now he got it. She was pissed off with him. Perhaps it was something he'd said, but hadn't he been very nice? From some far off recess of his brain there came some recollection of the disarming nature of this woman. She had sat across from him at any number of the settlement conferences, so pleasant despite her formidable reputation. It wasn't until much later that he'd realized how much she'd manage to grab for Skippy, and by then it was too late. A lot of good the big shot law firm had done for him.

Now he stood triumphant. Everything that Lucy had fought so hard to gain on behalf of her client was returning to him, and would soon be entirely under his control.

"Down the hall to your left. Or if you'd prefer, down the hall to your right."

She gave him a farewell smile and made her escape.

Consuela Birnbaum, escorted by her dapper Max, entered through the front doors into the busy foyer of Laurel Hall, intent on making a beeline for any available Brockhurst she could find. Andi hurried in moments later and was dismayed to see that her folks had already started in with the schmoozing.

Consuela was working the room. Once she had caught wind of the memorial evening, there was no stopping her. Upon hearing that their daughter was running late, the Birnbaums had set out on their own, leaving Andi in the lurch. Consuela didn't want to miss a minute of the evening. She left a message on her daughter's cell phone saying they'd get there on their own steam.

The couple moved through the crowd, Consuela introducing themselves as dear friends of the deceased, as she recited the same words over and over. "Such a beautiful girl, we knew her well. She witnessed our will, such a delicate thing." Max could only nod; he had no idea what his wife was saying, but he was certain she was saying all the right things. They shook many hands as they moved along with a grace and ease recently polished on their splendid cruise. But they had yet to land a real Brockhurst.

The inevitable was about to occur. Andi saw it unfolding before her almost in slow motion. She recognized the face of Denise Burden, a woman she knew from her former life as a personal injury lawyer. Denise's bland hair and pale makeup did nothing to camouflage her identity as Bantam Insurance's ruthless hatchet woman. The harsh lines around her mouth from years of smoking, and the permanent frown made the once attractive woman appear years older than she was; her grimace matched her personality. Andi realized at once that the woman was on site to dig up whatever possible on behalf of the insurance company, likely defending the hospital or perhaps the company affiliated with the ambulance. Skilled at her trade, Denise had purposely crash-landed onto enemy territory. Andi kept one eye on the investigator and another on her mother, who was busy making the rounds.

"I was truly concerned about her. But I never thought it would come to this!" Consuela shook her head, her onyx, chandelier earrings tinkling softly, as she spoke to Pastor Bill. She caught her image in the grand mirror of the entrance hall and silently praised herself for having found the perfect shirt to set off her necklace. The shirt's sequins were just subtle enough to not say "party."

"Oh dear, was she ill?" Denise cut in, with an exaggerated look of grief. She had dropped another conversation to turn toward Consuela and Max.

"Mom!" Andi interrupted, instinctively knowing where Denise was going with her question, and certain that her mother would fall right into the trap. Ms. Burden had skillfully targeted the big mouth in the room. Information about the medical condition of Skippy Brockhurst prior to the accident was exactly what Denise was after. Next thing, thought Andi, her mother would talk about Skippy's fainting spell in the office. From there it would only be a short leap for Denise's people to blame the accident on Skippy. They would argue that Skippy fainted in the street and no one could have seen her in time to avoid the accident. While it was certain that every potential defendant would already be inquiring into her medical history, Consuela's unguarded chatter was sure to make things worse for the accident case.

"You know you should have waited and let me drive!" said Andi, scolding her folks. "I don't know how you got here so quickly!" She turned to the little circle that had formed around her parents, including Denise. The woman's eyes narrowed as she and Andi looked at one another. Continuing to loudly address her mother, the lawyer found a way to throw Ms. Burden off the scent.

"Mom, I know how concerned you were about Mrs. Brockhurst. You're always that way when you meet one of my clients — even for a minute or two — and that's why I always say the office is off limits! You'd think she'd know my clients are in good hands, but no, she takes one look and wants to get in the middle of the case." She could see the rest of the story ready to burst out of her mother's glossed-up lips, but swiftly guided her parents over to Georgina Fiske, who while not a Brockhurst, was certainly among the evening's VIPs.

Denise Burden had been found out, but wasn't planning to let it stop her investigation. It seemed to her that Andi had done the appropriate thing, avoiding a scene rather than calling her out on the carpet. The company spy squeezed through the crowd, which by now had taken over most of the first floor. She followed a particularly garrulous waitress all the way down the hall and into the kitchen, where she tried to blend in with the help. Amanda, just returning with a large tray of empty glasses, took note of the woman standing there, out of place, and gave her the once over. She smelled a rat. One could attribute it to years at the Excelsior, but that had only sharpened her innate ability.

"Something you need?" Amanda asked.

"Just needed a break from the crowd for a minute."

"Did you happen to put your name in the guest book?" Amanda asked in her softest voice.

The others in the kitchen stopped what they were doing. They knew Amanda pretty well by now, and recognized that a standoff was underway.

"No?" the housekeeper pressed on. Ms. Burden stood in place, stunned. This flunky had put her on the spot.

Amanda finally came out with it. "You're a reporter, aren't you?" Vivian had warned her and the other members of the staff to be on the lookout for members of the press who might slip in. She told them that while the Adams Agency had been hired as security, even they couldn't promise a perfect barricade.

"If you haven't already, I think maybe you should meet Mrs. Brockhurst," said Amanda, now folding her arms.

Denise Burden sputtered something about not knowing what on earth the housekeeper was talking about. Andrea Birnbaum had let her off the hook, but this bitch posed a real obstacle. She was the type who would hound her until she left.

"So, why don't you come with me?" the housekeeper asked, leading the way out of the kitchen. But by the time Amanda turned around again, the woman had taken off in the other direction. Denise Burden was headed out of the mansion and back over the icy roads to Staten Island, with little to show for her efforts.

Lucy's headache had not abated despite the Advil, but had not become a full-fledged migraine. She wondered if the lavender-scented sachets adorning the massive guest bathroom might have helped a bit. Rather than rejoin the crowd, she walked down the broad hallway that separated the north and south portions of the mansion. The frenzied activity of the past few days seemed to have caught up with her. She just needed a few moments to herself. As she ventured down the hall-way, the din of the guests slowly fading away, Lucy noticed the majestic paintings lining the walls, each one set into its own lighted niche. The open archway at the end of the hall drew her, and as she grew nearer, light and warmth poured out toward her.

She stepped into one of the most exquisite rooms she'd ever seen. The southern portion of the room was filled from top to bottom with tropical plants, some reaching far up to the ceiling, some suspended from the carved beams that crossed the room. It was a perfect blend of conservatory and salon, reminding her of a picture she'd recently seen in a magazine; the elegant lobby of a grand, old hotel in Havana, restored to its former glory. This room offered the same perfect balance of opulence and comfort. Within the north-facing side of the room were great overstuffed chintz-cov-ered sofas and delicate tea tables, arranged in a few separate sitting areas. Fanciful statuaries, each with their own burbling, miniature lily pond graced the corners of the room. Steam heat poured in through vents along the perimeter, making the room cozy despite its expansiveness.

Lucy felt compelled to walk along the exquisite limestone floor toward the vista over the water. The lights from the other shore twin-kled in the wintry wind.

A chill crept through her. All of this majesty, and Skippy now gone. It was dreadful. And to think that this magical place had been a battle-field between those two parents. Lucy thought of the many wealthy clients she had, so many of them miserable in their charmed lives. Of course, the same could be said for the ones without much money; the contrast just didn't seem as stark.

"But we wouldn't screw it up," Lucy thought as she settled back into a deliciously comfortable settee. "Dan and I would appreciate every minute of it, and we'd keep our heads." Her cell phone turned off, the room still clear of anyone else, Lucy found a perfect moment of solace. Her last thought before dozing off was what a fortune it would take to heat this incredible room.

"Don't tell me," came the abrasive voice.

Startled, Lucy pulled herself up and out of her reverie. The cigar smell gave him away.

"Could it be the one and only Ms. Bennett?" He stuck his head right in front of her just in case she might not be the one and only Ms. Bennett. If it weren't, Nick DeBello would surely have handed his card out to whoever was sitting there in the event they might some-day require his services. His five o'clock shadow and raspy voice jarred Lucy right back into reality.

"Sad situation, eh, Lucy?"

"Very," she answered shortly.

"I'll bet you're wondering what I'm doing out here in these parts?"

"Sure am," Lucy said. "I had no idea you knew Skippy."

"I didn't," Nick said.

Lord in heaven, thought Lucy, *Nick and his games.* How long would it take for him to spit it out?

"Look, Lucy. You know how it goes. Each of us gets plenty of the big cases, and this time it's me. Georgina chose me for whatever rea-son." He paused. "I'm representing her in the custody matter." Nick DeBello would have done far better to have kept his mouth shut, but lately he'd had a surplus of zingers to distribute and Lucy was a prime target. He'd waited a long time for this opportunity.

This couldn't get any better, Lucy thought as she sat looking up at Nick in his dazzling pin-striped suit. He reminded her of so many of her clients who despite her strict instructions, just had to brag of some accomplishment or other while at a settlement conference or deposi-tion. "Well done, Nick," she said, rising to her feet.

"Hey, by the way, you didn't get back to me on Nixon. Wanna fill me in?"

"You know, Nick, let's do this on office time." Lucy sighed, as she headed back toward the hallway. Was nothing sacred to the man?

"Sure, sure…" he conceded, reluctantly.

The two attorneys moved through the now silent hallway. Lucy could just barely overhear the minister's voice resonating down the passageway. The evening's memorial service must have been ongoing for some time. Eager to shake off Nick, she planned to slip in among the guests, but found she couldn't even get past the overflow of people now pooled outside of the opened front parlor doors. She caught a glimpse of Andi and her folks standing far across the crowded room, but had no way of signaling to them. So there she stood, with Nick practically breathing down her neck until the service ended.

As the crowd started to disperse, Lucy made her way over to the Birnbaums, passing Beau and Emma and several other children along the way. They seemed absorbed in their own little world, and didn't even glance up at the adults surrounding them.

"Where were you?" Andi asked as the two partners finally found one another.

"Don't ask," Lucy said under her breath. "Assaulted by Nick DeBello, who couldn't waste a moment to tell me he's been retained."

Andi waited for the rest.

"Custody. Georgina," Lucy whispered as a waitress came by and handed them each a cup of coffee. The two women admired the delicate floral pattern of the porcelain china. "Gorgeous, isn't it? Recognize it?"

Andi separated the cup and saucer. Looking at the bottom of the dish to divine its origin, she said, "Royal Goyim! Who'd have known?"

"Hello there, cookie!" Consuela broke in. "We couldn't find you."

Lucy greeted her warmly, and promised to get over to the Birnbaum house for dinner after the holidays. After planting his customary kiss on the back of Lucy's hand, Max smiled and complimented her on the lovely suede suit. He was like a kindly uncle to her, someone who not only admired Lucy, but who looked on her as family. Here, with the Birnbaums, she had found a little bubble of welcome.

"Mom, Dad, I have to steal Lucy for a moment," Andi interrupted, steering her partner back into the hallway. "We just had an incident. An insurance investigator, Denise Burden, was trying to get the poop on Skippy, for whoever she's representing. I don't know how long she'd been here, but she found the one person who really loves to hear herself talk…" In answer to the look of dread on Lucy's face, Andi confirmed that it was her mother. "But, thank God, I cut her off before she said too much. Before I could find Georgina and tell her what was up, Denise was already being chased out — by one of the help, I think."

While her partner spoke, Lucy noticed Georgina and her husband walk by them and disappear into a room just off the hallway, closing a pair of massive doors behind them. She recognized Ron Fiske from the funeral, but had't seen him so close up. She could see how his wife might have been attracted to him, with his regular features, athletic build and full head of black hair. But Lucy could also see the thing that was wrong. He was too tightly wrapped.

"Can you believe they sent their investigator here?" Lucy said to her partner. "Reminds me of a few years ago when that house burnt down on Truesdale and the insurance company called everyone in the neighborhood even before the fire was out. They got Adam on the phone and asked if Mrs. Riley was a smoker! Adam, who was six years old at that time."

"Really? What'd he say?"

"He told them he didn't play with Mrs. Riley, so he didn't know." The two women giggled.

Surprised to see them in such good spirits at Skippy's memorial, Gary Vaughn didn't quite know how to approach the two attorneys.

"Hello, ladies," he tried.

"Oh my gosh, Gary," Andi said. "Were you here all this time?"

"I was over by the front. Couldn't get past the crowd. You know if Georgina's around? I wanted to pay my respects."

Lucy and Andi looked at one another, wondering why Gary would want to face Georgina. Perhaps he wanted to make a good impression before the war between them broke out.

"I'd just like to tell her how much I thought of Skippy."

"I think she's in there with the family," Andi suggested, pointing to the doors next to them.

As she spoke, a young boy emerged, leaving one of the doors open just enough for Gary to see into the enormous room. Georgina was slumped down on a couch, her niece nearby drawing in a coloring book. Lucy and her partner caught the same view.

"Well, if you're coming in, get in and close the door!" ordered a loud voice from across the room.

Ron Fiske wasn't expecting three adults to obediently walk in. Gary closed the door behind them, as instructed.

Lucy and Andi were perplexed. The vast size and central location of the room told them of its importance, yet it was set up like a gymnasium, a music room and a playroom all at once. In one corner, Georgina's husband oversaw two boys throwing balls to a pitchback.

Ron gave the intruders a glance, then went right back to his apparent coaching. Beau pitched smoothly into the net.

"Again," Ron said. "Now try the curve I've been showing you."

Beau tossed another one, and looked up to see his uncle's reaction.

"Beau, you can do better than that. How do you think Scott always ends up in the all-star game? He knows how to throw those tricky pitches."

Ron demonstrated, then motioned to Beau to give it a try. But Beau's cousin took the ball instead and threw a curve with perfect form.

"Actually, that's not great advice for a young player," Lucy said as she approached them.

Ron looked at Lucy and tried to remember if he knew her face. "Excuse me?" he asked.

"Well, I've coached Little League for years, and throwing a curveball at that age can really wreck a kid's arm." Lucy said.

In the silence that followed, Lucy smiled at Beau and his cousin, shrugged her shoulders as if to apologize for telling the truth. Beau remembered that this was the lawyer with the cool baseball collection. He wanted to return her smile, but didn't dare under his uncle's stern gaze.

"Do I know you?" Ron asked.

"Probably not. I was Skippy's attorney." She noticed the shadow that crossed his features.

Gary spoke quietly to Georgina, trying to keep an eye on Beau and an ear to the strained conversation going on between Lucy and what he took to be Georgina's husband. Lucy's voice was growing louder. Ron's glare hadn't stopped her.

"They've found that young pitchers can damage their arms if they try to throw curveballs. And then, by the time they get to high school, they've got no arm left at all."

"Really," Ron said, then turned away. "Try that curve now, Beau," he said.

Andi prayed that the lively discussion going on between Ron Fiske and Lucy wouldn't escalate into a real confrontation. Her partner would avoid making a scene, but surely would demand some concession from the man she'd cornered. At least, Andi hoped, the face-off wouldn't disturb Georgina, who looked so worn down as she sat there, politely accepting Gary's attempts to console her. The woman offered him a slight smile, but remained silent.

When she realized that the voices on the other side of the room were not subsiding, Andi stepped forward to express her own condolences, intentionally blocking Lucy from Georgina's view.

"I can see I've really made an impression," Lucy said, watching Beau as he followed his uncle's directions. He threw a few more pitches.

Ron wouldn't take this from another man, and he sure wasn't going to take it from some uppity female lawyer — a New York lawyer, no less. "You do whatever it is that you do," Ron said, "and I'll take care of my own."

"You know, I've heard the same thing myself," Gary called from across the room. "Kids have to be careful about throwing curveballs when they're young."

"Well, that's not what I've heard." Ron said. "That your husband?" he asked Lucy.

"No. I'm Gary Vaughn. I was a friend of Skippy's," the man answered, walking toward Ron and the boys. If he'd looked up, Beau might have recognized Mr. Vaughn, but he remained focused on his task.

"Actually, this room is supposed to be closed off. The kids need some privacy." From his icy tone, Ron's meaning was clear.

"Oh, that's fine. We were all just leaving," Lucy said.

On cue, Andi signaled a goodbye to Georgina. Lucy made her own small gestures of farewell and started toward the door. But Gary

Vaughn didn't move. He caught a fleeting glimpse of Beau's profile as he threw another pitch, then took one last look at Ron. If he'd bothered to read the expression on Gary's face, Ron Fiske might have gotten an inkling of what was to come. Gary shook hands once more with Georgina and left the room.

As Lucy drove home that night, the thought resurfaced: how could a person as normal as Georgina have wound up with such a bastard? As a mat attorney, she saw this sort of thing every day. She could imagine walking in Georgina's shoes, a seemingly reasonable person with a good heart, but she couldn't imagine spending more time than she just had with Ron Fiske, without strangling him.

As the last guests made their way off into the night, Amanda hunted down Mrs. Brockhurst. Finding her in the library, she prepared to convey to her the valiant job she'd done chucking out the intruder.

Vivian had no time for the housekeeper. She was preoccupied, watching her son slouch off into his boozy haze. Her husband stood off in the corner, face drawn and pale as he spoke softly with Charlie Fiske. It had been days since she'd had a moment just to think. Her place in this house had always given her strength. It was no longer so. Vivian stared into her glass of sherry and feared for the little world of her grandchildren. In a sudden wave, she felt the heaviness of the days ahead.

CHAPTER NINETEEN

"**M**arco!"

Jake disappeared into the water and resurfaced a few feet away with his answer.

"Polo!"

Dan stood at the side of the pool with his mother-in-law as she snapped another photo of her grandchildren's horseplay.

"Worth the hassle of getting here?" she asked Dan.

"You kidding, Gram? It was 10 degrees out when we left New York!" He looked across the pool at his wife stretched out on her chaise, the picture of relaxation. "It's just what we needed."

Gram, clad in her bright-toned cover-up, followed Dan's eyes and walked toward her daughter. Lucy appeared to be reading from her newest electronic gadget. Gram settled down in the chaise beside her.

"Good book?"

Lucy's fingers tapped across the tablet. "Not really. I just have to finish this one thing."

"I thought you came here to relax."

"I did. And I will. As soon as I finish this."

"If you died tomorrow, they'd find themselves another lawyer. Aren't you the one who told me about the lawyer who had a heart attack in court and the client just stepped right over his body?"

"Supreme Court," Lucy said. She put down her tablet. "Ma, this one isn't only about money. I represented a lady who just died. She had two little kids a few years younger than Jake and Adam and now a bunch of people are going to fight over who gets them."

"They'll still be fighting over them next week when you're not on vacation."

"I know, but I've got to make sure they end up in the right place. I'm editing papers that have to be ready to go to court with me the day I get back."

"There's always a reason. You know I lived with deadlines my whole life."

"Yeah, I watched you do it and I watched you meet every one of them. Everyone knew you'd get the work done, and now you're telling me not to do that? They count on me."

"They count on your office. Don't you have all those people working for you? I didn't have that. I had to do it all myself."

"Well, I must be doing something right to have gotten where I am. Right, Ma?" Lucy was surprised to hear the tone of her own voice. She never fought with her mother. It was as close to an argument as she could remember.

"You don't know how hard it is to watch someone you love make the same mistakes you've already made."

Lucy caught sight of Dan and her boys, now playing keep-away in the pool. She turned to her mother. She was squinting, but Lucy knew it wasn't the sun in her eyes. She closed her tablet and shoved it into the bottom of her beach bag.

"New teams!" Lucy shouted as she dove into the pool.

CHAPTER TWENTY

Gary could hear the kitchen clock ticking. He pushed back the hair from his forehead, and waited for a response, any response. The three women sitting around him didn't stir and didn't speak. He had brought the final meal of the holiday to an abrupt halt, but consoled himself with the thought that he'd at least spared them the news through the bulk of the vacation. He knew it would be wrong to wait any longer.

It was Gwen who finally broke the ice.

"Was this when you and Mom were —"

"Divorced. We were already divorced."

"So he's how old?" asked Lia, trying to focus.

"As I said, he's eight," Gary answered.

More silence followed.

"And I might as well tell you now that he has a little sister, which leads to a whole other set of complications."

The second bomb seemed to do the trick. His daughters all started in at once, mixing their rapid-fire questions with generous heaps of vitriol. As they all shouted in what seemed to be one voice, Gary couldn't properly respond to anyone. Finally, he pushed his chair back.

"Enough!" he said. "No, I didn't plan this! No, I didn't want to ruin your lives. No, I'm not being selfish. That's not why I'm doing this."

"You always wanted a son, we all know that," Becky charged.

"I wanted the children that I have."

"No, you also wanted a son," Gwen said, her voice trembling.

Gary took a deep breath and leaned back, surrounded by the many eyes that refused to meet his own. "Okay, maybe. Maybe I'd like to have a son. Doesn't every man have that in the back of his mind at some point? But I've always loved you girls. I've loved you with all my heart and soul and you know it. You all know you're the world to me." Gary's voice broke.

He had sworn to himself that he'd be strong and not cave. He was hell at the office, tougher than anyone he knew in business, tougher than even his old man had been and he'd been one tough son of a bitch. But here, facing his girls with this sort of news, he was terrified. He recognized it for what it was: a turning point. Gary had taken the terrible risk that his daughters might turn away from him.

"So why would you do this?" Lia asked. "What made you have to go and find out?"

Gary sighed and tried to make eye contact with his girls. Gwen was wiping tears off her face with the back of her sleeve, and Becky couldn't look at him. "After I was sure that Beau was mine, I still might have left things the way they were. But I knew too much about Everett, the man who was supposed to be raising him. He's never acted like a father to him, and basically abandoned both of the kids. I couldn't watch it go on, once I knew Beau was mine. I couldn't have that on my conscience."

"Well, that's a lot to pay for your conscience," Gwen blurted out. It was a personal wound to her, a blow to the heart. As eldest, she knew she was speaking for them all.

"Did you hear me?" he asked as gently as he could. "His mother's dead."

"But you would have wanted to get him, anyway," Becky said. She finally looked at her father.

He looked back at her, and could only answer those deep brown eyes with the truth. "I would have tried to see what I could do to become part of his life. I knew Beau was mine before his mother died, and yes, I was set on spending time with him."

The girls and their father had always shared a special, sheltered world of their own. Gary might not have been the greatest disciplinarian, but what he had given them instead was the pure love of life. As a dad, his easygoing, light-hearted nature drew his daughters to him and made him easy to talk to, even during the worst of the girls' turbulent teen years. The close bonds between Gary and his children had only grown stronger after the divorce. When they visited him, they had him all to themselves, without any other distraction. Eventually, Gary turned to them as confidantes.

They, in turn, became increasingly possessive of their father, even protective, shielding him from bad relationships, steering him toward the women they liked. The daughters guided him along, right down to obliterating his outdated wardrobe and setting up his new kitchen. They thought that they knew every detail of his life. It was unfathomable to the girls that their dad was capable of hiding such an enormous secret from them. The fact that he'd had another child hit each of them the same way: it was simply surreal. No matter how reassuring their father was trying to be, this was going to change the fabric of the family.

Gary watched as Becky and Gwen took off into the night. He wondered if each would make her own decision, or if Gwen might take the lead. Would they banish him entirely? At least Becky had said goodbye, but for the first time he could ever remember, Gwen had walked out without a word. It threw him. He suddenly doubted the gamble he'd taken. He could lose them all, and even Beau, for that matter. No guarantees had been made, far from it. Was it just as they'd said: selfishness, his last chance to have a son?

Gary walked back to the kitchen and started to clear the plates left behind. Another first. The girls always fussed and cleaned after dinner at their Dad's, but this time the kitchen was left in disarray. Lia had fled upstairs to her room. He could only imagine the phone calls that would now go on between the girls and their mother. It would only make it worse. He silently prayed that his daughters would find some way to understand and maybe, somehow, forgive. His brow creased deep in thought, Gary pushed up the long sleeves of his sweater, and started in alone on the pile of dirty dishes.

CHAPTER TWENTY-ONE

Lucy's return to the office was as she anticipated. Although everyone had done their jobs well while she was gone, there was an endless pile of messages stacked on her desk from clients who insisted on speaking only with her and were willing to wait until she got back. Her current popularity had lost its allure; at this stage in life, it was a burden.

Ruby knew just how to handle Lucy's return. She left the morning wide open without appointments so that the boss could sort through her messages and the overflow of mail that had accumulated. The lawyers had already taken out the important correspondence and court decisions that needed to be handled in Lucy's absence. In accordance with the boss's usual instructions, the lawyers made copies of whatever they took out so that Lucy could take a look at everything that had transpired on the files. While she was willing to delegate work, Lucy still wanted to know every detail about what went on in her firm. To some, she knew it might seem obsessive, but then, it was her name on the door. She knew no matter what happened at her office, it was she who would have to deal with the aftermath...for better or worse.

The boss settled into her specially ordered orthopedic chair, which had never lived up to its billing. In fact, on this first day back from vacation, it seemed to be giving her a backache. She buzzed Ruby, with whom she would need a good stretch of time to get up to speed on all the gossip around town and in the office, and to go through the mail and messages.

After hearing a snippet of Meg's New Year's "date to remember," letters were reviewed and responses dictated, phone messages were sorted and restacked in order of importance. Lucy asked Ruby to arrange telephone appointments for the few people who needed the boss's immediate attention. Lucy and her staff had learned to discern which emergency had to be handled first. By setting up phone conferences with the clients, the frustration of phone tag could be avoided and the clients didn't have to wait to see Lucy in person.

After going through everything on her desk and still seeing it in disarray, Lucy felt as though she'd only moved peas on a plate. But she had to get on with the day. She asked her assistant to call a meeting of the lawyers for 12:30 that day, rather than at 1:00 so that they'd have a little extra time to catch up.

While Lucy was on the phone with Judge Oser's chambers, she saw Ruby waving her hands in the doorway, mouthing that Maria DioGuardi was on the phone. Lucy whispered back that she'd pick up with her once she was finished with the current call. She didn't want to be chasing down Maria, but wanted to be sure to treat the judge's secretary courteously.

Once the call was over, Lucy picked up with the private investigator. "Hey Maria, got any good news for me?"

"Actually, I do. Is there a good time that we can get together? You know I don't like to talk on the phone."

"Can you make it here around 1:00? I'm up to my eyeballs, first day back and all, but I really do want to talk to you."

"Sure, I'll stop by then. Do you want me to pick up some food on the way over?"

"No, but thanks for the offer. See you in a few."

Lucy had yet to return a call when the attorneys started assembling in her office. A glance at her watch confirmed that it was already 12:30.

"So how were your folks?" Andi was the first to ask. There was just enough tan on her partner's face to tell her that Lucy had relaxed, at least for a little while.

"Terrific, as usual. I get tired just thinking of their social life. The kids had a great time and of course Gram and Pop spoiled them rotten. How were things with you while I was gone?"

"Let's see. Mr. Turner stole the Christmas ham from his wife's house just before the office was closing and just a few hours before her family was due for dinner. And yes, as crazy as that sounds and as upset as Diane was, I had a fresh baked one delivered to her house from all of us just in time for dinner. I called in a big favor."

"You did the right thing. Thanks, I owe you."

"Actually you don't owe me, we paid for it. And then, Felicia's kids didn't want to go to the Caribbean with Mort because he mentioned that a lady friend might join them. Glen and I arranged for a long weekend here before Mort left, so that worked out all right. And Mrs. Hecht called every day, just looking for someone to talk to. It was her first holiday without her husband in thirty-nine years, and she was a wreck. Heidi Herzog tried to play 'tag, you're it' one too many times on Mike Foster's case, so I forced her into court on an emergency conference on the morning of New Year's Eve. Steve and I didn't have any big plans, and I just wanted to piss her off after she started screwing with us again. Once we got there, we worked out the visitation just the way Mike wanted. We gave them New Year's Eve. Mike had a date and didn't really want the kids for the evening, anyway. He got them at noon on New Year's Day, and I think that put a crimp in his wife's plans.

"And while all that was going on, Meg and Claire were busting their butts on Gary Vaughn's motion and got a first draft done."

"So Claire, now that you've done all the research, what do you think our chances are of getting over the hump and at least being heard?"

"I think we've got a shot at it, Lucy, but it will be better if Maria has something we can throw in to make Everett look horrible."

"Funny you should mention that. She should be here any minute. I asked her to join our meeting. And where's Meg, by the way?"

"On her way back," Andi answered.

Just as Andi completed her summary of the week's adventures, Meg joined them in Lucy's office. "I saw Maria DioGuardi pulling into the parking lot. What's up?"

"I asked her to come over and fill us in on what she tracked down about our friend Everett Brockhurst." Ignoring the phone she'd just picked up in order to buzz her assistant, Lucy shouted for her attention.

"Why the hell does she pay for a fancy intercom system she never uses?" Meg searched the room for someone with an explanation.

"Ruby," continued Lucy at the same volume, "Can you get Maria from the waiting room?"

The others on the couch in Lucy's office made room for the PI. She wasn't quite one of them, but she was certainly a regular at the firm. She had started as Lucy's process server about ten years earlier. She and her brother had a knack for being able to serve papers on even the most difficult defendants, and eventually Lucy started to use them almost exclusively. They made sure to check in at Lucy's firm at least twice a week and more often if Ruby had a rush job requiring immediate service. Maria was relentless when it came to serving deadbeats trying to avoid service, and her good looks and small stature opened a lot of doors from fellows who might otherwise have dodged service.

As good as she was at it, Maria grew tired of the routine and wanted to make a change. She sought out Lucy's advice as to whether or not she thought the investigating business might be a good fit for her. There were few women in the field at the time. Knowing Maria's talents, Lucy encouraged her to give it a try. Since that time, the investigator had taken a variety of challenging courses in surveillance and marksmanship, worked briefly in the office of another investigator to learn some tricks of the trade, and was on her own for over four years. Her brother Vic kept the process serving part of their enterprise running smoothly, and their tandem operation had become a valuable resource for Bennett and Birnbaum. Lucy liked the fact that she could count on Maria to be part of their team.

"Glad you gave me this one, Lucy. I remember what a snot this guy was during his divorce and I have to tell you, it was fun to go after him again. One of the most condescending assholes I've ever met."

"Back then, you came up with some great pictures of him in that strip joint, and I particularly liked the close-ups of him smoking those funny-looking cigarettes. You got some good stuff…made my life a lot easier. When I called, I was hoping you could find something new."

"I guess you're in luck, then. I just had a feeling with this guy's substance abuse in the past, he might have moved on to bigger and better things."

"So come on," Andi said. "Don't keep us waiting."

"I can't give you all the details yet, but let's just say that it seems 'Mr. Wonderful' likes pills — like Oxycontin and hydrocodone with a side of benzodiazepine. You know, tranquilizers, mixed in."

Lucy was impressed. "How's he getting the stuff?"

"It looks like he has more than one drugstore filling prescriptions for him, from more than one doctor, for the same stuff or close to the same stuff and all at the same time. And there's not a prayer in hell he needs the amount he's getting for some toothache or backache or anything else he might claim to have."

"But I thought the state and the drug stores monitor that sort of activity," said Lucy, "so that people can't fill too many prescriptions for the same drug. Isn't it all on computer now, so they can track what's filled from store to store?"

"Sure, but Everett knows that too. He seems to be using a few different doctors and filling prescriptions at different stores."

"What about his insurance carrier? Wouldn't they pick up on it?"

"Not necessarily, if some of the prescriptions are in different names."

"Different names? How's he doing that?"

"I've got a pretty good idea, but don't want to be more specific 'til I get you all the proof. I just wanted you to have my preliminary info right away so you could know where I'm headed with this. But one thing's for sure. If — no, change that to when I get the proof, you'll have all the leverage you'll need. Everett will understand what's at stake. The prosecutors are hell-bent on pursuing these cases after the recent spate of drug store hold-ups, and that big shooting. They want to put an end to this sort of violence out here, and Everett could get caught in that net."

"You've made me a happy woman, my friend."

"That's what I'm here for."

"Do me a favor and spend a few minutes with Claire so she can get what she needs to finish Gary's motion papers. I think with what you've just told, she'll have enough to get Gary his day in court. And Maria, call me when you've got the details."

As the meeting came to an end, a smile came across Lucy's face. Not such a bad first day back after all, she mused.

CHAPTER TWENTY-TWO

The game was in full swing by the time Georgina and Matt got to Cedar Middle School gym. Among the players on the court was eleven-year old Cliff in the jersey she had stuffed into his bag, despite Ron's admonition that it was their son's responsibility to keep track of his own uniform and equipment. True enough, admitted Georgina, but she couldn't bear the thought that her son might miss the Boxers' important game on account of a missing shirt.

She wondered what would happen if every child on the team forgot his shirt on the same day, or if their mothers all forgot to remind them. Would the game be canceled? She thought of mentioning this, but knew Ron would find the question absurd. His instructions were very simple: no uniform, no game, no exceptions. He liked being in charge as the coach, she thought, as she and Matt wedged into the row just behind the seated players to grab a place next to her pal, Valerie. Ron was busy hustling along the sidelines and calling out to the players.

"He's doing great!" Valerie said, although she had no idea of what was actually going on in the game. She only focused on the action when her own son had the ball and when he tried for a basket. Other than that, she preferred chatting over watching.

"You mean Cliff or Ron?" Georgina kidded.

"I guess both, since we're ahead!"

"Not by much," said Matt. "Hey, look, Cliff's got the ball!" He stood up and screamed out, "Go Cliff! Shoot it! Shoot it!" He heard other voices chiming in from the top of the risers. "Hey, Mom, I just saw Scott and the other guys."

"Go ahead, hon." Matt scampered off to hang with his buddies.

"You know, you're lucky Ron's so involved. I wish Jim would come to a game now and then."

"Come on, Val. Be fair. Jim works late, and he's always doing stuff with your kids, so no complaining."

"I guess," she conceded. Valerie loved that about Georgina; she wouldn't let you whine.

The ref's whistle blew and the players gathered back at the sidelines. Georgina noticed something on Cliff's face. It looked like he had a bloody nose, but she wasn't sure. He was standing in the huddle that was gathered around Ron. Instinctively, she waved to her son and then pointed to her nose, with concern.

Cliff looked at her as though she had three heads, and ducked his face back into the group. Ron wouldn't care if he saw that his son was hurt; he'd just tell him to man up and get over it. She pictured Beau, alone on a basketball court without a ridiculously worried mother sitting in the bleachers. It was a crushing thought. She tried to block the intrusion, but it seemed to her that she was always worrying about the children who weren't with her. When she was up in New York with Beau and Emma, she thought constantly of her own children, and now she was obsessing about her niece and nephew, though she'd only left them days before.

Valerie leaned over and touched her hand. "You doin' all right with everything? I know this last trip was tough for you, Gina."

"Thanks, Val, I'll be okay. We're trying to get things settled, as much as possible. And I appreciate all you've been doing for the kids."

"Come on, you'd do the same for me."

The huddle was breaking up. Georgina could see her son with his head tilted back, holding his nose. Ron waved him back on the court, still oblivious to whatever was wrong with Cliff. They had a short conversation, the upshot of which seemed to be that the boy got back into the game with a tissue jammed part way up his nostril, one edge of it dangling out of his nose as he tore down the court. His little badge of courage, thought Georgina.

Ron hadn't yet made eye contact with her, hadn't even offered a nod of hello. Was it possible that he was so engrossed in the game that he hadn't even seen her yet? Yes, she thought, it was possible. It didn't take a game for her to be invisible to him; she'd grown accustomed to being ignored. Sitting in the bleachers amid all the noise, she wondered when it had started.

"You look really tired, Gina," Valerie said. "I bet you haven't had a moment to catch up on things. Why don't you go back and get some rest? You know I can keep an eye on Matt."

"No, no. I just have a lot on my mind today. Pass me one of those damned donuts and I'll be just fine."

Valerie dropped the large bag onto her friend's lap and gave her a soft pat on the back.

"Ah, cinnamon!" Georgina cooed as she opened the bag.

"Of course, you idiot. Think I wouldn't have brought your favorite along? Now, get me a powdered one."

Before long, the two women were chatting away about all Georgina had recently missed in the neighborhood. Time seemed to slip by. At one point, Cliff made an outside shot and the whole crowd cheered. But within moments, Devon, the star of the Razors, answered the brilliant move with one of his own, and at that, the score was tied once again.

"Close game," Georgina said. If they went home in defeat, like the week earlier, their home would be a scene of endless brooding. She prayed they'd win only so that she wouldn't have to deal with Ron and Cliff's disappointment. She'd endured Ron's post-game moods for years, and it never got any easier. Just a few weeks earlier, he'd put his fist through the wall in the family room. Cheap, crappy sheetrock, he'd griped as she tended to his bloodied knuckles. All of this on account of losing a bet on some college football game. It wasn't the little bit of money he'd lost; it was his need to be the winner.

Lately, this meant winning or being right on almost any level. His angry moods had escalated, becoming unpredictable. And more frequent. She could understand why he blew up at her during the stressful week at Laurel Hall and even about the laundry. Perhaps she should have given him better instructions, as he said, since the whole load turned out pink, uniforms and all. But why had he erupted at her over the heating bill? Just because she second-guessed his choice of fuel company? And before her last trip north, she and the kids had been forced to sit there at the diner and watch as he berated the waitress for serving him French fries instead of hash browns.

Then there was the shove. In the end, she'd dismissed it. Perhaps she was too quick to do so. Something was changing between them. Was it something in her?

Georgina stood up with the crowd as Cliff took an outside shot, missing by inches. She sat back down, with the collective sigh of dismay from the Boxer fans. Her son flew down the court, his face crimson, angry, the same as when he slammed down his books, or kicked something across the room at his brother. This new behavior, too, had somehow crept up on her. Had it started before or after they'd patched up the hole that Ron made in the wall? Bullying that boy on the bus, was that before or after? She could hear Valerie's chatter, but her mind was busy trying to put the timing together. Having recently raced back and forth between New York and home so many times, it was hard to distinguish one week from another. Perhaps, she wondered, Cliff was just turning into a teenager a little too early. Maybe it was just a coincidence.

It was at the end of the game, with the Boxers ahead of the Razors by only two points, when Ron called for a time out, gathering the team around him. Georgina and Valerie had their eyes on their respective sons in the huddle. One boy stepped back just a bit, and the women could then hear what Ron was saying to his team.

"There's twenty-five seconds left. We know they're all going to give the ball to Devon. We can't let him get off a last shot."

"You mean we should foul him? Is that what you're saying?" asked one of the boys.

"Not just foul him," Ron instructed. "We have to make sure he can't shoot. 'Cause as we all know, he's a great outside shooter but just like Shaq, he can't make a foul shot for the life of him." The coach's smirk was instantly mirrored on the faces of the boys surrounding him.

"Cliff, I want you to take him out."

"You mean I have to foul him, Dad?"

"Did I say foul him?"

Cliff's face fell.

"I said to take him out." Ron emphasized the last three words.

The boys got back on the court, Cliff the last to take his position. The whistle blew for the game to resume. Georgina knew enough about basketball to understand exactly what Ron had just instructed their son to do. Planning an intentional foul was a normal part of the game, but to tell Cliff to "take him out" was different. It meant that her son was supposed to purposely hurt another boy. The Razors' guard passed the ball in from half court to Devon, as predicted. The boy started to dribble as the clock was running down.

From out of nowhere, Cliff Fiske made a beeline for the Razor star, running full force at the boy and knocking his feet out from under him so that the child landed squarely on his shooting arm as he tried to break his fall.

"Good foul!" shouted Ron.

The stands grew quiet as Devon grimaced in pain. He got up slowly.

"Are you all right?" the referee asked.

The boy was not all right, as everyone could see. Yet, somehow he made it to the foul line. Georgina noticed Ron's satisfied grin. Her face flushed; she made a silent prayer. *Let that poor boy win. Let him make the shots.*

But Devon missed both.

The buzzer went off. The Boxers had won, but the usual jubilation was absent. Rather than running onto the court to celebrate with the boys, Georgina found herself out there yelling at her husband, the coach of the winning team. Her rage spilled out before she could control it, and for the first time in her life, Georgina leveled into her husband in public.

"Good foul? Is that what you think? Is that how you think? These are boys, like ours! How dare you tell our son to hurt that boy?"

Ron grabbed his wife by the wrist, cursing at her under his breath in the hope of silencing her. She broke away from his grip and took a step backwards.

Cliff heard all of it, along with everyone else nearby. His face contorted in confusion as he lashed out at his mother. "Are you crazy? Dad didn't do anything wrong! What the hell do you know?"

She did know, thought Georgina, and so did her son. With Ron's blessing, Cliff was defending something he knew was very wrong. She looked up at her husband and then back at Cliff, unable to form any words. Georgina fled the court, grabbed her purse from her seat and dashed for the exit without a word of goodbye to the speechless Valerie. It wasn't until she got into the car and started the ignition that Georgina realized she'd left Matt behind. She turned off the engine and shut her eyes.

A loud sound filled the air around her. Something was pounding against the car, or maybe it was the rumble of thunder. After a moment, she knew. It was the wild beating of her heart, in applause.

CHAPTER TWENTY-THREE

L ucy decided she'd take the motion papers to court on her own. She didn't normally hang out at the clerk's office, since that was a task for her staff, but this was a different matter. The afternoon before, she'd read and edited Claire's final version of the order to show cause seeking to have Gary Vaughn added as a necessary party to the already existing custody case between Everett Brockhurst and Georgina Fiske. Upon learning from Nick DeBello that he'd been hired by Georgina in her custody case, Lucy contacted her client to advise him that he needed to act quickly.

When they spoke, Gary made it clear that his goal was involvement in his son's life. However, the extent of the involvement he sought depended on where the case was headed. Under no circumstances, for instance, would he allow Everett Brockhurst to raise his son; he'd be willing to fight to the end to prevent that from occurring. On the other hand, he would accept Georgina raising Beau, provided he ended up with ample, quality time with the boy. He wanted sufficient time to counteract Ron's negative influence.

Lucy reminded her client that his chances of getting custody of Beau were slim to none. Even if the court had been tempted to grant him custody of Beau, it wasn't going to happen because he had no legal relationship with Emma. The law of New York does not favor separation of siblings, Lucy advised, and with what the children had been through, this was not a case in which the court would make an exception.

They agreed that whatever he sought to accomplish, whether it was custody or visitation, the time to act was now. He had to try and insert himself into the ongoing custody case, so that his and Beau's interests would be considered in any decisions involving the boy's parenting. The more time passed without his having access to Beau, the less likely it would be for that to ever occur. Once the court made its decision on the future of the children, it wouldn't want to revisit the matter and further traumatize them.

The papers that Lucy was presenting to the court included both a request for custody as well as a request for Gary to have immediate visitation with Beau, under the supervision of a child psychologist. There was Gary Vaughn's affidavit explaining in detail why he could prove he was Beau's father and attached to that was a DNA lab report showing a 99% likelihood that this was so. There was Lucy's affirmation explaining how the relevant law should be applied favorably to the facts she presented. The firm had anticipated that the opposing counsel was going to use the equitable estoppel argument and say it would be too disruptive at this late date to inject him into Beau's life.

The motion Lucy was carrying with her was intended to nip that argument in the bud. That was why she'd pulled Maria in at such an early stage, to have her collect the sort of dirt on Everett that might defeat the estoppel argument. Lucy and her colleagues carefully calculated how much information about Everett they needed to include in the papers. They had to have enough against him to get Gary's foot in the door, but not enough to prove the actual commission of a crime; in that case, the court might feel compelled to report the crime to the authorities. Lucy wanted to withhold the most damaging details to hold over Everett's head as a threat, giving her leverage in any future negotiations. Certainly, when he realized all that Lucy had in her pocket, Everett would want to resolve the matter rather than allow his misdeeds to come to light and jeopardize his livelihood. She felt that the firm had done its homework and struck the right balance in the motion papers.

At the courthouse, Lucy headed straight to the clerk's window and suggested that rather than having the motion brought up to the judge by a court employee, it would make more sense for her to bring it up on her own so that she could explain to the judge and law secretary the nature and import of the papers. The clerks knew Lucy to be a straight shooter and decided that her suggestion made a lot of sense. Joe clocked in her papers with the court stamp and gave a buzz up to chambers to see if anyone was available to take care of the matter. Lucy overheard the judge's law secretary telling Joe to send her right up.

The courtroom door was just being unlocked when Lucy reached the third floor. She walked in, taking off her coat as she approached the rail in Judge Thorpe's courtroom. The clerk of the court was sitting beyond the rail, checking over the day's court calendar. Lucy started to say that the judge's law secretary was expecting her, when Sandra popped into the courtroom with a warm greeting for Lucy, inviting her back into her office.

"So what's so important that you had to bring this up to me yourself, first thing in the morning?"

"Well, I know this is going to get a little ticklish, so I figured it might be best for me to explain what I've got before anything hits the fan. The case I'm talking about already has some notoriety and," Lucy said, waving the document in the air, "I think if and when the press gets wind of this they're gonna be licking their chops."

"I'm all ears."

"You know the Brockhurst case that you've got?"

"Yup."

"Well, that custody case is about to get even crazier. I represent a guy named Gary Vaughn and I've gotta tell ya', Sandra, I really do believe my guy is the little boy's father."

"Geez, Louise! What have you got?"

"Only a DNA test showing a ninety-nine percent likelihood he's the father."

"You kidding me? Is the test legit?"

"Yes, but we're willing to have him take a new one- which is, I'm sure, what everyone will want."

"But Lucy, don't you think your guy is a little late here? This kid is like eight years old, isn't he?"

"My client just found out. It seems he saw Beau for the first time close up a few months ago and put two and two together. Apparently, the kid looked just like he did at that age. Seems my guy and the deceased Mrs. Brockhurst had a little fling almost nine years ago. So when my guy saw the kid, he flipped out. He contacted Skippy. You know I handled her divorce, and I'm not going to bore you with all the details, but basically he told her that he wanted to know the truth. He wanted her to take the boy for DNA testing and that's when she called me."

Sandra shook her head. Another soap opera and the day had only begun.

"She was originally nuts over the whole thing," Lucy went on, "and didn't want everyone's lives disrupted. But, for a variety of reasons, most of them having to do with Everett being a lousy father, Skippy left me a message to go ahead with the testing. And then, she died."

"So, she never knew?"

"Well, I know she had her suspicions. But she never knew for sure. Turns out, Gary took matters into his own hands and found a way to get the testing done by a good lab, without Beau ever knowing, or anyone else for that matter. To make a long story even longer, Gary called me as soon as he heard about Skippy's death. I represented him in his divorce, too. So there I was, knowing that Skippy would have been willing to go ahead with the test, and Gary coming to me with the results, asking that I represent him."

"But what about the sister?"

"Georgina's not the problem. From what I know of her through Skippy, she's a nice lady. But, she's got the husband from hell and Skippy couldn't stand him. And with good reason, I believe. So that's how I got here."

"What's your application?"

"I want my guy joined as a necessary party and I want some visitation until a final decision can be made. We'll do it all with the proper therapeutic help, but we don't want to wait. We want Gary in this boy's life as soon as possible; his only other male role models he could do without. My guy's a great dad, that I can say for him. He has three daughters — all but one living on their own — and would love to have his son."

While Lucy and Sandra were chatting, the judge arrived at his chambers.

"Lucy, let me fill in Judge Thorpe. I'd like to explain the situation before he reviews your set of papers. How about you sit here for a few, while I talk with him. I'm sure you've got plenty of work you can handle on that fancy new gadget of yours."

Lucy loved her newest device. She started right in on her emails, texts and voice messages. Within a few minutes, Judge Thorpe came by to greet her and invite her into his chambers. Sandra was already seated at the conference table, ready to take notes.

"Nice to see you, Ms. Bennett."

"Thanks, Judge."

"I think the best way to handle this is for you to call both of your adversaries and let them know what's going on. I'm willing to sign the papers, but want to hold them until everyone has a say. I don't want to decide on temporary visitation until I hear from everyone. Let's try to get everyone in here as soon as possible."

"Makes sense. Want me to call their offices, or do you want your staff to take care of it?"

"Why don't you give Sandra some times that are good for you in the next two days, and she'll make the calls. We'll let you know what time works for everyone."

"Thanks again, Judge."

"And Lucy, let's try to keep this under our hats as long as we can. I just finished that hockey player's divorce that had the press crawling, and I really could use a few days' peace."

"You got it, Judge. Thanks, Sandra. I'll talk to you later."

Instead of staying to chat with her colleagues, Lucy left the courthouse. Doubtful as it was that Nick DeBello was somewhere in the building at this early hour, she wanted to avoid running into him. She believed that the best place to explain the new twist in the custody matter, preferably to everyone at once, was in the judge's chambers rather than along some courtroom corridor. Heading back to her office, she plugged in her new phone to listen to music and take her mind off the many problems she was supposed to be solving.

CHAPTER TWENTY-FOUR

Ruby was on the phone explaining to someone that "Ms. Bennett" was in court and should be back within an hour, when the lawyer walked in the door.

"So who was that?" asked the boss.

"Just your favorite hot-shot lawyer from Manhattan. Post was practically apoplectic! I kind of enjoyed telling him you weren't here. But he expects you to call him back."

"I've got a full dance card, so he'll have to wait. I have enough to do without having to talk to that stuffed shirt. Isn't Felicia Kornblum due in a few minutes?"

"I think I saw her black Mercedes pulling around the back. And don't forget, you told me to put Maryann Nixon in right after her."

"Do me a favor. Give me two minutes to get settled, and then bring in Felicia." Lucy scarfed down a few pieces of cut-up apple, thumbed through her message slips and realized that the calm she'd felt during her vacation had already worn off. She looked up to see her client crossing her threshold.

"So Felicia, how were your holidays?"

"How could they have been?" she answered, adjusting her tennis sweater. Nine times out of ten, thought Lucy, Felicia was off to a match just after their meetings. She imagined that the client, who typically left the office in a bad temper, took advantage of her mood to blow her opponents off the court. "I couldn't believe Mort left me with the kids. Not that I had that much to do, but it was the first time I'd accepted a blind date. So I cancelled the guy, and he didn't sound real happy about it. Something he said about putting my kids first rubbed me the wrong way."

"I'd say anyone who complains about your kids before you even know him is not a guy for you. So better you didn't waste your time on him."

"I know you're right, Lucy, but here's Mort again, controlling me. He decided he didn't want to take the kids, so I lose out on a date. He decides he doesn't want to pay his court-ordered support, and now I have to beg the oil and electric companies for basic services. Does that sound fair to you?"

"That's why I asked you to come in, Felicia. I think we have to ask the court to hold Mort in contempt and try to put him in jail."

"You might have just made my day. I didn't think you understood how much all of this was getting to me. I've never had to beg in my life. My bills were always paid on time. And there was always cash lying around, somewhere. Unfortunately, I had to use it all up and now I have to live like a pauper. Do you know how embarrassing it is for me to have to tell my friends I can't register the kids for camp? Do you know that last week my friend Phyllis actually gave me a gift certificate to Whole Foods? Can you believe that I'm reduced to this?"

"I know it stinks and it's not an easy time, but I told you from the start that in the divorce world, collecting from guys in their own businesses is one of the hardest things to do. Sooner or later the only answer for a guy like Mort is to put the fear of the Lord in him — or the fear of sharing a jail cell with Bubba. Usually, I'd have had to bring a slew of other motions before I could try for contempt, 'cause I'd have to show we exhausted every other method to get the money, and that nothing worked. And we're not only talking about the current money, there's the arrears. What was it, about $46,000.00 we already got a judgment for?"

"$46,758.00," said Felicia, "but who's counting?"

"Well, if Mort wasn't his own boss, I could have gotten you a wage deduction from his employer. Mort isn't about to deduct money from himself. So basically, that eliminates going after his paycheck. When the court sees that he's not paying you now, all your bills are behind, and he hasn't paid a dime towards the arrears — plus, that you've tapped out all your credit cards — I hope the judge will recognize the only way to get Mort's attention is to throw him in jail."

"Sounds great, but how's that going to help me get my bills paid? If he can't work, I won't see any money."

"Felicia, you aren't seeing any money with him working. If he isn't going to pay you when he has the money, why not let him sit in jail? Besides, my experience has been that when a guy is asked to bring his toothbrush to the next court appearance, most times they seem to find the money they couldn't find before," Lucy said. "Do you have enough time now to sit with Claire, so she can get what additional info she needs to draft the motion papers?"

"Sure."

Claire was far from delighted to hear that she'd have to spend the afternoon listening to Felicia whine. Nevertheless, the client was owed the money and Mort was being his usual wise-guy self. When she thought about it, it wasn't so bad; she was good at using words as a weapon.

No sooner had Felicia left for Claire's office, when Ruby buzzed her boss to say she had a guy on the line who sounded like he had a big case, but that he wouldn't book an appointment until he'd spoken with Lucy. She picked up the phone, sold herself as she always did and had Ruby make arrangements for the man to come in. Then she met briefly with Maryann Nixon to see if she was any closer to accepting her situation now that the holidays were over and the New Year had begun. After their conversation, Lucy wondered if Maryann would ever really be ready. Some never were.

On the heels of that discussion, she found herself looking into the weary eyes of a new consult with the same scenario: in this case, it was the man who'd been left behind. It was always the same story. Someone was ruining someone else's life. As tough as it was to listen to people in so much pain, Lucy nonetheless liked meeting with prospective clients like Robert. It was interesting to see how folks had found their way to her. Some referrals came from the oddest places; in this case, she'd represented the ex-wife of the man's best friend. The friend told

Robert that Lucy had taken him to cleaners and that he ought to get "that bitch" on his side.

As she spoke him, she could see the gears moving: he could tell she knew her stuff. That was the fun of it. She enjoyed seeing that look of acknowledgment. And who was she kidding? She loved signing up a new case and receiving a nice big check. It would have been nice to get paid without having to work for the money, but the exact opposite was true. She earned every dime she made. And, as she often commiserated with her colleagues, it was blood money.

Toward the day's end, Lucy was about to bring in her last consult when Ruby interrupted to say that Mr. Post was on the line.

"Arthur, what's up?"

"That is exactly what I'm asking you."

"I take it you got a call from Sandra over at Judge Thorpe's part. How much did she tell you?"

"She says you're representing someone who claims to be Beau's father and that you want him to be joined in our lawsuit, as a necessary party."

"That sounds about right."

"Don't you think that eight years is a little too late for your client to be waltzing in? You do know that this is going no place, don't you? And by the way, my firm will be seeking attorneys' fees for your frivolous motion."

"Arthur, I think we can agree that this isn't my first case. Obviously, we have differing opinions, but I can assure you I wouldn't be bringing this application if I wasn't quite sure it had merit."

"Do you want to tell me what merit you're talking about?"

"You know, since we're going to be in court soon, why don't we get into the specifics when we're there? I think that's why the judge thought that a conference with you, me and Nick would be the best way to go. We can all say what we have to say then. Did you and Nick agree upon a date?"

"Only one of the dates you left with Sandra worked for me, so I'll be seeing you next week. And Lucy, I was quite serious when I said we'd be looking for counsel fees. Everett Brockhurst should not have to be fighting with your client for his own son."

"We'll see, Arthur."

"Fine."

"Fine" didn't really mean "fine," but frankly Lucy didn't give a shit what Arthur Post thought. They hadn't indulged in any of the phony courtesies, and for that she was grateful.

Within almost an instant of hanging up with Arthur, Ruby buzzed her to say Nick DeBello was waiting on line two. She picked up, knowing that Nick wasn't going to be in any better mood than Arthur. At least, she thought, he could be amusing.

"So Nick, what's up?" Before the words were out of her mouth, Lucy realized it was a bad lead-in for their conversation; she knew exactly where Nick would go with that opening and tried to cut him off. "And don't start talking to me about your shlong!" she laughed.

"Am I really that predictable?"

"You're not really asking me that, are you?"

"All right, wise guy, you know what this is about. Sandra called to tell me you're representing some guy who wants in on the Brockhurst custody case. Why the hell didn't you tell me when I saw you at Laurel Hall?"

"Oh, Nick, you seemed so happy to have gotten Georgina as your client. I didn't want to burst your bubble. Besides, that just wasn't the time or place for us to get into that."

"She came to you first, didn't she?"

Lucy said nothing. It was true that Georgina had tried to come to her first, but having already agreed to take Gary's case, she was unable to help her. Why tell Nick that he was second choice? He was a blowhard and not the most popular guy, but for some odd reason there was something she liked about the arrogant bastard.

"What's the deal here, Luce? Who are you representing? I bet you got a nice retainer to get involved in this one." She ignored the comment. "Who's the guy?"

"I won't give you all the gory details, but let's just say I think the man who retained me is Beau's biological father. And in light of Skippy's death and what he's been told or knows about Everett, he doesn't want that guy raising his son."

"Look," said Nick, "I think we can both agree that Everett's a major shit, and that's why I think these kids need to be with their aunt. Honestly Lucy, I can't understand how you could think otherwise."

"I like Georgina, but believe me. I have my reasons."

"Wanna share or do I have to wait for the axe to fall?"

"It's not like that Nick, but since we're going to be in court on Thursday, let's just talk about it then, face to face."

CHAPTER TWENTY-FIVE

She had left everything she needed for the day ahead neatly at the top of the stairs. She'd finished up her prep work on Vaughn, stowed away the notes for the conference and felt prepared for the disaster that awaited her in Thorpe's part. She was ready for it.

Rushing down the hallway, she nearly tripped over her belongings. Apparently, "Houdini dog" had managed to open up all of her bags and disperse their contents along the whole length of the corridor. That dog had a sniffer unlike any other. He had managed to catch a whiff of the unfinished French toast bagel that she'd left in her briefcase.

Looking at the mess, Lucy could see that the dog had stuck his snout into her bags, and while rummaging around in his desperate search for the food, had pulled apart two formerly rubber-banded sets of papers. One set contained Lucy's carefully prepared notes for the morning's court appearance. If she didn't love that dopey dog so much, she'd be ready to kill him on a day like this. Of course, she could only blame herself for leaving a morsel of food anywhere within his reach, but all Lucy could think was that he'd deliberately screwed up her Thursday morning.

As she knelt down to gather up and reorganize the strewn papers, the culprit came skulking down the hall.

"Torts, you pain in the ass," Lucy said.

His head held down low, with huge mournful brown eyes staring straight up at her, the spaniel wagged his tail in a tentative, hopeful way that seemed to beg forgiveness. Damned if he didn't give her one of his guilty but adorable smiles. It broke whatever resolve Lucy had to punish that bottomless pit of a dog.

"All right, all right," Lucy muttered. She couldn't help but hug him and tell him she loved him. "If I didn't love you so much, you'd be off herding sheep in Bumblefuck," she said.

Torts stretched out his neck and tilted his head up to accept some apologetic scratching from his master. Lucy tried to suppress a grin.

"Jake, Adam! I'm leaving," she called as she threw on her coat. Reluctant though they might have been sometimes, no one got to leave the house for the day without hearing from Lucy that she loved them. After she'd given each boy her usual hug and kissed Dan good-bye, she was almost knocked over by Torts, who, wanting to be in on the affection, ran around her in a frenzied circle. Lucy gave him a final loving pat and headed down the stairs with her large pocketbook and rolling briefcase in tow, rehearsing how she'd approach the morning's conference.

Somehow, she'd let Arthur Post talk her into putting the case on for 11:00 instead of the usual 9:30. Now she was even more annoyed that she'd agreed to it. She far preferred to get to court first thing in the morning and handle office appointments and conferences all afternoon. To Lucy's knowledge, that was the way all successful attorneys scheduled their days — except, apparently, for lawyers like Arthur, whose New York City practice wasn't based on volume. Instead, his firm soaked a few rich clients at a time, and their lawyers didn't need to fill up every afternoon hustling new business and new retainers. An early start in court meant she could snag a prime parking spot not too far from the entrance and wouldn't have to risk the chance of getting stuck there for hours. Just like at the airport, delays in the schedule always mounted up over the course of the day. If there were too many lawyers ahead of her when she got to the courtroom and her case didn't get finished before the witching hour, twelve-thirty or so, she'd have to come back to court after the lunch break and kill the whole day. Ruby would have to reschedule an entire afternoon of appointments, which made for cranky clients, and an even crankier Ruby. Not a pretty picture.

Lucy stopped by the office; it made more sense to check on matters there than to sit doing nothing in the courthouse. But she was determined not to get involved in something at the office that might make her late for court. She pulled out her reassembled notes for one final review, trying to ignore the doggy drool, and wondered if she should tell the judge that the dog ate her homework. Just as she was filing her notes back into the red weld, she heard the door slam. The troops were arriving.

"Morning, Lucy!" shouted Andi. Seeing her partner's car in the lot, she'd wondered if Lucy was handling some sort of pre-court emergency. "Didn't expect to see you here. Weren't you supposed to be in court?"

"Don't remind me. It's going to be later this morning. But you know what, now that I'm here, what do you say we run through what's likely to happen on Gary's case?"

Claire and Melissa entered the room, also wondering why the boss wasn't in court.

"Glad to see the gang's all here," Lucy said. "How about if we run through my arguments on Vaughn so you can let me know if I'm missing anything?"

"That works for me," Claire said, pulling up a chair and resting her briefcase beside her. The others, equipped with coffee, settled into the room.

"Good, 'cause I'm really glad to borrow your brains. I've been playing out this morning's appearance in my mind. This whole estoppel argument's a tough one, you know?"

Lucy's colleagues nodded.

"Melissa, are you sure you got me all of the most recent cases on estoppel?"

"I'm pretty sure I did."

"Pretty sure isn't sure. Did you Shepardize them?"

"Yes, I checked each case through Shepard's to make sure none of them were reversed and to see cases where the other courts followed those decisions. I even went through the stuff with Claire before I gave it to you."

"So then, you're sure, is that what you're saying?"

"I guess so."

"For God's sake, Melissa, you have to learn to be more certain of yourself. 'Yes' would be the answer. Not 'I guess so.' Claire, you read Melissa's research. Think I'm gonna get by the estoppel problem?"

"Here's how I see it. Most of the cases seem to say that when a child is as old as Beau, the courts are not going to confuse him and allow random claims either denying or asserting parentage. They don't want to allow someone who has raised a child for seven or eight years to take themselves off the hook suddenly by denying they're the father. The courts also don't seem very anxious to allow someone to come into a child's life claiming to be a parent when the child's spent years believing someone else is his parent. It's clear the courts are worried about a child's stability.

"Having said that, I think a court is more likely to hear someone who's trying to take responsibility for a child, than someone trying to deny responsibility."

"Does it make any difference that Gary took action as soon as he discovered the possibility that he was the father?"

"Well certainly, the immediate action doesn't hurt."

"How about the fact that Skippy's dead? Does that make a court more anxious to find out who's the real parent?"

"Again it's something that can't hurt us, but not something that's going to be determinative."

"Okay, then how about Everett's issues with drugs and being a lousy father? Does that change anything?"

"Look, Lucy, there's no definite answer here. You've got a hard row to hoe. If I were you, I'd be pushing the DNA issue. Ask the judge what harm it can do to get that answer first, before he decides the estoppel issue. You can say that if Gary isn't the father, no harm, no foul and everyone can go on with his or her life. If on the other hand, this new test confirms that Gary's the father, I can't help but believe that it might tip the balance in Thorpe's mind a little in your favor. Then you can push hard on the issue. Remember, Everett certainly hasn't been father of the year. There is someone willing to step up to the plate who believes he is the father, and who is anxious to make sure his child is provided for. Let's just say, I think you have a shot — but I think what's going to hurt us is Emma. Remember, Gary has absolutely no connection with her. I doubt anyone would want to separate two children who've just lost their mother."

"Well, that's an honest assessment, Claire. I knew it was going to be a bear, but I'm glad you confirmed it. I know what I'm in for."

"Look, I'd just fight for the DNA test right now. If we get past that, we can see what else we can come up with before the results come in."

"You never know what will happen in between," Andi said.

"Okay, guys, thanks. I'm gonna try to return a few calls and then get out of here. Catch y'all later."

Against her better judgment, Lucy became so distracted returning calls that she didn't notice how late it had gotten until she heard Ruby yell that she better get going.

***

The parking lot was full, just as Lucy had expected. She took the first space she could find and prepared to dash through the rain. She flashed her attorney's ID card and smiled at the officer, avoiding the security line in the courthouse lobby.

As Lucy got into the elevator she ran into Glen, who was also on his way up to the third floor.

"Did you get a chance to pull Mort's foot out of his mouth and put together a proposal for us?" Lucy took off her rain hat, gently shaking off the beads of water.

"That was some session we had. I told my wife how disgusting some of those city hotels really are. She told me to tell you thanks for the warning."

"You never know what you're gonna learn from your clients. But seriously, you have anything for me?" The two stepped into the third floor hallway and lingered by the elevators.

"I couldn't sit down with him 'til this week, so I should have something for you by the beginning of next."

"That works. And Glen, do me a favor. Get him to be realistic, will you?"

"I think he's got the idea. He's not a big fan of the IRS and has come to grips with the fact that if he doesn't give your client the money, he will be giving it to them. So, like I said, give me 'til the middle of next week to get you something."

"Thanks, Glen, I'll be waiting."

"Who are you with this morning?"

"I'm in Thorpe's part. I've got Nick DeBello and this guy Arthur Post from the city."

"Well, Nick is always good for the entertainment value."

"Easy for you to say when you don't have to deal with him. Once, just once, I would like him to settle something."

"I hear ya. Well listen, have a good one and I'll catch you later."

On autopilot, Lucy dashed to the ladies room to try and do something with her terminal hat hair. She tried throwing a little water on it to fluff it back up, pushing the curls around. While it certainly wasn't perfect, she acknowledged a modest improvement as she looked in the mirror. Recalling the lines from a play, she told herself, Good enough "for all normal purposes."

As she got to Judge Thorpe's courtroom, the court officer gave her a welcoming smile.

"How ya' doin', bud?"

"Calendar's still looking pretty full. It's been that kind of day. How come the early bird's so late this morning?"

"Arthur Post, that guy from Manhattan, asked to put it on for eleven so he wouldn't have to get up too early, poor baby."

"Then he should have put it on for noon, 'cause you're not getting in before that."

"All right, so sign me in on Brockhurst. I'm assuming no one else has shown up yet." In all her years of practice in the county, she'd never once seen Nick show up in court on time. He preferred to make a grand entrance.

"No one's checked in with me yet."

She'd just finished checking through her phone messages when Lucy caught sight of a tall, thin man in a Burberry coat, carrying a large-brimmed hat and what looked like a designer messenger bag. The accoutrements alone announced "New York City lawyer." Before she could greet Arthur Post, Lucy heard the hearty voice of Nick DeBello.

"Lucy Bennett! So glad you brought us all in here on this rainy day, without telling us what's really going on."

"Nice to see you too, Nick."

"Seriously, Luce, what the fuck is up?"

The attorney didn't flinch. "Let's see if we can get Pete to bring us all in and we can have a nice chat about it." She gave Nick a bright smile.

Moments later, as the group was ushered into the judge's chambers, Lucy made a mental note to thank Pete for moving their matter to the top of the pile. Her annual box of chocolates always seemed to pay a few dividends. She and her adversaries stepped into the room to find the judge seated at his desk, his law secretary standing next to him.

"Good morning, Your Honor. And how are you today, Sandy?"

"Nice to see you, Lucy. Is everyone ready to talk about this mess?"

"Do you mind if I start, Judge?" Lucy inquired.

Without so much as a good morning, Post was quick to object. "Your honor, I don't see any reason for Ms. Bennett to even be in your court on this matter. I'm asking that you summarily deny her application to have her client joined as a necessary party. We have a boy here who is eight years old, who has never even met this man claiming to be his father. He doesn't know him and it would be upsetting and unreasonable to insert him into the child's life at this late stage."

"I have to agree with Mr. Post," Nick added.

Lucy couldn't stop herself. "You know, Judge, it's funny that Mr. Post should say that. Here he represents a man who believes he's Beau's father and yet he's barely made any time for him. Talk about inserting someone into a child's life. At least my guy stepped up to the plate the minute he thought he might be the boy's father."

She was about to launch into a tirade about Everett Brockhurst when she looked up and saw Judge Thorpe's face. Quickly she added, "I apologize, your honor, this case is really getting to me. And it's only just started."

Arthur and Nick began to speak at the same time.

The judge leaned back and put his palm forward, forcing a pause. "Look, everyone, let's start over. I asked you all to come here today without your clients because I think we have a situation on our hands. Mr. Post, I know the estoppel argument you want to make, that it's too late for Ms. Bennett's client to march in. You think the boy should stay with the father he already knows. I asked Sandy to do a little research for me and, while you have a point, I'm not ready to close the door on the guy just yet. The boy just lost his mother and I'd really like to know what all the facts are here.

"So this is what I am going to do. I am ordering both men and the child to give DNA samples to Ambro Lab and I'm going to ask you all to come back when the results are in. Whatever that result might be, I'm going to want an attorney to represent the child. Right now, I've got the aunt and the father fighting for custody, right?"

"Judge, I think you're a little premature in considering an attorney for the child, aren't you?" Arthur said. "After all, in a fight between a parent and a non-parent you need to find extraordinary circumstances before the child can be placed with anyone other than the parent. And right now, we have no extraordinary circumstances. It's not as though my client is an axe-murderer, rapist or drug addict. So, without anything like that, the boy belongs with Everett Brockhurst."

"You want extraordinary circumstances?" Nick snapped. "I'll give you extraordinary circumstances. Your client hasn't taken his kids on an overnight visit in more than a year. He canceled their holiday trip 'cause he couldn't find the time for them, and Arthur, I'm sure I wasn't the only one to read Lucy's papers. Looks like he's been a substance abuser for years."

"That's just mudslinging, DeBello. And while he may not be a perfect father, that doesn't rise to the level of extraordinary circumstances. The guy's been busy making a living."

"Hang on, all of you," the judge said. "Mr. Post, I'll hold off on an attorney for the child, as you suggest until, we meet again. I want your client and Lucy's client each to get to the lab within seventy-two hours. Who's going to get the boy there?"

"I think the easiest thing for Beau would be to have his nanny take him," Lucy said.

"I don't want anyone — do you hear me, anyone — telling this boy what the test is all about. There's no reason to confuse him or upset him further until I see a result and decide the estoppel issue." Judge Thorpe looked at each of them, in turn.

"Judge, doesn't it make more sense to decide the estoppel question before you subject everyone to the test?" Arthur Post asked in a tone that suggested the judge had made an error. He peered at Judge Thorpe over his reading glasses.

"I understand where you're coming from, Mr. Post, but I have some real concerns here. I'm persuaded by Ms. Bennett's moving papers that she might well overcome her burden on the estoppel argument. And you know what? I want to know what I'm dealing with, here. I want the test done. If your client turns out to be the biological father, then Ms. Bennett and her client are out of luck. So why don't we just find out?"

Arthur Post decided to take another tack.

"I think it makes sense for Everett to take the boy for the test."

"Really, Arthur? When was the last time Everett took his son to a doctor or a lab?"

Nick was glad Lucy had made the jab. For once he and Lucy were on the same side.

"I like the idea of the nanny," the judge said. "Let's tell her to take both of the children, so that Beau isn't singled out. You know what, Sandy, why don't we get her on the phone?" While the law secretary went to her office to make the call, the judge continued, "I expect everyone in this room to handle this case with sensitivity. It must be a terrible time for these kids."

"You're right, Judge." Lucy said. Her adversaries remained silent.

"Judge Thorpe, I've got Bridgette on the line. Would you like to speak with her or would you like me to handle it?"

"You know what, Sandy? You tell her what needs to be done, but give her as little information as possible. Just be sure to make it clear to her that the children are not to know what the test is about, and that under no circumstances – and I mean no circumstances — is she to say a word about this to another soul. Those are my orders."

"Gotcha, boss."

"Lucy, I want your client to pay for everyone to be tested. Let him know that."

"I already told him, Judge, that if you ordered the test, he'd have to pay."

"Lucy, you brought a full set of papers for each of your adversaries, right?" She nodded, and the judge went on. "I'm going to want all of the motion papers, answering papers and reply papers submitted to me three days before the next date you're back here, so that I'll have time to read your arguments. When can you all be back here about three weeks from now?"

The three lawyers got out their phones and coordinated a date that worked for them all, putting February 23rd on their calendars. Her adversaries left without a goodbye to anyone other than the judge, but Lucy remained to let Sandra and Pete know how much she appreciated their help.

CHAPTER TWENTY-SIX

Nick wasn't pleased to have to tell Georgina that the battle now looked tougher than before. Not only would she be fighting Everett for the children, but now there was another obstacle: Gary Vaughn. Nick buzzed his secretary to bring in his client and stood up from his handsome leather chair to greet the attractive brunette as she reached the doorway of his office.

"Georgina, thanks for coming in on such short notice. Since I heard you were in town for a few days, I thought it would be best for us to meet in person."

"Well, your secretary said it was important, so I dropped everything." She settled into one of the two sumptuous chairs across from Mr. DeBello's desk. "Can you tell me what this is all about?"

"I hate to be so blunt, but did your sister ever mention an extramarital relationship to you?"

"Excuse me?"

"Do you know if your sister had an affair before Beau was born?"

Georgina let out a short cough. On her drive over, she had been considering all the possible reasons Nick might have had for calling her away from her obligations at Laurel Hall. Announcing this nonsense to her came as a personal affront. "A relationship? An affair? You think my sister had an affair? What the hell are you talking about?"

"Well, there's a man, name of Gary Vaughn, who's come forward claiming to be Beau's real father. Now that Skippy's no longer with us, it looks like he wants custody of Beau."

"What are you talking about? My sister would never do that! I know her, and it's out of the question. Don't you think I would have known it if she was fooling around?"

"I know it's hard to hear this, Georgina, but I must advise you that this could have happened."

"I can't believe what you're telling me. Who is this creep? Where did he come from? And what the hell does he want from us?"

"I know it's a little out of left field, but —"

"I bet he's out for the Brockhurst money or something!"

"No, I don't think that's what this is about, Georgina. I don't know if it's reliable, but Gary Vaughn supposedly had a DNA test that shows he's the biological father. Lucy Bennett is representing Mr. Vaughn and seems to believe the results are valid. She included the results in her moving papers."

"Lucy Bennett?" Georgina repeated in horror. "This just gets worse and worse."

Nick nodded, but offered no comforting words to soften the impact of his last statement.

"I really trusted that woman! And so did my sister. Her "Rock of Gibraltar," that's what she called her, even in the worst parts of her divorce. Do you know Lucy had the nerve to turn me away after my sister died? I called to ask her a few simple questions about custody to see if I might have a case and she refused to give me any information — or even to offer any explanation about why she wouldn't talk with me. Now I get it! She already knew about this — insanity." Georgina put her hands over her eyes. Lowering her voice, she went on. "You know, Nick, I feel very, very betrayed by her."

Rather than try and explain Lucy's position, Nick again nodded sympathetically. He felt a certain pleasure seeing his adversary knocked about by his client. Irritated to hear once again that Ms. Bennett had been Georgina's first choice for a lawyer, and seeing his opportunity for a little Lucy bashing, he couldn't resist. "Well, you know some lawyers are motivated by things other than doing what's right. I know you're not from around here, but Lucy Bennett does enjoy the limelight. I'm sure that when this character gave her an opportunity to make a splash, she took it."

"I just can't believe she did this. I really thought she cared about us."

"Well, the good news for you is that you're in the right hands now."

Georgina stared off beyond Nick's face and at the gilt-framed diplomas on the wall behind him. She thought of Emma's delight that morning when they'd made the pancake shaped like a snowman. Sitting across from Nick, calm and cool as he presided over her in this rich, mahogany-paneled office, she wondered if he knew how very small she felt.

"I have to say, Mr. DeBello, I don't believe what you're telling me about my sister, or anything about what that man is claiming. But if you're saying we have to deal with this, where do we go from here?"

"I'll do my best to explain." Nick could see that she was still in shock. He spoke gently, clinically, like a doctor explaining the details of a terrible diagnosis. "Ms. Bennett has brought a request to the court that her client, Gary Vaughn, be added to our pending custody case." He let the words sink in. "She wants Mr. Vaughn to be granted custody of Beau, over you and Everett."

"But how can she just come out of the blue — and get a judge to let her client make such a crazy claim?"

"You're right, Georgina, she needs a lot more than just saying her guy is the father and showing test results from a lab no one's ever heard of. So yesterday, Judge Thorpe asked for Lucy, me, and Everett's lawyer to come meet with him in his chambers to discuss the situation. The judge hasn't made a decision yet as to what he is going to do with Mr. Vaughn. However, he did make an important decision which could possibly eliminate the guy from this case."

"What do you mean?"

"The judge has ordered that a new DNA test be done, through a closely supervised test at a well-known laboratory. There will be no chance of monkey business. I've used this lab before, and they're on the up and up. If the results show that Vaughn is not the dad, then that's the end of it. He's out of the case."

"So then what happens if this new test comes back saying this total stranger is Beau's biological father?"

"You know, it still wouldn't mean that he's in the case."

"I don't understand."

"Well, you see, we have a very strong legal argument that could be used to try to keep him from bringing his claim at all, and it's this: the law does not favor disrupting the lives of children and telling them the person they thought was their father, is not. There has to be a very good reason to make such an enormous change in a child's life. Obviously, it could be extremely traumatic for the child, so it's taken very seriously by the court." Nick watched as Georgina seemed to digest this information. She was one smart cookie, but even so, she would have to be spoon-fed after all she'd just been forced to swallow.

"The law recognizes that although someone might have a claim, such as the one for custody that Mr. Vaughn is trying to assert, there could be overriding reasons to block the attempt to do so. In this case that overriding reason to block the claim would be that if Mr. Vaughn prevailed, Beau would end up in the hands of a stranger, with his life turned upside-down. If we win on this point, you're done with Gary. And, I think we have a strong position on that legal point."

Georgina nodded. It had started to drizzle against the tall, majestic windows that graced the room. She tried to keep her focus, wanting to absorb it all, but other thoughts kept seeping in. Beau and Emma would be home in a few hours, and she couldn't afford to get stuck in traffic. What were her own children up to in school today, so far away? She turned back to her attorney.

"Can I just ask, isn't all of this supposed to be about what's in the children's best interest?"

"You might think so. But, as I told you when you hired me, where a child has a living parent, the law in this state presumes that it's best for the child to be raised by that person. And that's exactly what I tried to explain to you in our last meeting. Let's assume Gary's out of the picture, and this is just between you and Everett. When the fight is between a parent and a non-parent, the parent automatically wins. In New York State, it's presumed that any child born during a marriage is legitimate, the child of that marriage. So, in the fight between you and Everett, he wins. Unless, a court finds that there are extraordinary circumstances, either something terribly wrong with Everett like severe mental illness, drug addiction, or something odd about his relationship with the children — like he's been totally estranged from them for years."

Nick could read his client's face. He saw the small ray of hope in her eyes. "I don't mean just missing a few visitations, or even a lot of visitations. We're talking total estrangement. So, unless we can prove extraordinary circumstances, the court isn't allowed to hold a hearing on the question that you asked me, the question of what's in the children's best interests."

He let Georgina consider the information. "So, our job is to prove extraordinary circumstances with regard to Everett. And as you could see in her papers, Lucy Bennett gave us some pretty good leads on the drug angle. Her hope is to use the same evidence about Everett, not to prove extraordinary circumstances, but to have enough dirt on him to get the court to want to hear Mr. Vaughn's claim."

Georgina's head was spinning. Did her lawyer actually expect that she could comprehend all of this at once? He rose from his seat. Was this his signal that their meeting was over? She was filled with questions.

"Listen, Georgina, I'm sorry but I've got to run to a meeting at another lawyer's office. So think about what we discussed, and I'll be in touch if there's any news. You know you can always call the office if you need to speak with me."

Still in a fog, Georgina bundled up and made her way out to the parking garage, more alone than she could ever remember. Her sister was gone. Her parents were grief-stricken. She couldn't turn to Ron; he was angry at her, as well as at her lawyer, with all his bills and nothing to show for it. And yes, what about her lawyer? At their meeting, was he intentionally speaking gibberish? Was he trying to confuse her? Or discourage her? And Lucy Bennett, the one she might have relied on, had turned against her. She started the car and hoped to summon the strength to smile at those little faces awaiting her at Laurel Hall.

CHAPTER TWENTY-SEVEN

Emma and her best friend had gathered up every piece of material they could find in the linen closet, and draped the blankets and sheets and towels over the chairs and bed to form a covered hideout, spanning the entire bedroom. Hard at work constructing their fortress, the girls didn't notice Georgina as she passed by every so often to check on their progress and to peek in on Beau who was lying listlessly on the bed.

She was trying to pack, but it was an unbearable task. The kids would take it hard when she finally left, especially Beau, who'd stayed home over the last few days with stomachaches. He'd still been unable to return to his normal school schedule.

She wanted to stay until he was back at Aston, or at least was back to seeing his group of friends. Chris couldn't be there every day, as much as his mother tried to arrange it. There seemed to be little Georgina could do to comfort him. It wasn't for lack of trying. She took him out to the mall, since he needed a new coat for his upcoming class trip to Washington, D.C. The trip was to be a first: a whole weekend away on a field trip. Georgina thought that underneath the boy's sadness, she could detect a glimmer of his old self when he mentioned details about the things that were planned.

He'd outgrown his winter coat within one season, a fact that had tickled her sister. She'd mentioned how much Beau wanted to shop for that "cool" pea coat over at Abercrombie.

It was still on the rack in the store, when Georgina got there with Beau: the right coat, in Beau's size and in black, just as he wanted. With the music booming and the heavy scent of cologne wafting in on her from every vent of the store, Georgina didn't know if she'd make it through as the tiny teenager behind the counter rang up the sale, her baby fingers tapping away on the keys of the cash register. Yet, she didn't want to move an inch, for there it was at last: a grin on her nephew's face as he stood there in his new coat, watching himself in the mirror. Who did he see there? She hoped that all he saw was a boy, an everyday boy, smiling.

But now she was needed back at home, as Ron had repeatedly reminded her over the past few days. Matt was coming home with notes from the teacher about forgotten homework, and once again, Cliff had picked a fight with someone on the bus. It didn't sit well with Ron that his wife continued to "play nurse" to her niece and nephew, while leaving their children behind to fend for themselves. He disliked her visits to Laurel Hall when Skippy was alive and now resented them even more, no matter what had happened. Georgina headed back to finish her packing, knowing she was doing the best that she could.

***

As far as Ron was concerned, the Brockhurst children were spoiled rich kids with an endless supply of caretakers to tend to them. But when Georgina was out of town, he could only turn to Mrs. Lily, who never missed a chance to criticize him for one thing or another. Today, it had been his "foolishness" in keeping the kids out late the night before. Big deal, he'd stopped by with his buddies to see the game and it ran into overtime. If the old witch had made herself available, he'd have left the kids home with her. What was her important date, bingo? Did people still play bingo?

"Those children should be in bed by eight-thirty, and there's an end to it!" she said.

"Mrs. Lily, bedtime hasn't been at that time since 1910, and you know it," Ron returned.

"And just how would I know that?" she barked back. While everyone else in town knew better than to refer to Mrs. Lily's age, it was the exact sore spot Ron deliberately liked to rub. They rode in silence the rest of their way back to the old woman's dreary cottage.

God help me if I have to do this one more time, thought Ron, as he helped her up the frail steps of the front porch.

"When d'ya say Georgina's getting back?" Mrs. Lily asked as she worked the key into the lock.

"Not soon enough," Ron answered, relieved as the old lady stepped into her house and latched the door behind her.

CHAPTER TWENTY-EIGHT

Arthur Post had just about had enough of those hicks out in Abbott County. He was tired of their shoot-from-the-hip judges and their failure to give him the proper amount of deference, to which he was most certainly entitled. Although Everett Brockhurst was not his favorite client, he was, after all, a Brockhurst. The family had been excellent clients of the firm for many years. Hugh had been quite something to contend with in his day, generating millions in fees. He was tough in his dealings, but knew his business well and Arthur's partners had always spoken highly of him.

The attorney had never dealt with Hugh directly until Everett's divorce and then had only met him on one occasion: the day the retainer check had been written for Arthur's services. The lawyer had made his niche in the firm as the one who handled all of the family problems for the firms' wealthy clients. He had some knowledge of the business world from which the bulk of the firm's clients came, but his expertise was in matrimonial law.

The firm decided many years earlier to make Arthur a partner, to ensure that clients stayed in house concerning family law problems. They'd seen it happen before; a client consulted elsewhere on such matters, and the next thing you knew, they'd transferred all of their business to the new firm.

He shouldn't have been surprised that Vivian was there for the appointment, since she was the brains behind the operation, but he wished that Everett had let him know of his mother's intentions to join them. His approach would have to be adjusted accordingly.

Arthur greeted the two in the conference room as his secretary poured a cup of tea for Mrs. Brockhurst.

"From what Everett's told me, Arthur, something rather important has come up and quite frankly, I prefer to get the information directly from you rather than second hand."

"That certainly makes good sense. I'm always glad to get additional perspectives to consider. And of course, Vivian, you do have the ability to see through things rather quickly."

"Thank you, Arthur, if that was meant as a compliment."

Everett had run out of patience. "All right, Arthur, out with it. What exactly happened in court?"

"Lucy Bennett has inserted herself into the fray. She brought an order to show cause seeking to join her client as a necessary party in our custody proceeding."

Vivian blanched. "Who else could possibly have an interest in the children?" She wasn't happy about Skippy's sister being part of this, but understood why. It was easy to imagine that Skippy had disparaged Everett as a father, and Georgina must have believed everything she heard. But it made no sense that someone else was coming in on the attack, out of nowhere.

"The name is Gary Vaughn. He's claiming to be Beau's biological father."

"That filthy slut!" Everett snorted. Vivian sat motionless.

"Look, do you have any reason to believe that you are not Beau's biological father? Is there something you haven't told me? Something I should know?"

"I have absolutely no idea what this Vaughn character is talking about. If it's the same guy, I met him once or twice at some charity thing or other. He's a builder or an architect, right?"

"Architect. Can you think of any reason he'd make this claim?"

"No. Of course I'm Beau's father! The guy's claim is ridiculous." But, as the words came out, he thought back to the time it had taken Skippy to conceive, all her trips to the fertility specialist, the trouble conceiving Emma.

"What are the finances of this gentleman? Have you looked into his need to be picking our pockets?" Vivian cut straight to the potential motive.

"From what I can see so far, I don't think money is a problem for him. Since he's hired Bennett and Birnbaum, he must have paid them a substantial amount. And you have to consider why anyone would want to take on the responsibility of a child if he didn't think it was his. It's usually just the opposite and they're trying to wiggle out of it."

"I'll see what can be found out about the good Mr. Vaughn," Vivian declared. "If he's looking for us to buy him off, I can assure you I will leave no stone unturned."

"DNA testing was ordered by the court yesterday, to establish paternity. Everett, please sit down. I want you to listen. I'll give you the details on how to contact the lab. The cost of the testing is being borne by Ms. Bennett's client."

Everett opened his mouth to speak but his mother cut him off.

"What about Beau? Does he have to be tested as well? Do we need to make arrangements to take him someplace? We don't want the boy upset, Arthur, is that clear?"

"I couldn't agree with you more, Vivian. The court has already contacted the nanny to make arrangements to take Beau for the testing. I believe the suggestion was made that Emma go too, so that Beau would not feel singled out."

Vivian was outraged that Bridgette knew something so important and hadn't told her; the woman was under orders to let her know every detail about the goings-on at Laurel Hall.

Continuing, Arthur looked directly at Everett. "Since you really were not the one who took the kids to their doctor visits, we thought the decision to have the nanny handle things made good sense and might be the least upsetting."

"How long will it be 'til the results are in?"

"The twenty-third. We're all to be back in court that day. The judge has ordered that no one try to contact the lab or court in advance of that date regarding the result. He wants all of us to learn the identity of the biological father at the same time."

Everett needed some clear answers. What if it turned out that Vaughn was the father? Would he lose one kid, both kids, no kids...

and what about Laurel Hall? "Arthur, is it fair to say that if the tests show I'm the father, then we're done with him?"

"Yes, I think that's a fair conclusion. If that's the result, we'll have seen the end of Ms. Bennett and Mr. Vaughn."

"And what if it turns out the other way, and Vaughn is the father? Is he going to be rewarded for fooling around with my ex-wife?"

"Well, that's an interesting question. The issue is extremely complex, highly technical…" And very, very expensive, the attorney nearly added, to complete the phrase in his head. "I do want to try and give you and your mother as much information as I can," he went on. "In New York there's a presumption of legitimacy which means that a child born during the marriage is presumed to be the child of the married partners. That means, of course, that you are presumed to be Beau's dad. Then, there's an important legal argument that I'd make on your behalf, which would be persuasive. I'd argue that Mr. Vaughn should be stopped from asserting his fatherhood at this late stage in the game, since it's not in Beau's best interest to upset and confuse him and take him away from the only father he's ever known."

"Well, that certainly makes sense. But that slippery Lucy Bennett must have something up her sleeve. I had enough of her last time. You remember what I went through. She's just unrelenting," Everett fumed.

"There's an argument she might make and while I think it's a tough one, she's likely to try it. This one comes down to you. If you've done something particularly egregious – so bad that it would make the court want to overlook the rule, then it's possible the court would allow Mr. Vaughn into the picture. Everett, I told you that Bennett raised the drug issue in her papers. I have to ask you again. You aren't doing anything I should know about, right?"

"Do I have to defend myself to you? I told you before, there's nothing Georgina and her lawyer or Lucy Bennett will find out about me."

"It's my job to ask you these things, Everett. And this is the one time that Nick DeBello and Lucy Bennett are both looking for the same thing; to find something that's going to make you look bad… really bad."

"Then they have their work cut out for them," Everett said with an air of cockiness that couldn't help but worry Arthur.

Vivian, likewise, was concerned. Her son had trouble with the truth. She hoped that just this one time, he would not be a disappointment to her.

CHAPTER TWENTY-NINE

Hugh pushed the tiller out and swung the boom in one motion, turning the boat in a neat reverse, then headed downwind on a broad reach out of the mooring field and into the bay. Vivian had put her foot down and wouldn't let him go alone on the *Black Heron* anymore, but he could handle the little Sonar. He'd picked it up for the kids to use on their visits, and after Vivian's phone call, it was the only thing he could think of to clear his head.

Hugh's favorite time with his grandkids had always been out here on the bay where he could literally show them the ropes, supremely confident that they'd pick up more skills with him in a few hours than they did in a whole summer at the Waterfront. Pete and the other instructors would disagree, no doubt, but Grandpa believed in his own methods, honed over a lifetime of boating. He'd made his grandson tie a giant bowline around the pine tree with a knot strong enough to hold up both children, with all their weight on it. Emma tried to do as her grandfather demonstrated and "put the rabbit into the hole" to create the sturdy knot, but couldn't quite get the hang of it.

"We'll work on it next time," he'd assured her, "at Christmas."

They had met again in December, as promised, but only to mourn. Since Skippy's death, he and Vivian had a single focus: to help Beau and Emma get through the cataclysm. Yet their concerted efforts to soften the blow now seemed futile. A complete stranger had appeared out of nowhere to set in on his grandchildren. A complete stranger, she'd told him on the phone. What was it they'd always said — that a court would act in a child's best interests? A child's best interests? Well, of course they should, and that would be the end of it! All of the money and power and clout that the Brockhurst family could bring to bear, and yet Arthur Post could promise nothing.

He felt that old heaviness rise up in his chest, but rather than turn back to shore, Hugh was determined to stay out on the water for as long as he could, if nothing more than to try and shake off his black mood. Even here, facing the wind, he could feel his grandchildren falling away from him, as Brandt had fallen away from him all those many years ago. This was different, he assured himself; the grandchildren would still be fine tomorrow.

Brandt would have talked sense into that thick and boozed-up head of his brother and fired him up to fight for his children. Brandt would have seen to it. But Everett made no damned effort at all, not for his own children, and not even for a moment to live up to his brother's legacy. There was no getting away from it, Brandt had been the one. Hugh adored that boy. And now, to be torn up again, he couldn't do it. It was too hard at his age.

The *Cloud of the Sea* came into view. As it drew closer, he could see Jack and Lizzy Hewitt sending him their usual jolly wave across the water. Lizzy seemed to call out something, but her words were eaten up by the wind. He waved back, as always, but hoped they couldn't tell. It would have been an awful sight for them, a tough old salt like him, reduced to tears.

CHAPTER THIRTY

Vivian was oppressed, this early Monday morning, by the abundance of tackiness surrounding her in the small office. The cheesy paneling and smoky atmosphere had to be purposeful, she thought, as she sat waiting for Jerry to finish up with his phone call. He was the best in the business, or she wouldn't have been sitting here on the slippery leatherette couch that had already become uncomfortable. All that was missing was a ceiling fan and the buzzing of flies. The whole scene seemed arranged to assure her she was getting what she paid for: the talents of gritty, gutsy Jerry Frame, PI.

At last, Jerry plunked the phone down on his cluttered desk and swung around in his chair to face Mrs. Hugh Brockhurst. Old Hugh and he had done a lot of work together over the years. From time to time, Hugh had been forced to deal with the sort of harrowing troubles that plague anyone reaching his stratospheric level of success. Hugh's integrity was a trait that attracted a certain type of adversary who would go to any length to try and cut him down to size. Often, he sought out the PI to dig up what he could find about his enemy. Such investigations were repugnant to his client, especially since the information uncovered was often unseemly.

Jerry doubted that Vivian knew anything about the sordid details, but he was wrong. Vivian was always involved from behind the scenes, making sure that every effort was used to protect Brockhurst interests. This was the first time they'd met in person, and Jerry was intrigued as to why she'd sought him out.

He reached across the desk to shake hands and felt only her fingertips meet his. The massive diamond and emerald ring did not go unnoticed. Jerry thought of the money he'd made assisting her husband,

and how profitable the instant transaction might prove to be. "Mrs. Brockhurst, it's a pleasure."

"My husband has always spoken very highly of you. I'm hoping you might be able to obtain some information about a certain individual."

"Name?" Jerry asked as he held his pen over a scrappy notepad.

"Gary Vaughn, he lives somewhere in Drexel County. An architect."

"What sort of thing you looking for?"

"Any and everything there is to know about that man."

"Can you tell me why?"

"No, we just want the information."

"Got it," answered Jerry. He came up with a figure they could both live with, and they settled on a first payment she readily handed over in cash. Jerry promised he'd be in touch shortly.

Within the hour, Vivian was washing her hands at the club locker room, before reuniting with a few of her cronies from the old days. During lunch, she would say nothing regarding the difficulties at Laurel Hall, but everything about the lovely new boat Hugh had his eye on.

CHAPTER THIRTY-ONE

Smoke hung heavily over the billiard table in the walnut-paneled study of Laurel Hall. Lately, the guys had been enjoying the hospitality of their old chum, Everett, who'd solicited their help in dealing with the tragic death of his ex. They tolerated his nonsense about how traumatic it all had been for him, his ludicrous claims that he loved Skippy until the very day she died. But they knew he just wanted to take advantage of their sympathy and use it as an excuse for his usual self-indulgence.

Far from being upset about Skippy's death, Everett felt a certain degree of freedom. He no longer had to answer to any more of her demands. He certainly wasn't going to miss her incessant complaints about his being "missing in action" when it came to the kids.

And as for them, he was annoyed to find himself burdened by responsibilities he'd always managed to avoid. The calendar that Bridgette had emailed him seemed designed to swallow up his time, with dates for parent-teacher conferences, band and sports events, deadlines for camp program applications, as well as dates for those pointless family therapy sessions he'd postponed twice already, resulting in a tirade from Vivian. Naturally, Bridgette had ratted him out.

After a few grueling nights trying to get through Beau's math homework with him, Everett realized it was futile. These tasks were too complex to be done at home. It was just another sign of teachers shirking their own duties, he'd explained to Vivian when she got wind of the school's concern over Beau's incomplete assignments. Vivian disagreed, and arranged for a tutor.

Recently, Everett and Bridgette had tangled over the nanny's insistence that he and Emma go through her backpack with her. For God's sake, thought Everett, the girl was only in kindergarten, and her pack was filled with homework assignments and cryptic notes from the teachers about bake sales and Valentine's cards…and a list to be filled out for the Student Book Club. He had to scrounge up seven dollars and change, which meant beseeching one of the help to break a twenty for him. It was maddening! Why Skippy would have chosen to handle all of these irritating details herself was beyond him. That was Bridgette's job.

Everett took some consolation in the fact that he was back on his old stomping grounds, in his rightful position as the master of Laurel Hall. He might have been able to actually celebrate his return if not for the feeling that he was constantly under the prying eyes of Bridgette. When Skippy was alive, the nanny seemed merely indifferent to him, but now she treated him like an intruder who had to be instructed on all the rules of the house and on everything that concerned the kids. Worse was the fact that his mother supported Bridgette's every decision and cut him no slack.

Heeding their old friend's call, the guys had been showing up a few nights each week at Laurel Hall, with a copious amount of liquid refreshments. Everett arranged for these soirees, confining them to his private library, hidden from the "surrogate mothers". But he was becoming bored with the dull nights in no-man's land, as he called the suburbs; Everett needed something more to lighten the mood. As he had loudly proclaimed to the guys one dreary February evening, there was a time for everything and this was a time to get over his gloom — with women and drugs. He alerted them that they should be prepared for some unusual fun the following night.

The fellows were perplexed by the email they received from Everett the next day inviting them to a "share a bag", since this wasn't part of their lexicon. Everett was in a great mood when he got back to Laurel Hall in the evening along with Dave Reynolds from the office, who'd promised to orchestrate the party. Everett's young co-worker took a stroll around the mansion while Emma spent some time with her father before she was dismissed to have dinner. Everett, who rarely if ever shared mealtime with the kids, was taking his dinner in the library as usual, to watch the hockey game in peace.

As Everett's pals arrived over the course of the evening, they were struck by one thing in particular about his friend Dave: he was light years younger than the rest. Everett was supposed to have been the guy's mentor, but it seemed that the tables had turned. He'd become fascinated by his new underling's self-described lifestyle. Apparently, Everett was missing out on a world of good times. He liked to hear Dave talk up one of his favorite subjects: drugs. The underling came up with some fresh ideas, offering a whole new range of possibilities.

Besides that, Dave's weekends seemed to be filled with Lisa Sweeney and her cohorts from Operations. Everett's were filled with the recent parental burdens that had fallen in his lap. He blamed Skippy for imposing a new leash on him by the very act of dying. Playing parent was cutting into his hoped-for social plans. While finding women had never been a problem for Everett, the type of women Dave hung out with were in a different league entirely. They were answerable to no one, far more daring than the women he was used to, and in some cases could even be viewed as sexual predators. And they were younger, much younger.

Of course, as Roger Graham, his client-turned-pal from Farber Chemical, pointed out to him over the phone, with the right type of drugs you don't need the company of women. Jim seconded that motion, especially since he'd recently caught hell from his wife when she discovered he'd been flirting online with an old girlfriend. He was finally back in his wife's good graces, and didn't need her to hear any rumors about some wild orgy over at Laurel Hall.

In any event, there would be no women present for the evening. Vivian forbade it. She'd preempted her son by stating how traumatic it would be for the kids to have "that sort of thing going on." The sort of party Everett was anticipating would have to wait until he was back in the city.

On this icy February night, as they settled into the grand leather chairs set out before the majestic fireplace, the fellows were content to share their finest brandy and splendid cigars with Dave, who in a fair exchange, gave a detailed and graphic description of his most recent exploits with the ladies. In addition, as he'd promised his superior,

Dave brought along a lovely plastic bag as his own special gift: the basic ingredients necessary for the "pharma-party."

Everett didn't sufficiently warn his friends, but advised that they'd be staying the night and should each bring along a sample of their favorite prescription drug. Each of the invited wondered what their host was up to this time, but figured they'd leave their options open. Dave, ready to reveal what the group was in for, explained that there was going to be a game, though one usually reserved for a younger bunch of daredevils. It sounded to the guys like a sort of Russian roulette, using prescription drugs instead of bullets; the pills were mixed together in one bag, a handful to be taken randomly by each partier. The fun would be in the effects, said Dave: a surprise in every mouthful.

Ward sheepishly dumped his contribution into the bag, not disclosing that it was limited to Sudafed and Motrin. While not the required prescription drugs, they were all he had around other than stool softener – and that he absolutely refused to bring for fear of overdose, having taken his daily quota just that morning.

George Rusk, Everett's old friend from prep school days, was the most reluctant to participate, due to his memory of a certain night in college. His first and last indulgence in fog-cutters, a random array of alcoholic beverages mixed in a vat, had ended rather poorly, at least from a physical point of view. It was the campus equivalent of a pharma-party, based on alcohol instead of prescription pills. The brew hit everyone differently but George took it the worst of his fraternity brothers, ending up in the on-campus hospital. After having his stomach pumped, he was released from Mary Hitchcock Hospital and, still disoriented, curled up on the front steps of the first dormitory he passed. Cece liked to recount the story that when she discovered him lying there in a stupor, the sweet, dopey expression on his baby face, she realized it was her life's mission to save this fellow from himself. They'd married upon graduation.

Now, it was Cece herself who had urged her husband to join Everett for an evening at Laurel Hall. She knew that George missed his incorrigible friend who, after his divorce, had moved to the city and until now, rarely spent a night out in the country. George was fully aware that his wife would have been furious if she knew about the evening's basic agenda; if he fell off the wagon after all these years, it would threaten to undercut the great job Cece had done with him.

"Hey, I've got a great idea." Everett suggested, grabbing the bag of pills from Dave's hands as he headed out of the room.

"God help him if he downs them all himself!" shouted George after him, laughing but already concerned.

"Have no fear!" Everett called out, his voice echoing down the long, marble hallway. He soon returned with a lovely Baccarat bowl. It was filled with pink and red Valentine's Day candies. Bridgette had set the bowl out in the front hall in accordance with Vivian's instructions, though Skippy would have never done so; the kids had no self-control when it came to sweets, and she had only permitted healthy snacks to be left out. Upon leaving for Florida that afternoon, Vivian insisted on leaving the children their Valentine gifts, and a huge bag of candy hearts and jellybeans were among them.

Set out that afternoon, the bowl had already been refilled twice. It wasn't just Emma who indulged. The entire household seemed to take a bunch of goodies each time they passed by.

"Don't eat too much candy. You should save some for Beau," Bridgette had warned Emma earlier that evening, as she'd kissed her good-bye. The nanny had accepted Everett's kind offer to take the night off, so she made last minute plans to stay with her niece until the next day. With Beau away on his school trip and Amanda available to help out, Bridgette agreed it would be a nice break. She convinced herself that Everett was capable of caring for one child overnight. She wondered if his sudden generosity might herald a turning point. Perhaps he just needed a bit of time on his own with that little cherub to realize all that he'd been missing.

"Help yourselves!" Everett roared, setting down on the pool table the bowl, now overflowing with candies and pills. The guys all laughed, but no one was taking.

Finally, Dave made the first move. He plunged in, grabbing a few pieces from the bowl. "Mmm, jelly beans!" he chuckled. "And maybe... more?" he added as he rummaged through the bowl and came up with a few choice items. He chased them down with a swig of Johnnie Walker Blue. "And that's how it's done!" Dave said as he passed the bowl around. "Go for it!"

Ward and George watched as Everett and the others followed Dave's lead, but they would have no part of it. Ward told himself that if his own son ever tried anything as stupid, he'd kill him with his bare hands. George refilled his glass of brandy, feeling comfortable with his preferred intoxicant.

***

In the glow of her nightlight, Emma could see her American Girl doll staring at her. "Why did you wake me up, Samantha?" she asked.

She got out of her bed, shifting as slightly as possible the special bed-top positions of her many stuffed animals, and grabbed the doll from her little bed in the corner. "Okay, if you're quiet you can stay with us," she advised as she pulled the doll into bed with her. She folded the covers back over her doll and adjusted the stuffed animals so they wouldn't fall out of place. Then she tried to get back to sleep.

From far off in the house, she could hear music playing. She thought she could hear Beau in his room. But she remembered he was away, and so was Bridgette. Her Daddy was downstairs with his friends. She could hear laughter.

"It's Valentine's Day tomorrow," she whispered to her doll. "If you're good, I'll make you a card." She closed her eyes and thought about the Valentine card that Hadley had given her. She pictured the one she would make for Samantha, with hearts all over it.

A loud noise from downstairs interrupted her thoughts. It was followed by another loud sound, like a door being slammed shut.

"You're keeping me up, Samantha!" The doll's eyes were shut, but the child lifted her to a standing position so that they snapped wide open. "I'm going to go tell Daddy."

Emma took the doll in her arms. Together, they left the bedroom and embarked on the trip through the mansion and toward the source of the noise on the main floor. The pair first passed by Bridgette's room, where in the grip of her headphones Amanda was absorbed in her iTunes. Before leaving for the evening, the housekeeper promised Bridgette she'd spend the night upstairs in the nanny's room, next to Emma's; it was the first time since the death of Mrs. Brockhurst that everyone was away, Georgina, Vivian and Doris. Even Beau was gone. Amanda reluctantly agreed to stay in Bridgette's room, though she had no intention of playing the role of Mommy.

"Hey, did anyone close the door back there?" Jim hollered at the others as he moved ahead in the dark. "I closed it!" shouted George as he approached them, barely able to see the shapes of the other men farther in front if him. He and Ward were trying to keep an eye on Everett and the others as they half-ran, half-slid across the ice encrusted back lawn. By now, the partiers were flying high, the assorted drugs having started to take effect.

"It's fucking cold, God damn it!" screamed Ward, hoping to round the guys up and bring them back indoors. Everett had different plans. He was ahead of them all, on his way down to the boathouse, the site of many a youthful indiscretion. This time, no one was around to put a damper on the fun. He was giddy with the thought.

When they realized that the party wasn't coming back to the main house, Ward and George returned to retrieve all the coats from the front closet, as well as the paraphernalia for the intended poker game. Running back, they tried to help their fellow revelers downhill in the dark toward the glimmer of light from the boathouse. By means of sheer habit, Everett had managed to find the light switch, his faculties all but failing him as he yelled at Dave. He was trying to tell him to get the fire going, but it came out as "gutta fire blowing." Dave, laughing uncontrollably, dragged over a few folding chairs from a dusty corner of the room, and started to set up camp in front of the fireplace.

George, steering the stragglers into the boathouse, saw right away that there was no wood by the hearth, where it used to be neatly stored. The old propane heater would take forever to get going. Aside from freezing their asses off, they'd be stuck at the boathouse without even the chance of a decent poker game, since Everett and the others were by now barely coherent.

Everett had thrown a musty old beach blanket over his shoulders. He stood shivering in the middle of the room, still making loud, word-less noises. George tossed him a coat, but realized that in his rush he'd pulled out Beau's jacket. There stood the heir to the Brockhurst for-tune, wrapped in an old, frayed blanket and the arm of a child's coat, his mouth agape and a blank expression on his face. For a moment, he seemed to recognize his old buddy George, but then, as his eyes glazed over again, Everett threw his head back and howled.

***

She entered the room and looked around. The music was still blaring and smoke filled the air. But the room was empty.

"Daddy went out," Emma said. "And look, he was eating our Valentine's candy from Grandma!" There on the pool table was the lovely glass bowl filled with all the sparkling goodies, colorful and invit-ing. Bridgette had warned her not to eat too many Valentine's sweets, but with no one watching, it was just too good to resist. She put her little hand into the bowl and grabbed a bunch of candies, munching on them as she ran out of the room and up the stairs. Something in her mouth tasted bad, but the thrill of getting away with her midnight snack tasted just wonderful.

CHAPTER THIRTY-TWO

Under the glare and endless buzzing of the floodlight in the hospital parking lot, George sat in his Lincoln Navigator, the seat heater set to max yet doing a minimum to help his throbbing lower back. Splayed across the back seat under his signature cashmere overcoat was his involuntary passenger, one moment moaning, the next moment spurting out a string of garbled words. Everett was in bad shape, but George had no doubt he would survive. He was certainly having an easier time of it than was his daughter, in the emergency room having her stomach pumped.

George sent out a silent prayer of thanks that Cece had answered his call. Standing in the cold in front of Laurel Hall and blubbering to her on his cell phone, he watched as the ambulance pulled away. Please, he begged his wife, get to the hospital for Emma.

Everett wriggled around in his stupor, grunted, sighed, was silent again. George's cell phone vibrated. The call was from the other front, Laurel Hall, where Ward remained stationed. George was glad to report to him that Emma was in good hands and that Cece had gotten to the hospital in a flash. From the mansion, Ward's report was also promising; Jim was in the bathroom vomiting, but very much alive. Dave was passed out in the den, less green than an hour earlier and breathing rather evenly, with Roger lying on the floor a few feet away from him. A lovely night all around, thought George.

And where was the housekeeper? George wanted to know. Back in her room, Ward told him. She remained there in accordance with their on-the-spot decision to banish her and strip her of any further responsibility for the child. It was the right choice, Ward confirmed, after the way she'd burst into the boathouse to announce she wasn't the nanny, wasn't supposed to be on duty all night, and didn't need to have risked injuring every bone in her body crossing the frozen tundra just because the "Little Princess" wasn't feeling well. They could only guess what might have happened had they not flown up to the house to find Emma. When they found her, she was at the top of the stairs, slumped against the newel post, too dizzy to stand. Had they gotten there a moment later, she might have fallen down the stairs or passed out.

As though an afterthought, Ward inquired about Everett. "He's in the back seat, breathing," answered George. Everett thrashed about again, then wedged his head under his coat and out of range of the harsh floodlight.

"Seems like we both have our hands full. Oh, here we go again, Jim's yelling for something. Gotta go!" Ward signed off.

Another twinge signaled to George that his back had gone out again. He had long accepted the burden of his friendship with Everett and now added to the mental anguish of it was this new layer of physical pain. They'd been through a lot over the years, but this time he couldn't seem to drum up an ounce of compassion for his pal.

George wondered if Cece had an Advil with her. Or had he taken them all to use at the party? He shifted about and played with the buttons to reposition his seat, but nothing helped. He was getting too old for this. So was Ward. They'd tried to carry Everett up the hill, but he was too unwieldy; his legs kept giving way. Ward finally figured out that they could drag him over the icy surface of the hill. Moving as quickly as they could against the bitter wind, they hauled him all the way up to the top of the driveway.

Maneuvering the big oaf into the back of the car: that's what did it. Lift and twist, the perfect combination to wrench your back. But a little pain wasn't anything to complain about when he considered what Emma was going through, the poor kid.

Now settled down, Everett started to snore. George cut the engine. It would be so easy to get him right into the doctors' hands. Just roll the car right over to the front of the emergency room entrance and slide him out onto the red carpet. Sure, the shit would fly, but so what?

Maybe it would be the best thing for him, he'd finally get some treatment. George sat for some time, wondering if it would be the right thing to do, but couldn't force himself to go through with it. What if Everett resisted help and somehow crossed paths with Emma? It could make for an ugly scene, not something the child needed to see. Abandoning the idea, George went back inside to find his wife.

Cece clutched Emma's hand. She looked so small lying on the cot in the dismal, oversized hospital gown. Her eyes were shut, her voice too weak to answer any of the nurse's questions. Cece spoke up on her behalf as the nurse jotted down her words. She explained that she knew only what her husband had told her. He said that according to the housekeeper, the girl took something from the medicine cabinet that made her sick. She became dizzy and unable to speak. Her husband had called 911 to report the girl's condition and to say she had taken an unknown substance.

"By the time I arrived, the ambulance had already gotten here and Emma was about to have her stomach pumped." Cece said. "I'm the neighbor," she added.

"I know," said the nurse as she scribbled down her few final notes.

It was at least the third time Cece had given the same explanation, each time speaking to a different member of the medical staff. By this point, her repeated statement rang false in her own ears, the holes in the story looming larger than the story itself. She left out the fact that the only men sober enough to have driven the child to the hospital were instead preoccupied with protecting the Brockhurst name, tending to a bunch of drunken idiots. She left out the fact that everyone was being strangely mum about what exactly the child might have taken to make her so ill. Now and then, she'd seen Emma and her brother over at Laurel Hall or the club. They seemed well-behaved and were always friendly to her daughter. Kids could get into the medicine cabinet if they had a mind to, but she couldn't imagine the sweet, obedient Emma doing something like that.

She also left out the part that still puzzled her, about how Emma ended up all alone in the ER. The Brockhursts always kept a nanny as well as a live-in housekeeper. She was sure one of them would have met up with her at the hospital, though as she raced along, she wondered what might be so urgent that it also called for her to be there, as well. On arrival, she was shocked to hear that other than the medical attendants, Emma was alone. She was being prepared for the procedure.

Frantic, Cece finagled her way past the border guards, who surely would have wasted her valuable time with insurance forms and authorizations rather than escorting her to the frightened little girl. When the automatic doors opened to admit a very pregnant woman and her excited, extended family, Cece snuck in along with them, pretending to be part of the entourage. She easily located Emma, who was still in a fog.

Assuming that the person standing by the child's side was her mother, one of the doctors assured her that Emma's vital signs were looking better and that the procedure itself would be brief.

By the time George caught up with his wife, Emma had already been treated and was back in the monitoring area of the emergency room — but to Cece, not far enough away from an older woman on the other side of the curtain, who in an irritating sing-song voice asked over and over, "Am I going to die?" Now and then someone came by to calm her down, but as soon as they left, the hideous song continued. George saw it coming: Cece collared one of the interns who was walking by and swore to him that if the child woke up to hear that crazy patient's question, she was going to answer "yes" and proceed to make good on her promise. The staff had little room to work with, but the vocalist was finally rolled out on a gurney into the hallway where she could be more thoroughly ignored.

George smiled at Cece, despite the depressing scene around them. He loved to see his wife in action. There was absolutely no one like her, especially in a crisis.

Later, while George was out at the car once again tending to Everett, Emma's eyes finally opened. As the space around her slowly came into focus, the girl saw a face she recognized: Allison's mom. Allison was one of Beau's friends. The lady was smiling and holding her hand. That was strange, thought the little girl. And there were curtains around her, and a man in a green outfit, like when Beau broke his arm. To answer her growing look of panic, Cece stared straight into Emma's eyes, and told her she was fine, that she ate something not so good and now she was getting all fixed up. She was in the hospital just for a little while, and then they would go home.

"Where's my Daddy? Where's Beau?"

The tears streamed down the child's face and onto the pillow, while Cece did her best to answer her questions and comfort her. She could see the faintest hints of future frown lines on this little one's forehead. Without a second thought, she ran her hand over them to ease the worries away.

As Cece stroked Emma's brow, she realized it would soon be morning. Her own kids would wonder where she was. Before she took off for the hospital, she had woken the housekeeper to say there was an emergency and that she'd be back as soon as she could. Yet here she was, promising Emma to stay by her side. She bent over the child and gave her a kiss on the cheek, and watched as Emma slowly returned to her slumber.

CHAPTER THIRTY-THREE

During the lunch meeting in Lucy's office, Meg mentioned having fielded a call from Howie Gassner, the doctor who had last treated Skippy. He said he was being harassed by a woman named Burden who wouldn't let him alone. First, she insisted on obtaining the medical records for Skippy, which he refused to provide since they were privileged. And now, she wanted to know the exact circumstances surrounding the accident. She told him he was an occurrence witness, with no privilege attached to what he actually saw, just like any other bystander.

"Howie wants to know if he should just meet with her and get it over with."

"Ruby! Get me Howie Gassner on the phone!"

"Caufield's still holding for you."

"Howie's done me enough favors. She'll have to wait."

Meg took one last bite of her turkey sandwich and set it down on a folded napkin. She took out her legal pad and turned to her colleagues. "Now, can I ask a few really important questions? Who's bringing what to Andi's, and what are we wearing?"

"Lucy, you've got to bring your brownies," Claire insisted.

"Only if you bring your artichoke dip," the boss responded.

Ruby interrupted. "I've got Howie on three!"

Intermission had come to an end.

"Hey, Doc. I hear that Burden's been hounding you."

"What a bitch! As much as I hate you lawyers, these insurance people are even worse! Do I have to meet with her?"

"Hey, you insult me and now you want my help? Just tell her to go to hell."

"You really mean that?"

"Yeah. You told me you didn't see the accident at all, right? Anything that happened before that in your office goes toward diagnosis and treatment and is privileged. So, you have nothing to say to her. If she keeps bothering you, give her my name and number. And by the way, you better take back what you said about lawyers, or you can call your plumber next time."

"Mrs. Caufield's getting cranky!" Ruby called.

"Hello, Julie. You're not going to believe it, but I'm in the middle of —"

"I know, an emergency. You're always in the middle of a fucking emergency. Why don't you let me know when you're not in crisis so we can have a chat then, hmmm? I'm about to get on a plane." The speaker carried the client's voice loud and clear across the room.

Andi whispered, "Why don't you put her on hold long enough for her to miss her flight?"

Lucy switched off the speaker to cover the snickering of her cohorts. "Call me when you land," she said, trying to sound solemn amid the giggling.

"We'll see about that," the client answered cryptically, and hung up.

Lucy was her fourth attorney in the matter, a statistic that had gotten around. Lucy doubted she'd want to find a fifth.

"God, does that lady have timing or what?" Lucy said. "Now, where were we when we were so rudely interrupted?"

The sisterhood went on horsing around for some time. Lucy smiled at the faces surrounding her. She wondered if it was like this at any of the other firms. How could any group of professional women act as silly as this bunch of knuckleheads? Most of them Ivy Leaguers, to boot. They were something to behold. Her heart was light; she was among friends, having fun. She grabbed a Post-It and scribbled down the ingredients for her signature brownies.

CHAPTER THIRTY-FOUR

Flowers adorned the kitchen table. Each rose in the Waterford vase was in full, sumptuous bloom. He loved the way she feigned surprise each year, pretending she had no idea he was planning to send them. His spitfire of a wife, he adored her. George nibbled on one of the last of the Perugina chocolates, this time finding his favorite, the one with a layer of caramel. The air had cleared from their final argument on the subject. He was going to do what had to be done. The phone was in front of him, he had her number, but the call would mean the end of a long friendship.

What was it that Cece told him? When she called to see how Emma was doing, the nanny had told her it was a shame that the child had gotten into her father's bathroom cabinet and become so ill. But she was now doing very well, thank God. So, as Cece reported to her husband, Everett's version of the story was now the official one. He wasn't taking any responsibility for endangering Emma, and instead was making sure everyone was on the same page as to what had occurred. In fact, she added, Emma probably accepted Everett's rendition of the story as much as did anyone else. George was loath to butt into Brockhurst business, but not Cece. They had to confront Everett, she insisted, or if George was unwilling to do so, they had to tell someone else what had actually happened. The past few days had been a struggle between them: Cece badgering her husband to take action, and George reluctant to follow her suggestion.

That afternoon, just as George was about to leave his office, Everett called him to say that Child Protective Services had already interviewed the family and staff, and now wanted the names and contact numbers of whoever else was present when Emma became ill. He didn't have to remind George of the substantial powers that CPS wielded.

Everett asked his old pal to tell the same, simple story to the authorities if they contacted him: Emma got sick from something she took from the medicine cabinet. Everett made the request sound perfectly reasonable, and asked for one more favor. He wanted George to call the other guys who'd been at the party and refresh their memories about what had happened.

George put it as delicately as he could; Everett would have to make his own phone calls. The last time he'd been asked to "clean up" for his buddy was years earlier, the night at the pier. There was the usual ruckus, the boys drinking as much as they could hold and flirting with the girls. The pier was out on the neck and far from any road. They were always willing to make the long trek by foot, since the gathering place was beyond the eyes of the Florida cops. All week they'd partied out there, more and more out of control each night. The others drank beer and fog-cutters, smoked some pot, but Everett was mixing it all with cocaine.

Concerned about his buddy after he didn't turn up back at the hotel one morning, and knowing he couldn't call the police and risk any publicity, George had put in a call to Brandt. Big brother was already on his way down to Florida when Everett finally turned up late the following evening. Brandt had responded to the plea for help; even if Everett was located, his little brother was on a binge. He needed to be straightened out.

The Brockhursts were delighted to learn that Brandt was on his way to join his brother in Florida, since their boys never seemed to make time for one another. Had they thought it through, it might have seemed odd that Brandt had changed his plans. As a senior it was his final Spring Break, a time to celebrate the end of his college years with his own group of friends.

Instead of thanking George for handling things below the radar, Everett scolded him for getting his brother involved. But he told him it really didn't matter: Brandt was not going to ruin his vacation.

Hearing Everett orchestrate another alibi triggered George's memory of the terrible night on the pier. The balmy Florida air had been the same as on the other nights, with the same group of kids, the keg in its central location, the music playing and the distant lights from the boats out on their moorings. But one thing was different that evening. The tide was out. In fact, Brandt mentioned that fact as he sat back in one of the director chairs. The water had pulled away from the pier, revealing a mass of jutting rocks lying many feet below them. But hours later, who cared, who noticed? High as a kite, and in his lurching dance across the pier, Everett had started to topple over the edge.

This was the part where George always tried to press pause and rerun it, so that he might have time to fly across and grab the son of a bitch before he fell. But that night, his mind had been moving too slowly. The only one on the ball was Brandt, who leaped out to pull Everett back and in so doing saved his brother, but stumbled and rolled off the pier.

Later, George was forced to support Everett's version of the facts. The story line was that only the 21-year-old Brandt had been drinking that night on the dock. The others, all underage, had organized a birthday celebration for Brandt, but they remained sober. The birthday boy overdid the fun and ended up falling off the pier. All of them were ordered to give the same information to the medical authorities and police. George knew that Brandt himself would have covered up for his brother, had he been able to do so. He would have excused the whole thing by stating the obvious: Everett hadn't purposely caused his brother's injury. It was just a horrible accident.

George often wondered which of the two of them, he or Everett, felt more to blame for the tragedy. It was Everett's wild behavior that had caused Brandt to be there on a pier in Florida that night, tending to his brother. But if George had waited for Everett to show up the next day rather than panicking, what then? Brandt would likely be a husband, a father, a great man ready to step into Hugh Brockhurst's shoes – and Everett might be doing something other than escaping into his perpetual fog. George imagined that the guilt was shared by the two of them, a bond of sadness. It was a bond about to be broken.

CHAPTER THIRTY-FIVE

Vivian closed her laptop for the day, having finally caught up on her work for Fairmount. They were nearing their goal, the fundraising campaign in its final weeks. Thank goodness the organization had been able to nail down Dr. Whitcomb. With his addition to the staff, Fairmount would retain its status as the state's finest rehabilitation center for brain trauma victims. The annual drive always focused her energy so that she felt able to move mountains.

This year, with all her absences, she had to make up for lost time. The other women were well-meaning, but didn't have what it took to raise the serious money they needed. Those funds came through the relationships Vivian had honed over the course of many years. She sat down at her vanity, thinking ahead to the quiet dinner with Hugh when he came in the room to tell her that George Rusk was on the phone.

Vivian held the phone to her ear, while applying make-up with her other hand. "Nice to hear from you, George."

"Hope you're all doing well."

"We're fine. Glad to be back here for a bit." She set the phone to speaker and started to brush her hair.

"I can imagine. You must have just left when everything happened up here with Emma and all."

"Yes, and I wanted to thank you. It's a good thing you and Everett got her over to the hospital right away."

There was a pause on George's end.

"Yes, well, actually she got there by ambulance."

"An ambulance? She was taken by ambulance? She must have been terrified!"

"We weren't sure if we should drive her or get EMS to the house right away, but, we didn't want to take any chances. She was pretty out of it by the time they got to her, so...they took her to the hospital."

"I see." Vivian put down the brush and stared at herself in the mirror.

"And, uh, I guess you know about how it happened."

"Emma took some pills...from the medicine chest."

"Well, actually, that's the reason I'm calling."

"Please, go on."

"There was a party. A few guys over, and there was a bowl of candy."

Vivian wondered what in the world candy had to do with any of this.

"And some of the guys, they added some pills to the bowl of candy."

"Why on earth would someone do that?"

"It's so stupid, Vivian, I can't even explain it, but I think that by mistake Emma took a handful of what she thought was candy, and it was actually some pills."

"What kind of pills?" Vivian watched in the mirror as her face paled, even through the make-up.

"Well, it could have been almost anything."

"George, I cannot believe what you're telling me." Vivian stood up. She started to pace. "And can you tell me who would be so insane as to put pills into a bowl of candy...and with a five year old in the house?!"

"It was a party, so some guys..."

"A party? No one told me anything about a party...not Everett, not Amanda—"

"Some of the guys came over with some pills and..."

"Everett! I suppose it was one of his brilliant ideas!"

"It wasn't Everett who came up with the idea... it was a guy from his office who thought it might be..."

"Are you trying to defend my son?"

Vivian waited.

George finally spoke. "No. I'm not defending him or myself. Actually, with everything going on with the children and custody, we...

Cece and I thought you should know about all of this. And that I suspect Everett has a real drug problem."

Vivian sat on the edge of her bed. So, it was back. Hadn't Everett promised after the custody case to clean up his act? He seemed to be functioning at that high-level job of his. She wondered how much George knew about her son's past use of cocaine. Was that what he was talking about, or was it something different?

"What sort of drug problem?"

"I'm not sure, Vivian, but I think he may be using prescription drugs. At the party, he seemed to make a large contribution from a personal supply."

Vivian was shaking. She couldn't speak. She imagined Beau and Emma at Laurel Hall and thanked the Lord that her fool of a son was nowhere near them. He was back in his city apartment. Bridgette was in charge, the children were safe.

"I'm sorry, Vivian. This is not a call I wanted to make."

With effort, Vivian composed herself. She was determined not to crumble the way she once had, years ago. The children were safe, and this time she could do something to make sure they remained so.

"George, it must have been difficult for you to make this call. You've been a good friend to my son."

"Thanks, Vivian. But there's an additional problem you should know about. Child Protective Services came to Laurel Hall over the weekend and talked to everyone."

"Yes, I was told that it was a formality, since Emma took the medication."

"The story that Everett told you and CPS, about Emma taking something out of the cabinet. That's the same story he asked Cece and me to tell, if they call us about it. Do you think we should tell them what really happened?"

Vivian considered the ramifications of contending with a force outside of the family. If the truth came out, would the authorities consider the children to be in danger? What if Beau and Emma were taken away altogether?

"I'm afraid we have no choice, George. We have to stick to the story. Not for Everett's sake, but for the sake of the children."

The pause in the conversation signaled its possible conclusion, but George wasn't quite finished. While he had this moment to speak with her, despite the reluctance he always felt, he had to ask.

"How's Brandt doing?"

"Oh, George, he's doing all right. Same as always. We saw him on Sunday, and he looked fine. Thanks for asking, really."

George knew better than to mention what he'd read in the Times, the latest experiments using stem-cells to help regenerate brain tissue. The Brockhursts were experts, having spent the last twenty years helping to advance the center. If anyone knew about the cutting edge in brain injury treatment, it was Vivian and Hugh.

"Well then, Vivian, if there's anything else Cece or I can do to help with the kids, please let us know."

"Nice of you to offer. Please send my regards and thanks to your wife," she said, ending the call.

Cece stepped into the kitchen. George sat in his chair, the phone still in his hand. His back was to her, but she knew without seeing her husband's face that this hadn't been easy for him. He was loyal to a fault. He would view the call as a betrayal of his old friend. Leaning over his back, she wrapped her arms around her husband and over his chest.

"You did the right thing, hon."

George remained locked in his wife's embrace, his eyes closed. He wanted to believe she was right.

CHAPTER THIRTY-SIX

Without consulting her daughter, Consuela, whose own housekeeper was away, contacted Miracle Agency with a last-minute request. She needed two ladies to help with a Sunday afternoon party. When she got nothing but static due to the short notice, Consuela asked for Sonja Virag, the manager. Intimating that she was a close friend of the Brockhursts, Consuela reminded Ms. Virag that it was she, Mrs. Max Birnbaum, who had referred the agency for work at Laurel Hall. As she recalled to Sonja, there must have been a dozen women who ended up handling the one job. It wasn't long before Consuela got a return call saying that they had at least one available worker, and possibly two. By Saturday afternoon, she was assured that two women would be waiting at the train station the following day, at 2:00 p.m.

Experience told Andi that capitulation was in order. Giving in to her mother's decree so readily wasn't a good precedent, but these were desperate times. "You're wonderful, Mom." Consuela was surprised to get no argument whatsoever. Apparently, her lawyer-daughter couldn't negotiate her way out of this one.

"Great, I'll be there with the housekeepers tomorrow, a little after two. That should give them plenty of time to get things ready, and I'll be there to help out." The only problem Andi foresaw was how she was going to manage her mother until the guests arrived.

Sunday afternoon, Consuela, Max and the two housekeepers arrived amid much fanfare. They carried in presents, balloons, and wine as well as the little dessert Andi had agreed to, which when translated by her parents into "Birnbaum-ese" included an array of pies, cheesecakes, pastries and a specially-decorated, gargantuan seven layer anniversary cake.

Steve fulfilled his pledge to steer his in-laws out of the kitchen and into the family room where the festivities were to occur. He preferred to celebrate their anniversary with a quiet dinner at their favorite restaurant, but Andi had coaxed him into inviting over the family and a few close friends. He realized from the beginning that it was likely to get out of hand. Yet, now that all the preparations were over, and with the last-minute offer of help from Max and Consuela, he was actually looking forward to it.

The children exchanged hugs and kisses with their grandparents, then started in on a general rampage around the house. Andi's brother had thought it a wonderful idea to drop his kids off early, so that the five cousins could have more time to play together.

"Beth, did you brush your hair?" called Andi from the kitchen. "Can you guys please settle down?"

Oblivious to the commotion, Max took his usual place at the end of the big couch and announced that he was ready for the concert.

"Sari! Front and center!" called Steve. "Papa Max is waiting!"

"I'm coming!" the ten-year-old answered. Sari extricated herself from the tangle of cousins and returned to the family room, obediently sitting down at the piano. Meanwhile, the other children snuck off to the playroom, avoiding any chance of being called upon to perform. As usual, they left the entertainment in Sari's capable hands. She loved to play her original compositions for the one person who was, as always, her most appreciative audience.

From the kitchen, Andi was happy to hear the concert begin. Finally having a moment to greet the housekeepers, she did a double take. She knew she'd seen one of them before.

"Amanda Gray," said the sturdy blonde, introducing herself and rubbing her hands together as though ready to get right down to business. The other woman introduced herself as Bette.

"Great to have you here on such short notice," Andi said to both women. "I think we've met before," she said, with her friendly smile. "Wasn't it at Laurel Hall?"

"Might have been. I was working there for a while." The dour-faced Amanda had nothing further to say.

Andi laughed. "Well, as you can see, it's a bit smaller here."

Amanda raised her eyebrows and looked around the kitchen with a scowl that Andi couldn't miss.

God, this one's a real charmer, thought the lawyer, *a fun way to start the party.* She stood motionless, wondering where to begin. It was a relief to hear Steve call out that the caterer had just pulled up. Now, she could put the women straight to work. A relay was set up between the caterer's van and the kitchen, with Andi calling out instructions as to where all the food should be placed.

But before she could get far, Consuela found her way into the kitchen, and Andi's plans fell by the wayside. Great trays of food flew past her in all directions, some set into the oven, some onto the stove, some in the family room, all in the wrong places, but all where Consuela thought best.

"And you're not wearing that, are you, honey? Did you even get a shower today?"

"Mom, I'm not dressed yet! Why is the turkey going out there when it has to be warmed up first?"

"It's too late for that, they'll enjoy it cold. Andi, it's an afternoon party. No one expects a hot meal. What did you decide to wear?"

Andi saw no sign of Steve. Where the hell was he? Oh God, he must have dropped the ball despite all her warnings, and was off somewhere fiddling with the CDs, and here she was stuck in the middle of the very pre-party pandemonium she'd been determined to avoid. She was fielding calls from guests who needed directions despite her absurdly over-informative invitations, fending off the wild pack of kids who'd emerged from their hide-out scrounging for snacks, and trying to appease her mother, who continued to harp on why her daughter always waited until the last minute to get dressed.

By the time Lucy walked in, a little early as promised, her partner was in bad shape. She still hadn't gotten off the phone or out of the kitchen. She stood surrounded by workers bustling about in all directions as they tried to avoid bumping into her mother whose head was now wedged into the refrigerator, her generous rear end protruding far into the room.

Lucy appraised the scene, placed her package of homemade brownies on the kitchen counter, grabbed her friend by the shoulders and ordered her "Out!" Pushing Andi down the hallway, she told her not to join them until she was damned ready to. Meanwhile, her trusty partner would handle whatever was necessary, including answering the phone and managing Consuela. No different from handling a challenging client while juggling everything at the office.

"You're a goddess!" cried Andi, as she closed the bedroom door behind her.

Back in the kitchen, Lucy faced with grace and courtesy the great overflow of creative ideas Consuela wanted to take the party to the next level. She suggested a dance contest. Unfortunately, said Lucy, they'd have to decide on that later, since she first had to attend to answering the phones and properly greeting the arriving guests.

This was my real anniversary gift, thought Lucy, as later she watched Andi make her grand entrance into a room full of guests, radiant in her ravishing outfit, her hair in order and — what was that? Make-up? As Andi took a twirl in her flirty dress, Steve made an appreciative comment and Consuela practically swooned. Music filled the room, guests crowded in, drinks were sent all around and the party swung into action.

The celebration went on from there, wending its happy way through the afternoon. It was well into the evening by the time Amanda and Bette started gathering up the dessert plates and coffee cups from the long buffet table. Amanda reached out to grab the remnants of the anniversary cake when she was commanded to halt.

"Andi, tell them dessert is never over for this bunch," Claire advised. Adding emphasis to the statement, she helped herself to an additional piece of cake and brought two brownies to her husband, Keith. The revelers, having whittled down to the tight-knit nub from Bennett and Birnbaum, were serious about it. The night was still young, there was much more eating to be done, and they needed time to indulge in the all-important post-mortem. They were all in agreement that the party had been splendid, the caterer had outdone himself and that the video montage had been one of the party's

highlights. But the Merengue, as danced by Max and Consuela —
now that had truly taken the cake.

Meg, holding up a glass of Champagne, noted how resplendent
everyone looked. "You all clean up real well," she said. "And Andi, that
fantastic dress. And how did you do that to your eyes?"

Fluttering her eyelashes, Andi answered, "I have to keep a few
secrets, don't I?"

Claire tugged on the sleeve of her own blouse and asked, "All right,
how much?"

Andi took the first crack. "Forty. It's from Ann Taylor Loft. Doubt
it's silk, but it looks good."

"Sorry, Claire, I saw it at T.J.'s first," Lucy said. "Looks better on you,
with your dark hair. When I saw it, I think it was around twenty-three."

"Wrong!" Claire said. "Final sale, sixteen bucks. And the skirt?"

"Including the belt?" Ruby asked.

Claire swung her long, straight hair back, her chandelier earrings
jingling. Her title as Discount Queen was hardly threatened. Even if
they were close on the skirt, they were going to lose big time on the
scarf or boots.

"Skirt and belt, twenty-eight."

To the astonishment of the whole group, these words came out of
the mouth of the fellow who'd accompanied Meg to the party. They'd
heard very little from him up to this point, as Meg had monopolized
all of his attention. It had been a surprise to everyone that she arrived
with a date; her colleagues were intrigued at how well she'd hidden
the existence of this good-looking fellow.

"She helped you!" Claire accused Jeff.

"Not a word," Meg said in his defense.

Jeff leaned forward, looking directly at Claire. "If you think you're
good at this, you don't know my mother. She played this game all my
life- and won against my dad every single time."

"He's a keeper!" shouted Lucy. "One of our kind."

"And this?" he asked, pointing to his fleece vest. Claire pounced on
the challenge before anyone else had a chance.

"Eighteen!" she shouted. "Including tax!"

Keith grinned at his wife. She loved a challenge.

"You kidding? That doesn't even cover the material! I'm 6'4", 220. This is not from the boy's department!"

No, you're certainly not a boy, thought Melissa, taking the longest sidelong glance she dared. He was built like one of those perfectly proportioned sculptures she'd studied in college…and his eyes, his smile. Much as she tried, it was nearly impossible to look away.

Jeff leaned back on the couch. "I think I've got this one."

Dan looked at the upstart and said, "You know, that looks a whole lot like the vest Lucy got for me on clearance from Land's End." The attorney nodded at her husband, allowing him to steal the glory.

"I say $24.50, shipping and tax included."

"On the button, so to speak," Jeff conceded, smiling. "Your wife and my mother seem to share the same talent — finding unbeatable sales online." At that, he got up and courteously excused himself.

He'd barely left the room when the game came to a sudden halt, the ladies of Bennett and Birnbaum pouncing on Meg with their multitude of questions. Wasn't he cute? Where had she met him? Who introduced them? How long had they been dating? Why hadn't she told them? What about this company he said he worked for? Did he make any money? Could this be the one? In the midst of the inquisition, Meg asked for a time-out.

Lucy glanced down the hallway. "Relax, I think he's still in the bathroom. You think you could get away with it, just waltzing in here with that on your arm, without penalty? You got lots of 'splainin' to do, missy!"

Andi was cuddled up in Steve's lap, finishing a slice of anniversary cake. She made one observation: "Too good-looking. Must be gay."

"Oh no, I'm not taking that bait, honey," Meg said. "I'm not giving out any details on that score!"

"Why doesn't anyone ever mistake me for gay?" Dan asked. "I'm a good-looking guy. Fine, even."

"I always thought so," said Keith.

"So, what did I miss? Who won the game?" Jeff asked as he reappeared.

"We voted you Rookie of the Year," Lucy said, wondering how much of their conversation he'd overheard.

"Enough with the party games," said Ruby. "We need to get down to the nitty-gritty. Andi, what's up with your next-door neighbor? She waltzed in here with some attitude! Her poor husband. Tell me she isn't always like that."

Andi laughed, as she put her arm around Steve. "Are you talking about the shrill part or just the nudgy part?"

"Pick, pick, pick. That's what I'm talking about."

"That marriage is a train wreck waiting to happen," added Meg. "When they're bad, you can smell 'em a mile a way."

"I don't know how he stands it," Andi admitted. "I expect he'll be someone's client one of these days."

Meg laughed. "Maybe ours. But don't be so sure it's all her. There's bound to be something wrong with him, also. After all, elephants don't marry giraffes. There's a reason we always say that."

Lucy nodded in agreement. "And it's easier for us to spot. In our line of work, I think we develop radar for bad marriages."

"I like your line of work," said Dan. "It's been great for us. You spend all day looking at screwed-up relationships and the worse the husbands behave, the better I look!"

"Works for me, too," Keith said. "When she gets home, she practically kisses my feet — and all I do is take out the garbage!"

Claire looked at her husband in horror. "Kiss your feet? In your dreams! That's for your next wife."

Amanda Gray, unsmiling, stood just outside the family room while Bette was finishing up at the sink. In Andi's estimation, Ms. Gray had been trying to put an end to the festivities for quite some time. She'd finally won. The hostess tried to sneak into the kitchen to conclude her business with the helpers, but her guests picked up on the clue. Rising and stretching, they agreed it was time to get going. As Lucy headed for the kitchen carrying some of the glasses, she overheard the workers express their concern about making it to the train.

"Andi, we're going right by the station, so we can drop them off, no sweat," she offered. Dan seconded the motion. He'd already grabbed his and Lucy's coats, hoping they could get back home in time for him to prepare for his next day's meetings. Andi accepted their suggestion. Though she would have preferred to schmooze all night with her good friends, she was glad for their help with her final chore of the day. She watched the couple dash off with the two workers.

***

Lucy was behind the wheel, not that Dan was woozy, but just because they both knew she had a special talent for getting people where they had to go precisely on time. And she was the maven of shortcuts in the area. As she drove along, she pretended to chat with Dan, but was actually intent on listening to the conversation going on between the two women in the backseat.

During the evening, Andi had pulled her partner aside to remind her that Amanda Gray was one of the housekeepers they'd seen over at the Brockhurst memorial, and in fact, the person who'd chased Denise Burden out into the cold. Apparently, Ms. Gray recognized Andi, yet, as Lucy was glad to see, nothing in her manner suggested that she recalled ever having seen Lucy before. Her motive in offering a ride to the workers was not confined to helping her partner. Even the smallest bit of information as to what was going on at the Brockhurst mansion would be like gold to her.

From what Lucy could glean, the two women were comparing the length of their respective journeys home, then moved on to some annoyances concerning the agency, then to the benefits of being unattached. This was a rare opportunity.

"Uh, ladies, sorry to interrupt but I know someone who might be in need of some help coming up. Any of you ever worked a really high-end party? I mean like socialites, diplomats?"

Bette launched into a long story about a job she'd handled in Greenwich, an evening fete on the Sound. She handed Dan her business card from the agency.

Amanda spoke up next. "Well, I've done a lot of work at the big venues, the Hamptons, debutante balls, that sort of thing. And snobby places, like Laurel Hall."

"I'll take your card, too, if it's okay," Lucy suggested. Amanda passed her own card forward. Lucy thanked them both, and then turned to Dan, feigning a sudden interest in the details of his upcoming week. But she'd started the motor running in the backseat. Lucy was pleased to see the ladies' chatter turn to the subject she'd hoped.

"Laurel Hall? I thought that place was in the news a while back," Bette said. "You worked there?"

"Just got out, actually. I feel like I escaped a madhouse! Big snobby name they've got over there. But let me tell you…a bunch of nut jobs." It made her smile, just to say it out loud. Those bitches had stabbed her in the back. Teresa and Bridgette, ganging up on her when it was she who'd run through the snow like a maniac trying to get help, while the real culprit was let off the hook. And after everything, Vivian Brockhurst had the nerve to blame it on her, without even giving her a chance to explain. She just threw her out like a piece of trash. It was all over in one lousy phone call, all her high hopes dashed. "Your services are no longer needed here." What a load of crap!

"I saved the kid's life and they gave me the boot. Can you believe it?"

"You saved the kid?"

"The daughter. She got into something and ended up in the hospital. But if I hadn't found her when she passed out, she'd be as dead as a doornail."

Lucy glanced in her rearview mirror. Dan was going on about his schedule for the week, a speech he was going to be giving, but his wife's ear was glued to the talk in the backseat. She eased up on the pedal. She wanted enough time to hear everything Amanda had to say. The hell with the train. If she had to drive each one of them straight to their front door, she'd do it.

"She was passed out, had to get her stomach pumped, the whole nine yards."

"What did she eat?"

"God only knows, but it wasn't from dinner. I ate everything she did, and more of it, you can be sure. They thought it was something from the medicine cabinet in her father's room, but I don't buy that.

She's just a little kid, too short to get up that high, and I didn't see anything moved around like a stool or a chair. No, she got into something else…"

"Like what?" Bette asked, breathlessly.

"I don't know, but her father had a pretty wild party going on. Really out of control, know what I mean? My thought was he left something around the house."

Dan had become aware of the conversation. As he stopped to listen, Amanda fell silent.

"You better step on it, or they'll miss the train," Dan cautioned, noting that Lucy had brought the car to a crawl.

There was to be no more from Amanda. The only words exchanged during the remainder of the short trip were between Lucy and Dan, wondering aloud what the boys were up to and taking bets on whether or not they'd both done their homework. The Lexus and the train pulled up into the station at the same moment. With a few quick words of thanks, the women bolted from the car and flew to the platform, glad to make the 9:05.

"Was that what I think it was about?" Dan asked as they started for home.

"The Brockhurst saga continues."

"That was about those kids?"

"Sure was. And I just got some incredible dirt on the case, all on a trip to the station. Could be one of the most worthwhile rides I've ever given."

She didn't want to bother Andi, but it was too important. She pressed her number on the car speed dial and waited for an answer. "It's incredible I was able to hear anything over your recitation of your calendar for next week," she said to Dan, and laughed.

"No, I should get the credit," he said. "If I hadn't been yapping, she would have stopped talking a lot sooner."

"Fair enough."

Andi answered the phone, and let out a victory whoop that could have woken the dead. Her children rolled over in their beds, but slept blissfully on.

CHAPTER THIRTY-SEVEN

While the principals in the Brockhurst case were unable to get much sleep, each of them arrived at the courtroom of Judge Thorpe at 9:00 a.m. sharp, along with their respective counsel. Even Nick, in recognition that this might be the seminal moment in the matter, made it his business to be punctual. Gary Vaughn was confident as to what the DNA testing would reveal, yet his nerves were as frayed as the others. Lucy had explained to him on more than one occasion that even if he was found to be Beau's biological father, that still didn't mean the judge would let him into the custody case.

Everett sat at the back of the courtroom, distractedly reading through the morning's emails on his smart phone. Lucy Bennett was, once again, making his life miserable. He'd been angry to hear about Skippy's supposed affair, but he couldn't really believe she'd been unfaithful to him. In those days, she'd loved being a Brockhurst. She never would have jeopardized her position by doing something so foolish. He would have known if his wife had been cheating on him. He was positive that he was the boy's father, although he'd never really cottoned to the role. Children simply bored him, but it didn't mean that Beau wasn't his.

Vivian sat quietly looking through notes she'd kept about the meetings with Arthur, reviewing the various issues the lawyer had highlighted. She appeared composed despite her inner turmoil. Rather than talking with her son, she kept her thoughts to herself. If called upon, she was ready to make her position clear and to encourage her son to make the right decisions.

And then there was Georgina, at loose ends. She was still unable to believe that her sister might have fooled around. Wouldn't she have revealed something of this magnitude to her? Hadn't they been the closest of sisters? And if for some unimaginable reason her sister had hidden this fact from her, but later discovered that Gary was Beau's father, there'd be no question she would have told her.

The day at the Frick Museum came back to her, when they had renamed one another. Doris and Charlie had refused to let Georgina visit New York City on her own, although their daughter pointed out that she wouldn't be alone. After all, she was going to be traveling along with the entire art class. Nevertheless, since she was barely sixteen, her parents insisted that the two sisters go on the trip together, and found the money to make it happen.

The girls had wandered through the Frick mansion, falling behind the group of art students as they all toured the museum together. For that one day, it seemed to Georgina that Suzanne actually showed an interest in artwork, so she was in no hurry to move her along with the others. The sisters stood for a time admiring the paintings in the dining room of the mansion, stopping before the lovely painting of Lady Skipwith in her fancy hat. Georgina remarked that the elegant young woman had a bit of Suzanne's likeness.

"And that's you, Gina," Suzanne chuckled as she walked just a bit to the right and gazed at what seemed to be the matching portrait. "Lady Taylor," Georgina said, reading the faded title. It was from that time on that they referred to one another as Lady Skipwith and Lady Taylor, to the amusement of their parents. A year later, when Georgina was helping her sister move her things into her college dorm, their pet names were overheard. For several days, the fellow freshman girls on the floor continued to address Suzanne as Lady Skipwith, but it was soon abbreviated to "Skippy" and the name stuck. In some ways, Georgina felt she'd helped recreate her sister. She'd shared her most intimate secrets with her, remaining close until the day she died. Yet, she was now expected to believe that her sister would not have told her about an affair. It couldn't be.

She could see the culprit from the corner of her eye, as he sat seemingly engrossed in a paperback. She recognized him from the memorial. He was the one who'd made trouble with Ron, something about Beau's pitching. Just being in the same room with him upset her.

On the other hand, she was no fan of Everett's, the man sitting silently on the other side of the room alongside his mother. To anyone else, she thought, he'd pass for normal, but she knew too much. The thought crossed her mind that it wouldn't be such a dreadful thing if it turned out he wasn't Beau's father. But in that case, she wondered, how would all of it impact Beau? And Emma? And what did she know about Gary Vaughn? She braced herself for the possibility that she'd now have to fight him as well as Everett. The whole business sickened her.

Before she left, Ron told her to stop wasting time worrying about it when it was clear what the outcome would be: the court was going to grant her custody of both children. Vaughn was a complete stranger, Everett was a rotten father, and she was the aunt they'd always known. He didn't seem surprised at all that Skippy might have cheated on her husband, and, in fact, made some rather unkind remarks about her. Ron, of all people, to be the judge of character.

The parties waiting in Judge Thorpe's courtroom had all managed to sit as far away from one another on the benches as they could. Yet Georgina could see all the lawyers standing together, chatting amiably. Her attorney and Lucy Bennett seemed to be cutting up over some joke with one of the court officers. Their laughter seemed inappropriate. Lawyers were a funny breed. Remarkable, she thought, how they could seem so friendly, yet turn on one another as soon as they began their presentations to the judge. She hoped Nick DeBello would have the upper hand when it came down to it.

The court officer entered through a small doorway behind the judge's bench and called out, "Attorneys on Brockhurst. Is everyone here and ready to go?" All three lawyers answered in the affirmative and moved up to the front of the courtroom to join the court officer. Georgina and the others watched from their respective locations in the courtroom as their lawyers disappeared behind the doorway.

"Good morning, everyone," Judge Thorpe began, greeting the attorneys as they entered his chambers. "Rather than keep the suspense going any longer, I've asked Sandra to bring in the DNA results we received from the lab and open the report right in front of you."

Inviting the law secretary into the room, the judge tried to lighten the mood. "Here's the woman of the hour! You've never been in so much demand, have you?"

Sandra entered the room with a brown manila envelope in hand.

"Okay, let's get this done. What've you got for us?"

The law secretary opened the envelope and flipped to the last page of the report, which contained the answer everyone was seeking. The attorneys sat motionless as Sandra read silently through the conclusion.

"Well," she said at last, "it says here there's a ninety-seven percent likelihood that Gary Vaughn is Beau Brockhurst's father. Do you want me to read any more of the report, Judge?"

"No, thanks. I think the lawyers have just heard all that they're interested in right now." He turned to the attorneys. "I've read your papers, and now that we have these results, is there anything any of you would like to add to your arguments at this time?"

As all of them started to speak at once, Judge Thorpe interrupted. "Why don't we start with ladies first? Lucy, go ahead."

"I think everyone is aware of my position. Everett Brockhurst has always had a substance abuse problem. He had it at the time of the divorce and he seems to have only gotten worse over the years. As indicated in detail in our reply papers, Everett's problem seems to have escalated to the point where he's having multiple narcotics prescriptions filled simultaneously at a variety of drugstores. And now, his drug habit has endangered Emma."

"Is this something new?" demanded Judge Thorpe. "I certainly didn't see anything about him endangering a child in anyone's papers." As he spoke, he looked directly at Arthur Post.

Lucy continued. "Judge, between the time we submitted our papers and today, it seems that Emma ended up in the emergency room quite ill because she got her hands on some of her father's drugs."

"Is this true, Mr. Post?"

"Your Honor, it's true that Emma visited the emergency room, but certainly Ms. Bennett cannot possibly have any direct knowledge of the events in question."

"Mr. Post, did the child get her hands on some drugs, be they prescription or nonprescription?"

"I believe those are the allegations, but they are just allegations."

"And wasn't she in your client's care and control at that time?"

"Well, yes, Your Honor."

Judge Thorpe did not look pleased. In actuality, he was even more displeased than he looked, since one of things he hated most was a surprise, particularly in a custody matter. He went into overdrive.

"Okay, that's it! I want an attorney for the child involved in this case as of today. I'm appointing Sarah Golden, who I think would be good with these children. They could use a motherly figure right now. Does anyone have a problem with that?"

Taken aback by the judge's swift action, everyone remained silent. The judge asked, "Ms. Bennett, did you finish what you wanted to say?"

"I'd just like to sum up by saying that we have some rather extraordinary circumstances here, Your Honor. We have a paternity test, telling us the identity of the biological father, another man who's a father in name only and who's never been much of a father to these children, and who has now allowed his substance abuse to endanger them."

"That's an allegation!" Arthur Post interjected, cut off by the judge, who responded in a terse monotone.

"We're all very clear on your position, Mr. Post."

"I apologize, Judge."

Judge Thorpe instructed Lucy to continue.

"Well, I think this boy, who's just lost his mother, is entitled to have the love of his biological father. I'm asking that you grant our application and join Gary Vaughn as a necessary party."

"Mr. DeBello, is there anything you would like to add?"

Nick was still processing the revelation about Emma, news he hadn't heard until moments earlier. He hesitated. Lucy was like a dog with a bone. If there was anything to uncover about Everett, she was going to find it. That was certainly going to be a help to Georgina's case. By letting Lucy into the case, however, he was signing up for a formidable adversary. He liked his odds better without her.

"Your honor, I agree with Ms. Bennett. There are extraordinary circumstances here. However, we have the children's aunt ready, willing and able to raise these children and there is absolutely no need to upset the apple cart and bring a person into the case who's a total stranger to the children. Further, Your Honor, Emma has no relationship whatsoever to Mr. Vaughn. Therefore, I can't imagine that it would be in either of the children's interest to learn that Beau has one father, and Emma has another. It is certainly not in the best interest of either child to allow Mr. Vaughn into the case."

Lucy was disappointed to hear Nick make one of his better arguments. The problem with her case was the fact that Gary and Emma were strangers in every sense of the word. She did not want Nick to have the final say on that issue. She also had an interesting idea that she felt might work in her favor.

"If I may, Your Honor…" Lucy started. The judge nodded at her, signaling that she could go on. "Allowing Gary Vaughn into this case is not determinative of the outcome. At this stage, you'd just be deciding that my client deserves to be a part of the process and that he's entitled to be heard. So, I'm asking that consistent with my moving papers, that you include Gary Vaughn in the custody matter and that you appoint a child psychologist to assist us all in determining the best way for this unusual set of circumstances to be handled. You've already appointed an attorney for the child to represent Beau, so I can dispense with that request."

Arthur Post spoke up. "Your Honor, I don't see why we need a psychologist, since the child's attorney can handle whatever's necessary."

"Sarah Golden is just like you or me, Arthur," Lucy interrupted. "She isn't trained at all to deal with something as complicated as this. We need a professional, a psychiatrist or psychologist who would not only be equipped to help these children, but who is capable of deciding whether to introduce Gary Vaughn as Beau's father."

"The judge hasn't even decided to let your client in, Ms. Bennett, and you're telling us who else we should include in this mess?"

"Let's face it," said Lucy, "no matter what we do here, someday Beau is going to find out that Gary Vaughn is his biological father.

None of us can stop that from happening. But if you let my client into the case, then he's subject to the judge's orders; Gary would be told what he could tell Beau and when. That's exactly why I'm asking for the psychologist, to help us determine the best time and manner for revealing something potentially so upsetting."

Judge Thorpe listened closely to Lucy's approach to the matter, and was struggling. A son needed the love of his father. From what he knew, Everett was the boy's father in name only. And now the child had a shot at a caring father, but at what cost? Further trauma? Was it fair for him to force the boy to deal with it now, on the heels of this mother's death? After all, there was the mother's sister, who both of the children knew and loved. Wouldn't she be the simplest solution? Then again, thought the judge, even if he allowed Mr. Vaughn into the case, he could still choose to give the children to the aunt in the end. Wouldn't he just be preserving his options by adding Gary Vaughn into the mix, and wouldn't this give him a measure of control over him?

"I'm inclined to let Mr. Vaughn be joined as a necessary party. However, under these very unusual circumstances, this court would like to appoint its own mental health expert to get an advisory opinion as to the ramifications of inviting Gary Vaughn into this boy's life. Ms. Bennett, this is not exactly what you asked for. I'm appointing an expert not as a treating or consulting therapist for the boy, but someone who will examine the circumstances and report to me on the pros and cons of allowing Gary Vaughn into this boy's life at this time. If he advises that this should occur now, then I'm asking him to recommend how it's to be done. Of course his advice won't be binding but I sure want to hear what an expert has to say. So, I'm appointing Dr. Alan Sundgren as the court's expert. Counsel, I recognize that this is unusual, but the Court is supposed to act as *parens patriae* and I want to do all I can to get this right.

"I'd like all three of your clients to share the costs of the attorney for the child and expert at this preliminary stage. In the meantime, until I get more information from them, this is how I want to do things. Will this be on consent or do I need to render a decision?"

Lucy wanted clarification. "Judge, so you're reserving your decision on whether you're letting my guy into the case?"

"Yes, I want to see what the expert says first, before I make a decision."

The lawyers eyed one another. None of them wanted to be the first to speak. Arthur held his tongue, since the Judge had seemed ready to jump down his throat. The attorney's primary concern was to avoid adding any further fuel to the fire now that the dangerous allegations about his client's drug behavior had been aired. Judge Thorpe could have referred the incident to the local prosecutor for further investigation and Arthur was well aware of it. From his earlier experiences with this judge, he knew he was unpredictable. His methods were often unorthodox, and as some would say, wacky. Normally, a judge would decide whether or not to join someone as a necessary party and then decide whether or not the case required the services of a psychiatrist or other expert. In this case, the judge was making the parties pay for an expert to essentially make the decision for him.

Lucy stepped back. She had no role to play at this point. She watched as Arthur and Nick fell in line, indicating their consent to the judge's plans. For now, her foot remained in the door, and like the others, she'd have to wait for Dr. Sundgren to make a recommendation.

***

Lucy went directly from the conference in Judge Thorpe's chambers to the ladies' room and found it filled with women trying to shake off their soggy coats and take back some control of their windswept hairdos. The unrelenting storm had wreaked havoc all morning with the appearance of anyone daring to cross the courthouse's vast parking field. Umbrellas were useless against the vicious wind and rain. In fact, a pile of broken umbrellas filled the garbage cans at the entrance of the Supreme Court building.

Seeing the mob of women in the bathroom, Lucy thought of rushing down to the lawyers' private rest room, but noticed Georgina. She was standing there at the mirror, washing her hands. Lucy waited for another person to step away from the next mirror, then moved to stand beside Georgina.

"Jesus! It's a miracle they gave me any respect in there, looking like this!" Lucy exclaimed, pulling a brush out of her bag.

Georgina glanced over and to Lucy's surprise, didn't snub her.

"Your hair is naturally curly, so it's fine."

"Yeah? You people with straight hair just don't get it. A little rain and I suddenly have a mop like Carrot Top! And I thought I took care of it before I walked into court." The room was starting to empty out, and Georgina was taking an inordinately long time at the hand dryer.

She wants to talk, thought Lucy.

Sure enough, Georgina came back to the mirror, this time taking out some lip gloss.

"You know Lucy, I haven't had a chance to talk to you since…" she broke off, awkwardly.

"I know, Georgina, and I'm sorry — but under the circumstances, with you being represented by counsel, I'm just not ethically permitted to speak with you directly."

"Well, I really didn't want to talk about the case. I'm just trying to sort out a few things in my mind."

"As long as we're not discussing the matter itself, I suppose I can listen to what you have to say. I can't answer anything for you, since the rules of ethics are pretty strict. Whatever happens, I can't violate confidentiality, and I can't give you answers."

Lucy's warning did not dissuade Nick DeBello's client from doing what she wanted to do. The room seemed to be empty, so Georgina felt she could speak. "I read the will. And I have to say, I was angry to find out I wasn't mentioned at all regarding guardianship of the children. It makes no sense. Skippy and I always said we'd be there to take care of each other's kids if something happened to either of us. Divorce or no divorce, she knew I'd be there to raise the children. She didn't care what the law said, she wanted me to take care of them, not Everett. Since you wrote the will, I thought maybe you made a mistake and left out what she and I agreed on. Or then, I wondered if maybe Skippy changed her mind without telling me. Or if she felt somehow I just wasn't up to the task…"

Lucy, looking straight at her, was obliged to be silent.

Georgina felt that if she hit upon the correct reason, the attorney would show some indication, some change in her expression, but her countenance remained unchanged. So, it hadn't been an oversight. She'd been deliberately left out of the will, and not because her sister doubted she could handle the job. Her heart sank as she realized the likely reason. She was about to come out with it, but hesitated. If she was guessing correctly, would Lucy use it against her somehow? Could saying it hurt her chances of gaining custody? The answer she needed to hear was far more important to her than the case itself.

If Lucy confirmed what Georgina had begun to recognize, it would be shattering. Her sister's opinion meant everything to Georgina, and after her death, seemed almost sacred. And the only one who might know Skippy's mind on this particular issue was standing right next to her.

"It was about Ron, wasn't it?" she continued in a sad and quiet tone. "You didn't make a mistake, did you? Skippy told you not to make me the guardian because of him. That's what you can't tell me."

The slight tilt to the attorney's head, the lift of her eyebrows told Georgina she had guessed correctly.

Without a word between them, the damage was done. The confirmation shook her. It brought her back to the basketball game and all that had occurred there. And Cliff's behavior on the bus, his bullying. In the resulting meeting at school, the principal asked her and Ron directly: was anything going on at home that might be affecting their child? This sort of behavior, he said, "didn't come out of thin air."

Sitting beside her husband, she had offered no explanation. Though she'd begun to question the way Ron interacted with the children, and was alarmed by the intensity of his recent outbursts, the words remained stuck in her throat. She could barely admit it to herself; her husband's temper was changing all of them. Was this what Skippy had seen before anyone else, the impact he was having on the boys? Was this why her sister would not entrust her children to the Fiske family? And, if so, what did it say about her own judgment, her willingness to ignore what needed to be dealt with at home?

"Well, if my sister didn't want Ron's influence on her children, then I'd have to think about honoring her wishes."

Lucy was shocked; it was practically a concession.

"But if not me, then who else should it be? Not Everett. He's worse now than he was at the time of the divorce. He was always a lousy father and a big drinker. But now, according to your court papers, he's added prescription drug abuse on top of it. And I can't imagine what else my attorney's going to find out about him. Even without this new information, we both know Skippy would never have wanted Everett raising them. Then there's my folks, but they're not leaving Henryetta. Dad's business is there and he'd never leave it. It's all they have. And it's the last place on earth Skippy and I wanted our children to be — back in the town we both escaped from."

Lucy was memorizing every word Georgina had to say about the other potential candidates.

"And I guess, there's Vivian and Hugh. They're not bad people, but you have to admit, they're cold as ice. You can't say affection comes naturally to them, and that's what the children need now more than ever. And, to have a son who's so dysfunctional…well, that doesn't come out of thin air." The words used by the principal bounced back at her off the tiled walls.

Georgina realized that her own attorney was waiting for her back in the courtroom, where he intended to return after handling another matter.

"But this Gary Vaughn character…no matter what the DNA says, it's not fair to let a total stranger into the children's lives. That's one thing I know for sure. Skippy would never have wanted that." This time, she didn't look to the attorney's face for answers. There was no further reason to do so, since Nick DeBello was now available to tell her everything he'd just learned in the conference, including what the DNA results showed. What she needed from Lucy Bennett, she'd already gotten.

"Goodbye," said Georgina. She turned and left the room.

Lucy had listened closely. The same thoughts had run through her mind, but with all she knew and couldn't divulge, Lucy's assessment of the various contenders was far different from Georgina's. Both of them were worried about what was best for the kids, but for Lucy, that was exactly why she had chosen to represent Gary. Yes, he was a stranger to the two children, but as someone who'd always been dedicated to his daughters, he was likely to be a positive influence on Beau and Emma. Skippy had considered that as well, and so had said to go ahead with the DNA testing. It was unfortunate, thought the attorney, that she couldn't reveal this fact to Georgina. It might have saved her a great deal of angst.

Vivian, one of the only women who actually followed through when announcing she had to go and powder her nose, closed her compact with a snap and left the back stall of the ladies' room a little wiser than she'd been a few minutes earlier. As always, her timing was impeccable.

CHAPTER THIRTY-EIGHT

The first thing she noticed was his five o'clock shadow. That was bad enough, but beyond that was the creased black sports jacket along with the apparent decision to pair it with a navy tie. And then there was his hair that appeared to have gone through a wind tunnel. Thank God we're not meeting at the Club, she thought. It was the end of a workday, so perhaps it was possible he'd not had a chance to freshen up – or so it seemed, to even take a look in the mirror. His disheveled appearance did nothing to assuage Vivian's concerns about the man who might, by a twist of fate, end up at the helm of her grandchildren's lives.

"You must be Mrs. Brockhurst." Gary stretched out his hand to Vivian. He had seen her at the memorial and then, in court, but hadn't caught the entire effect. He almost blushed as he felt her eyes bore through him, her jaw set square as a boxer's. The woman exuded power, even in repose. Looking into her green eyes he could also see the beauty, a thing totally unexpected. She brought to mind a faded film star, still glamorous, regal, perfectly put together.

"Sorry my hand's so cold," he apologized. "I've been on-site all afternoon, and came straight over to make it on time."

"Cold hands, warm heart," Vivian returned, unsmiling. She noticed a little scar above his cheek, a few deep lines across his brow. That was all she was able to discern upon scanning his features for any obvious trouble that might be written there.

"Yeah, warm heart," Gary said, hazarding a smile as he moved onto the seat across from her in the private booth. With her eagle eyes still on him, he realized that this meeting might turn out to be even more grueling than his past two hours arguing with that sleazy bunch of bastards at Gold Cove Development. But at least he knew how to handle them. Vivian Brockhurst posed a bigger challenge.

A waitress appeared. Gary, noticing the glass of red wine set before Vivian, asked for the same.

"Mr. Vaughn," Vivian started.

"No, call me Gary, please."

"Gary," she continued. "It's good to meet you." Her face said otherwise. "We do have an awkward situation, as you know, and I thought we could iron out a few things just by talking face to face."

"My thoughts, exactly." Why, he wondered, did he feel she already had the upper hand?

"Beau and Emma are of paramount concern to us. Hugh and I expect to be very involved, no matter how this turns out. We've advised Arthur Post to do whatever necessary to see that we have at least as much time with the children in the future as we do now."

"Of course," Gary said. "That's perfectly understandable. I'd have no objection to that."

"Well, depending on how this goes, you may have no real say in the matter." Vivian's lips turned up ever so slightly at the edges, as though toying with her prey.

"I guess that's true for you, too." Gary was beginning to get a better read on the lady. "At least I have a crack at becoming a principal in the battle. Are you throwing your hat into the ring, as well?"

"I don't need to. Everett and I are of one mind."

"Well, I suppose the judge could make decisions we both would have to live with, but it's not going to stop me from doing everything within my power to have Beau in my life."

"I have to ask you, Mr. Vaughn — Gary. What made you decide to stake a claim to this boy, when you knew it could hurt him so badly?"

Gary stared back at her. She certainly knew how to go for the jugular. The waitress set down a glass of wine before him. He took a long sip and let Vivian's words hang in the air a bit longer than she might have liked. "I wouldn't have pursued this if I thought it would hurt Beau... or Emma. I'm sorry if that's how you see it."

"Well, what I see is that you're willing to put your own interests first, no matter what damage is done. You want to get what you think is yours, and deal with the consequences later. I see that as selfish, if you want to know the truth."

"So, just forget I have a son? Get on with my life, and let your son raise mine?" Gary felt his heart start to race, then realized that a person had approached their table, and it wasn't the waitress.

"Viv! Sorry to interrupt! What a surprise to see you here!" The petite brunette leaning over the table had just overstepped all acceptable bounds with Vivian, starting with the abbreviation of her name.

Lord in heaven, thought Vivian, she'd picked out the restaurant for the precise reason that it was located in no-man's land, up north of Sloatsville, an area not frequented by any of her acquaintances. And now Margot Baynes' perky face was directly in hers, the travel agent addressing her by a nickname she despised.

"Yes, I'm up to see the grandchildren." Vivian responded, shortly.

"Oh, I hadn't heard from you in the longest time, and …gee, I heard about your daughter. So, so very sorry."

Vivian was too annoyed to point out that it had been her daughter-in-law.

Glancing at Gary, Margot proceeded to stick her other foot in it. "And this must be your son!" The sympathy in Margot's voice continued, unabated.

"No, I'm afraid I'm not her son." Gary broke in before Vivian could answer. He'd seen her look of dread, and though bemused by her reaction, carefully smothered his smile. "I'm afraid we're in the middle of a business meeting," he said, and stared up into the eyes of the pretty intruder. He said nothing else.

The silence did its work. "Oh, I see, of course. Excuse me, really. Well, Viv, I'll be in touch…hope to get together real soon!" She gave a little wave as she moved off, though she would have liked to stay and get the real scoop.

Private booth, red wine. What a hunk her fellow was, with those fierce, dark eyes. *Makes sense*, she thought, *that Viv Brockhurst would be the ultimate cougar.* And now, what an opportunity to help the pair arrange some travel plans that would assure them a lot more privacy than they had out here in the open. She entered a note into her Blackberry to reach "VB/ASAP."

"My travel agent," Vivian explained after Margot returned to her table. The only one who's ever..."

"...called you Viv." Gary completed the sentence with a chuckle.

It was then that Vivian saw the resemblance. The funny lop-sided grin, the pronounced dimple. It was Beau's very smile.

"You make a poor 'Viv', I'm afraid."

"I never was one, and I never hope to be one!" Mrs. Brockhurst agreed, a smile forcing its way up to the surface. They each took a large sip of wine, and eased back into their respective seats. Regarding one another, each recognized a thaw. "Well, Gary, in the remote event that you somehow prevail in your efforts, how would you possibly propose to take care of two little children...while handling that all-consuming career of yours?"

"All-consuming?"

"You think I haven't read your papers? You describe yourself as the county's top architect."

"Among the top..." Gary interrupted.

"As I said, how could you handle that and the lives of two children who have just lost their mother?"

"I'm not sure you realize that I had joint custody of my daughters. I did what I think was a great job with them while building my career. And now that I'm established, it's a lot easier. There are busy days like today, don't get me wrong, but I've got more free time than I did back then."

Vivian was silent.

"On a day like today, I'd be only too glad to come home to those two kids. I've just spent several hours again dealing with the gang over at Gold Cove and their plans for the Bay."

"Peacock Bay? Everett said they'd given up on the project." It was a topic Vivian was concerned about, since the same company had been trying to develop several acres not far from Laurel Hall.

"Not at all. I've been working with them for over two — no, make that three years, and every time we're about to move ahead, there's another change. Now they're pushing some type of restaurant-barge out over the water, like that will ever off get off the ground. Everyone knows the approval's only been given for condos and a mini-mall. I'll tell you right now, Vivian, I'm off the project if they keep pushing for the barge."

"Don't give me that, Mr. Vaughn, you'll follow the money, especially if you end up with two young children on your hands. Let me tell you, it will cost you a pretty penny to raise Beau and Emma." Realizing what she'd said, she added, "If you were ever lucky enough to get the chance."

Gary, who had been fiddling with his wallet, set photos of his three daughters out on the table. "They're pretty annoyed with me right now," he muttered.

"Pretty girls," Vivian admitted as she took a close look at each picture.

"They'd agree with you. They think I'm being selfish."

Vivian put the pictures back on the table and said nothing.

"They think I just want the son I never had."

"And isn't that so?"

"Partly, yes. But really, the biggest thing for me is this. I loved my old man, and I can't imagine having gone through life without him. That's the kind of father I want to be to Beau." Gary took the last sip of his wine and leaned back. "You know, on one of my hikes with my Dad when I was just about Beau's age, he sat me down on a rock and tried to have a man to man talk with me. I was too young to understand what he was trying to say. He said, 'Gary, you know I'd do anything in the world for you. 'Yes, Dad, I know you would,' I answered. 'Well, son,' he said, 'if a person was standing there with a gun, about to shoot you, you know what I'd do, don't you?' I tried to imagine the situation, and I thought I knew what my Dad would do."

Gary started to chuckle, then went on. "So I said, 'Yeah, I know what you'd do. You'd shove that man out of the way so he couldn't shoot me!' I thought that was a pretty good answer. Dad started getting steamed at me. He said, 'No, you don't get the point!' 'What point?' I asked. I was so confused, I just wanted to give him the right answer and show him I was smart. 'Let's try it, again,' he said. 'You're standing there, and I'm next to you and a man is going to fire a bullet at you. What would I do?' I thought about it again and told him, 'You'd get that man and grab his gun!' 'No!' he shouted. 'I'd take the bullet for you! I'd stand in between you and the gun, and take the shot instead of you!' 'Why would you do that?' I said."

Gary looked at Vivian. The arch of her brows told him he had her full attention. He allowed a dramatic pause before going on.

"My father had lost it altogether by that point. 'Because I love you!' he said. 'I'd take the bullet for you! It's symbolic!' So I said, 'Why would you go get shot when you could just stop the man instead?' At that point, my Dad looked very disappointed with me. That was his first attempt at a father-son talk, and I really can't recall him ever trying it again. Wasn't 'til years later that I remembered that day and what Dad was actually trying to say to me."

Vivian shook her head and smiled, seeing Gary Vaughn as far less the enemy she'd imagined just an hour before.

"You think we should order?" he suggested. "I've heard their lasagna Bolognese is out of this world. Even better than mine."

"Oh, and he cooks too?" remarked Vivian as she finally opened the menu.

"I have a lot of hidden talents," Gary answered, flirting.

Absorbed in the menu, Vivian barely heard him. She seemed to have found her appetite.

CHAPTER THIRTY-NINE

"**H**ey. Mom, what do you know about Indian divorces?"

Lucy could barely hear her son's words with all the noise in the background.

"God, I thought there was something wrong! Isn't this your lunch period?"

"Mom, I'm sitting here with Rahme and he said his aunt's in some kind of trouble 'cause his uncle went and got a divorce and now she's living at Rahme's and…don't Indian divorces have something to do with going around in circles?"

Ruby buzzed in that she had Andi on the line, but first, Lucy had to get this right with her son. Clearly, he'd overheard some discussion she must have had with Dan comparing divorce laws of different countries. She'd probably mentioned the kind of divorce that required a person to simply walk around in a circle, repeating the words, "I divorce thee" three times, and that was that. No lawyers, no fees, no rights. Apparently, what Jake had heard made an impression on him. He'd filed this little tidbit in his young and empty memory bank, until it came up for use.

"Jake, listen to me. This isn't something you should be talking about with Rahme. If his aunt needs to reach me, remind Rahme of my office number and I'll be glad to talk with her. But I don't want you in the middle of something like this, okay, honey? I have to go now. Is everything else all right?"

"Yup. Hey, those are mine, get outta here…!" Jake's words faded away into the general commotion around him.

Lucy was glad to know he was back to what he should be doing: horsing around with his buddies instead of talking nonsense about divorce. The boys knew next to nothing about the subject, and she purposely kept it that way. There was no discussion in front of them about the particulars of any case, to ensure the clients' confidentiality and to protect the children from the subject matter itself. Now and then, the boys asked questions about her work and at those times, she enjoyed speaking about what she did for a living and explaining the law in its most simplistic terms.

For the most part, Jake and Adam seemed to be interested in her job as a source of bragging rights; their mom was like the lawyer on "The Good Wife." Lucy was unaware that the inspiration for Rahme's inquiry was her son's claim that his mother "kicked ass in court."

Lucy put down one line and picked up the other.

"I wrote down everything I could of Sundgren's report— not only the highlights, but the whole goddam conclusion!" Andi told Lucy, who appreciated what a chore it was to do the writing.

The reason for the handwritten account was the court's unwillingness to give out copies of the printed reports themselves after what had occurred in the case of *Hassell v. Hassell*. Mrs. Hassell's lawyer had received from the court the forensic expert's printed report and evaluation concerning Mrs. Hassell and her then husband. The lawyer sent the report to Mrs. Hassell for her review and comments, but instead of limiting herself to the attorney's instructions, she took it upon herself to fax the report to each and every one of her husband's business partners. It made for interesting reading, since the report spelled out John Hassell's hitherto secret dalliances with his partners' wives. Sylvia Hassell enjoyed her moment of catharsis, but the court was not pleased.

From that day forward, in any divorce court in the county, an expert's report would no longer be released to an attorney and would only be available for review at the courthouse. Lawyers could make as many notes as they wanted. Some, like Andi, preferred to take the time and write out the conclusion word for word. Having found out that the report was in and well aware of how important it was to Lucy, Andi had gone to Judge Thorpe's part to write out the important parts of the document.

Upon reviewing the report, she was maddened by its length. "It's a damn treatise!" she'd shouted at the law clerk as she started to scribble it down. She said the same thing to Lucy, when asked to repeat everything she'd copied.

"Look, I've got to get to Klark's before I get home. Sari needs new shoes for her school concert tonight, and I'm flat out of time. Why don't we meet at the shoe store and I'll go over the report with you, and get the shoes at the same time. And Lucy, they're having a huge sale, so it could be a good thing all around!"

"Like I have time to shop!" Lucy responded.

Still, it was hard to pass up the late winter sale at Klark's, when this could mean picking up boots close to half-price. The two partners had been looking for a way to knock Claire out as Discount Queen for the month and they both knew that this sale could do the trick. They always did particularly well at Klark's, its member discount card taking a prominent position in their respective wallets.

With a sigh, Lucy added, "You know I can't get out of here. And I need to know what's in that report."

"You'll find out as soon as I pick you up — and I promise we'll get there and back in a flash. Not to mention I just did you a big favor. And by the way, when was the last time you took a minute out of the office, even for lunch?"

Andi was right. Lucy rarely made an escape from the grind on a work day, and if she did, it was usually just an emergency trip for office supplies or to drop off her car for repairs.

"I know, my life sucks."

"So, get your coat and get ready, missy, 'cause you owe me one!"

"All right, all right, but I have to be back for my two o' clock."

No sooner had she hung up with Andi than Ruby buzzed in to announce that Mrs. Nixon was on the line. "And J.J. Brice is on hold," she added.

How the hell did Andi think she could swing a trip to the shoe store when she still hadn't caught a bathroom break all morning? "Tell Mrs. Nixon I'll be with her in a minute — and as for J.J., I know she has an appointment coming up, so I'd rather deal with her then."

"Yeah, I see that it's next Tuesday."

"Ruby, just handle it, okay?" Lucy glanced at her watch. Friday was always a killer. Hoping to keep it short, she picked up with Maryann Nixon.

"Hi, there, Lucy!" The client's voice struck Lucy as unusually cheery. "I thought I should give you a heads up about something. I'm going to Atlantic City for the weekend."

"Well, that's great," Lucy said, unable to imagine why her client thought this merited a call to her attorney.

"With Bruce."

Without flinching, Lucy spelled out her usual advice to a client planning to spend time with an intended "ex" right in the middle of a divorce.

"Maryann, I'm sure you've thought this through carefully, and you know I wish you well. Just be sure that you don't get talked into anything over the weekend." Lucy refrained from telling her what she was really thinking. While she thought there were some couples who should try to find a way to reconcile, she rarely saw that happen. Usually, one party misled the other into believing in a possibility of reconciling, while it was only sweet talk; what they were really doing was tricking the other into agreeing to a rotten deal. The typical line was that they could work things out as long as they could just stop fighting over every penny. The other spouse, wishing to keep the marriage alive, would soften his or her stance in the negotiations and go along with more lenient terms.

In this case, Bruce was probably looking for a better deal, aware that his great salesmanship was matched only by his wife's gullibility. Apparently, he guessed correctly that she still wanted to be married, despite all she'd been through with him. Either she really loved him, or it was for practical reasons: her house, her cars, her school district, her lifestyle. It was difficult to protect a vulnerable client like Maryann in this sort of situation, since Lucy had to leave room for the possibility of reconciliation, but had to ensure that the client didn't lower her guard. She was able to obtain the client's sworn promise to say nothing at all about the case while on her junket with Mr. Nixon.

"Ruby, take my calls. I'm going out for a minute!" The words struck her secretary as strange. Before she could respond, Lucy charged down the hallway toward the ladies room, nearly knocking Meg's papers out of her hands as she whisked past her. Meg and Ruby exchanged puzzled glances when, what seemed like moments later, Lucy dashed by them in the other direction with her coat and purse.

Stopping for a split second beside her secretary's desk, she announced that she was off to meet Andi. "Text me your orders, I'll pick up at Panera's!" she shouted as she flew out the back door, slamming it behind her.

"The garden salad!" Ruby called, but it was too late.

Meg caught a glimpse of the partners streaking by the office window in Andi's car. "Weird, or what?" she asked Ruby.

"Really weird," was the ready answer.

***

"Andi, slow down!" Lucy said. "I'd like to get there alive!"

"You're not gonna believe it," said the lawyer, easing up on the accelerator for a moment. "Check it out." A legal pad was set out on the dashboard with several pages covered by Andi's hurried script.

"What the hell, did you write this in Swahili?" Lucy began, but her partner cut her off.

"No complaints! I worked as fast as I could. The conclusion itself was five pages long."

Lucy skimmed through her partner's notes. "God, how many pages did the shrink need to say if Gary's in or out of the kid's lives? Tell me, Andi, what's the frigging answer already?"

Her partner continued tearing down the road, Lucy hanging on for dear life until they stopped at a light.

"Bottom line, he said he's in, but exactly how he thought this could happen, I'll tell you in the store. It's a bit convoluted because the doctor wants to be careful. The kids are fragile, with their mother having died, and he was trying to come up with a sensible way to reunite Beau with his real father."

Deciphering Andi's scrawl, Lucy's eyes lit up. "Holy shit!"

Andi took off once more, speeding down the road and making it through a yellow light, then swerving into the store parking lot. Lucy hadn't uttered another word. She sat in wonder, thrilled that her thoughts on the Brockhurst matter had been corroborated.

Like her, the forensic expert had been forced to struggle with the same questions about what was right for the children. Lucy faced the same issues from the outset, when forced to decide whether or not to represent Gary. She was extremely pleased that she and the expert doctor had reached the same conclusion, since she had seen other experts miss the point entirely or fall prey to deception by a wily, interested party. As sharp as he was, even Dr. Sundgren was capable of being snowed, on occasion. Anything was possible with the cast of characters in this case.

"What's the big emergency with these shoes, anyway?" Lucy asked as they rushed into the store.

"I told you, the concert's tonight and we bought the shoes a month ago but when Sari tried her outfit on last night, the damned shoes were too small! She's been texting me all morning 'cause I promised to get the next size and have them home in time."

As promised, Andi found the display, the correct shoes and an available cashier practically all at once, at the same time recounting to her partner what the expert psychiatrist had recommended. Dr. Sundgren wanted to introduce Gary into the children's lives, little by little, through normal activities, with a special event thrown in from time to time. Lucy was so engrossed in hearing about the report, she barely noticed the signs for the fabulous annual boot sale, though she did make a little mental note to return over the weekend.

The sales transaction was underway, the partners about to get in and out of a store in record time, when Lucy felt a tap on her shoulder.

"The other register," said Andi under her breath. Lucy took a furtive glance at the far register. There was Becky Slade, her voluminous hair piled high on her head as usual, the giant eyelashes casting a soft shadow over her Botoxed features. She looked particularly diminutive next to the tower of boot boxes stacked along the counter.

"Can you fucking believe it? Didn't she tell you at her last appointment that she was eighty-six thou in debt, and now it looks like she's buying …what? Seven pairs of boots? Can you count the boxes?" Andi added in a whisper, "Look. I'm gonna get a little bit closer and see what she's really got."

Lucy begged her partner, "Please, just don't let her see you."

Andi gave her the thumbs-up, pointed to the door and added, "Meet you there."

To her dismay, Lucy was left to handle the exchange of Sari's shoes, while Andi was off on her mission.

As the two caught up on the way out, Andi asked Lucy with a little grin, "So, which do you want to hear about first? The boots, or the rest of the shrink's report?"

"The boots of course, you idiot!"

Andi obliged, reading off the list like a who's who of expensive boots: "Jimmy Choo, Lanvin, Dior, Cavalli, Givenchy — oh, make that two, and I also think she had the ones you saw Sharri Alderon wearing in court, and said you wanted, but they were way out of your range."

"The Pradas?"

"Yeah. So I guess our client's over eighty-eight thou in the red by now."

"It's pitiful. If she wears those damned boots to her next appointment, I swear I'm going to stick 'em where the sun don't shine!" The two partners burst into laughter.

"Don't tell me this wasn't worth it!" Andi demanded. "We got to discuss the report, snag the shoes, see a client and pick up lunch, all in less time than it would take to get a Frappuccino!"

On their drive back to the office, after a quick stop at Panera, the two settled down and discussed the expert report, and how Dr. Sundgren might have reached his conclusion.

CHAPTER FORTY

Thursday at 2:00 p.m., the whole crew on the Kornblum case descended upon the offices of Bennett and Birnbaum. The clients and their respective attorneys were ready to meet for a conference, in Mort's words, to "hash it out." The previous day, Andi asked Melissa to join in on the four-way to get a glimpse of how such meetings were conducted.

Rather than the expected enthusiastic response, Andi was greeted with a wide smirk.

"Sorry, I just can't get used to that phrase." Melissa hoped her short explanation would suffice, but noting the look of puzzlement on her superior's face, she tried again. "The first week I started here, I was in your office while you were on speaker with Glen Ellers, and he suggested a four-way. Then he said something about a Hotel Excelsior, and…well, I started wondering if I was intruding in some really private conversation, except you looked so nonchalant chatting about it all, and with me sitting right there in front of you. So then I really started to wonder if this stuff was normal for you — like you had friends with a LOT of benefits."

Andi chuckled.

"You'd think it would be better to avoid using, I don't know, obscene terminology since after all, we're dealing with matrimonials," Melissa added.

"It really is pretty dumb," admitted Andi, "but it's just part of the jargon. And come to think of it, there've been a few times when I had to spell it out to a client, so there'd be no mistake! Well, whatever you want to call it, Melissa, I'd like you to be in on it."

She went on to explain the purpose of the four-way meeting in the Kornblum case, its purpose in facilitating settlement discussions and what sort of outcome they might expect. Melissa would learn a great deal just by sitting in on the meeting.

"Now, that's a beautiful shade!" Dina exclaimed as Felicia Kornblum stepped into the waiting room. After buzzing Andi to announce the arrival of the client, the receptionist asked, "And are those lowlights or highlights?"

This was exactly what the client was hoping to avoid; she didn't want to draw attention to the effort she'd put into her appearance. She just wanted Mr. Kornblum to wonder how he could have forgotten how beautiful she was. Her trip to the hair salon had been carefully timed to occur just before the meeting. Mr. Kornblum, however, was oblivious to his wife, absorbed as he was in the new issue of Golf Digest.

Before she could find a way out of an answer to the receptionist, the waiting room door opened and Andi ushered her in. She delivered the client to an empty office, to separate the couple. This arrangement was certainly not uncommon, since Andi and Lucy each had seen more than one waiting room confrontation sabotage a settlement meeting before it even got off the ground.

Andi ran back to grab hold of Glen Ellers, so they could spend a few minutes in a pre-conference meeting. Her adversary spoke candidly with her. As she anticipated, Glen had already advised his client that he'd made a mess for himself at his deposition, first as to the accuracy of the income he reported and second, by inadvertently crediting his wife with a significant contribution to his business success. Neither of them needed to make a living by milking a case and billing for hours of unnecessary litigation. The time was ripe, both attorneys agreed, to put an end to the disaster that was Kornblum v. Kornblum.

"Now, remember," Andi said to Melissa as the two walked down the hall toward the conference room, "all you have to do is watch. After all, it's your first four-way!"

"Don't get me started!" Melissa laughed.

Andi smiled. She had accomplished what she intended, to relax her intern so that she would appear natural rather than nervous. Her client would be on edge already, and wouldn't appreciate seeing a worried novice in the room. While she certainly knew how to lighten the mood, Andi anticipated a very serious meeting, since the Kornblum case had to be settled. Mort simply had too much at risk, and needed to make a deal happen.

Dina had straightened up the conference room. She set out the freshly baked chocolate chip cookies she'd been instructed to bring in that morning. Andi invited Mort and Glen into the room and seated them next to one another on one side of the table. Then, as instructed, Melissa brought Felicia into the room. Andi took her seat at the table opposite Glen and motioned to Felicia and Melissa to sit beside her. After everyone was situated, Andi began with some introductory remarks.

"The purpose of this meeting is to see what we can do to try to resolve this matter without being forced to have a judge make a decision. I think I can speak for Glen and myself when I tell you both that we think parties are happier making their own deals. Otherwise, you have someone who's met you for a few hours or days deciding your whole future. Especially in this case, with all that's come out, I doubt that's something either of you would want to risk. And remember, whatever's said here in our conference cannot be used in court in any way, should we fail to reach an agreement. We want you to feel free to speak and offer your thoughts. I do have one important rule, though: you are not to be rude to one another. I, of course may be rude to Glen. You know I'm just kidding, buddy."

He smiled very slightly, but just enough to let Andi know he appreciated her familiarity.

"Is there anything you want to add?"

"Thanks. Folks, I agree with everything Ms. Birnbaum has said so far, which is not so common among adversaries. Really, the point is we can keep this case going and believe me, we will both make money that way. But settlement in a case like this is something that would suit you both best. Remember, if we don't settle this, you both may have exposure with the IRS. While you might think that only one of you is at risk, I want to remind you, without being adversarial, that you both signed those tax returns and there is no guarantee as to who may find themselves with trouble on their hands. That having been said, can we start with some of the less controversial topics, first?

"I assume you have no problem with Felicia being the residential custodial parent. Is that fair to say?"

Glen gave his quick consent. "I don't see that as a problem, provided that Mort has input in major decisions."

"Is that okay with you both?"

The parties nodded. Both had discussed the issue in depth with their attorneys separately.

"I would like to be able to see the kids whenever I have the time," Glen's client said.

"Mort, we're going to make a schedule, so that everyone has some structure. It will give you plenty of time, alternating weekends and an evening or two during the week. That's what we normally do, but that doesn't mean you two can't work out something else by agreement. The reason we put in the schedule is to keep you from having to run into court if you can't agree."

Andi was pleased with how Glen presented the need to implement a visitation schedule. He took the words right out of her mouth. She added that Mort would get alternating holidays and vacations, as well as time during the summer.

"And Glen, if there are any holidays or dates particularly important to your client, let me know. The Jews make holiday visitation easy because there are two seders, two days of Rosh Hashanah and plenty of days of Chanukah. So, we'll switch who gets the first night each year unless anyone has a problem with that. Thank God we don't have to fight over Christmas."

Glen moved on to the next big topic, distribution of property. "I'm hoping this will be fairly easy. Mort, you want to keep your business, and Felicia, we've been told you want the house." Both clients nodded. "The way the appraisals shake out," continued the attorney, "it looks like the numbers are close enough to make an even trade."

"But he's gonna keep making all that money," interrupted Felicia.

Andi turned to her. "Hopefully, that will be taken care of in the support provisions," she said. "So, why don't we assume that we'll make this trade subject to the support numbers. If we can't come to an agreement on that, we can always come back and revisit this distribution of assets. The rest, like the cars and boat will be whacked down the middle."

Again, Felicia jumped in. "But all that money he's got socked away. I want half of that. We've already run through all the cash that was in the house."

Mort snapped, "You ran through it?"

"I used it to pay all the bills you were supposed to be paying!"

Andi lifted up her hands to silence the two. "This isn't productive. Let me suggest the following. We'll never know how much money you've got hidden, Mort. But based on what was in the house, I'll bet there's a good deal more. So how about Felicia keeps the furniture and furnishings, the artwork, the coin collection and all her jewelry. And Mort, you get to keep all the cash you say you don't have."

"I want his golf clubs. I gave those to you as an anniversary gift. And that was when you were off banging that waitress!"

Melissa blanched. This wasn't how she'd pictured the settlement conference.

"What are you going to do with a set of men's left-handed Calloway golf clubs?" Mort spit out.

"Don't tempt me, Morty."

The attorneys were reaching the same conclusion: the atmosphere had grown contentious, and the parties needed to be separated.

"Why don't we each spend a little time with our clients?" Glen suggested. "And then maybe we can see if the rest of the issues can be resolved by shuttle-diplomacy."

"Good idea," answered Andi. "I'll take Felicia to my office and you can stay here with Mort."

The negotiations continued for another two hours, the lawyers getting plenty of exercise as they took the messages and proposals back and forth to their respective clients. The biggest fight was over the amount and duration of support; no one was sure of Mort's real income, not even Mort himself.

Ultimately, the man's desire to keep his business outweighed his desire to short-change his wife in the support department. They settled for high enough payments to keep Felicia and the children comfortably in the house until the youngest was out of school. Mort was to post $100,000 security, which he seemed magically able to raise. In the end, the two sides came to terms.

Sitting in Andi's office after the parties left, Melissa congratulated her mentor.

"You'd like to believe it's done," said the attorney. "But it will probably take two months of going back and forth between our offices on contract language before the agreement will be ready to be signed. And, by the way, who do you think should be doing the drafting?"

"I don't know. Mr. Ellers? Didn't Lucy just mention that we've been swamped with agreements?"

"Yes, she did. And there's a reason we're swamped. We like to write every agreement our clients sign."

Melissa looked confused.

"If we write it," Andi explained, "we include every term we agreed upon, but phrase it in a way that's most beneficial to our client. Also, we can organize the document so that we know where to find everything we're looking for. That way, we don't have do a search and destroy mission for errors or omissions by the other side. Most of our adversaries are only too happy to let us do the extra work." She suggested to Melissa that it would be a good learning experience for her to review the drafts and responsive comments, to be sure that the terms discussed in the negotiations were all included and that there was sufficient detail in the document to make the agreement work.

***

The ladies were gathered around the giant Ghirardelli bar, a gift from a client whose divorce papers had just been signed. The only effective method they'd found to break up the massive block into manageable pieces was to use Meg's heavy-duty hammer. Crowded into the small kitchenette, each attorney took turns wielding the weapon, enjoying the effort it took to "mine" a few chunks.

The party atmosphere was broken by Ruby, who reminded everyone they were expected in Lucy's office. The group straggled down the hallway, Andi with a paper plate of choice shards for her partner.

As her colleagues assembled in the office, Lucy noted that they looked more eager and attentive than usual. Must be the quality of the chocolate, she imagined, starting in on a rather large piece she selected from her plate.

"Okay, guys," she began, "I spoke to Maryann Nixon. Even though we caught him red-handed in court with all that money in his pockets, she still wants him back. He's suggesting a reconciliation."

"Sure, so he doesn't have to share his money," Claire said.

"Look, she's hoping for a miracle," added Andi. "She still loves him."

"That's right," said Lucy. "Let's bring her in as soon as she's back so we can see which way to go with this. It might be a good time to suggest a marital agreement to her. If he does want to get back together, this would be a great time to have that kind of an insurance policy. We'll know exactly what the terms will be if things don't work out."

Andi turned to Melissa. "You probably haven't heard much about marital agreements. Not that many people think of using them. Everyone's heard of a pre-nuptial agreement. Well, this is a post-nup. There's specific language in the New York statutes that allows people to make enforceable agreements at any time during their marriage. We like to suggest post-nups when the marriage has been on the ropes, but there's a possibility that the parties may try to make things work. So, if someone like Mr. Nixon wants to get a second chance, he'll have to put his money where his mouth is. We'll tell his lawyers that our client is willing to reconcile, as long as he will agree to give her a certain amount of support and a percentage of his business if things don't work out. We consider that a litmus test of his sincerity."

"Melissa, what she means is if Mr. Nixon isn't willing to sign that kind of agreement, then he's full of shit."

"It's Mrs. Caufield," Ruby announced from her desk. "Line two."

A collective groan issued. Meg suggested they disconnect the client to see if that might drive her right over the edge.

Nearly the entire staff was aware that Julie Caufield had been calling daily to see if the firm had received the business appraisal on Braintree Designs. Rather than using one of Lucy's regular appraisers, Julie had insisted on selecting an accountant she'd handpicked. Based on Lucy's experience, this could be a disaster. Many of the private accountants, while competent enough to do audits or tax returns, were unprepared to properly handle a matrimonial appraisal, since they were typically unaware of the applicable revenue rulings.

Lucy shouted back, "Tell her we're in a meeting, and when the mail comes, we'll let her know!" Looking around the room, Lucy said, "We've got a little work to do on Vaughn. Sorry, but we've all been up to our eyeballs with work, and I haven't had a chance to explain to everyone what happened in court yesterday. Instead of just conferencing the case, Thorpe realized that what he was about to do was going to be dicey. So, on the spot, he asked us to orally argue the motion to join Gary as a necessary party.

"If you remember, when we originally brought the application several months ago, that whole episode with Emma hadn't happened, we didn't have the final DNA results and Dr. Sundgren had not yet issued his report. When I argued to the judge, I asked him to deem my motion papers amended to include everything that's come to light since the original motion."

"Including the stuff Maria dug up about Everett filling prescriptions in the children's names? And filing phony insurance claims?" Meg asked.

Lucy waited two beats to get the full attention of her colleagues.

"Look, I had to make a quick decision. It looked pretty clear that with the confirmation of the DNA results and Sundgren's report, things were headed in the right direction for us. The judge already knew plenty about Everett's drug use. What he didn't know were these new details Maria dug up. If I gave them to the judge, then I think he would have been compelled to report the criminal activity. And then, all hell would have broken loose. Everett would seek to delay the custody case because anything that he says in Thorpe's court can be used against him in the criminal case. And Arthur Post is smart enough to know that. No matter how you slice it, a delay would not be good for those children."

"So, what you're actually telling us is that you'd rather use those tidbits to encourage Everett to make a deal," Meg observed.

"The judge heard from each of us, and there was a pretty extensive record made," Lucy said. "Nick and Arthur did their best to oppose me. You should have been there just to see the looks on their faces when Judge Thorpe issued his order from the bench. Not only did he join Gary as a necessary party, but he even gave him interim visitation, as well. It was un-fucking-believable!"

Andi raised her signature wine glass in a mock toast to her partner, while Claire took out her note pad. She knew what was coming next.

"You know, there's always good news and bad news," Lucy continued. "Good news is, we won in Judge Thorpe's part. The bad news? Claire, you've got a lot of work to do. We've got to submit a written order for the judge to sign on three days' notice to the other side. We need to include as much information as we can because the judge wants enough of a record to hang his hat on. He knows our adversaries won't wait a second to challenge his order and try to stop the interim visitation from ever starting. Nick and Arthur know that once that genie's out of the bottle, there's no going back. So, they'll take Thorpe's order right up to the Appellate Division, where those folks can give it the once over. No judge likes to be second-guessed, and if the Appellate Division doesn't uphold his order, it'll look like he made a mistake. And this matter is odd enough and sexy enough to get the attention of the press. Let's face it, this is a tough case and the judge went out on a limb on this one."

Andi agreed, noting that the press had followed the Brockhursts closely since the day Skippy died.

"Claire," said Lucy, "as well as preparing the order, you're going to have to write some really convincing papers opposing the application to stay the visitation. Now, we've already looked and there aren't any cases on all fours with this one, right Melissa?"

"Affirmative," she answered without hesitation.

"You're going to have to be a little creative, Claire, but we're all gonna look damn good if we win this one — not only us, but Judge Thorpe, too."

Lucy's colleague assured her that she could knock out the order for Judge Thorpe's signature first thing in the morning and still be thorough. As for the Appellate Division papers, Claire was chomping at the bit to see what her adversaries might say. She anticipated a fierce fight to block Gary's visitation. Though prepared with any and all possible ammunition, she and her colleagues realized that the Appellate Division might well overturn the judge's order. The challenge would be her delight.

"Which one of us do you think should handle the argument?" she asked. "I mean, if I've been doing all the research, shouldn't it be me before the Appellate Division? Or maybe it should be you, since you're the one who's been arguing it all along."

Lucy smiled. "I know what you'd like, Claire. But let's wait and see."

Meg's stomach started to growl, proclaiming that it was high time they all got home for dinner. Andi lingered, and exhausted as she was, remembered to tell Lucy that after the day's four-way, she saw the possible making of a good attorney in their intern.

CHAPTER FORTY-ONE

At the end of a long, winding driveway, the black Excursion pulled up to the gravel courtyard and came to rest beneath the vine-covered porte-cochere of Cedar Golf and Tennis, former estate of D.L. Penning. A young attendant darted from behind one of the massive fluted Ionic columns to eagerly help Gary out of his car and to usher him in through the main entrance. To Gary's surprise, the fellow took him for a club member and left him to his own devices to make his way into the building.

"Must be a newbie," thought Gary, keenly aware of the scrutiny to which he was usually subjected at the other clubs. During the handful of fundraisers he'd attended at Cedar, Gary would have liked to spend more time in the entry hall, just to admire its design. Now was the perfect opportunity to take a closer look.

The long, vaulted hallway built of Caen wall was lit from above by a spectacular iron and stained glass light fixture, with its unusual silhouette of a lady on horseback. On his last visit to the club, he'd rendered a sketch of the item on the back of his business card, and later commissioned a copy of the light to grace the entry of a new home he'd designed. But the real thing put it to shame. Far more seasoned hands had cast the original, a true work of art.

His eyes were drawn toward the far end of the hallway and on through the windows of the splendid Great Hall to the dormant, formal gardens and the grand sweep of lawn beyond. His delight in the view was interrupted by the figure of a deeply tanned, willowy woman, tottering in her sling-backs as she came forward to greet him. Her even, white teeth shown out at him from behind her leathery skin, and she looked at him with a mixture of graciousness and puzzlement. One thing stood out to her: the man was chewing gum.

"I'm here to see Mrs. Brockhurst," Gary announced, without further ado.

"Yes, I see," the lady responded, betraying a tinge of curiosity as she stared at his leather coat. It was black. His shoes were brown. She stood staring at him, her wide eyes trying to make sense of what he was.

"I'm Gary Vaughn," he repeated. To meet Mrs. Brockhurst... for lunch." He expected that his explanation would suffice.

"Lunch. Indeed." Her smile continued, but the eyes said something else altogether. While the two faced one another in the ensuing silence, another woman came up beside them. She had caught a snippet of their conversation.

"Oh, you must be Mr. Vaughn. Mrs. Brockhurst told me to look out for you."

"Gee, and I thought I'd stumbled into the wrong place!" he chuckled. The woman smiled back, and offered to take his coat, explaining that a few of the regular attendants were out sick. "She's already in the dining room, so let me take you there. By the way, I'm Chloe."

"Nice to meet ya, Chloe," Gary offered, shaking hands heartily. They walked off together, leaving the older woman to look after them in wonder.

"And please forgive Mrs. Dory," whispered Chloe. "When she's not in Bermuda, she practically lives here, like she owns the place! So, it's almost an imposition when someone new invades her territory."

"Oh, I just chalked it up to snobbery," Gary chided.

"The members of Cedar? Snobs? No, that's at the other clubs, not here!" Chloe responded as though she actually meant it. "I've worked here for quite a while, and I must say, they're just the friendliest people."

Gary was amused by her attitude. He knew very well that Cedar was an exclusive club, whose members were derided by outsiders for their infuriating elitism, especially by those who couldn't get in. Many assumed the members were outright racist, no different from the club's original founders back in the '50s. Even now, if a Jew, Catholic,

Latino, African American or Asian managed to become a member, it still made big news around town and came along with an intricate explanation of just how it had occurred, perhaps through an inter-faith marriage or, as in one notable case, the conversion of a long-term member from Presbyterian to Buddhist.

Gary and Chloe stepped into the main dining room, where Vivian awaited her guest at a window table. Despite her move to Florida, she continued at Cedar as a house member, retaining various special privileges such as the use during her visits of the dining table that overlooked the magnolia, with the lovely view she'd always preferred. Chloe escorted Gary across the sun-drenched dining room filled with tables of chattering lady golfers and a handful of gentlemen. She brought him over to Vivian's perch, where the woman sat facing the tree, its first flowers in blossom. The Tiffany glass lights set into the ceiling above Mrs. Brockhurst cast a soft glow across her face. How far superior they were to modern skylights, Gary mused, as he recognized a mastermind at work: Vivian surely knew she looked her best in this exact spot, with the gentle light filtering in on her from all directions.

"Make yourself comfortable, Mr. Vaughn."

"Gary."

"Oh, here we go again," she said lightly, "And it's Vivian."

"And am I supposed to say 'we have to stop meeting like this?'"

Vivian laughed as Gary sat beside her.

"This place never changes," Gary commented, "And that's what I love about it."

"Yes, I've heard your designs tend to be influenced by what might be called a sense of nostalgia."

"Very good." Gary was impressed. Apparently, she'd made inqui-ries about his work as an architect. "But not everything I do falls into that category. This place- well, it's just a work of art. Thank you for inviting me here."

Vivian smiled. "I have a plan, and I know you'll be interested."

Gary's eyes told her to continue.

"Hugh and I have discussed it. If this situation ends up in a full-fledged custody trial, there's no telling what will happen. From what I have heard, this judge is a loose cannon. It would be a terrible gamble for us to let him decide what happens, with the lives of our grandchildren at stake. We need control of the outcome."

Gary wondered where Vivian was going with this. Did she want a concession from him? Was she going to ask him to back off?

"We spent a great deal of time and effort considering all of the possible options and are in agreement that you might actually be the person best suited to have custody of the children."

Her words didn't register with Gary at first.

"Everett would relinquish custody, and after a period of transition, you would become their parent."

The second wave hit as hard as the first, and Gary adjusted his glasses. He looked closely at Vivian, trying to get the best read possible. Ignoring her former invitation to call her by her first name, he spoke in a more formal manner.

"Mrs. Brockhurst, I'm certainly intrigued by your proposition. But as you can imagine, I'm shocked. Are you and your husband actually taking sides against your own son? I'm sure he still wants the children, doesn't he?"

"Perhaps so, but let's just say he has other concerns."

"What kind of concerns could be more important than his children?"

"Oh, don't be coy, Mr. Vaughn, you saw the legal papers. We both know what Everett's been up to."

Paulette, who was well aware of Mrs. Brockhurst's luncheon tastes, had been waiting for an indication that she was ready to place her order. Now, looking over at the table, she caught the woman's nod.

"The usual for me, and Gary, I would suggest the fresh fruit and seafood salad."

This woman was too much. Not only was she trying to control his destiny, thought Gary, she was even ready to control what he ordered. And she expected him to acquiesce to both.

"Now, didn't I once have some great onion soup here?" he asked.

"You're right," Paulette answered agreeably. "With extra cheese?"

"You've got my number," Gary said.

Vivian, a bit disquieted by her guest's display of independence, went on to order for them both the large Perrier with a twist of lime.

So, Gary thought, *she just has to win.*

Continuing with the business at hand, the two faced one another. Vivian looked him over once again. Gary was no fool, no matter how nonchalant he appeared. He would surely require some further explanation, but he'd have to ask for it. She sat in silence as she turned her eyes back to the magnolia.

"Mrs. Brockhurst, really. I'm sitting here wondering what's going on. I mean, did you just tell me that if I wanted the children, I could have them? Because, frankly, if that was some kind of joke, it's not a very nice one. I think you know what this means to me. You can't imagine that I would talk about this, let my children know and risk everything they are to me, if I wasn't dead serious. The fact that I have a son came as quite a shock to them."

"And I wouldn't have asked you here if I wasn't equally serious. This is certainly no joke, Mr. Vaughn. I can no longer support my son's position. After what happened with Emma, he's a risk I am no longer willing to take. I've been through that before with him, and I can't do it again and I won't do it again."

"Before? Did he endanger Emma or Beau before?"

"My reasons are my own."

"So let me get this straight. What exactly is it that you're proposing?"

"Mr. Post has told me that the forensic expert thinks Beau will need a good male role model in his life and that Everett can't seem to provide that. I understand he thinks you might be a good influence."

Gary was familiar with the expert's recommendations, since Lucy had happily summarized them in their recent meeting. He let Vivian continue.

"If, in fact, you are capable of fulfilling that role, then I would think that may be the best answer for my grandchildren. Of course, I would continue to play an important part in their lives. Hugh and I talked seriously about taking them ourselves, but we felt that relocating them to the south would be too disruptive after what they've been through. And we have certain obligations in Florida that will never allow us to leave the state."

"Does Everett know about all this? Does he know we're meeting?"

"Everett will not be an issue as long as you'll agree to uphold your end of the bargain."

"Oh! So, now we can get to the point. Mrs. Brockhurst, what exactly is it that you want from me?"

"It's a simple request. You probably have no idea, but in Everett's divorce the stumbling block was always the house: what was going to happen to Laurel Hall. My former daughter-in-law's eminently qualified attorney," she started with disdain, "oh, that would be your lawyer, too, wouldn't it?" She paused for a moment, and then went on. "She managed to wrangle the family home away from Everett. As a compromise, it was agreed that when my grandchildren finished their educations, Laurel Hall would belong to them, through a trust that was established. Until they graduated from college, Skippy was allowed to live at the house and maintain it for them. In order for you to get the children, the ownership of Laurel Hall must be restored to Everett. And obviously, the children will need to be compensated for the loss."

"Laurel Hall must be worth over four million dollars! Are you selling your grandchildren to me for four million dollars?"

At the nearby tables, heads turned.

"Of course not," she assured him. "Hugh and I are willing to share this cost with you, equally."

Gary had been wondering what the catch was going to be, but this idea struck him as outrageous. Was it even legal?

Paulette chose this inopportune moment to deposit the fruit salads in front of Gary and Vivian. "The mango's straight from heaven, I tell you," the waitress gushed. Vivian gave the signal and Paulette retreated as quickly and gracefully as she could.

"Maybe we should just see what the judge has to say."

"Well, of course, you could make that choice. But as I'm sure your attorney has told you, your odds of getting custody are slim to none. Your status as Beau's biological father won't get you that far, at least, that's my understanding. I'm well aware that my son's position is shakier now than it was before, but even if he doesn't prevail, Georgina would certainly be the next in line. At least, Arthur seems to think so. And despite what we discussed earlier, if it came down to an all-out court battle, who knows. Hugh and I might just have to throw our own hats in the ring. As far as I can see, you've got a weak case. I'm offering you an opportunity to get just what you want — including, I assume, getting my son out of the picture."

So, then, it was going to come down to the money. Gary knew better than to underestimate Vivian Brockhurst, but it was really something to see her in action, wheeling and dealing between dainty dips into her raspberry yogurt. He tried to imagine the little chat between Vivian and her son as to the sale of the Brockhurst children. Had Vivian suggested this buyout, or had Everett come up with this brilliant idea? A fabulous pay off for that asshole, that's what stuck in his craw. The number was enormous, Then again, it was only money. And Vivian had offered to spend as much of hers as she was asking of him.

"Have you already discussed this idea with Everett?"

"That's not your concern."

Gary nearly choked on his spoonful of blueberries.

"Let's leave that out of our equation for the moment," she added.

She'd already had the chat, Gary realized. Had that bastard given up without any fight? How eager had he been?

"Well, it certainly is a tidy sum." Vivian gave no response. "And it may take me a little time to raise it. But if you're telling me that this is what it will take, I'd have to consider making the deal. But I do have to ask, have you cleared this with Georgina?"

Vivian knew he'd get to this, eventually. But she couldn't approach Georgina about the idea unless she'd already struck a tentative deal with Gary. Recalling the conversation overheard in the courthouse bathroom, Vivian felt that under the right circumstances, Georgina might back off.

"I have good reason to believe I can bring her around. But first I need to know if you're on board with this. Before I go to her, I have to be assured that you'd uphold your part of the bargain and honor all of your obligations."

"Other than the money, what other obligations are there?"

"Hugh and I will continue to be actively involved in the children's lives and Georgina will also be given appropriate time and deference. The children love her. So, she'd need to visit them on a regular basis. We'd contribute to a fund to cover her travel costs, and we'd expect you to split those expenses with us."

Gary was impressed that she had included Georgina in her proposal. Before him was the formidable Vivian Brockhurst, who despite her cold exterior, clearly loved her grandchildren and cared about their welfare above all else. The steely determination reflected in her eyes made him almost believe that this insanity might work.

Lunch was served and completed in due course, and while he might have slipped once or twice in his oafish handling of the onion soup, Vivian felt satisfied that Gary could pass muster at any club. It didn't hurt that when Grace Harlan came by the table to say hello and learned who the gentleman was, she praised the work he'd recently completed on her niece's new home. Vivian liked hearing that Gary's work was held in high regard from that particular corner, since she respected her old friend's opinion. Gary could never be one of them, but he was accustomed to being among them. That much, she could see. And after all the polishing she was prepared to do, he could become proficient enough to raise the Brockhurst children in the appropriate manner.

CHAPTER FORTY-TWO

Gary Vaughn appeared in the solarium fresh from his morning meeting at the work site. This would explain the dirty boots, Vivian imagined, while offering her guest a seat across from her on the elegant chintz-covered couch. She made a mental note to have Teresa check for mud deposits throughout the hallway, along every inch of the route Gary had taken.

"Vivian, thank you for inviting me."

"I'm glad you could make it." As she leaned forward to pour some tea, Georgina entered the room.

Gazing across the room at her, Gary took a closer look. On the few occasions his path had crossed with hers, her face had been hidden behind her mass of full, dark hair. Now, as she moved toward him, Georgina seemed to emerge from the shadows. He was startled to perceive the resemblance between the two sisters. There they were: the finely curved lips, the high, open brow, the strong cheekbones. And he was pleased to notice that the few extra pounds on this version had landed in all the right places. Her hair pulled back in a ponytail, and in her faded jeans, Georgina took her place on a wicker chair.

As they shook hands, he observed a small, fleeting smile that evaporated as soon as she glanced at Vivian. It had been an awkward morning between the two women, as each anticipated the meeting, yet avoided any mention of it. At breakfast, they were cheerful for the sake of the children, but said nothing at all to one another. Georgina was particularly apprehensive now since true to form, Mrs. Brockhurst held all of the cards and revealed very little.

Upon requesting the meeting, all that Vivian had said to Georgina was that the three of them might be more productive than their high priced lawyers, who profited greatly the longer the case continued. After giving it some thought, Georgina agreed that getting together was worth a try. She hadn't mentioned to Vivian that she would walk away if it turned out to be an ambush rather than a meeting.

Teresa came into the room with a tray of cookies, Bridgette at her heels. The nanny was carrying a large watering can, hoping this would provide a pretext for lingering nearby long enough to learn what Mrs. Brockhurst had on her mind.

"Isn't it refreshing to meet without our lawyers here to muck up the works?"

Georgina, her face brightening for an instant, confirmed Gary's opinion. "Good point."

She had no idea what to expect from this discussion, but then again, she never knew what to expect when she was at her attorney's office, either. Nick always seemed to have some unwelcome surprise up his sleeve. For the moment, she felt relieved to be on her own.

"Let's get to the point," Vivian began, "since my driver is due here in a few hours. I want to make the most effective use of our time." Turning to Georgina, she continued. "Gary and I met privately several days ago. But we quickly decided that you had to be a part of any decision."

Georgina felt grateful for the recognition.

Before Vivian went on, she noticed that Bridgette had overstayed her welcome. She gave her a brief nod of dismissal, and the nanny left the room. Vivian then outlined the proposal, as Georgina sat stony-faced trying to absorb what the others had come up with in her absence.

Apparently, neither she nor Everett would get the children. Of all the scenarios she'd considered, she had not imagined one in which Vivian agreed to eliminate her own son from contention, though on some level, she had prayed for the woman to recognize how unsuitable he would be for the children, leaving "Aunt Gina" the obvious choice. But Gary? Her mind scrambled for answers. Had the other two found out something about her and Ron? Had the doubts she expressed about her family's suitability for the children somehow been revealed?

Amanda! She could have been eavesdropping on her conversations with Ron at Laurel Hall. In retrospect, she'd noticed that annoying woman hanging around at the oddest times, but thought little of it. And then there was Lucy. Now she regretted having said anything to that woman. If Nick learned about their little encounter, he would have killed her. And she could only imagine how furious he'd be if he got wind of this outrageous proposal!

Georgina sat silently as Vivian continued. When she got to the part about the millions in trust fund money that was to be put up by Gary and the Brockhursts, Georgina wondered if they'd eliminated her solely on account of her financial limitations rather than due to possible revelations about her life with Ron. Georgina was about ready to pull the plug on the whole discussion, when Vivian offered her an olive branch. As an integral part of the deal, Georgina was to have generous involvement in the children's lives.

"And since we know that you would always have the children's best interests at heart, we would like for you to own the life insurance policy on Gary's life," Vivian said. "This way, he could never change the beneficiaries from the children to anyone else, and we know you certainly wouldn't do that." She was pleased with herself. She had been up late reading and rereading her son's divorce agreement. Bennett had shrewdly inserted several carefully worded clauses, the importance of which had become clearer to Vivian, now that she was the one controlling the deal.

Georgina realized just how clever Vivian had been, in assuring that Aunt Gina would be the protector of the children's funds. It made her a critical figure in the arrangement and also was an attempt to heal the wound they surely knew had been inflicted upon her.

As for the second million that Gary was also obligated to provide, Vivian and Gary had decided that a reliable financial advisor would be the right one to manage those funds. The several million in Brockhurst funds, which they had likewise agreed to provide for the children's benefit, would continue to be overseen by Vivian and Hugh, and on their demise by their young crackerjack of an investment advisor. The entire funds together were to be equal to the value of Laurel Hall, to which the children were entitled under Skippy and Everett's divorce settlement. Apparently, Everett had been willing to trade the children for regaining sole ownership of the mansion, something he had long considered his legacy.

Most important, Vivian and Gary agreed that it was essential for Bridgette to stay on. They both felt confident she would be willing to do so.

It seemed to Georgina that the others had planned everything out very neatly, down to the last detail. After Vivian finished laying out the proposal, there was a long silence. Georgina glanced at Gary, whose expression revealed nothing. He had to be quite satisfied with the arrangement, if not ecstatic, she thought.

"You just said that I'm the one who'd always have the children's best interests at heart. So how was it that you both decided I'm not the best choice for them?"

"It's not you, my dear," Vivian said.

Georgina looked at her closely and saw her reach for something on the low table beside her.

"I'm not a home-wrecker," Vivian said as she handed Georgina the envelope. "This is for you, and I want you to know I bear you no ill will. Use this as you see fit."

Gary wondered what was in the envelope, but Vivian Brockhurst never acted without a purpose.

It would be hours later, after Gary had departed and Vivian was off to the airport, that Georgina at last took a look at what Mrs. Brockhurst had handed her: a copy of a report from the office of Jerry Frame, P.I.

CHAPTER FORTY-THREE

At the same time that the deal was being proposed at Laurel Hall, Arthur Post and Nick DeBello were busy preparing papers to serve on Lucy's office. They were each doing all they could to put a stop to any contact between what they considered an interloper and the children. For once, Nick and Arthur were on the same team, united in their common goal: to get a stay of the visitation order from the Appellate Division.

While each had consented to allow a forensic psychologist to investigate the pros and cons of having Gary in the children's lives, they had most specifically not consented to allow that report to be determinative. There was an enormous difference between consenting to an investigation and consenting to be bound by the investigator's recommendations. Judge Thorpe had, nonetheless, issued an order based on Dr. Sundgren's recommendation. Nick and Arthur were seeking to stay the enforcement of that order.

A day earlier, Lucy had made the obligatory call to her adversaries in an attempt to arrange the visitation between Gary and the children, as ordered by Judge Thorpe. She was delivering on her earlier promise to the children for seats to a Yankee game, although she knew there was not a prayer in hell that Nick or Arthur would consider accommodating her request. In fact, Nick responded exactly as Lucy expected, telling her to go fuck herself. Using more refined language, but in a similar vein, Arthur told her to hold onto her expensive tickets, since there was no chance Gary Vaughn and the children would be sitting in those seats.

Lucy was on her way back to the office when Dan called to say one of them had to get over to school to pick up Adam. He'd just been injured at recess, and the nurse was fairly certain his ankle was broken. Adam always preferred her to go to the orthopedist with him. He dreaded the thought of having to wear yet another cast, and was sure his mom would negotiate better terms with the doctor than would his father. The last time, she'd managed to whittle down Dr. Kanter from his initial recommendation of a five-week cast to only three and a half weeks. He was hoping his mother could work her magic again.

After telling Dan she'd handle the situation, she contacted Ruby about her most recent emergency. Her assistant responded with news of her own: she'd just received a joint phone call from Nick and Arthur providing alternative times to appear before an Appellate Division judge, to argue a stay of Judge Thorpe's order.

"Just great," Lucy responded. "Please tell me that wherever it is, I don't have to be there within the next few hours."

"No problem, it's tomorrow at noon. They got Judge Samuels over at her chambers in town."

"Good thing, because my most important argument is set for later this afternoon, before Doc Kanter. And my client has only the highest expectations."

"That's because he knows you can get him out of almost anything."

"Yeah, in this case, a Goddamned cast."

"That doctor must be planning his retirement around the Bennett-Hammond family and all their disasters."

"Can you hold off my one o'clock or see if Andi or Claire can handle it? God, I just remembered it's Mrs. Caufield. She'll just love to hear I'm not available."

"Why don't I send her straight to x-ray and have her meet you there?"

"Delightful! Always thinking, aren't you?"

***

Georgina didn't know any other way to handle the meeting with Nick DeBello than to just come out with it. "Thanks for fitting me in. I know you're not going to be happy with what I have to tell you and I didn't want you to hear it over the phone.

Nick instantly thought, *I've been fired by better than you, lady.*

"And I know there's a time concern about this," Georgina continued. She took a breath and then told Nick that she'd just come from a meeting with Vivian Brockhurst and Gary Vaughn. She summarized the details as best she could. Nick's face grew red. If anybody was capable of sabotaging their own case, Georgina Fiske appeared to be the perfect candidate. Here she was, talking to her two formidable adversaries, giving away 'who knows what' to them.

"You've got Nick DeBello as your lawyer and you think you can do better by negotiating directly? We're this close to getting you everything you want and now at the eleventh hour you decide to take things into your own hands? Georgina, you better tell me what it is you want, because honestly, I'm mystified."

"Nick, you don't know Beau and Emma. You don't care about them the way Gary and Vivian do..." Nick steamrolled over her words, continuing his tirade. "So, what exactly did you three geniuses discuss?"

"We agreed to allow Gary visitation, just like the psychologist recommended and like it said in the judge's order. So, when I heard that tomorrow you were going to try and stop it..."

"Who told you that? I haven't even had a chance to talk with you about this!"

"Vivian told me."

"I see. Apparently, what she has to say about this matter is more important than what I have to say."

"No, that's not true. She has the children's best interests in mind, just the same as I do. And we're all in agreement that if Gary is eventually going to let Beau know that he's his father..."

"Says who?"

"Well, isn't it true? Someday that boy is going to know the truth. There's no real way to stop that from happening."

"Oh, did Mr. Vaughn threaten to tell the child? Because if so, I'm letting Lucy Bennett know right this..." He reached for the phone.

"No! He never threatened anything. It just makes common sense; someday, Beau will find out about Gary."

"Okay, that might be true, but sometime down the road, the boy should be better equipped to handle it."

"Funny, that's not what the psychologist said. Didn't he recommend Gary's involvement now rather than later?"

"Those shmucks! Every shrink is more screwed up than the next. And so are most of their kids. So as far as his moronic report, I wouldn't trust it as far as I could throw it!"

"Then why did you agree to it?"

Nick was taken aback. Was this hick questioning his professional judgment? "Because," he started, "I knew the judge wanted it done. Alienating Judge Thorpe is not what you want me to do. That's not the lawyer you hired. And remember, I only agreed to have the shrink write the report. I never agreed to listen to it!"

"But Nick, I'm only agreeing to allow Gary visitation right now. I'm not agreeing to give him custody yet."

"Yet? Did I hear "yet"? What kind of snow job did these people do on you? How could you even consider that, when I'm running around convincing everyone that you're the best choice? And are you telling me Vivian Brockhurst is on board with a plan like that?"

"It was her idea."

Nick was dumbfounded. It made no sense. What was his client not telling him?

"Look, allowing this visitation doesn't mean he gets custody, right?"

"No, but it certainly gives him a better shot. Once he gets to visit the kids, how can we argue he's a complete stranger to them?" He let his words sink in. "And it sounds to me like the bunch of you have thrown Emma into the mix. And there's no law in this state that would give that child to Mr. Vaughn when her own father is alive."

"Yes, but doesn't the law say you shouldn't separate siblings from one another?"

"Usually," Nick admitted. "But this is quite a unique situation. These two children don't have the same biological father. They're half-siblings."

"Even so, there's no way I could separate them." Georgina looked directly into her attorney's eyes. "Isn't this really about Beau and Emma and what's best for them?"

Nick paused before he responded, fumbling around in his drawer. He carefully placed on his blotter what Georgina thought was a fountain pen. It only looked like one. Nick glanced at the object to be sure the device was in recording mode, and then continued. "Just understand, honey, that this little agreement of yours to allow visitation will seriously jeopardize your chances of getting custody of both children. And if the visitation goes well, and it continues, it's Gary who happens to live where the children have always lived and Gary who's the boy's blood relative, so you better be damned sure about what you're doing. 'Cause if you come back tomorrow and realize you made a mistake about allowing the visitation, don't blame me when you don't win your custody case. Hear what I'm saying?"

"I hear you."

"And I'm assuming you've discussed this with your husband."

"Ron has nothing to do with this."

"Then, in that case, are you telling me that you want me to cancel tomorrow's meeting with the Appellate Division judge?"

"Yes," she mumbled.

"Is that a yes?" he asked as he leaned forward, his recorder in hand.

"Yes," she said more clearly. She pushed her chair back, and left the room without a further word.

Wonderful things these gadgets were, Nick thought as he swiveled back in his seat. He synced the recorded conversation into his desktop computer. Then he summoned his secretary to arrange the necessary calls to the offices of Arthur Post and Lucy Bennett.

CHAPTER FORTY-FOUR

Her blouse was loosened the way he liked, her auburn hair gently pinned up and ready to be released at a single touch. They toasted one another as they shared the appetizers she'd so carefully prepared. She let him go on pretending for a few minutes that it was the farthest thing from his mind. They role-played just as they had done during their many meetings as attorney and client. How well he used to hide it from her in his office, reading over the dreary documents, consoling her, advising her. The photo of his wife and their grown children was always prominently displayed in its heavy, ornate frame on the desk, the wedding band always gracing his ring finger as he reached out to shake her hand. He remained professional throughout the case, never letting on that he was as interested in protecting her ass as he was in grabbing it.

She slipped her shirt down over her shoulders, revealing ample breasts that she positioned perfectly just before Arthur walked in. Now, they cooperatively poured out over her skimpy, lace push-up bra. Dr. Dingle's brilliant boob job made up for much she knew was lacking in her other areas, but, she thought blissfully, the rest could be attended to in due course. This generous man would surely pay for all the necessary upgrades, especially since they would be of mutual benefit to them.

She nibbled on his ear and then tucked herself behind him, to spoon for a while. There wasn't a crevice, a crack, a particle of Marlena's frame he hadn't already explored endlessly during their weekly interludes, but today, he was intent on re-discovering every inch of her delicious body.

"I need something big, honey," she giggled.

He was floored. "You don't think this thing is big enough?"

"Oh, God no, not that! I mean next week's present! You're as big as they come!"

He was relieved. If she needed anything bigger, he'd have had to reassess his opinion of her. "You didn't do enough shopping?"

"I want some furniture, honey, something for the foyer…kind of dazzling, you know? Maybe a better chandelier. And I was thinking about a few more cushions for this room. You know, for better angles."

"Mmm…better angles. Sounds good. I'll have you speak to my guy over at Roche Bobois."

"You're such a sweetie pie." She snuggled into his armpit. *The cleanest man*, she thought. *Must shower three times a day.*

"So, what's going to be your favorite part of our afternoon?" he asked teasingly, fondling her bottom.

"Oh, that's easy," she answered. "The part where I'm screaming."

The cell phone buzzed. He'd made the cardinal sin of forgetting to shut it off.

"Oh God, Marlena, I can't…I have to get it…"

She drew back from him. Their brief session was over before it had even begun.

Arthur sat back on the couch to check his phone. There was a text message he could not ignore. Knowing the drill, Marlena turned down the music. It was time for business. He was going to return the call.

"Post here, for Mr. DeBello." Marlena came back to her lover to give him a peck on his cheek, pouted at him and left for the bathroom. He watched her walk away, her rear swaying as if to taunt him. Was it just fortuitous, or did his colleagues wait around all week to call with their most urgent messages during his few moments of pleasure? His frustration only grew as he got the run-around from DeBello's new secretary.

"No, I need to speak to him directly."

"He's on a conference call, sir, so can I take a message, or would you prefer his voice mail?"

"Young lady, it was Mr. DeBello who called me and said it was urgent."

A moment later, the gruff voice came through Arthur's phone.

"Nick DeBello. Thanks for getting back to me so quickly."

"You said it was urgent. If it's the papers, you should have received them already. They were forwarded to your office as well as Ms. Bennett's."

"No, no, they're here. I was calling to see if you got the same crazy-ass instructions I got."

"What are you talking about?"

"Georgina was just in here telling me to call off the dogs. She told me she's been having private meetings with Vivian Brockhurst, along with Gary Vaughn. And now they've decided to give Gary the go-ahead so he can have visitation with the children. Can you fucking believe that?" The curse slipped out before Nick could block it. Arthur was the only attorney he supposed might be offended by his language.

"Are you telling me that they no longer wish to pursue the matter with the Appellate Division?" Arthur asked.

"That's certainly what Georgina told me, and I would think you'd want to check this out with your own client."

Arthur considered how much effort, time and money had been expended on the recent Brockhurst papers. Of course, he'd have to confirm the news with his client. Either way, the Brockhursts would pay the substantial legal bill, no questions asked. "Have you spoken to Lucy Bennett?"

"Not yet, and you know, Arthur, I wouldn't put it past that bitch to have cooked up this whole thing."

"I might agree with you if it was a different case, but frankly, I've yet to see Vivian take instructions from anyone, myself included."

"But I just can't stand the thought of Bennett gloating about a case you or I should have won, hands down. I guess there's no way around it. We better get in touch with her since she's already got our papers."

"Yes, we should try to reach her before she answers them."

"If she is answering them. Remember, I bet she's in on it."

Marlena returned to the room dressed only in her spiked heels and refreshed lipstick, just in case Arthur had anything more to add before he left. She handed him his glass of Johnnie Walker Blue and cuddled up next to him on the couch.

"In on it or not, we have to deal with it," Arthur said. "But do me a favor, Nick. I should be back to my office in about a half hour. Can we handle this then?" He took a sip of his drink.

"Let me guess, you're over at the club...in the middle of a nice malt. Enjoy. Maybe one of these days I'll get to join you there." That stuffy old hang-out, Nick thought, recalling his several occasions as a guest at the Princeton Club. Perfect place for that drip.

Arthur said a polite goodbye and then turned back to his lover. "Afraid I've got to go to the office...but maybe I can get back here tomorrow. Some time just freed up for me."

"Two days running? I think I'll faint!"

He gave Marlena his last smile of the day and then with great reluctance, broke from their embrace and left.

CHAPTER FORTY-FIVE

Adam lay on the couch in Lucy's office, surrounded by the chatty group of mat ladies. While the lawyers suggested that the answer to his suffering must be a chunk of chocolate, Ruby had a better read on the boy. She procured for him a bottle of lime Gatorade from Lucy's mini-fridge. Adam took a sip, but all he really wanted was to be home moping in front of his X-box. This injury meant that once again, he'd miss the beginning of the season's baseball practice. Just like with soccer the year before, he would have to work his way back into the starting line-up with teammates already on the field for weeks.

With one eye on her son as he tried his best to abide the ladies' unwelcome attention, Lucy tried to coordinate the workload and calendar with her colleagues. Pretty picture, she thought, her child beside her, leg in a cast, while she attended to business; wasn't this what they called "having it all?"

The day's phone slips having accumulated, Ruby was dividing them into categories marked "urgent," "very important" and "who gives a shit."

"Are these three messages all equally urgent?" Lucy demanded as she waved the top pile of slips in the air.

"Yes," her assistant said.

Lucy took the slips and methodically distributed one each to Andi and Claire, keeping one to deal with herself. "Now we each have one 'urgent' to start off with."

Andi, wine glass in hand, looked at Lucy. "You couldn't have meant to give me Gary Vaughn, could you?" She took a long sip of water, knowing she was off the hook.

Lucy shook her head, having had no chance to even read through the messages, and said, "I'll trade you two Humphreys and a Bonfiglio for three 'very importants'."

Claire offered to take the entire pile of "very importants" for six "who gives a shit."

Adam came to life and blurted, "I'd give two shits for another Gatorade."

"Excuse me!" said Lucy in mock horror, as the rest of the office rolled in their seats. Her son was still just young enough to enjoy getting away with bad language.

"Now Claire, on Vaughn. How were the moving papers on the stay application?"

"Post's were written better than Nick's. Big surprise. But I have to say, as I've said all along, they have good arguments. At least this time, I've got the DNA results to work with, but more importantly, I've got the shrink recommending Gary's involvement. I asked Melissa to do some more research before I started writing and while there are plenty of estoppel cases, the facts here are pretty unusual. We didn't find anything on point, but I think I can extrapolate enough from the favorable cases to make a decent argument. I'm maybe half-way done, but remember, it's a stay application so the papers aren't going to be that long.

"Oh, and Mrs. Hecht just called," Claire added. "Believe it or not, she says she's made some real progress on her net worth statement. Of course, I think she used some of her husband's numbers for the household expenses, but it still makes sense to get her in here to spend some time with you, Meg."

"She's never going to be able to explain the figures if she keeps taking them from her husband," her colleague said.

"If the numbers look out of whack, you can call Bill Davies to get copies of the actual bills."

Lucy turned to Melissa and explained that this might be the one case where the husband was actually trying to be helpful by providing information, perhaps because he felt genuinely guilty.

"Guilt is a gold mine, to be tapped whenever possible," Lucy said. And now was the time to take advantage of it, before Mr. Hecht lost patience. "So, Meg, this might be a prime case for a four-way. See if you can get enough financial information from our client to go forward with a meeting."

Lucy looked down at her papers and wondered how this one had landed under "very important."

"This one's a fucking nightmare!" she said, decoding a handwritten memo on the Nixon case that read, "weekend great, co-signed small loan, no biggy, only 100,000, will call."

"Mom, I think that one stays in your pile."

Lucy gave her son a half-hearted shrug in apology. She'd completely forgotten he was there. "You know, when I ask her to pay her outstanding $7,500 bill, that's a biggy. But signing a $100,000 mortgage isn't? Hope the weekend was worth it."

"What, did they do it from chandeliers?" Meg asked.

The intercom buzzed at the same time as Ruby called from her desk, "Nick DeBello's on line two! He says it's important!"

"Hey, Nick, I've got you on speaker. What's so important?"

"L.B., I just want to know how you managed to orchestrate this one."

"Orchestrate what?"

"You know damn well what I'm talking about. How'd you get them to drop the appeal?"

"Are you kidding me?. In fact, I cleared my calendar to meet you at the Appellate Division tomorrow. Are you telling me it's off?"

"Georgina told me, and Vivian told Arthur that they're agreeing to let your client have visitation. I just don't get it. We would have gotten that stay."

Lucy looked across the room at the raised fists and the mock applause.

"I guess we'll never know now, will we?" Lucy answered. "But now that I have you, does this mean we're all going to the Yankee game together? Like one big, happy family?"

"Cut the shit."

Lucy raised an eyebrow toward her son, knowing he was enjoying this. "I guess we better check and see if they've arranged that, too.

Honestly, Nick, I don't know what's going on, so let me touch base with Vaughn and I'll get back to you right after I speak with him."

As soon as Lucy ended the call, the chatter began. Everyone had a different idea as to which client had pulled the strings. Ultimately they agreed: it had to have been Vivian Brockhurst. The general mood was light, but Claire was the exception.

"I guess now I'll never know what would have happened, either. I really wanted to give this one a shot. If we won, we would have made the *Law Journal.*"

"Claire, remember. We would have made the *Journal* if we lost, too. And the good news is, we didn't get the chance to lose. It's a win-win for us. The client got what he wanted, and we freed up tomorrow. And we'll be paid for all the time you put into those papers. Happy clients are paying clients."

After the lawyers revised their calendars for the next day and everyone cleared out of Lucy's office, the boss had one more call to make before she could come up for air. But before she could get Gary Vaughn on the line, a sheepish Dina appeared in her doorway. "Ruby thought I should give you this myself."

The phone slip was stained with some sort of oil. Through the smeared writing, Lucy recognized Gary's cell number.

"It got stuck to my sandwich wrapper. So sorry." Dina tiptoed backwards out of the office, into the hallway.

Lucy grabbed the phone and made the call to the client. Gary recounted all that had occurred at Laurel Hall. By the time Lucy hung up with him, she was satisfied that her client had done very well for himself. She had to admit that she couldn't have done better. In fact, there were several terms that sounded surprisingly familiar, as if they had been directly lifted from a divorce agreement she had written.

Her next call was to Dan. Adam, still lying on the couch, started to grin as he overheard his mother congratulating herself.

"Yep, my best work of the day," Lucy bragged. "Only three and a half weeks 'til Adam's a free man."

CHAPTER FORTY-SIX

She walked into an empty house, having spent the entire plane ride rehearsing what she was going to say to Ron about her choice. On the surface, things looked like they were in good order and better than she might have expected. But a few peeks here and there revealed signs of her long absence. The dishwasher hadn't been run, the inside of the fridge was looking pretty sorry and the boys' rooms were strewn with clothes. She emptied her suitcase on the bed and grabbed her bundle of wash.

At the bottom of the basement steps, a pile of laundry greeted her. So, here was the rest of it. There was no reason for her to expect that the guys would have attended to the things she always did around the house, but she still held out hope the day might come. She was pouring detergent into the washer when she heard heavy footsteps above her. The kids couldn't be home, since it was only mid-day. And Ron had told her he was too busy to pick her up at the airport, forcing her to ask Val.

So who could this be, and how had they gotten in? Georgina slowly backed away from the laundry area and into the dark alcove with the workbench. She reached for the largest hammer she could find, and stealthily positioned herself behind the basement staircase.

Upstairs, a phone rang. She heard a familiar voice answer it, and although she knew she should have been relieved to hear her husband speaking, she would almost have preferred to confront a burglar. Hitting someone over the head with a hammer seemed easier than facing Ron right now. She'd caught him in a lie; he had been available to get her, but chose not to. And apparently, from what she'd learned from Vivian, he'd lied to her about a lot of other things. Now, she was about to reveal her decision, despite the angry reaction she anticipated.

She made her way up the stairs and into the kitchen to find her husband sitting with his back to her, beer bottle in hand.

"Hi, Ron."

He didn't rise to meet her.

"What are you doing home at this hour?" she asked. "I thought you had a meeting and were too busy to get me."

"Well, who's too busy for who? I'm not the one who's been away from the house and kids for over a week. Again."

"You know I had no choice. It hasn't been a vacation."

Ron slogged down the balance of the beer and took a long look at his wife. "No vacation, but Laurel Hall isn't exactly slumming it. Who was waiting on you this time, one of the usuals or was it that snot-nosed lady from the agency?"

"Mrs. Brockhurst let her go. And none of them wait on me, you know that. I made breakfast and dinner for the children every day, just like I always do."

"Glad you were cooking for somebody. We sure as hell could have used some home cooking around here."

Georgina took a glance at Ron. He wasn't wearing a one-beer look. "I made a decision when I was in New York."

"Oh, really. Without talking to me?" he asked.

"This whole thing is about my sister's children. It's about what's best for them."

"So what kind of bullshit decision did you make?" Ron's response destroyed Georgina's small ray of hope that a fight could be avoided.

"I don't think the children belong here. And I told it to the others."

"You don't think they belong here? You're their aunt. Those kids should be right here with us, with this family!" he shouted, pounding on the kitchen table.

Georgina shook her head. It was going to be ugly, after all.

"What were you thinking? Were you thinking at all? Do you understand what this means for our family? Did you think about what you were doing to us?"

Georgina stood in the middle of the room. Even from there, she could see that his eyes were glazed over. He'd been drinking at lunch, she thought, or maybe even on the job. "What does my decision have to do with 'us'?"

Ron rose from his chair. One fist clenched, the other holding the bottle, he moved toward his wife. "It has everything to do with us. Gina, where do you think all the money is going to go?" She had no answer. "Don't you get it? The money is going to go where the kids go! And if the kids go to Everett, he'll run through the dough like it's water! And that weasel, Vaughn, don't you see why he wants them? Everyone seems to get the big picture here except for you! We know what would be best for those kids!"

"So it's the money? That's why you're upset?"

"I'm upset that you changed the whole game plan without even talking to me! We're supposed to be in charge of those kids... and the money. And that expensive lawyer is supposed to make that happen. Why else are we paying him?"

"We're not paying him. I'm paying him with the money my sister left me, just for me."

"Oh, don't give me that crap. You probably used it all up already. For what? So you can just give the kids away? Well, Gina, you better fix this. Tell me you can take it back."

"I won't. This is my decision."

Ron raised his fist, as though threatening to knock her out. Instead, he threw the beer bottle in the opposite direction, where it smashed against the wall with a loud bang, the glass shattering. He grabbed his wife and shoved her against the counter. "Don't tell me you won't!"

Georgina cowered, her courage retreating.

"Those Brockhursts did a great snow job on you. They want to keep it all in the family. Your sister's gone, so they can get it all back, everything Everett lost in the divorce. Can't you see what's going on here? You fucked up, Gina. You fucked it up for us."

Georgina broke away from him. At what she measured to be a safer distance, she spoke up softly. "It's you. The reason we're not going to have custody of Beau and Emma." Ron's eyes narrowed. "Mrs. Brockhurst got some information about you."

Ron started to smile. "Oh, this is good, just like I was telling you... she'll do anything to keep it in the family."

"You beat up your own son."

"I never touched our kids and you know it."

"I mean Sean, your son with Patty. You beat him up. He was just twelve and you beat him up."

"Where are you getting this shit? How would you know what happened with Sean? You talk to him?" he asked in a flat, deadened tone.

Georgina went on. "I don't even know where he lives. I never see your checks go out to him. It was in the police reports that Patty filed. Vivian Brockhurst found out. She hired an investigator."

"That fucking bitch hired someone to investigate me? And she's looking into stuff about my old girlfriends? And about Sean? That doesn't make you wonder what's really going on here?"

Georgina felt as though she was looking down at herself from above, aware of the danger but unable to stop. "And there was a report from the owner at Greene Street, where you did all that work. You hit him. When we were visiting Mom, I guess. The police were called. You gonna tell me it was his fault? And what about the fight with the guy at the bar? He started it, too? Jimmy, at the precinct — was he the one to get you out of it?"

Ron started to pace as she spoke. "So, you believe all this crap?"

"The Brockhursts believe it and they don't like it. And I'm not sure what to believe anymore." The man cocked his head slightly, daring her to go on. "I watched you tell our son to beat up another child on the basketball court." Georgina held her breath. He didn't respond. "You've got a problem, Ron. You need help. And unless you get it, you won't only lose those children, you'll lose your own children."

"Is that a threat?"

"No, it's a promise. You'll lose me, Ron. Me and the children."

"You'll never leave me," he scoffed. "What would you do?"

"I don't know. But I'm going to leave if I have to."

Ron studied his prey. Make a move, his eyes dared her. One little move.

Georgina didn't flinch under his glare. Her tears hadn't helped last time, or the time before that. They only seemed to make it worse. She was going to be brave no matter what came next.

"You're not goin' anywhere."

"If I have to…"

"I supported your ass since the day you left that stinking town and I've busted my chops paying every fucking bill and dealing with all your family shit and then you give me this? I told you before, Gina, you're not leaving. And if you try, you know I'll follow you. I'll hunt you down." He could smell her terror. "And don't even think of going off with the kids."

"Ron, I can't take this, I can't. You've got to get help, or I swear I'll …"

In one motion, she felt herself thrust to the floor, her legs collapsing out from under her as she landed hard on one arm. His knee against her chest, Ron held her down. He choked off her cries of anguish as he seized her by the neck. Then he threw her over onto her stomach, twisting her arm behind her, under his weight.

Unable to move, Georgina steeled her body to receive the inevitable blows. She couldn't catch her breath; her screams remained frozen in her throat. She prayed it would be quick, like the last time. Just a few blows, and with God's help, not to her face.

But Ron had something different in mind. With one hand, he started to loosen his belt. She could hear it fly out of the last loop. A whipping?

With fury, his strength easily fending off her struggle, Ron Fiske laid siege to his wife.

***

She was still shaking when she started to pick up the shards of broken glass. The shower was no help; she just couldn't stop the flow of tears. She told herself to go through the motions. The kids would soon be home. Would they see that she'd been crying? This one was close, what with her arm. He could have broken it. Before, he just left bruises and expected her to cover it up. Going back to the center was out of the question. They'd notice her injury and would want her to do something about it. It wasn't the right time.

Still trembling and despite her pain, she mopped the floor. A thought came to mind. She could kill him. Not impossible. It gave her a little solace to believe she might be capable of doing it. But murder? She could leave him, but not if it meant leaving the children behind. With nothing but Ron's influence, they'd turn into angry, brutal men. They could be halfway there already, she feared. It might be too late, but maybe not. She was not going to abandon them. She heard her husband's footsteps as he walked down the hallway toward her. He entered the kitchen.

"I told you I'd help clean that up." He had to be kidding, she thought. Seeing that he wasn't, she propped the sponge mop upright in the bucket and left it there. She slowly walked over to the sink and ran warm water over her hands. She let the water run for a long while.

Looking back, the rest of that afternoon and night were obscure. She couldn't remember Ron in the kitchen, helping. She couldn't remember the kids coming home, what they said, what the family ate for dinner. She couldn't remember how she finally stopped shaking. This time, she wanted to remember. She didn't want to forget what he'd done.

CHAPTER FORTY-SEVEN

Doris was uneasy as her daughter drove her from the airport along the Interstate to the outskirts of town. Instead of enjoying their usual conversation, she ended up giving a soliloquy about her local news and gossip. She reported that back at home, the Davis family had just given up their last few acres to a developer, generating another round of talk about some big box store that might be coming in. Such rumors always rattled the small merchants in Henryetta, including Charlie. Wearing out that subject without any response from her daughter, Doris forged on with a tale of the mayor two towns over who'd absconded with a large portion of funds from the annual cattleman's convention. Still, no response. The long silences weren't like Gina. But Doris was determined not to pry. Things were bound to unfold as long as she remained her usual patient self.

The house looked fine from the outside, but as she entered, she sensed that something was off. The rooms were all tidy, but she noticed a starkness she hadn't seen before. Washing up in the little guest bathroom, she was sure something was missing. One, old frayed hand towel sat in its lonely position on the rack. The wall paint was faded. She hadn't been to her daughter's home for a long time, but from what she remembered it had always looked more welcoming than it did now.

"Did you move some furniture around?" she asked, as she took a seat in the kitchen. She peered through the alcove into the shadows of the living room.

Georgina was preparing coffee and putting some snacks together. "I've spent the last few days cleaning out some junk. But it's the same old furniture in the same old places." She put coffee cups and a plate of cookies onto the table, and still standing, sorted through the day's mail.

Doris frowned, noting the discolored areas on the kitchen wall. She could hear the hum of the refrigerator. "Gosh, now I know. It's your paintings. The paintings are gone."

"I moved some of them to the basement."

"Oh." Doris started on an oatmeal cookie. Her daughter still hadn't looked up at her.

"Thought I might finally set up a studio for myself."

"But it's so dark in the cellar, isn't it? Don't you need natural light?"

"A little comes in from the basement window. Besides, there's no other place to set it up. The attic's too cramped with that roof line. It's all eaves up there." She sat down beside her mother and glanced over a letter.

"Well, I miss your pictures. They really do cheer up the place."

"Thanks, Mom. It's hard to believe anyone would notice."

Doris shook her head. Her daughter, the artist; so different from Suzanne. Bold and confident, Suzanne had been comfortable with praise. But to Gina, talented as she was, it still came as a surprise that her artwork might garner any attention. She painted for the sheer pleasure of it. Doris understood. It was the same for her when it came to sewing and quilting. She did it because she couldn't do otherwise. She found herself in fabric shops, buying pieces of possibilities in yards and bolts, imagining, dreaming. She reached out and patted her daughter's hand. "You know I've always loved your work."

"Oh, Mom. Well, here's some good news for a change," she said, holding out the letter she'd been reading. "Looks like I'm all set to start again in August." She poured the coffee, adding just the right amount of cream to her mom's cup.

Doris smiled. "They certainly appreciate you. I'll bet they can't wait to have Mrs. Fiske back in the art room again." The ice seemed to have broken.

The women chatted over coffee until Doris announced that it was getting on, and that they should work on a shopping list; she was going to make good on the promise she'd made to her grandsons to make their favorite short ribs. She wanted to get cracking. The ladies headed downtown to collect groceries.

It was in the meat section of Barstow's that Georgina finally told her. "Mr. Vaughn wants to meet Beau." The color went out of her mother's face as she gripped the large package of short ribs she'd just been inspecting. "It's going to happen soon."

Doris felt bone through the package. Bone under cold flesh. She had not prepared for this turn of events. Doris turned away from her daughter, dropped the package into a plastic bag and tossed it on top of the other groceries in the cart. Then she slowly pushed the cart along, pretending to study the contents of the poultry bin while actually trying to keep a lid on her anger. She was determined to be different from her own mother. Troubling news like this would have sent her straight into a frenzy.

Doris avoided interrogating her daughters. As they grew into women, she had vowed not to interfere in their lives, even at the cost of sometimes appearing indifferent. By taking a step back from them, her girls would always have room to open up to her.

However, holding in her feelings was now becoming more and more difficult. A permanent groove must have formed in her bottom lip by now, she mused, from all the recent times she'd had to bite it rather than say her piece. From the start, she and Charlie made it clear that they were counting on their daughter to monitor the situation with Beau and Emma, knowing she would do her very best for them. In turn, Gina assured them that things were going well, even after the shocking news about Mr. Vaughn and the confirmation of his paternity claim. Word was that the lawyer was sharp and knew how to keep the man at bay.

What had changed to allow him any contact with Beau? Wasn't it the job of that expensive lawyer to prevent this from happening? She glanced at her daughter, wondering how she could have been so calm in breaking this sort of news.

Georgina placed a package of chicken legs into the cart. "I talked to Mr. DeBello. I had to choose whether or not to stop Mr. Vaughn from seeing Beau...and Emma. I was forced to decide, and so I did."

"This was your decision? You decided?" Doris heard herself shout. It was unlike her to speak sharply at all, and rarer still for her to raise her voice to her own child. But to do so in public was completely out of character. Georgina could feel eyes upon them. Even the butcher raised his eyebrows, looking at them through the glass barrier.

"I had to," Georgina said under her breath, pushing the cart along.

"And you didn't think of mentioning this to us? What decision did you make?" She hadn't lowered her voice.

"Mom, please. The court appointed a psychiatrist who looked into everything. He thinks Gary should meet the children and spend some time with them. After really thinking about it, I'm in agreement. We could have temporarily stopped Mr. Vaughn from having what they call 'visitation', but I met with Vivian and Gary Vaughn, and we made a plan that might work out. So I decided not to stop him. He's going to meet the children."

Mrs. Lily chose that particular moment to cross their path as she emerged from the frozen section. Her shopping cart contained a stack of sticky buns. Georgina dreaded the thought that the babysitter might have witnessed the little interchange between her and her mother.

"Oh my, if it isn't Doris and Gina."

Doris did her best to cover her distress, despite what she'd just learned from her daughter. She prayed silently for Mrs. Lily to make it brief, but it was not to be.

"I'm deeply sorry about everything. It's such a tragedy. I remember what a lovely girl your Suzanne was." She gave Doris a little squeeze on the arm. "But I've done my best to help over at Gina's house."

Georgina took the opportunity to express her thanks, once again, for everything she'd done for the family.

"Not easy over there these days," Mrs. Lily commented, shaking her head. She then added her own thanks for the lovely bouquet of flowers sent by the Fiskes in gratitude. The woman didn't seem to mind that her frozen food was in danger of melting as she continued with her pleasantries. She turned a sympathetic gaze back onto Doris. "Is Mr. Granger doing well?"

"He's just fine, thanks."

"And the store?"

"Same as always, we're getting by."

Mrs. Lily had that in common with Doris: their men had each inherited family-run hardware stores, once a secure livelihood in small towns but now struggling outposts threatened by the approach of behemoths like Home Depot and Wal-Mart. Randolph had died years ago, the hardware store given up when the Lily children moved away. It comforted the older woman to hear that Charlie was still keeping his head above water out there in Oklahoma. If he was anything like Randolph, that store was who he was and who he would always be, that is if he was lucky enough to survive the tough times.

"Send him my regards, please. And again, I'm very sorry for your loss."

As Mrs. Lily walked away, Georgina moved off into the next aisle. She hoped to avoid the discussion she'd been having with her mother, and scolded herself for bringing up the subject right there in the store as if it were some minor issue. Her mother's unusual outburst struck a nerve. It was a pipedream, she recognized, to think her mother would comprehend her reasons for allowing Gary into the children's lives. No matter what explanation she might offer, it would make no sense. And, Georgina realized, it would make even less sense when her mother learned she was prepared to withdraw from the custody battle. As understanding as her mother was, she would never accept her choices concerning Gary Vaughn.

In fact, looking at it now from her parents' perspective, Georgina saw that they would fight her decisions unless the entire story was laid out before them, a story Georgina could barely admit to herself. Her marriage was unraveling. With all the grief her parents had endured, it seemed unfair to add this to their worries.

At the end of the dairy aisle, Doris caught up with her daughter. She turned to face her and spoke calmly, in a very low voice. "We need to be included, Gina. They're our grandchildren, and this should be a family decision, not just yours or the lawyer's...or God help me, Vivian's." She took the milk and yogurt out of her daughter's hands, added them to the cart and struck a path towards check-out.

***

The aroma of Gramma's short ribs permeated the house. The children were expected on the late bus, after sports. Doris was trying her best to appear upbeat. She bided her time, pretending to focus on her kitchen chores. Georgina, meanwhile, tried to look as busy as possible, peeling the potatoes while wondering how she was going to make it through a weekend trying to avoid the painful topic. Her mother wasn't likely to let it go. She found it wrenching to cross her.

Their relationship had always been an easy one, much like that of two best friends. They had so little history of confrontation that when it was upon them, it was like being struck. At those rare times, her mother's pleasant exterior seemed to barely cover her coldness.

She'd been this way when Georgina told her about planning to move away with Ron. Her mother opposed her not by histrionics but through a subtle pulling away from her, her banter evaporating, the few choice words coming after many long hours: "If you go off with that man, you'll have to live with the consequences." Georgina recalled thinking her parents' opposition was on account of their old fashioned attitude about couples living together before marriage. Soon after she left with Ron, they eloped. Now she wondered if her family had actually objected to the man rather than the decision to go off with him. But if they did object to Ron, her mother would have been loath to say what she really felt. It would only have created a permanent distance between them. Mom was wise to stay out of it, Georgina thought. There was no way she could have stopped me.

"What is this horrible thing?" Doris had come across a crinkled up bag of food wedged into the far recesses of her daughter's refrigerator.

"Must be from last week. Ron kept buying the boys Taco Bell and McDonalds."

Doris winced as she gingerly gathered up the leftovers and dumped them in the garbage. She went back to her task of searching for the carrots, confronting more obstacles along the way.

"Egg roll, French fries," she said, identifying each item in turn and discarding the desiccated remains. "Didn't you say he makes dinner, now and then?"

"It's been hard for him with me away. And real cooking? Well, that was a long time ago, Mom."

Doris remembered Mrs. Lily's comment about things not being easy at the Fiske house. As she dumped a bunch of parsley that had seen better days, some of it dropped behind the garbage pail. She moved the large can towards her to clean up, and noticed a dent on the wall, level with her knee. It looked fresh, somehow, a deep, sharp dent like a raw scar. She moved the pail back into its place, covering the blemish.

"Boys should be home in about an hour," Georgina remarked, finally locating the carrots for her mother.

"Well, that should give us time to talk. About the children."

"Oh, they're doing great. They're doing well in sports…and I think now that I'll be home more they'll do better in school."

"I mean Beau and Emma."

"Mom, I don't want to talk about this." She dropped the potatoes into a pot of water and lit the stove. Doris stood at the kitchen counter, peeling the carrots and then set out a cutting board and knife. She started to chop. The stillness of the kitchen was punctuated by the even rapping of the knife against the board. Georgina watched her mother's steady hands. Golden hands, everyone called them. She, rather than Suzanne, inherited them from her mother. A soft chime from the hallway clock echoed through the house. Somewhere down the street, a dog barked. It was a standoff neither woman offering a word.

The silence weighed down on her. Georgina realized there was no way out of it. Her mother deserved an explanation. She sat down at the table and looked up at her.

"Mom, I'm trying to do the right thing. The psychiatrist gave his opinion suggesting that Mr. Vaughn spend time with Beau, and the judge agreed. It made sense to me. And if he meets Beau, he should see Emma. It's only right. I met with Mr. Vaughn and Vivian, and we decided it would be the best thing to do."

"The same people you're fighting? They're the ones you made the decision with? And your lawyer went along with it?" She was trying to get it straight. Everyone had been consulted about this but her and Charlie.

"I didn't need to ask the lawyer, Mom. Mr. Vaughn is going to meet Beau someday. He'll make it happen, no matter what result we get in court. I'd rather have it happen the right way."

"That sounds like a big change from what you've been telling us. You thought that man wouldn't have any chance of meeting the kids."

"You're right, I did think that. But the psychiatrist had a different view from what we expected, and the judge was influenced by that opinion. Basically, the idea is that Beau should have the chance to get to know a parent who really wants to care for him. You, of all people, know how little Everett has ever cared. And now with Suzanne gone, we all feel that the attention of a caring father would be good for Beau. And for Emma. The more I thought about it, the more I felt that spending time with Gary could be a good thing for them."

"Now it's 'Gary'?"

"I've met with him a few times and yes, I call him Gary."

Doris moved the chopped carrots into the bowl, and set it aside. At last, they were getting to the point.

"Let's say they spend time together. What then? Is Beau going to find out that Mr. Vaughn is his biological father?"

"He'll find out during therapy — and only when he's ready for it. So it will be handled right."

Doris sighed. She and Charlie had little belief in psychiatry. They viewed therapy as a lazy way for rich people to handle their personal problems, problems that could be resolved if faced squarely. "More therapy for those children?"

"They've done well with Dr. Backus. Beau's doing better and Emma seems to be coming along very well. They've been through trauma, Mom, and she's been there to help them."

"But to throw this at them, a different parent and after all they've been through? The judge and that court psychiatrist should realize that this is just too much for the children. It's another trauma to find out about some other father."

"It can't be avoided forever."

Doris got up and walked to the sink. She let the warm water wash over her hands.

"Gina, we're not going to see eye to eye on this." She wiped her hands and opened the fridge to get the cucumbers. "And I don't see where it leaves you. Are you going to be running back and forth taking the children to see Mr. Vaughn for these visits? Where are they going to be staying? In that giant house with a nanny?"

Georgina took a deep breath. There was no point in beating around the bush; it only prolonged the torture. "Well, visitation hasn't started yet. We're going to see how it goes. If Everett agrees to it, and Gary does well with the kids, we might consider having them live with him. We'd all go to visit them at Gary's home, or they'd come to visit us."

It was the cucumber's turn to come under the knife. Doris wielded the weapon without looking up. Her mouth was taut.

"You and Dad would be welcome anytime." Georgina's voice trailed off.

"Are you're telling me that as long as Mr. Vaughn and the kids get along, you're ready to give up the kids?"

"I didn't say I'm giving them up, I'd still see them as much as possible."

"That's giving them up. Are you going to let that man take them? Or risk Everett keeping them?"

"Mom, I have no intention of letting Everett have custody. I'll do whatever I can to stop that from happening. But Gary seems to be a good man, and he really cares about the children. He's come forward to be Beau's father when most men would run in the other direction, to avoid the responsibility. I spoke with him in person and he really seems to have his heart in the right place. He has three daughters who he loves very much. He just wants his son, too. And since we wouldn't split up the children — well, he'd take both of them."

Doris held the knife up as she stopped. "So, let me see. Now, you're against the idea of bringing the children down here to live with you. I thought that was what this whole lawsuit was about."

"I want to have a say in what happens to the children. That's why there's a lawsuit. And if Gary is unsuitable, then yes, I'll still fight for custody. But if Gary turns out to be good with them, then Beau and Emma will be able to keep their lives as normal as possible, by staying in New York and continuing at the same school with all of their friends."

"If I'd known about all this, maybe Charlie and I would have butted in. They could have lived with us, if you couldn't handle all four of them."

"It's not that we can't handle them. If we had to, we would. But Suzanne didn't want her kids living in Henryetta or here in Greenwood, anymore than she wanted either place for herself. She made a different life for them up in New York, and that's what she wanted for them. I know she would have wanted Beau to stay at Aston."

"The children are young. They could get used to living here very easily, don't you realize that? And they could do very well in school and go on to some fancy, Ivy League college if they have a mind to do it. The important thing is who you live with, not where you live! You should know that, Gina."

Georgina didn't want to insult her mother. She couldn't say that she'd have blown her brains out if she'd been forced to spend the rest of her life in Henryetta. Her sister felt the same way not only about her hometown, but about Greenwood, too. Skippy had once asked her how she could stand her isolated town which, though larger than Henryetta, was still a "goldfish bowl," where a different hairdo raised eyebrows, a new outfit stirred up commentary, a new car incited envy.

Georgina's recent travels were already part of the local gossip mill. People were aware that she was visiting New York to help her niece and nephew, yet it didn't stop tongues from wagging. Someone had started the rumor that she was suddenly rich, ready to pull up stakes and move north. In fact, the thought had crossed her mind that living in New York might have been a better fit for her, not only as a person who cherished privacy, but as an artist. Perhaps, her life would have been different. She could see her sister's point of view.

"You're right, Mom. People are more important. But when Suzanne got divorced, she had to make that same choice: to move here with me or back with you, to the people she loved, or to stay in New York. She made her choice and was willing to give up a lot to stay there. Believe, me, Everett would have signed off as fast as he could if she had wanted to leave New York with the children and give up Laurel Hall, but she never even considered moving away. She made a life for herself there and that's what she wanted, both for herself and her children."

"She didn't know what was to come, Gina. If she thought this might happen, she would have wanted them to be with you, no matter where you were."

"That's not what she said in her will. She could have suggested I take them if anything happened to her and Everett. But she didn't put that in her will. And she didn't include you and Daddy, either."

"Oh. She didn't mention us?" Doris hadn't expected to be included in the will, but hearing the actual words hurt.

"That's right, Mom. She could have done it, but she left us all out."

After a pause, Doris folded her arms across her chest. "Well, I wish she'd thought about a guardian and given some sort of instruction. I can't believe she would have allowed the children to be handed over to a complete stranger to them. And nothing you can say will change my mind about that."

Georgina had no answer. Her mother was right. She was just missing a very important part of the equation: Ron.

The boys tumbled into the house, with their backpacks, sports gear and sweaty clothes. Doris had a big hug for each of them, sweaty as the boys were, and apologized for her long absence. The intoxicating scent of the food had her grandsons scrambling for showers to get ready before the special meal.

"They've shot up, even since the winter," Doris commented, helping set the table.

"I know. They've both been on growth spurts with no end in sight."

"Gina…"

Georgina could feel the tide turning again, her mother ready to resume their wrangling. "Mom, I can't keep doing this. Can we talk about this later?"

"Sure. But I have one last thing to say, please."

Georgina looked at her mother. She saw the lines that had formed under her eyes and around her mouth. She wanted to smooth the lines away along with all of the grief they'd both suffered.

"I suggest you get to know this man, this Gary, very, very well. Because otherwise, I don't see how you could even consider letting them live with him."

"I know, Mom. That's just what I'm going to do. I'm going to find out everything I can about him."

The kitchen door opened, and Ron entered, carrying a package. Georgina knew it contained what he needed to get through the weekend: a few six-packs of Bud to tune them all out. Wouldn't it have been nice, she thought, if he'd picked up some flowers for her mom? She chided herself for confusing him with some fictional dream-man. Even if a guy was out there who would of his own accord do something sweet for his mother-in-law, Ron was not that man. And Georgina wasn't going to ask him to do her any favors.

***

Charlie wasn't one for talking on the phone, but Doris had to speak to him. It was her chance to do so, with the boys and Ron out shooting baskets down the street and Georgina downtown getting a few things. With the excuse that she needed a little nap, Doris vanished upstairs to her sanctuary. The guestroom, usually used as the boys' TV hangout, was filled with family memorabilia. The shelves displayed assorted shells from their trips to the beach, Ron and Georgina's wedding pictures, Ron in uniform graduating from the academy, Georgina's diploma from art school, the boys' trophies and class pictures, and one familiar portrait of Doris and Charlie with the family at a Christmas dinner in Henryetta. In the photo, the boys were little and Ron had his muscular arm around his wife. Her fingers were touching his. All was well.

Now, she sat on the old twin bed with its woolly, red plaid coverlet and wondered exactly how to say what she had to say to Charlie. Their own marriage had been challenging at times, but she couldn't remember a bad patch that looked anything like what was going on with Gina and Ron. The tension between them was obvious. It didn't take a brain surgeon to figure it out, as Charlie would have said.

The weekend had started off well, with a lovely dinner and silly stories being shared around the table. But as the hours went on, it became clear that Ron and Gina were at odds. Her son-in-law made disparaging remarks about the letter from school, viewing the offer to take her back in the fall in the worst light possible: the school had failed to hire her for the summer. He tore into Gina about the latest bill from the attorney, and, perhaps hoping to expose her for bad behavior, told Doris that his wife was thinking of abandoning their niece and nephew. Yet, when Gina spoke of visiting them again soon, he complained that she was leaving her own kids in the lurch. Ron had never struck her as being particularly warm to her daughter, but this was different. He was rude to Gina. It was unpleasant and awkward for both of the women.

During the weekend, Doris noticed that the boys had begun to follow their father's lead. At first, she wrote if off as the beginning of pre-teen nonsense. But then, she noticed the way they joined Ron to gang up on Gina. Gina had become a second-class citizen in her own house. She couldn't suggest a movie, a place to go, a meal they might like or, it seemed, any plan at all without inviting mockery. Her daughter didn't protest. She seemed to ignore their words.

So Doris was not surprised when, in a moment to themselves, her daughter finally admitted to serious trouble at home. Gina couldn't say when it had started with the boys, but she thought that Ron had been different for some time, perhaps even before her sister died. No, he wasn't drinking more, she said, but he was becoming a nasty drunk. And if he didn't drink, he eventually got irritable, anyway. The stress concerning Suzanne's death and all the recent traveling had worsened the situation, but Gina felt that their relationship had been going in the wrong direction for quite a while. Doris couldn't believe that the words came out of her own mouth, but she mentioned counseling.

"I tried that, Mom. He thinks it's ridiculous. Ron told me there's nothing wrong. Except with me."

Doris listened as the full story started to emerge. What concerned her most was Gina's fear for her sons. As her daughter told it, Ron was the influence behind Cliff's bullying incidents; watching his father get away with it at home made it seem acceptable to model the same behavior in school.

When Doris asked whether the bullying at home amounted to physical abuse against her or the children, Gina was hesitant. She didn't give her a straight answer. She admitted that Ron's temper had erupted on several occasions, but said no more about that. Doris thought of the strange dents in the walls, even the one in her daughter's bedroom. The one in the hallway. The missing vase. Evidently, his displays of temper had occurred on more than a few occasions.

When Gina told her mother about the basketball game, it set off an alarm. What could be done? Gina didn't have any answers, only questions. She asked, "How can I bring Beau and Emma into this home when I don't even know what to do with my own family?"

Doris knew Gina was speaking of her marriage. Her daughter apologized for adding her troubles to the heap and when Doris reached out to say it was no burden at all, Gina did just as she had as a little girl; she folded up into her mother's arms and dissolved into tears. And so they sat for a long while, Doris promising they'd figure it out together.

Cell phone in hand, Doris tried to think of the words to say. How could she possibly get all of this across to Charlie? It was awful news, and she wouldn't be there to comfort him. He would certainly agree that these were treacherous waters for their daughter to try and navigate on her own. She knew he'd be ready to do anything to help Gina. Sitting there alone in the room, Doris couldn't summon the courage to make the call.

When finally she and Charlie did have their long talk, it was after she was back in Henryetta. They were opening the store early in the morning, before deliveries. He took it better than she thought he would, and said he'd had an idea that there might be some problems, but had brushed it off. The thing that most surprised her was his calm suggestion that they meet Gary Vaughn for themselves. If he was a bad egg, said Charlie, he would know it in a minute. There wasn't a chance in hell that man was going to have anything to do with his grandchildren if he didn't measure up.

"And I don't mean measure up like Ron. That mistake ain't happening twice." Charlie's voice softened. "How's Gina taking it?"

"She'll be all right, honey. I know she'll be all right. She's got to be, for all the kids."

CHAPTER FORTY-EIGHT

"**Y**ou totally guilted me into this. And you're gonna pay for it!" Lia waited for a reaction, but met only her father's steady gaze and uncharacteristic silence.

After a moment, he cleared his throat. "Thank you, honey, with all my heart. Thank you." He gave her a hug, aware that it was going to be one-sided. Lia seemed to shrug it off. She turned her eyes toward the end of the driveway where a black Range Rover was pulling in, a woman at the wheel. "And I suppose you're gonna tell me to play nice."

"I'm not pushing my luck," Gary said. Getting ready, he'd tried to convince himself that it was just going to be a little outing. But, he couldn't. It was huge. It was the first step, even if the children didn't know it. For them, the day was going to mean only one thing: the excitement of being at the stadium to see the Yankees play the Sox.

With arms outstretched wide the same way he always greeted his family, he came forward to welcome the children. His broad grin was meant to reassure them, to say he was a good guy, a person you could trust. Beneath the smile, though, Gary felt every bit as vulnerable and awkward as a boy on his first date. The fear of rejection overshadowed what could have been a moment of joy.

"You remember Mr. Vaughn, don't you, Beau?" asked Georgina.

The boy gave a little nod.

"Call me Gary, you guys, okay?"

"Hi, Gary," Emma said, staring up at him.

"Hey, are we all ready to see our team kick butt? Where are your Yankee caps?"

"We don't have any."

"Well, Emma, we'll certainly have to take care of that. Do you want a pink one to go with your sweatshirt? 'Cause they have special pink ones just for the ladies."

"Hey, cut the sexist stuff," Lia interrupted. "The Yankees wear blue and white, Emma. They're known for their Yankee pin stripes." She pointed to her own cap.

The six-year-old smiled. "I want one like hers!"

Beau had been watching the interchange between his sister and the woman named Lia, but all the while keeping an eye on Gary. He remembered him not just from the few days at school, but from the night at Laurel Hall. The man had disagreed with his uncle. It was about pitching.

"And how 'bout you, Beau? A pitcher as good as you must have a Yankee cap. Unless you're a Mets fan."

"Chris's dog chewed it up." Emma covered her mouth and giggled.

The sudden scorch across Beau's cheeks reminded Gary of his own torture as a child. His fair face, too, had reflected even the slightest degree of embarrassment.

The boy mumbled, "I'm a Yankee fan."

"Well then, two caps it shall be. And you can choose them as soon as we get there. Deal?" Beau nodded, but was quiet, still trying to figure out why Mr. Vaughn and the woman were going to be with them for the day. His aunt said they were her friends. And he knew they were also friends of Ms. Bennett, the lawyer who gave them the tickets she promised. But he'd seen his uncle argue with Mr. Vaughn that night in the playroom. Looking again at the man, he remembered what it was about. Mr. Vaughn told Uncle Ron not to let him pitch a curveball or it would ruin his arm. And that was the same thing his coach at school told the team. He warned everyone about it. Beau felt a little better thinking it through. He hopped in the car next to his aunt and Emma, ready for a little excitement.

***

"Ever tasted a better hot dog?" Beau and Emma shook their heads in tandem, their mouths stuffed with food. "That's right, because nothing tastes as good as a hot dog at Yankee stadium. It's a well-known fact."

Georgina glanced sideways at Gary's face. He'd picked up a tan since the last time she saw him. Was he thinner? He seemed completely relaxed, natural. She noticed that when he talked to the children, he didn't patronize them. He seemed to assume they'd understand his grown-up conversation without his having to dumb it down. To Georgina, it was a sign of respect toward Beau and Emma. Probably the same way he related to his own kids, she thought. Lia struck her as a smart, strong young woman, and a very good sport in what had to be an unsettling situation. Instead of shying away, the young woman was earnestly conversing with Emma's bobble-head Jeter doll. The little girl took on the role of the doll, speaking gruffly in her best imitation of a man. Glancing at Lia, Georgina recognized a familiar look. Her squint, despite the sunglasses, matched the one on her nephew's face as he watched the game. They could certainly pass for the sister and brother that they actually were.

Gary sprang from his seat, fist raised, cheering, as the inning ended with an out at first base. Beau accepted his high-five, fired up to have witnessed the pitcher's signature pick-off move. Emma tried to join in, but was encumbered with a hot dog in one hand, the doll in the other.

As the crowd settled back for the seventh-inning stretch, Lia announced she was off to the bathroom. Emma looked at her aunt, and got the nod to join her. The girl left with Emma, taking her by the hand.

"Hey, Beau, so what do you think?"

The boy smiled at Mr. Vaughn.

"Think Mo's coming out in the ninth?"

"Hope so."

"Me too."

"Who's Mo?"

Beau and Gary looked at one another with the same expression of incredulity. Then they laughed. "Lady, you are no New Yorker," Gary said.

The brunette responded with a little flutter of her eyelashes. "I don't pretend to be one."

Gary nudged her with his elbow. "You do know that they're going to play 'God Bless America' now, don't you?"

"Of course!" she lied, smiling at him.

By the beginning of the next inning, she started to worry about her niece. With such a large crowd in such a huge stadium, she hoped the two hadn't become separated. When they finally returned, Georgina knew that something was wrong. Emma was sniffling, Lia's arm around her.

"She'll be fine," Lia assured Georgina. Gary was concerned, but before he could say anything, Lia shook her head at him in warning. Over Emma's head, he mouthed the words, "What's wrong?"

"Please," Lia begged. "She's fine. She just needs a minute." Emma turned her tear-streaked face to her aunt. She reached out for her and scrambled into her lap. Emma whispered into her aunt's ear that she thought she saw her Mommy. She said it looked like her, but it wasn't her. Georgina gave her a hug.

Whatever was wrong with Emma, Gary knew one way to help: distract her. Luck was on his side. "Now, this time we're not going to miss it!" he insisted, addressing everyone in his contingent, "So get ready — and this means you, Little Miss Emma!"

Emma broke away from her aunt and got back into her own seat, watching intently as "the wave" came her way. As the crowd around her surged, she jumped up with her hands in the air, shouting along with everyone else.

The music started. The theme of "The Sandman" blared across the stadium as Beau's dream came true: he saw his idol, Mariano, jog out to the mound. The crowd cheered as the pitcher took his place, easing his slender body into its stance. For Beau it no longer mattered who would win that day; it was a sight he would never forget.

Later that evening, when Lia was alone in the kitchen with her dad, she told him what had happened with Emma. They'd followed the lady, since the little girl was so upset, so insistent. And when they stopped the woman, Emma just stared up at her. The woman seemed to realize she'd been mistaken for someone else.

"The strangest thing came out of her mouth," Lia told her father. "The woman leaned down to Emma and said, 'Sorry, honey. But you're so sweet, I wish you were mine.' That poor kid," Lia muttered. "And Beau..."

Gary was preparing the steak for the two of them. He turned it over in its marinade as he listened to his daughter.

"They're adorable, they really are," she went on, "but I can't imagine after all they've been through, what it's gonna do to them to find out you're Beau's dad."

Her father was placing sliced onions in the pan. He started and stopped a few times as he tried to put his words together. "Lia," he finally said, "The last thing I'd ever want to do is hurt those kids. You have to trust that it will come out all right."

Before stepping outside to put the steak on the grill, he turned to her with a smile and thanked her for what she'd done that day.

CHAPTER FORTY-NINE

She did the dangerous thing and stepped into the office. One foot in the door and she might never get out. It was even riskier with all the lawyers still in court except Claire. But she had to get the file for the next day's appearance, or get stuck coming in for it in the middle of the night.

"Hey, Lucy, what're you doing here? I thought I'd have some peace!"

"You still do, Ruby! I'm just here to pick up my stuff for court tomorrow and then I'm out of here." Lucy looked through her messages, grabbed her file and was about to exit when she heard a familiar voice from behind the waiting room door. It was Julie Caufield, speaking to Dina.

"No, I don't have an appointment. But I have to see her!"

Lucy snuck back into her office and buzzed Claire. "You have to help me," she begged. "I have to get out of here, and Julie Caufield decided to drop in for a visit."

"I do papers," said Claire, "not people. I hate people."

"Life's a bitch, I know. But you've got to come down here. Everyone else is in court! And this isn't one I can hand to Melissa."

"What do I get for it?"

"My undying appreciation."

"Not good enough. Try again."

"Fuck you."

Within a few moments, Claire appeared outside of Lucy's office. "And my day was going so well," she said. "So what's up with her?"

"I don't have a clue. She just showed up — and I've got to get out of here!"

"All right, so let's get on with it. But you're going to have to tell her what you're doing in golf clothes that's so important you can't see her."

Lucy stepped into the waiting room. She wished she hadn't opted for the pink, plaid shorts.

Mrs. Caufield looked at her attorney with disdain and wondered once again why she remained with the firm.

"Julie, even though you didn't have an appointment, I've asked Claire to drop what she's doing and meet with you." *Be nice*, Lucy wanted to add. But she knew that client wasn't capable of it. The attorney flew out the door to make her important appointment.

***

His Titleist club had landed his first drive onto the 16th fairway instead of the first, but Gary was nonetheless in a cheerful mood as he deposited Lucy at the red tees. He moved into the driver's seat of the cart, ready to go and locate his ball.

"Nice to see that you hit it down the center of a fairway. Not the right one, but a fairway nonetheless."

"Is this how you're going to be all afternoon?" Gary shot back with a smile.

She wanted to add a few jabs about all his bragging, but the cart was already flying down the hill. If his performance on the first drive was any indication, Gary's talents were not going to be as advertised.

By the time they finished at the first green, Lucy was relieved to see that she wouldn't be spending her afternoon with a duffer. Her first question answered, she wondered which direction the conversation would take. So far, they'd only discussed the beauty of the grounds, the quickness of the greens and the cooperating weather. When golfing, her business guests tended to behave in one of two ways: they were either the no-nonsense type and got down to business, or they took their time and casually discussed their business over the course of a leisurely eighteen holes. Gary's relaxed pace and manner told her she'd have to be patient, but that over the next few hours, she'd find out plenty. Eventually, he'd have to tell her how Emma and Beau were getting along with him.

By the fourth hole, Gary had finished covering the latest news about the waterfront project he was handling and was starting to turn to personal matters. But just as he seemed ready to open up, Lucy saw her coming. There was the old biddy with her huge broad-rimmed cap, hanging out of her golf cart, her hand flapping in the air as though she was hailing a cab. Some indiscernible words were coming out of the woman's mouth.

It was her former client, Edith Howger, all geared up to spoil Lucy's delightful May afternoon. As their carts approached one another, the attorney decided she'd be better off just accepting her fate. She stopped her own cart far enough from her client's to provide room for a quick escape.

"This won't take long," Lucy promised Gary. Her guest used the moment to check his cell phone.

While Lucy usually sympathized with clients who blew it by ignoring her advice, this was not so when it came to Mrs. Howger. The woman could be downright nasty. Her marriage late in life had turned from unpleasant to intolerable for both parties, yet when it came to Mr. Howger's suit for divorce, Edith wouldn't budge. She claimed he had no grounds, and she was correct. So, he couldn't get his divorce unless Edith agreed to it. The only way he could get out was by offering her a very sweet financial settlement. When he did so, Lucy strongly advised her client to consider taking it. She also cautioned Edith that no-fault divorce was being mulled over in the halls of the New York legislature and that if the law changed, her husband would have no reason to offer so handsome a deal; he could get his divorce without needing to prove grounds and so, he would have no reason to offer his wife any incentive.

Edith refused the warning. She wanted to remain married even if in name only, but mostly to ruin Mr. Howger's dream of making his sweetheart into his wife. She preferred to force them to live "in sin." The fact that he resided elsewhere with his paramour was fine with Edith since she had the marital residence to herself, with Mr. Howger continuing to pay the bills as well as her club fees. To Edith's satisfaction, her husband realized how awkward it would be for them to continue sharing their club membership. He gathered up his irons and left in search of greener greens.

A few years later, Lucy's prediction turned out to be correct: the New York law changed. No-fault divorce arrived in all of its glory. Predictably, Mr. Howger wasted no time in bringing a suit for divorce. As soon as Lucy heard that Mrs. Howger had called for an appointment, the attorney knew why the case had cropped up again.

This time, however, Edith was in for her comeuppance. As much as Lucy might have enjoyed saying "I told you so," she was prepared to do everything within her power to prolong Mr. Howger's frustration and get her client as much money as was possible.

The deeply tanned woman hollered out into the soft breeze, "He's a bastard and I'm not going to stand for any more of his horse pucky!"

Lucy noticed Edith's partner in the golf cart, a tiny, wizened woman of the same vintage who appeared equally miffed. She leaned forward along with Edith, united in the attack.

"Jesus," Gary muttered with a grin. "This is going to be fun."

Before Lucy could respond to either comment, Edith continued. "Did you see his papers? It's an absolute travesty and I'm not going to be cowed!"

"At his age, he should be ashamed!" added her diminutive companion in a munchkin voice.

Lucy tried to keep a straight face with the two of them squawking at her in their various pitches. She tried to settle them both down with a simple question to her client.

"Edith, I believe we have an appointment about this later in the week, isn't that right?"

"He's barking up the wrong tree, let me tell you! He doesn't know what he's in for!"

"Welcome to my world," Lucy whispered to Gary under her breath. "We'll talk when you come in, Edith, so let's handle it then, okay? How's your game going?"

"How can I concentrate when I have to deal with this sort of nonsense?" she asked, and added with annoyance, "I'm three over my handicap for the front nine, dammit."

"Catch you later, Edith," Lucy said with a wave as she drove away toward the next hole. "Sorry about that, Gary."

"Come on, it's the same for me. It's what we do for business."

"But it would be nice to relax a little." She brought the cart up to the course's highest knoll. The glistening water of the lake emerged as they came across the rise. Gary got out of the cart, taking in the dramatic view. He gazed out toward the far shore and the hills beyond. "What I wouldn't give to build right on this spot."

"Thank God you can't."

The two strolled across the lawn toward the tee box.

"I've been hunting around for something on the water. In case everything goes well."

"You kidding me? If everything does go well for you, you've got some huge expenses."

"I'd make it my showcase. Doesn't have to be huge. And I've got plenty of equity in my house. Plus, there's money in a few of the spec homes."

"So, a house on the water? Would you be doing this for you or for them?"

"Well, they could be closer to Aston…"

"Don't get in over your head, Gary."

He took an easy swing and drove the ball down the fairway. Then he turned back to her. "Lucy, I'm already in over my head when it comes to those kids. But I've got the money to handle it."

"I have to admire your enthusiasm about all this. Can't imagine wanting to raise young kids at this point."

"Beau and I were at Guitar Center last weekend."

"Ah, the bribes are already starting."

"He was playing around on a Fender. The guys in the store dropped what they were doing. I mean, the kid's got something."

"You sound like a proud father, kvelling."

"Kvelling?"

"Bragging!" Lucy said, teeing off. She sliced the drive very far right. "Thank you, Edith Howger," Lucy commented as she and Gary set off on another search and destroy mission. On their way to find her ball, Lucy asked what was up with Emma.

"She's aiming to get a karaoke machine," Gary said. "I know, I know, she's probably too young for it, but she likes to sing. Told Beau she wants to join his band."

"Oh, no. He must be thrilled."

"Yeah, he was just dying. She wouldn't let him alone about it. Let me tell you, that little Emma is one stubborn kid! So, I told her the really cool thing would be to have her own 'chick' band."

"Did she go for it?"

"Crossing my fingers."

"Are your own girls musical?"

"Becky plays piano by ear. They all can sing, but none of them really pursued it."

Lucy stopped the cart at the base of the fairway. She grimaced upon finding her golf ball. It was wedged into the crook of a grand old Beech tree.

"And the other two, they finally talking to you again?"

"Well, this thing coming up will be a sort of litmus test. Everyone knows it'll be Emma's birthday. Lia's organizing it and invited her sisters. We're making it a big deal. Georgina's flying in, and even Vivian and Hugh are supposed to come."

Finally reaching the green, Lucy was about to putt. The shot was a cinch, but just as she came forward with her club, Gary spoke.

"Quite a lovely woman, that Georgina."

Lucy overshot the putt. The ball went dribbling off in an unintended direction. She looked up at Gary, ready to kill him. "Thanks," she muttered. "And by the way, isn't that how you got into all this trouble in the first place?"

"I didn't say anything. I just said she's lovely."

"She's married."

"Miserably."

Lucy's business was handling the unexpected twists her client's lives had taken. Sometimes, she could see things going awry right in front of her eyes.

"Watch out, Gary. Those kids have enough to contend with. One more thing and they won't make it."

"Little bit of an overreaction there, counselor, don't you think?"

"After all I've done to help you with Beau and Emma, I just don't want to hear you're fooling around with their aunt."

"Don't worry, you won't hear anything!" Gary laughed. To assuage his lawyer's concerns, he added, "There will be nothing to hear."

Finally sinking her putt, Lucy put one hand on her hip and pointed the end of her club at Gary. "All right, pal. You've been tiptoeing around it all day. So tell me the truth: how did the kids do with it? Your message said it all went well at Dr. Backus's office. But come on, what'd she do? How'd she break it to them?"

"By the time the doctor brought me in the room, Beau and Emma had already been told they'd be living with me. I don't know exactly what happened before I walked in the room. The kids looked confused. I tried everything the doctor suggested in advance. I schmoozed, I hugged, I was upbeat...but no matter what I did, the situation was still very awkward."

"Sounds a lot rougher than you said in your message." The two got back in the cart.

"The doctor told me that before the meeting, she explained to the kids that I'd be acting as their daddy, that their father still loves them but can't take care of them the same way I can. We're not telling them about my connection with Beau. It's much too soon, she advised, and the kids can't handle it. They're still grieving, and it could take a long time before they're mature enough to find out. For now, they just know I'm the one who'll be best at taking care of them. All in all, the session ended up on a good note — and we have more meetings with the doctor ahead of us. I'd say things are running pretty smoothly."

"So, what's going on with the deal? Is everyone on board, now?"

"Yes, we're all on board, but I need you to take care of the mechanics. How long do you think it's all gonna take?"

"A while," Lucy answered as she pulled the cart up to the halfway house. They put in their lunch order and took a table in the shade.

"First," said the attorney, "I have to draft the agreement, and then everyone involved has to be satisfied with it, including their lawyers — who, as you well know, will have to put in their two cents. And, it's not only you and Georgina and Everett, but Vivian and Hugh have to sign on as well, since they're putting up a portion of the money. Then, you have to realize, we have to take care of the real estate and the adoption, which will involve the Surrogate's Court. And the adoption's not going to be simple. While this is all consensual, it will require your medical history, financial history and the court's approval. Remember, you're a single parent who's no spring chicken, adopting two young children."

"What d'ya mean, two children?"

"If the case is discontinued, there will have been no finding that you're Beau's father. Since the law presumes a child of a marriage is born of the marriage, Everett is still Beau's father. Technically. So, you'd need to adopt both children. Frankly, I think it's healthier that way, for the children to be treated the same. And by the way, I'm sure you'll have to discuss that with Dr. Backus. If the adoption works out, she's probably going to want you to keep that quiet, as well, until the children are old enough to know."

"I don't love it, Lucy, but it makes sense."

"I'll start drafting the agreement and we'll get you in to start working on the adoption packet. How 'bout you finish that burger so I can kick your butt on the back nine?"

"Wanna wager your fee on that?"

The remainder of the day was a pleasant one for the two players, capped off with dinner at the club with Dan. The threesome was enjoying dessert when Edith Howger strolled over to say a word or two.

As part of the planning committee, Mrs. Howger was fielding talk about expanding the women's locker room and the pro shop. Some members wanted to add a large extension to the main building. It was a mere idea at this point. Lucy handily steered the conversation so that Mrs. Howger soon learned about Gary's brilliant redesign at the Cedars Club. Edith exchanged contact information with him and then mentioned to Lucy, *sotto voce*, that she had advised Marguerite Fletcher to give her a call; her son was on the hunt for a good divorce lawyer.

While listening to Edith, Lucy had the satisfying thought that interruptions to her golf game and to dinner were a small price to pay for the opportunities the club provided. It was a major hub of business, both for her and her guests.

She glanced over at Gary, who was checking his cell phone — perhaps, she thought, entering Edith into his list of contacts. Lucy hoped he'd get a first crack at it if the club was headed for renovation. And what was good for Gary's pocket would be good for those kids.

After all of the innumerable custody battles she'd handled, it was Beau and Emma who stood out. They had a special place in her heart. Gary had read her correctly; she was deeply concerned about what was in store for them. She was determined to make sure their lives remained on the right track, even if it meant hounding Gary Vaughn for the rest of his years.

CHAPTER FIFTY

"**L**adies, this will take us half the time if we can all just shut up and focus!" Lucy sounded her warning as she started to go through the stack of files behind her desk. She wanted to move the meeting along as quickly as possible on this perfect first day of summer. The secretaries sitting among all the attorneys, were murmuring mutual compliments on their respective manicures, Andi scolding them both for throwing good money away on nails that were sure to break under the stress of the firm's weightier files.

The boss was getting crabby. "What's this scribbled on Benton? That's your handwriting, right?"

Dina picked up her head. "Oh, yeah, he's coming in to drop off the tax returns tomorrow."

"Well, grab this, will you? It's got to be broken down. Ladies, we can't work with these monster files! They have to be subdivided." The buzz in the background grew louder and louder.

Ruby interrupted the meeting, which still hadn't gotten very far, to announce that Georgina Fiske was on the line. The fact that the agreement had been signed eliminated any conflict, so Lucy was comfortable about taking the call. Abandoning her mission, the boss sent everyone out of the room and picked up the phone.

"Ms. Bennett, I'm calling from my mother's house." The words did not come through clearly and sounded muffled.

"You know you can call me Lucy."

"I'm done with him." It was still hard to distinguish what she'd said, but Lucy could hear the anguish in her voice.

"What happened?"

"He beat me up. He really beat me up." Her words broke off, and for a moment there was silence on the line.

"Are you hurt?"

"Better than yesterday. I'm feeling a little banged up. But my friend drove nonstop to get me out here. I had to leave, Lucy. It's over."

"Well, where are your kids?"

"When the police took him, I had the boys come with me. I needed to be here with my folks for a few days, just to get my head together. It isn't for long. We all have to get back to school."

"Have you spoken to a counselor, or a lawyer?"

"I just needed to get out of there. I didn't speak to anyone but the police. I figured I'd call you first. I knew you'd give me the right advice."

"Georgina, you know I'm here for you to talk to, but we've got to find you the right lawyer, where you live."

"Could you do that for me?"

"Consider it done."

"Ms. Bennett, Lucy, you know I was angry at you while this whole thing was going on. But now, I understand. You and Skippy both could see what I couldn't."

"There's nothing to be gained by beating yourself up over it. Let's see what we can do to turn things around for you." A tearful thanks from Georgina was the last she heard before the troops reappeared at her doorway with the birthday cake and broke into song.

CHAPTER FIFTY-ONE

Kimmy rolled over in bed. Still in a fog, her head throbbing, she reached out and groped for the clock on the bedside table. Her hands found nothing. Finally able to focus, she could make out the ornate bedpost. With a start, she realized where she was. How she had gotten there was a bit fuzzy, but she did recall arriving at Laurel Hall with the bunch from work.

"Oh, God," she murmured, "This sure looks like the master bedroom." She tried to sit up but the headache crashed in upon her and she fell back onto the plush bedding. This time she had gone too far. It wasn't Jason or Billy. This was her older boss. She closed her eyes, hoping to erase whatever she might have done over the past twenty-four hours and any thought of what repercussions at work might face her come Monday morning.

Downstairs, Everett set down the mug of black coffee on the desk. The windows over the back garden were open wide. Last night's party had overtaken almost every other room of the house, but his library doors had remained closed, keeping the crowd from infiltrating his private domain. What's-her-name was still upstairs, the only one left after the guests had all finally departed.

Now, in the stillness, he was left to reflect on all that had happened over the last few months. The movers had been in for the last of the children's things on Friday, just as he arrived. The toys were gone, the bedroom furniture, the video games and books, even the sleds and bicycles had been taken from the garage. He imagined that he could hear their voices coming from off in the kitchen. But, then he remembered that this was over now. He would never again hear or see the children at Laurel Hall. What little he might see of them would be limited to a few hours now and then, as a guest in someone else's home. He gazed out the window at the budding dogwoods lining the edge of the forest. Alone with his thoughts, Everett Brockhurst recognized that in essence, they were all gone from his life, his wife, his children, his brother and even his parents.

He took another long sip of coffee and closed his eyes. It had been a long time coming.

"Perfection," he thought, inhaling the fresh air and the smell of success.

Lynne's Acknowledgments

Anyone who has ever contemplated engaging in a business or project with a partner knows the challenge and terror of entrusting your thoughts, goals and dreams in another human being. You know the gravity of the choice you are making, and you also know just how much depends on your judgment. I could not have exercised better judgment in my choice of a partner, and first and foremost must thank my friend and co-author Jane Dillof Mincer for making work fun and for taking this journey with me.

My husband Fred Eisenbud and my children, Joshua and Benjamin, have inspired and encouraged me in any and every crazy endeavor I have embarked upon, and have put up with years of my trying to strike a delicate balance between my work life and home life. They have done so with grace and humor, and I hope I have given to them as much as they have given to me. My love for them is endless.

I am lucky enough to have had parents who told me I could do anything I wanted to do and have damn near tried to do just about everything imaginable as a result. My dad loved his work as a lawyer and encouraged his argumentative daughter to follow in his footsteps. He read every word of my manuscript in his 93rd year and still offers me his wise counsel. My mother gave me a love of reading and writing and was the better writer of the two of us. She was a role model as a professional woman and as a mother, and I have spent a lifetime trying to emulate her and make her proud. I wish she had lived long enough to have read this book and seen that I got out of the rat race soon enough to have time to write…something she never got to do.

I have a collection of wonderful friends and relatives who have served as sounding boards and proofreaders. Each of you know how special you are to me and how much help you have been in making this book a reality. Thank you to Lucy Buxton, Ellen Kanner, Brian Donovan, and Marcia Frank; my book group of Kathleen Moran, Rochelle Donnino, Cheryl Zagorsky, Karen Sommers, and Andrea Levenbaum ; my law professor critics, Deseriee Kennedy, Ann Nowak, and Eileen Kaufman. Finally to my brother Stephen Kramer and his wife, my sister Sheryl Goldstein, who share my odd sense of humor, thank you for being there for me in any number of ways.

To all of those folks I have spent a lifetime representing, I hope you understand how much I really did care about the work I did for you and hope that in some way, some part of your life was better as a result of what I did.

And finally, to all of the Mat Ladies (and men) out there who have busted their butts in this crazy field and who have given so much of themselves to clients and colleagues, this one's for you. LAK

JANE'S ACKNOWLEDGMENTS

There was this person huddled in the stands at our sons' Little League games, always wearing an inordinate amount of layers, with enough food and drinks in her coolers to take care of both teams. Oddly, she actually knew what was happening on the field. She regaled me with stories of her life as a divorce lawyer, and despite her words of warning, I joined her firm. Mentor, former boss, tennis partner, and now co-author, Lynne Kramer has always nudged me to do my best – and to get the job done; I would still be re-writing had she not forced a deadline! Our collaborative effort could have been a chore, but instead, we balanced the hard work with lots of coffee, silliness and kibitzing, making a book out of our simple wish to reveal what goes on in the strange corridors of divorce law. Lynne, thank you for your trust in me, your candor, and above all, your friendship.

After a family trip overseas, my father supplied me with legal pads and pencils along with a special briefcase for storing the drafts of my first novel. Inspired by the Russian portion of the trip, I started my book with a boy strolling along Nevsky Prospect. The boy never made it down the street. The briefcase grew dusty. I was seven years old.

Dad, you must be annoyed that it took me so long to complete a novel- if it's possible to be annoyed in heaven. Although this book has nothing to do with that trip to Russia, it is about law. Even if you hadn't been a lawyer, I think you'd get a kick out of it. Crossing the finish line at last, I feel your loving pat on the back and thank you for seeing the writer in me.

I learned to write by running back and forth between my room and my mother's, asking her, "What's that word I'm looking for? How does that phrase go? What's the best way to say...?" Mom, your skill, patience (and extensive vocabulary!) helped me find joy in writing. I have kept every note you've ever given me, not only for your precious thoughts, but because you are the finest writer I know.

Kate Mincer DiSanti, thank you for reading this book early on and promising me it had legs. Your encouragement kept me motivated and your suggestions were spot on. I have given up trying to emulate your clear, natural style of writing, but it will always inspire me.

Ted Mincer, you know very well that mothers are put on Earth to embarrass their sons. I try not to. So, I am happy to blame anything you dislike about this book on my co-author. Please be assured that whatever you might like about it is my doing!

Dobro Dick Dillof, thanks for your thoughtful suggestions and advice about the storyline.

Elisabeth Dillof Dreizen, you confirmed that this project was real and allowed me to weave a sense of you into the book, even if by just a few brushstrokes.

To the members of the Fort Salonga Book Club on our silver jubilee, thank you for proofreading the book and for your words of encouragement and advice. Thank you Katy Anastasio, Pat Casella, Chris Colacino, Toni Denis, Toni Dunican, Fran Gorman, Kathy Graf, Annamarie Hyne, Yvonne Langer, Linda Levins, Lene Morawski, Marie Perico and Judy Travers.

To Roger Erickson, I did not get the book to you in time. I didn't know you were ill or that you might soon be gone. You were my greatest teacher. Thank you for encouraging me to continue writing.

Last, but always first in my life, Larry. You are my one true love. Thank you for urging me on even when it meant facing my glazed expression whenever I was re-working a scene or thinking of a character's next move. You gave me a favorite line for the book, but I'll never tell! I would describe in detail what it's like to have you as my personal chef, but know that it is ill-advised to advertise your man.

Authors' acknowledgments

A masterpiece of this magnitude cannot be created without the help of many people. OK, so it turned out to be a "good beach read," but still....

We are grateful to Charles Salzberg, David Henry Sterry, Ann Collette and Rosemarie Tully for their guidance and encouragement and to Ellen Clair Lamb for her editing work and advice.

Thanks also to Joan Silverman who put up with our weekly updates and Stella Bacus who lived through and helped us survive our collaborative sessions.

About The Authors

Lynne Adair Kramer, an AV-rated attorney, has spent thirty years negotiating and trying complex matrimonial and custody cases in the suburbs of New York City. She and her law firm of fifteen women broke ground in the field of family law. Kramer has lectured in the areas of matrimonial and family law as well as trial advocacy as a member of the faculty at Touro Law Center, Jacob D. Fuchsberg College of Law, and as a former bar association president. She continues to practice matrimonial law and act as a mediator in New York, while serving on the full-time faculty at Touro Law Center.

Jane Dillof Mincer is a writer, attorney and real estate broker who lives with her husband, Larry, in Northport, New York. She is an alumna of Friends Academy, graduated with honors from Wellesley College and earned her Juris Doctorate Degree at New York Law School. Mincer is a founding member of the Fort Salonga Book Club whose participants have read, discussed and dissected over 250 books to date.

Made in the USA
Lexington, KY
21 May 2015

Cover pictures: Left: The ribbon is one of the events in modern rhythmic gymnastics. Top right: A women's pair perform in sports acrobatics. Bottom right: Trampolining is great fun.
Inside covers: A spectacular display of synchronized gymnastics.

Contents

Picture acknowledgments: All-Sport, Norman Barrett, J. Allan Cash, Colorsport, Purnell Books, Sporting Pictures (UK), Supersport Photographs.

ISBN 0 7166 3163 6

Copyright © 1983 Walt Disney Productions Made and printed in Great Britain by Purnell and Sons (Book Production) Limited, Paulton, Bristol, a member of the BPCC group of companies
a/hc

Walt Disney's

SPORT GOOFY

ENCYCLOPEDIA
All About Gymnastics

Published by
World Book Encyclopedia, Inc.
a Scott Fetzer company
Chicago

What it's all about

Gymnastics is about keeping fit. The exercises you do in the school gymnasium are designed to keep your body healthy. Different routines and apparatus are used for exercising different parts of your body. Working out in this way will help to improve your agility and strength, and keep all your muscles in good shape.

Modern gymnastics is exciting to watch and perform. There are all kinds of things you can do, from acrobatics to trampolining. At the highest level, these sports call for the sort of agility you see in an acrobat. But they are great fun to do. And so is modern rhythmic gymnastics, which is more like ballet. On the other hand, you might just enjoy loosening up in a keep-fit class in the company of friends.

Left: The ribbon, with its colorful, moving patterns, is the most popular apparatus in modern rhythmic gymnastics.

Gymnastics is one of the fastest growing sports. This is due largely to the spectacular Olympic performances in the 1970's by such stars as Olga Korbut of the Soviet Union and Nadia Comaneci of Romania. These young girls thrilled the world with their daring skills on the bars or the beam and with their wonderfully entertaining routines on the floor. They inspired millions of girls from many countries to take up the sport.

Men's gymnastics has long been an important part of the sports programs in the United States and many European countries. Now, with increasing exposure of the sport on television, more and more boys are taking it up.

You can read about the classic gymnastics events in *Olympic Gymnastics*, another book in the *Sport Goofy* series. In this book, we take a look at other competitive branches of the sport, as well as general aspects of gymnastics such as safety in the gym and keeping fit.

GOOD TO LOOK AT

If you are the kind of person who marvels at the skills of a drum majorette as she twirls her baton, throws it up high and plucks it out of the air with amazing ease, then you will enjoy the sport called *modern rhythmic gymnastics*. Known as MRG for short, it is a marvelous sport to watch. And it is now in the Olympic program.

Based on dance movement, MRG is performed only by women and girls. All the events are performed to music, on the floor, either on your own or in groups. All the events call for graceful artistry and a good eye for movement, as well as perfect coordination.

In each event, you use a small piece of apparatus — a rope, hoop, ball, clubs, or ribbon. Performers are judged on technical ability, difficulty of the movements, and general impression. Originality and harmony with the music are also important.

The balancing routines in sports acrobatics competitions are thrilling to watch.

In MRG exercises, the ball is delicately balanced on the gymnast's hand. It is never held.

8

ANOTHER FINE SPECTACLE

Acrobats and tumblers have been popular entertainers since ancient times. But it is only in recent years that acrobatics has become a competitive sport. It is called *sports acrobatics*, and it provides a fine spectacle as well as thrilling competition. Both men and women take part.

The routines of the pairs and groups of three or four gymnasts are very much like what you might see at the circus. They perform breathtaking balances and throws with considerable grace and skill. And the tumbling is like the most athletic part of the floor exercise in Olympic gymnastics, with spectacular twists and somersaults performed at great speed.

TAKE YOUR CHOICE

One of the great advantages of gymnastics as a sport is that you can compete in individual events if you prefer to perform alone, or in group

Young children delight in the joys of trampolining.

work if you like to be part of a team. This is especially true of MRG and sports acrobatics. Even in trampolining there is a *synchronized* event for two competitors. And if you really enjoy contributing to a large-scale event, you can take part in those magnificent outdoor displays with a "cast of thousands."

Everybody out!

Gymnasts and acrobats have to follow a long and difficult program of training in order to strengthen their muscles and at the same time make their bodies flexible enough to perform the routines. But physical fitness is not something just for gymnasts who want to become stars. If you are fit and look after your body, it will function well. And that will mean that you will be able to work and play more efficiently and so be a happier person.

It's a good idea for everyone to work out a program of exercises that suits them. If you do your exercises regularly, you will gradually be able to do more difficult ones.

KEEPING FIT

Physical fitness programs are part of almost every child's education. On the simplest level, such programs include simple exercises. Such exercises are practiced all over the world. They are called *calisthenics*, or keep-fit exercises.

These exercises aim to stretch and stimulate the whole body. Gymnasts do calisthenics to warm up before training. Such exercises can be done anywhere, because no equipment is needed. But exercise classes are popular, because people like the encouragement and the companionship of a group.

A HEALTHY HEART

Aerobics is a form of exercise that needs a lot of air or oxygen. The term was invented by an American fitness expert. It is really *cardiovascular* exercise — that is, it is your heart and blood vessels that really benefit.

Aerobic exercises are performed continually for at least twenty minutes,

Movement training exercises help children to develop grace and coordination.

using large parts of your body in a constant rhythmic movement. The exercises must be vigorous enough to keep all your body active.

During this non-stop routine, your heart and pulse rate become very rapid, because you use up oxygen at a fast rate. In effect, it's like doing your exercises at a jog. If you do this a few times a week, it really increases your strength and stamina.

YOGA

Another system of exercises used to stay healthy is *yoga*. It is particularly good for improving your flexibility and

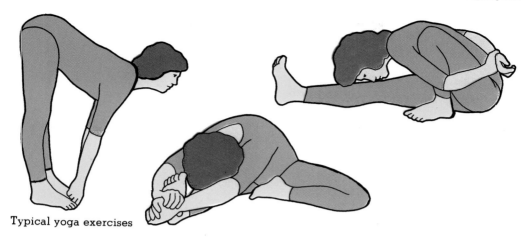

Typical yoga exercises

for relaxing from stress and tension. It is not, however, a way of building up strength and endurance.

Yoga originated in the East, and is a complete philosophy of life. It deals with your mental and spiritual well-being, as well as your physical health.

Some of the poses of yoga are similar to gymnastics positions, but they are far removed from the hectic pace of competitive gymnastics. When you do yoga, you move slowly, without strain. Your aim is to find mental and physical calm.

Wear and beware

It is important to wear the proper clothing when you do gymnastics. Neat, well-fitting clothing will show the movements of your body as you do the exercises. And how you dress is also important for safety.

A gymnastics training session, with neatly dressed gymnasts in a well-equipped gym.

DRESSING FOR THE PART

In gymnastics competitions, women and girls wear leotards, usually with long sleeves. Gymnastic slippers and socks are optional.

Men and boys wear long white trousers, a sleeveless athletic shirt, and gym shoes with or without socks. For the vault and floor exercise, they may wear shorts, with or without footwear.

Track suits are sometimes worn during training. They will also keep you warm during competitions while you are waiting to perform.

The best shoes are special gymnastic slippers that fit well and are very light. Socks may be worn with them.

Hands get very sore when you work on the bars and the rings, so handguards are worn. They protect the palms of your hands and have a rough surface that gives an additional grip. They fit over your middle fingers and fasten around your wrist.

TRAINING SESSIONS

Before a training session begins, all apparatus should be properly erected and checked. There should be mats around the areas where a gymnast dismounts or where someone might fall.

Gymnasts must never wear anything such as rings, bracelets, or hanging earrings that might interfere with their

12

hands or vision, or that can catch on the apparatus. Eyeglasses should be securely fastened around the head. Hands should be kept dry with "chalk," a magnesium carbonate powder that absorbs the sweat and helps you to keep your grip.

Girls practicing wrap-around and bounce movements on the uneven parallel bars can wear foam rubber padding across their stomach and hips to prevent bruising.

Coaches must be expert at *spotting* — that is, supporting or assisting a gymnast making a move. This is usually done by hand, but some gyms have special equipment. For instance, a belt that fits around the waist and is supported by a coach on either side can be a help when you first learn to do somersaults. For work on the higher apparatus, the belt may be supported by overhead pulleys.

SAFETY IN THE GYM

It makes sense to be careful in the gym when you are training. Gymnastics is not dangerous as long as it is done sensibly and the rules are followed.

Gym Care

Never go into a gym and practice on your own without a coach.
Never try a new move without consulting your coach.
Never start a session without a proper warm-up.
Never engage in "horse play" on gymnastics equipment.

Getting ready

The human body is very strong, but it is also very delicate. If you build yourself up slowly and thoroughly, you will one day be able to do very difficult exercises. But don't expect to do everything right away.

Young gymnasts listen to some advice from their coach.

BODY CARE

In competitions, your health and general appearance are very important. Try to look your best. Keep your hair neat, and tie it back if it is long. Take good care of your hands. Make sure your nails are short. Don't let calluses build up. File them down with pumice-stone, and use hand cream after sessions to keep the skin soft.

A healthy diet is important. You will need lots of energy-giving foods. Even when you are not training, try to exercise regularly in the gym, to keep your body flexible. Make sure you shower regularly and keep your body clean.

LOOKING AFTER INJURIES

Gymnastics is a sport in which you can suffer lots of minor bruises, sprains, and strains. It is always essential to have a qualified person present who can take responsibility for any injuries. Every gym should have a medical kit at hand, so minor problems can be treated.

Two important things to remember are: *Never train if you are injured*, and *allow time for your injuries to recover*. Report any injury, however minor, to the coach.

WARM-UP

One of the most important rules of gymnastics is to have a proper warm-up session before you start your training or your competition. If you exercise and stretch your body by easy stages, you gradually warm and relax your muscles. This prevents strains and pulled muscles.

The warm-up session should last for about twenty minutes. You should try to exercise all parts of your body. If you wear a track suit or something warm, it will help you raise your body temperature more quickly.

First steps

The first exercises in a warm-up session should be simple. The best way to start is with some jogging on the spot, skipping, or jumping, for about five minutes.

The remainder of the warm-up exercises are for stretching the muscles and joints. Before you start stretching, remember:
(1) Make sure you are warm.
(2) Use slow, smooth pressure, never violent movements.
(3) If you are going to stretch a bit more than usual, ask a coach to help.

Stretching exercises

Back bends are good for stretching the spine and shoulders.

Stretching

Feet and ankles Stand on tiptoes and jump in the air, landing gently. This will stretch your feet and ankles and improve your spring.

Shoulders Stretch and swing your arms forward, backward, and sideways.

Waist Put your feet about shoulder-width apart and stretch your arms above your head. Lean to one side and then the other, keeping your back straight.

Legs (1) With your legs apart, bend forward from the waist and let your upper body hang loosely. Try to put your chest on your thighs. Twist and turn to stretch your leg muscles.

(2) Place your legs wide apart, with your arms out to the side. Lunge forward, bending one knee. Then repeat, bending the other knee.

(3) Sit with your legs wide apart, extend your arms above your head, and stretch forward to place your chest on one knee, then the other. Hold the stretch position.

(4) Sit with your legs together, straight out in front. Stretch your toes and point. Then stretch them back toward you.

(5) Sit with your legs together in front of you, with your arms extended above your head. Lean forward and put your chest on your knees.

Back and stomach Lie on your stomach and clasp your hands behind your back. Lift up your head and chest.

Spine and shoulders Lie on your back and push up into a back bend.

Tumbling

Tumbling consists of rolling, leaping, turning, and twisting movements. These skills are performed in sequence, one after another, on a long strip of mats. Tumbling plays an important part in the training of a gymnast. The movements form the basis of many skills performed on other apparatus.

Once you have mastered the basic movements described and illustrated on these two pages, you can put them together to form a tumbling sequence.

A gymnast practices her tumbling routine along a strip of mats.

Basic Tumbling Skills

Forward roll Start by standing upright, feet together. Then bend your knees so that you are in a squat position. Put your hands on the mat, and roll over with your head tucked in. Then stand upright.

Backward roll Bend your knees so that you are in a squat position. Allow yourself to fall backward. Roll over on your back, and push up to a standing position.

Cartwheel Begin with your arms above your head. Lift one leg parallel to the floor. Then step down with this leg and follow with your arms. Keep your back straight, your arms and legs extended, and land on one foot at a time.

Headstand and handstand These can be reached by a kick-and-swing method, or by pure strength. The aim is to balance yourself with your body perfectly straight.

Walkovers The forward walkover is an extension of the handstand, continuing the rotation until your body is upright again. In a backward walkover, the body makes a bridge, then one leg at a time is moved in a step and over.

Roundoff This is a cartwheel in which you land on both feet at the same time. You bring your legs together at the top of the movement. Then, with a twist of the hips, you snap your legs to the floor, landing facing the way you began.

Handsprings, headsprings, and necksprings These are springs from the hands, head, or neck that bring you back to your feet. They have to be perfected if you are going to get the momentum to go into a somersault or further movement. A back handspring is called a *backflip, flic-flac,* or *flip-flop.*

Somersaults These are complete rotations in the air. They are a marvelous sight in tumbling routines. For a front somersault, you must leap with a lot of height and tuck your body in by grasping your knees as you rotate.

Freewheel This is a walkover, or cartwheel, done in the air. It takes a great deal of flexibility of the back and hips.

Now you should be ready to start training.

Knowing the gym

To start training as a gymnast you need only a large floor space and a mat. Soon, however, you will need special equipment for more difficult exercises. These will help you to develop the body in particular ways, and prepare you to use full-sized Olympic apparatus.

The equipment you will find in the gym and use for training includes the ladder, the wall bars, the rope ladder, the rope, the bench, and the springboard and vaulting horse.

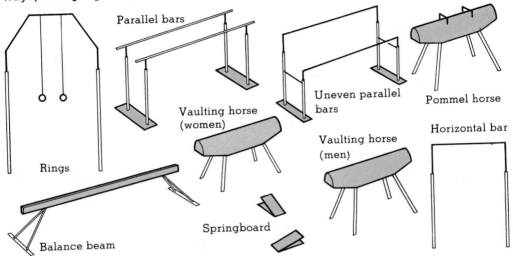

Rings

Parallel bars

Vaulting horse (women)

Uneven parallel bars

Vaulting horse (men)

Pommel horse

Horizontal bar

Balance beam

Springboard

Using the Equipment

Push-ups Using the arms to raise and lower your body. These can also be done with your feet raised on a bench or wall bar.

Pull-ups Start by hanging straight down from a wall bar. Then, pull yourself up until your chin is above the bar.

Hop jumps Do hop-ups over the bench, lifting your knees to your chest.

Hang and pike Hang from a high bar, *pike* your feet to the bar without bending your legs.

Leg stretching Holding on to the wall bars, stretch your legs up to the side, the back, and the front.

Back arching Lie on a box or horse, bending forward over the end with your feet held firmly by a partner. Put your hands on your head and lift your body as high as you can.

Vaulting The springboard and horse can be used for practicing your vaults and for learning to jump onto apparatus.

Balances The bench is ideal for practicing the balance and control needed on the beam.

Ludmila Tourischeva leaps as the uneven parallel bars collapse beneath her during the 1975 World Cup competition. Luckily, she was not injured.

I got rhythm!

Modern rhythmic gymnastics (MRG) is a competitive sport for women that is based on gymnastics and dance. It has its own World Championships every two years. It will also be included in the Olympics for the first time in 1984.

Movements in this form of gymnastics are very attractive, showing flexibility, gracefulness, coordination, and poise. Floorwork is the basis of the sport. The gymnasts use small hand apparatus while they do the exercises. The pieces of apparatus, which can be any color except gold, silver, or bronze, are the rope, hoop, ball, clubs, and ribbon.

An attractive MRG group exercise with balls and ribbons.

MUSIC

Music plays a very important part in MRG. It must be expressive, rhythmic, lively at times, and played by one instrument. The composition of the exercise has to display an interpretation of the music, which shows drama, mood, and gracefulness. It must be composed to suit the character of the gymnast.

COMPETITIONS

The area in which the exercises are performed is 12 meters (40 ft.) square, the same as for Olympic floor exercises. The area may be covered by a mat, or uncovered. In top competitions, areas of both types are provided. The gymnast can choose between them.

An individual exercise lasts between

1 and 1½ minutes. Four *judges* mark routines and are overseen by a *head judge*. The highest and lowest marks are discarded. The middle two marks are averaged, to give the final score. Exercises are scored on a basis of 10.

Seven marks are for content, difficulty, variations in rhythm, use of floor space, floor patterns, and the harmony between the dance and the music. The other three marks are for technical performance and expression.

Basic Skills for MRG

The sequences are built up from certain skills that are part of all the exercises. Each piece of apparatus also has its own special features.

Steps are taken from ballet and are always performed on the toes of the feet, and with the toes turned out.

Jumps and leaps Lightness and poise must be displayed when jumps and leaps are made. Different shapes are made in the air, such as the *split leap*.

Turns are made on the toes, with the heel well off the ground. A *pivot turn* is one of the basic turns.

Balances The gymnast must briefly freeze her routine in poses that show beauty and balance.

Waves are a rippling movement through the body, starting at the feet and moving upward.

Bends Body bends show the flexibility of the gymnast.

Rope tricks

The *rope* is made of either hemp or synthetic fiber. Its length is in proportion to the height of the gymnast. Knots may be tied at the ends to help the performer grip the rope. There are three special skills used with the rope — skipping, swings, and throws.

LIGHT AND SPRINGY

Skipping is the main feature of ropework. Skips are done on the toes, and should be light and springy. Feet and ankles are stretched. The arms are held out straight, away from the body. There are three aspects of skipping: the turn of the rope, the pattern of steps in the skips, and the timing or rhythm of the skips.

NO KINKS

Swings of the rope can be made with the rope open or folded, but the rope must always be in unbroken curves, with no kinks.

THROWING THE ROPE

Throws of the whole rope can be made. For instance, you can throw a double folded rope behind you, then, as the

The ropework exercise in MRG involves light and springy skipping movements.

ends part, catch it again in each hand. There are also many ways of throwing just one end of the rope.

There's always hoop!

The *hoop* is made of wood or plastic. It has a diameter of 80 to 90 centimeters (31-35 in.) and weighs 300 grams (10.5 oz.). A variety of grips are used for the hoop. You change your grip for the different movements. There are six special movements you can do with the hoop.

Hoop Moves

(1) *Swinging* or *circling* movements around the body are done with your arm extended. (2) A spinning movement around a part of your body, such as your leg, foot, hand, or waist, is called *rotation*. (3) You can *turn over* or *twist* the hoop with one hand or with two. (4) *Rolling* the hoop is performed either on the floor or across some part of your body, while you are moving. (5) You can *pass through* the hoop, with part of your body or with your whole body. (6) You can *throw and catch* the hoop with a smooth, flowing movement, as part of a sequence.

Gymnasts find graceful ways of passing through the hoop or swinging and turning it around their bodies.

Ball control

The *ball* is made of rubber or plastic. It is 18 to 20 centimeters (7-8 in.) in diameter, with a circumference of 57 to 62 centimeters (23-25 in.). It must weigh at least 400 grams (14 oz.).

Using the ball presents special problems, because it can never be held, even when it is caught. It has to be carefully balanced on the palm of the hand with your arm extended away from your body.

Ball Movements

Bouncing the ball must be done with a flexing movement of the wrist. Various patterns can be made by bouncing the ball low and quickly, or hard and high, so you have time for a turn or a held balance.

Rolling movements can be made across the floor or along the body.

Swinging and **circling** and **throwing** and **catching** are also movements performed with the ball, without gripping it.

Rolling the ball along the arms, while other steps are being performed, is a feature of the ball exercise.

Club room

The *clubs* are made of wood or plastic. They must be 40 to 50 centimeters (16-20 in.) long. Each one must weigh at least 150 grams (5.3 oz.). The head of the club is a bulbous shape, about 3 centimeters (1.2 in.) in diameter. The clubs are the greatest test of skill, probably because there are two of them.

Clubs become extensions of the arms when performing graceful swinging movements.

Club Work

The main movements with the clubs are:

Large swings in which the clubs become extensions of the arms. Movements can be made in the same direction with both arms, or in opposite directions, or alternately in the same direction.

Small circles, or twirling movements, are made from the wrists.

Throwing and catching of the clubs is more difficult because there are two, but it does lead to a lot of interesting movements. Some of the throws almost resemble juggling.

Beating the clubs against each other or against the floor gives the added element of sound to the routine.

Pretty ribbons

The *ribbon* is, without doubt, the most attractive section of modern rhythmic gymnastics. The ribbon is made of satin. It is 4 to 6 centimeters (1.5-2.4 in.) wide and 6 meters (20 ft.) long. The first meter (yard) is double thickness. The ribbon is attached to a slim wandlike stick, 50 to 60 centimeters (16-24 in.) long. The attaching link gives the ribbon lots of freedom of movement.

The ribbon is used to make spirals, snakes, and other moving patterns.

Making Patterns

Most features of ribbon work involve making spectacular moving patterns:

Swings and circles made with movements of the arm from the shoulder produce circular patterns in the ribbon. The patterns must stay in an unbroken curve.

Snaking patterns, either up and down or sideways, make waves in the ribbon that must run along its entire length.

Spirals are made with a stirring action of the wrist and forearm. The ribbon makes a series of circles from end to end that are the same size, or that gradually increase in size.

Figure-of-eight patterns are more complicated, and made with a swinging action like that for the large circles.

Throws with the ribbon can be spectacular, but they are difficult to do and not an essential element.

Teamwork

There are few more impressive sights in gymnastics than these exercises performed by teams for 2½ or 3 minutes. The group is usually made up of six gymnasts. The exercise has to show harmony, various floor patterns with changes of position, and exchanges of apparatus between the members of the group.

Because of the complex nature of group work, two judging panels are used. Panel A judges the content of the exercise, while panel B gives marks for technical performance.

Moving Ways

Teamwork is based on the same body movements and apparatus skills as in the individual exercises, but the group moves in different ways.

Unison All move together with perfect timing and direction of movements.

Changing unison All move together in unison, but in different directions, so as to create floor patterns.

Canon A series of movements performed one after the other.

Alternation Members of the group do the same movements, but part of the group moves first, then the others move, and this is repeated.

Contrast Some members perform one movement, while others perform another.

MRG teamwork usually consists of six gymnasts working together in a complex routine.

Circus tricks

Sports acrobatics is a tumbling and balancing sport, really more like a circus performance than a gymnastic exercise. It's fast and exciting, with lots of breathtaking somersaults and balances. There are two main sections: one is pure *tumbling*, the other is *pairs* and *group* work.

In tumbling competitions, performers do their routines on a long straight run, combining their movements to form a sequence which is called a *pass*.

In pairs and group work, performers work together on a mat 12 meters (40 ft.) square. They combine balances, tumbles, and somersaults in a carefully prepared routine. In sports acrobatics, there is no equipment apart from the mat. Performers balance and somersault from their own partners.

There are seven events at the international level: women's tumbling, men's tumbling, women's pairs, men's pairs, mixed pairs, women's threes, and men's fours.

MAKING JUDGMENTS

Judging is similar to that of other artistic sports, such as ice skating. At major competitions there are 8 judges — a *master judge*, or *arbiter*, and seven others. They follow strict rules for marking. For example, all elements in the routine must be done in the right order; balances in the pairs and group work must be held for set periods of time.

Competitors must submit details of their exercises before they perform. The elements in the exercise are graded for difficulty and a *tariff* mark, out of ten, is given.

At the end of the exercise, the arbiter will give the judges the tariff mark. This is used as the maximum mark for the exercise, from which the judges make their deductions.

After each judge hands in his score to the arbiter, he displays it to the audience. The final mark is the average of the four middle scores.

A women's acrobatic trio performing in a tempo routine.

Ski run

Tumbling is performed on a sprung track, or *ski run*. This track is 25 meters (82 ft.) long and 1.5 meters (5 ft.) wide, with a 10-meter (33-ft.) approach run.

The first ski run was made in the USSR out of snow skis with the curved ends cut off. The skis were supported by two strips of wood, and covered by a plywood and matting surface. This sprung floor gives a performer a chance to get more height and so do more difficult movements, such as a triple somersault. It also provides a better landing surface.

A gymnast combines his movements in a sequence called a pass.

PASSING BY

Two routines are performed in tumbling competitions. The first is known as the *straight pass*. At least three kinds of somersaults, without twists, must be shown in this routine. To rate the full marks for difficulty, men must include a triple, and women a double, somersault. The second is the *twisting pass*, and here different kinds of twisting somersaults are performed.

In both routines, the competitor must maintain or increase the initial speed.

The nonstop combination of flips, springs, and turns, must be performed in a perfectly straight line and must end with a firm stand.

ROUTINES

Once the basic tumbling techniques have been mastered, you have to train to get enough strength and stamina to be able to start joining some of the moves together. The faster skills, used for tumbling competitions, include handsprings, back flips, and somersaults.

Forward walkover

33

Two at a time

Pairs work often produces the most fascinating acrobatics of all. Women, in particular, get a chance to demonstrate their agility, balance, and grace.

Pairs routines are all based on one person of great strength and stability supporting a partner of less weight and great agility and powers of balance.

An elegant handstand balance is performed by a pair of women sports acrobats.

BALANCE AND TEMPO

Two routines are performed, each for a maximum of 3 minutes. The first involves *balance*, the second *tempo*, or pace.

The balance routine must show at least five balance elements, such as handstands, headstands, and footstands, all choreographed into a routine. The balances must be held for a set time.

The tempo routine is made up of throws, springs, and somersaults, all done to faster music.

MUSIC

The choice of music often contributes to the success of a performance. Any music can be used. But it must suit the movements of the performers, be interesting, have a good rhythm, and be planned to fit perfectly with the movements and pauses for balances in the piece.

WOMEN'S PAIRS

The upper partner must be very supple in her legs and back, as well as having the necessary firmness. The lower partner must have strength enough for lifting and supporting her, without her feet moving. They must work together and display a dancelike grace.

MEN'S PAIRS

Men perform more difficult routines than the women. Usually, these require greater strength. Arms have to be kept extended throughout the performance. The lower partner often has to perform a movement while holding the other partner aloft, as in a one-arm handstand.

MIXED PAIRS

These routines take advantage of the strength of the supporting man and the agility and balance of the woman. One of the main features of mixed pairs is the tossing and catching of the woman performer. She needs to have a good awareness of her body in flight, and confidence in her partner.

Back swan on feet

Front scale on one knee

Thigh-stand balance

Building pyramids

In group work, the women perform in threes (trios) and the men in fours. Some of the most spectacular routines involve building towers or "pyramids," just like acrobats performing in a circus.

WOMEN'S TRIOS

In women's trios, there is an emphasis on music and choreography. Both individual and group work is judged. The first girl must be strong and good at supporting. The second needs climbing and balancing skills, as well as being a good support. And the third girl must be light, supple, and have good balancing skills.

Supports form an important part of routines in women's trios. Usually two of the girls lift the third. There must be a varied selection of *balances*, some on the floor, others upward. The greater flexibility of the girl gymnasts allows them to build pyramids that are varied and attractive, though they are not usually as high as the men's pyramids. In the *tempo* routines, two girls throw the third.

MEN'S FOURS

The men's group is different from all the others, because in their *balance* routine they build a column, rather than perform an exercise. This balance is done without music, and may be one of great difficulty — such as a three-man-high pyramid, with the fourth man holding himself in a one-arm balance on the head of the third man. The top man is often a young boy, who is light and supple.

The tempo exercise is full of throws and somersaults, and is set to music. Moves include spectacular feats such as somersaults from and back on to the shoulders of the support man. This is just like a circus act.

The men's fours are responsible for amazing feats of balance and strength.

In the women's trios, the balances are not as difficult, but they are more varied, and often very attractive.

A lot of bounce

Trampolining is great fun. You bounce up and down in the center of a canvas or nylon sheet stretched tight by springs on a steel frame. Because you can jump quite high, you can stay in the air longer and perform all sorts of turns, twists, and somersaults before landing.

Trampolining is very strenuous exercise, but it takes time to become an expert. Simple movements must be mastered before the difficult leaps or combinations of movements are tried.

Trampolining is great fun and wonderful exercise!

Trampoline Safety

Certain safety rules must be followed.

(1) Know and work within your limits.
(2) Jump for short periods.
(3) Never get on the trampoline until the previous jumper is off.
(4) Keep all jumping to the middle.
(5) Make sure you have at least four spotters standing by ready to assist you. Never use a trampoline on your own.
(6) Do not wear jewelry, glasses, or anything sharp. If you are a beginner, wear something to protect your legs and arms.
(7) Use the overhead spotting belt when trying new moves.
(8) Make sure there is nothing underneath the trampoline, and that there is enough headroom above it.

COMPETITIONS

There are trampolining competitions for *individuals*, for *teams*, and for *synchronized pairs* — two performing the same routine on two trampolines 2 meters (6 ft.) apart. Routines are always made up of 10 movements.

In individual and synchronized competitions, there is a *compulsory* routine followed by an *optional* routine. You give the details of your optional routine to the judges before the competition. The judges mark these for difficulty.

For team competitions, five members perform one compulsory and two optional routines.

Two *difficulty judges* check what you perform against what you proposed. Four *form judges* give marks for execution. The highest and lowest form marks are discarded, and the average of the other two is recorded.

Skills used in trampolining include bounces, landing positions, twists and somersaults, and dismounts (the way you come off the trampoline when you finish).

BOUNCES

Foot bouncing is the basic movement on the trampoline. Once this is mastered, three basic jumps can be made: the tuck jump, the pike jump, and the straddle jump.

LANDING POSITIONS

When you land, there are several positions you can use. The seat landing is one of the basic positions, knee landing, hand-and-knee landing, front-drop landing, and back-drop landing are others. These can then be linked up with bounces to form, for example, feet-to-knee bounces, or feet-to-front bounces.

TWISTING

Rotating on your vertical axis — while your body is straight — is known as *twisting*. A simple twist can be made from a vertical bounce. More difficult twists are made from front drops and back drops.

SOMERSAULTS

All sorts of somersaults are possible on a trampoline. The spotting belt is useful when you are first learning. The *barany* is a forward somersault with a half twist, so that the body lands facing in the opposite direction.

DISMOUNTING

As a beginner, you must step down very carefully from the trampoline. The floor will feel very hard after the spring of the apparatus, and may jar your ankles. Later, special dismounts with twists and somersaults can be learned.

In this synchronized pairs competition, the two gymnasts seem to be in perfect harmony.

Spaced out

Spaceball is a ball game played on a trampoline. The trampoline has an extension at either end, on top of which a *rebound net* is fitted. In the center of the trampoline is a *gantry*, which divides the court in half and has in its center a two-way *basket*. As the players bounce up and down on their side of the court, they try to score points by pushing or throwing the ball through the basket into the scoring area on the other side.

The server throws the 8-ounce (227-gram) ball through the basket to start a rally. The ball is in play until one team or the other scores. A *game* is 7 points up, and a *set* is the best of 3 games.

Players must keep bouncing, but there is no limit to the number of bounces you can make, with or without the ball. Points are won by timing, and varying the way you shoot the ball through the basket.

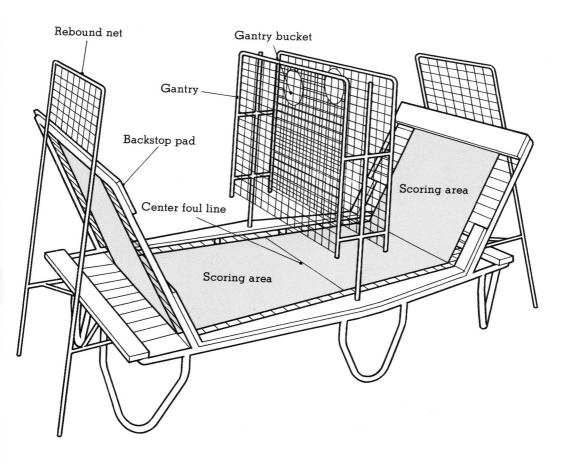

Spaceball court

Cast of thousands

Gymnastics work performed by large numbers of gymnasts — groups of several hundred or even several thousand — is very effective for displays.

Big sporting festivals, particularly in Eastern Europe, put on performances using many of the principles of group work in MRG. Good timing and rhythm is vital, along with variations in speed, style, and types of movements. It must all be performed with faultless synchronization, of course!

One of the most famous mass gymnastics displays is the spectacular *Spartakiade* in Czechoslovakia.

A gymnastics display featuring held balances was part of the finale at the Moscow Olympics.

Hoops and ribbons used together in a coordinated MRG display provide an almost carnival atmosphere.

"Gymnastistics"

Rope Climbing

In the first of the modern Olympic Games, at Athens in 1896, there was a gymnastics item called "arm exercises with smooth cord." It turned out to be rope climbing. The event was won by a Greek whose name was Nicolaos Andriakoupolos. He must have been up the rope and down again before the announcer finished calling out his name!

Rope climbing is no longer an international event, but American records are regarded as world records. A time of 2.8 seconds for the standard climb of 20 feet (6.1 meters), with hands alone, was set by Don Perry at Champaign, Illinois, in 1954.

Full Circle

An event for men's teams (of 16 to 40) "performing free gymnastics or exercises with hand apparatus" was included in the early Olympics. And a form of rhythmic gymnastics for women was included in the 1952 and 1956 Olympic Games as "team exercises with portable apparatus." There were also world championships at this time. But rhythmic gymnastics was not a separate sport. It was performed by the gymnasts who also took part in the regular events. After 1956, it was dropped. Because of this, it became a sport in its own right, with world championships dating from 1963. It returned to the Olympic program as a "new" sport for 1984.

All-around Champion

To win an Olympic overall title you have to be an all-around gymnast. The first Olympic champion had to be more than that. At the Paris Olympics in 1900, there was only one set of gymnastics medals to be won — for the combined event. Gustave Sandras of France won the gold. He had to compete not only in the classic six Olympic disciplines that men perform today, but also in the following: long jump, rope climbing, combined long and high jump, pole vault, and heaving a 50-kilogram (110-lb.) weight!

Bouncing Eskimos

The Eskimos have practiced a kind of trampolining for many years. They stretch walrus skins across stakes wedged in the ice, and jump up and down on them for amusement.

The Perfect Pair

America's leading women's pair in sports acrobatics in the 1980 and 1982 world championships were Pamela and Gail Isaacson — identical twins. But they were not quite a perfect pair — the best they could do was a bronze medal. They won this in the tempo routine in 1982 — by tying for fifth place.

How could they win a third-place medal by tying for fifth place? Well, it's because of a curious rule in sports acrobatics. If there is a tie for any place, the tie stands. The next competitor, or team, moves up one place. The Isaacson twins were very fortunate. They finished behind ties for both first and second place. That is, four pairs finished in front of them. So they were placed third, tied with a British pair who had the same number of points. And six pairs shared three medals!